Under A Velvet Cloak

Incarnations of Immortality Book 8

Under A Velvet Cloak

Incarnations of Immortality Book 8

Piers Anthony

Mundania Press

A Mundania Press Production
Mundania Press LLC
6470A Glenway Avenue, #109
Cincinnati, Ohio 45211-5222

To order additional copies of this book, contact:
books@mundania.com
www.mundania.com

Cover Art © 2007 by SkyeWolf
SkyeWolf Images (http://www.skyewolfimages.com)
Book Design, Production, and Layout by Daniel J. Reitz, Sr.
Marketing and Promotion by Bob Sanders
Edited by Daniel J. Reitz, Sr.
Based on a summary by Stephen Smith, used with permission.

Signed Limited Numbered Hardcover Edition ISBN: 978-1-59426-251-7
Signed Limited Lettered Hardcover Edition ISBN: 978-1-59426-039-1
Trade Paperback ISBN: 978-1-59426-294-4
eBook ISBN: 978-1-59426-295-1

First Edition • December 2007

Production by Mundania Press LLC
Printed in the United States of America
10 9 8 7 6 5 4 3 2 1

TABLE OF CONTENTS

Chapter 1
On Velvet

It was the time of a great king who ruled from a shining city. He had been trained in statesmanship by a powerful mage, and had united the warring clans to form a kingdom that would be long remembered. He had gathered a prominent group of knights under his banner of chivalry. They met at a table in the shape of a circle, so that there was no seeming order of rank among them. But this is not that story.

In a small village in this kingdom was a family with two daughters. The lack of a son might have been unfortunate, but the elder sister was beautiful, outgoing, talented in the arts, intelligent, and good natured. She would inevitably be courted by many eligible young men, fall in love with the handsomest and wealthiest, marry, and have many excellent children. Some of her distant descendants would become Incarnations of Immortality, and others would marry them. But this is not that story either.

The younger sister was fair of feature, but slow to develop, so that at age thirteen she still lacked breasts. This was awkward, as other girls her age were already fascinating young men. She was quiet, introspective, observant, and sometimes given to flashes of intuition. That would have been acceptable, had she not made the error of expressing them. She was simply too smart and nervy for a girl. Her prospects were bleak.

This is her story. As seen by a ghost.

✐✎

Jolie quested until she found the correct girl. She could tell by the feel of her. She had to get it right, because once she entered, she would probably be confined to that body, until her long mission was done. She couldn't just flit about, because she was out of her timeline and could readily get lost.

This second sister was the one. She fit the description, and she felt right. She had vastly more potential than she knew, and she was the pivotal figure in the divergence of realities. What others did didn't matter; only this girl's actions were responsible for the key changes.

Jolie entered the body and was subsumed. Her awareness became the girl's awareness, but Jolie retained her own identity to the extent she wished. She could assert herself any time she needed to, but it was too much of an effort to bother with routinely.

Kerena did not know what to do. She was so much in her elder sister Katherine's shadow that she was in effect invisible. She seemed destined to remain a drag on her parent's household. There was barely enough to go around as it was; they could not afford to feed her indefinitely.

That's what you think, girl. Your life is about to change significantly. Jolie was not really talking to Kerena, who was not aware of her presence. But the pretense made her feel better. She could influence the girl's thoughts, and thus her actions, but it was essential that she not do that unless it was absolutely necessary. Anonymity was golden.

Then a Seer visited the village, really just passing through on his way to somewhere more important, and Kerena suffered a flash. If she could somehow persuade him to take her off their hands, that would be almost as good as marriage. They would be free of the burden, and she would get to travel. Of course it would not be a completely pleasant existence, but she could gather herbs, scrub pots, and do whatever else a servant girl did. Men traveling alone were always in need of such services; they were incompetent housekeepers.

That's it, girl. He is a good man. Do it. If for some obscure reason the girl didn't do it, then Jolie would have to encourage her, because this connection was vital.

In fact vital rather understated the case. There were a seemingly infinite number of timelines, alternate realities, each slightly different from its neighbor, the differences growing as they progressed. The tiniest deviance could generate massive change farther down the timeline. If a girl was walking at dusk to a love tryst, and made it, and conceived and birthed a baby, that baby could grow up and have descendants of lesser or greater significance. But if that girl happened to see a large spider and took a fright, and fled home instead of making her tryst, there would be no baby, and all of what that new person did in life would be lost. All because the maiden happened to see the spider instead of missing it. The change of the direction of one glance could alter the fate of that entire timeline.

This was not academic. In Jolie's timeline the Incarnation of Good had made a study of adjacent and nearby alternate timelines, and discovered that only one achieved salvation: her own. All the others, as far as the Incarnations had fathomed, expired in hellfire, chaos, or some other dreadful doom. It was hardly possible to discovery why, as that would require in-depth studies of an infinite number of variants. God—the Incarnation of Good—could not check directly, because few folk could cross between timelines. Only those who had no similar selves in the others, and there were not many of those.

Instead they had sought the closest variant, and prepared Jolie to go there, to its earliest point of divergence, so she could in effect change the girl's glance and salvage the situation. Jolie could not affect her own timeline, because of the paradox of changing her own existence, but she could touch this adjacent one. They called it Timeline Two, or T2, the original being T1. There might not be a Jolie here, but by the time she brought it into alignment there would be a Jolie. That would be a different person from herself, with an independent existence, but very similar in all the ways that counted. Including, unfortunately, her tragically early death. That was uncomfortable to consider. Suppose the Jolie of this timeline survived, and she had to change it to make her die? She hated the very notion, yet knew she would do it if she had to.

The hope was that in this straightforward manner a second timeline could be saved. Then the Jolie of that universe could do the same for the third timeline, and so on in a chain, saving many that were otherwise doomed. T1 to T2, T2 to T3, and so on, in theory. Perhaps there were many routes to salvation, but the only pattern they could be sure of was the first one. They had to make the second align with the first, at least until it was close enough to achieve salvation on its own.

Thus her mission was literally to save a universe. She had no certainty of success, but it was something that had to be tried. The folk of this timeline did not deserve the cruel fate that awaited them otherwise. Meanwhile she was learning things about the prior course of her own timeline, because of the alignment. These supposedly dull details were thus made fascinating. Here was an innocent girl proceeding to a tryst of a sort. Let her not see a spider!

Kerena walked to the verge of the commons where the Seer had made camp. He was a man of middling-early adulthood, halfway handsome despite his worn clothing. His great velvet cloak was hanging from a tree branch; it was decorated with stars. She came to stand before him, unspeaking, for respectable maidens did not address strangers.

"Hello, child," the man said.

She looked up, meeting his gaze, though this was another unmaidenly thing to do. "I am not a child. I am thirteen." There was something about his eyes she found compelling.

Trust him. He is your early love. Jolie could see some distance along the girl's life. This was necessary to be sure of alignment.

"My apology for misjudging you," he said jovially. "I was not using my Sight." He focused, and Kerena felt the special power of it. "Well!"

"You need a helper," she said. It was hardly a guess, and she knew it was especially true for him.

"And you need training, to become what you can be."

"You will take me, then." She was not asking.

"Of course." He considered. "But you must understand, it is not entirely for routine chores."

"As an apprentice."

"That also."

There was too much to assimilate. "Please, tell me in simple words."

"You have marvelous potential as a Seer; I recognize it in you as you recognize the reality of this power in me. But you are also a lovely young woman. This complicates it."

Kerena shook her head. "I am not."

You are.

"I see you as you are two years hence, grown. I will fall in love with you. That is not wise."

She caught another flash. "And I with you. Is that bad?"

"Not bad in the sense of evil. But it will interfere with both our powers, especially with respect to each other. That could be dangerous."

"What have I to lose? I have no future at home."

"Your comfort. Your reputation. Your life—all are at risk."

"You risk much also."

He sighed. "I have tried to warn you, but your coming beauty overwhelms the foolish male in me. So we are decided. I had better talk to your parents."

And we are on our way.

"This way." Kerena was somehow not even surprised; her flash vision of the future was not a picture so much as a feeling of rightness. This was her destined course.

"Perhaps now we should exchange our names," he said as they walked. "I am Morely."

"Kerena."

"Already I like the name too well."

She understood. Never before had she related so swiftly and completely to a strange man. But he had ceased being strange the moment their eyes met. She recognized in him the power she sought, though she had not known until now that she sought it. He would complete her.

They came to her house. Her father emerged, scowling. "What is going on here?"

"I am Morely the Seer. I wish to take this young woman as my apprentice. In accordance with standard practice, I proffer these three pieces of silver."

The scowl faded. The silver would see them through the winter with far greater comfort, especially considering that they would no longer have to support her. It might be that the real nature of her service would be as a child mistress; it was nevertheless a very good deal for the family.

No, he is not a child molester. But Kerena already recognized that, thanks to her Seeing. In any event, she did not consider herself to be a child, as she had said. Whatever this man wanted of her, she was ready to give. It was part of the bargain.

Her father accepted the silver. Thus was the contract made.

Kerena gathered her few belongings. Katherine came to hug her. "Send word," she said tearfully. They had always gotten along reasonably well together, in significant part because Kerena had Seen the futility of showing her jealousy.

"I will."

Kerena spent the night at Morely's camp, sharing his meager food by the fire. "I had no idea you would pay so much."

"The expectation is that you will be bonded to me until you work off that amount. That is academic; you owe me nothing."

"I will nevertheless try not to disappoint you."

"Take my bed. I will sleep on the other side of the fire."

She did not argue, though she was nervous about sleeping alone outdoors. What monsters did the darkness conceal? Yet this was a price of her commitment; she would endure.

He had made a bed of pine needles with a blanket above and his voluminous velvet cloak below. The fire had driven off most of the bugs. It was sufficient.

The situation reminded Jolie strongly of her own introduction to the realm of the Incarnations of Immortality. She had been a terrified French girl, seven or eight centuries hence, associating with a Sorcerer's apprentice. It had taken her so long to trust him, but when she did, she had loved him. This girl Kerena had the gift of Seeing, so understood such a process much more rapidly. Still, it would require much work before she had full use of her talent, instead of occasional flashes.

Next day they traveled. As they walked, Morely explained the business. "Part of the power is real, but most of it is showmanship. People have to be persuaded to part with their wealth. We need sustenance; it is a complication of mortality. So we dazzle them with incidentals to satisfy them. What is real will take time to develop, but the other is readily learned."

Kerena was pleased that already he was saying "we." It confirmed her legitimacy as his companion.

She learned. Divination with dice or entrails was largely a matter of fathoming what the subject wanted to hear, and providing it with enough vagueness so as not to be directly caught in an error. If true Seeing was negative, a way had to be found to make the news palatable. If a love potion was desired, caution was recommended: potions did not work perfectly in every case, as they could incline the recipient to the wrong person. So there was no guarantee, but the one who bought one could take a small sip to verify its effect. Since folk truly wanted such magic to work, they generally felt a rush of passion when they sipped, verifying it to their eager satisfaction.

"And some merely like a diversion," Morely said. "When you fill out, you will dance in clothing that proffers tempting glimpses of your young flesh. This will attract a group of prospects."

Who will slaver at the titillation of those glimpses. Men are typically crude. You'll get used to it.

"I will do what is expedient," Kerena agreed, not entirely pleased. She had never respected the way males of all ages acted toward her sister. Nor, for that matter, the way her sister responded, liking the attention.

"Think of it this way: you are controlling them, without being affected yourself. It is a worthwhile ability."

"And will you be slavering too?"

Oops. That thought must have slipped through.

Morely glanced at her, and for a moment Jolie feared he had perceived the ghost. Then he chuckled. "I will be enchanted by your presence."

"Thank you."

"A lesson in observation and judgment: what just occurred?"

Kerena considered. "You just lulled me by saying the same thing in palatable language."

"Very good. All things are as they are, but perception is largely guided by language. Never be fooled unless you want to be."

"When should I ever want to be fooled?"

"When I tell you I love you."

Oh, this man is sharp!

Kerena considered again. "Because that would justify giving myself to you."

"Exactly. Always be guided by reality rather than passion. But at such time as *you* desire it, let the passion flow."

"But when you speak of love, it will be true."

"Not necessarily. I will speak love to you, but I will say it to others too, so my words are not to be trusted. Men speak of love when they want sex. They are not at all the same thing. So heed your own feelings, understanding the deceptive conventions. Words and feelings differ, even when they are the same."

Kerena wrestled with that. "As the word for a stone is not the stone itself, the words of love are not love itself?"

"Correct. The words are merely a guide, and can be true or untrue. Always be aware of the distinction."

"I will try."

And that awareness will be one of your defining aspects.

"You are an apt student."

Kerena felt a thrill. Then she quelled it. She might be apt, but should not believe it merely because he said it. "Thank you for those words," she said carefully. "I appreciate the compliment without necessarily believing it."

"Exactly," he repeated, seeming pleased.

"But please, what is the distinction between love and sex? I have heard of sex as making love."

"Love is an emotion. Sex is an action. Love can't be forced. Sex can be, either by violence or seduction. The two can overlap, but their underlying natures differ. Love cherishes the welfare of the other person; sex is for one-self. A man demands sex of a woman; a woman grants it to a man. You must learn and heed the signals of friendship and desire, and always know them apart, for you own comfort and safety."

"My comfort? My safety?"

He shook his head, nevertheless pleased with her again. "Use your Seeing. You are or soon will be sexually desirable. You must anticipate a man's approach in time to escape it, lest you be caught victim of molestation."

Kerena used her Seeing, and was amazed by the graphic accuracy of the warning. What he said was absolutely true. She was in potential danger from any man, except Morely himself. He desired her but would not force her. Not that he would need to.

Still, she slept alone, on his velvet cloak. Her nervousness about the night diminished but did not entirely fade. She wished he would join her there, and not merely for that reason. She was thoroughly smitten with him.

Morely also taught her the value of logical thought. "Most people be-lieve in magic, but they are too credulous. Real magic is hard to come by, and it accomplishes little that could not as readily be accomplished by ordinary means. You must learn the techniques of extrapolation and interpolation, then how to go beyond their boundaries through inspiration and intuition. Form a solid basis of logic and sense, then build on that as necessary. You must always be rational at the root. Fool the others if that is necessary; never fool yourself."

"I love your mind. You know so much." Kerena was not trying to flatter him; she was speaking her thought as it occurred, a liability she would have to learn to control.

"You are able to understand. That is a significant part of what makes you worthwhile to train."

"And you will love my body, soon."

Stop that, girl! But Jolie was already becoming fond of her innocent directness.

"Soon," he agreed. "It is not too early for you to learn the ways of flirtation. They will work only partially now, but when your body arrives, they will be extremely effective."

"Teach me!"

He nodded. "When you walk, move your hips, so." He demonstrated.

She laughed. "That's ludicrous!"

"To be sure, on a man." He fetched the blanket and draped it around him. "Picture me as a woman." He moved his hips again. Masked and exaggerated by the draping, they suddenly exuded sexuality.

Kerena appreciated the effect. She imitated the walk, thinking of her sister, who did it whenever in the presence of a man, even one she didn't want.

Morely nodded. "Practice it when alone, but avoid it when in public."

"Avoid it?"

"It is already effective. I don't want you attracting men until you are ready to handle them."

"But no one ever notices me."

"Past tense, girl. No one noticed you when your sister was near. But we will encounter groups of men. They will notice you as the only person of the female persuasion, and some are more than ready to relate to a girl your age. Be a child, for now."

Oh. "Only when with you," she agreed, walking in a circle, moving her hips *so.*

"I spoke of two years," he said sharply. "Do not make me think of one year."

Oh, again. Her Seeing and his Seeing saw their future, and already it seemed much like the present. It tempted her, as a challenge. She pondered, and decided to see if she could make him think of less than a year. He would know what she was doing, but might not object. Why wait unduly for the inevitable?

Faulty logic, girl. Death is also inevitable. But Jolie read the determination in the girl: she wanted to impress Morely, and fancied this was a way.

Yet there was a reservation. It was sex she would use to capture his fancy. She wasn't sure she knew how to do it. Oh, she knew the motions, but what about the essence? Suppose she stiffened involuntarily, turning him off? She wanted very much not to have an initial failure.

Ask him, girl, Jolie thought, amused.

"Morely, when—when the time comes—how can I be sure to please you?"

He laughed. "Be assured you will please me, just by being you."

"But because of my inexperience—"

"Inexperience is a virtue, in a maiden."

"Still—"

"You are really concerned," he said, frowning.

"I confess it. I want—your love—yet I fear it. I don't want to scream or cry and make you regret it."

"I think this is unnecessary," he said, rummaging in his pack. "But it's something you need to know anyway, to help girls who have similar concerns." He brought out an object. It was a small figurine, a plump bare woman. "This is an amulet, an ancient love goddess, carved from a mammoth bone, imbued with magic. I suspect women have used it to facilitate love for twenty thousand years."

"An amulet? Is this a matter of faith?"

"Faith never hurts, but no, this is real magic. A woman puts it in her love channel at night, and it matures her internal configuration, so to speak, making her capable of handling almost any size or shape of male member. Try this tonight, and you will have complete confidence." He handed it to her.

Kerena studied it. The thing was, yes, about as long and thick as an erect male member; it would no doubt fit, if she applied it firmly. But it was hard and irregular, surely uncomfortable. She distrusted it. "I don't know."

He shrugged. "There is surely no need. I was wrong to suggest it." He reached for the amulet.

She snatched it away. "No, I'll try it. I want to know. As you say, if I am ever to advise a wary girl."

"As you wish." His mild amusement remained.

That night she tried it. She put the figure to her cleft, expecting discomfort, but discovered that its touch in that region generated immediate warmth and moisture. Encouraged, she poked it at her vagina, and it slid inside, summoning further warmth and moisture. Soon it was all the way in, with only the base outside, not uncomfortable at all. She had more room in there than she had thought, or it had caused her to expand.

She left it there, basking in the muted pleasure of it. And dreamed of having sex, over and over. The amulet not only made her ready, it made her want it for itself.

She removed it in the morning, cleaned and pocketed it. Morely seemed to have forgotten the matter, as he did not ask for it back. *The hell he's forgotten, girl! You have already made him desire you, but he doesn't want to demand it, so he's letting you come to him when you're ready. This will make you ready sooner.*

The fact was, Kerena was already more than ready; she was eager, thanks to the amulet. But she fathomed that Morely was not yet ready, perceiving her as still a bit young. So she bided her time, awaiting the right moment.

They traveled from village to village, entertaining and educating the villagers, making a living. Kerena learned the multiple minor ways of magic and superstition, making sure she knew them apart even if the villagers didn't. Meanwhile Morely did teach her the techniques of extrapolation and interpolation he had mentioned, broadening her mind. She soon discovered that when she learned a fact, she pleased him somewhat; when she learned a technique, she pleased him more; and when she learned a better way of reasoning, she pleased him greatly. He liked her to be savvy as well as talented.

Men like him are rare treasures, Jolie remarked.

He also taught her rudimentary magic of the elements: fire, water, air, and earth. Her nature as a Seeress hinted at her larger potential, and this was part of that: the talent for invoking the inherent magic of nature. She was an eager student.

The right combination of focus and spell could ignite tinder. "But mask it with a spark from a stone," he advised. "Do not let others know you can do such invocations. Some have very negative attitudes about it."

"Like the church," she agreed. "Though I don't understand why."

"Because it wants to have control of magic," he said. "If too many others learned to do it, they would no longer need the church for spot healing or miracles."

Another focus and spell would cause water to flow from the ground. "But say you have talent in finding springs," he said. "Find it, do not openly make it."

"Maybe that's what the spell actually does."

He tapped the top of a projecting stone. "Perhaps." Water spouted from a hitherto unseen crack.

With air, it was a swirl that could stir up fallen leaves and dust, making a little funnel shape. With earth, it was a vibration that could shake foundations. "Do not overdo any of these," he said. "Keep them limited, for they are dangerous when overdone, apart from branding you as a sorceress."

"I can see how fire can spread and become dangerous," she said. "And too much water could make a flood. But where's the harm in a little swirl or vibration?"

"A big swirl can fling cows around and destroy huts. A big vibration can shake down all the houses in a town."

She was amazed. "All that?"

"If you have enough power. Not many do, but you have such aptitude you may. Never test your limit except when the need is dire."

She was happy to agree.

There was immediate application for the things she was learning. At one village, there was a problem with fire; several houses had burned, yet the people were not at all careless with their hearths. Morely was busy with others, as the villagers flocked in to demand his services, so Kerena tackled it alone.

Her Seeing gave her the hint, and her new technique confirmed it. "You have a salamander," she told them. "This is an elemental fire spirit that plays joyously in natural fires, and shows sometimes as the Will-o-the-Wisp. This one is a rogue, spreading unnatural fires. You can see it if you focus properly." She showed them how to do that, taking deep breaths, observing the tongues of flame closely, listening for the salamander's crackling smoky voice in the singing embers. Once observed, it could be dealt with, either tamed or banished. Soon the villagers were seeing it, and knew their problem would be solved.

At another village there came a messenger from the estate of a wealthy trader: "Master wants to know do you interpret dreams?"

"Of course; we are expert," Morely said with his public air of confidence. "My girl will handle it."

Thus rapidly, and not quite confidently, Kerena found herself following the boy to his master's house. She had memorized the dream symbols and standard interpretations, because Morely had impressed on her the importance of dreams in the popular mind. "I think they mean nothing, other than fragments glimpsed as the mind sorts out feelings," he said. "But there is extensive literature, and belief is strong." So she was prepared, but not at all sanguine about tackling it alone.

"I dreamed I was in a garden surrounded by marvelous blooms," the merchant said. "But when I went to take one, lo, it was an arrow. Then it was a thread, which wrapped around and bound my hands, and I felt horribly helpless and afraid. I woke sweating and uneasy, but I have no idea why."

Kerena's apprehension faded. There were symbols here, and she could work with them. "I will not presume to question your business," she said. "I know nothing about it. But I can tell you that blooms indicate productivity."

"Of course," he agreed. "I am quite successful."

"But an arrow means sending a letter which you may rue."

He winced. "I did write a letter to a prospective client, but it was very positive. I have new exotic cloth from afar that is not only better than local cloth, but cheaper. He can do very well with it."

"And thread means tangled situations. Tied hands is difficulty in getting out of trouble."

He looked stricken. "I just remembered: his wife weaves similar cloth. He will not be pleased by this competition. He may cut me off entirely. Why didn't I think of that before?"

"Your dream knew," Kerena said, seeing the rational explanation. "It was unable to warn you until you slept."

"I must get that letter back. I sent it only yesterday, and my messenger is not a swift traveler. I'll send a faster one to intercept him." He looked at Kerena. "Thank you, apprentice. Here is silver for your master's fee." He gave her a piece that would readily cover Morely's normal charge.

She was exhilarated as she returned. She had done a professional dream interpretation and the client was satisfied. She was a success!

Another time a woman approached her in tears. "I was away too long and my hearth fire went out!" she wailed. "That means terrible bad luck. What can I do?"

"Go check her situation," Morely told Kerena, because as usual he was tied up with another client.

She went to the woman's house. There was no doubt: the fire was completely out, and incapable of being revived. If she had to light it again, the bad luck would be locked in, because it would no longer be the original fire.

Kerena wanted to help her, and not just for the fee. The woman was in great distress. But what could she do?

She looked around somewhat desperately. In the corner of the room was a small dim lamp. That gave her an idea. "That lamp—how did you light it?"

"Why, from the hearth, of course—a brand from it."

Exactly. Fire was not that easy to make, so was spread about as convenient. "Then that's a trace of the original fire. Use the lamp to restore it, and it will be as if it never expired."

An expression of pleased wonder crossed the woman's face. "Are you sure?"

This was the place for proper confidence. "Yes. The fire knows its origin. There will be no bad luck."

Soon it was done, and the woman was overjoyed. Since luck was mainly in the mind of the person, as Morely had told her, this was a fair fix.

"You are doing very well," Morely told her, pleased. "Many clients are asking for you instead of me, and not just the horny young men."

"I am but a reflection of your genius."

He shook his head. "It's a shame to have such lovely false flattery wasted on a non-client."

Kerena didn't argue, but neither did she agree. It wasn't false, and it wasn't, she hoped, being wasted.Six months into her apprenticeship Kerena lay on the velvet cloak and stared up at the night sky. It was unusually clear, and the stars were bright in their myriads. Jolie knew the girl was ready to make her move. For one thing, she had the love goddess figurine in her channel. Her passion was mounting.

"Please, speak of the stars," she said. "I am sure you know of them."

She was not guessing; he had evinced fascination with the stars, and of course they were on his cloak.

"That is a subject larger than the world we know, and less believable," he demurred.

"I am restless with curiosity. What is that one there?" She pointed.

"Describe it; I can not see which one you mean."

"Come here so you can follow my gaze."

Jolie had to admire the way the girl got him to come close. If he was not amenable to what she had in mind, he would avoid it.

Morely came and lay beside her on the cloak. He put his head next to hers. "Where?"

"There." She pointed again, so he could sight along her arm. "That bright triangle to the north."

"Ah. That is Cepheus."

"Who?"

"By Greek legend, he was the king of Ethiopia. The triangle forms his loin, abutted by additional stars to fill out the rest of his figure. Beside him is his wife, the vain and heartless Queen Cassiopeia."

"You were among the Greeks?"

"I have known some in my day."

"What is their story?"

"She annoyed the powerful Nereids, or sea nymphs by boasting of the beauty of her daughter Andromeda as greater than theirs. They persuaded the god of the sea to send a sea monster to ravage the coast. The only way to stop it was to sacrifice Andromeda to it. So the queen did so, chaining her lovely daughter to a rock by the shore. Fortunately a hero came to rescue and marry her. Now they are all stars in the sky."

"They are *represented* by stars in the sky."

"True," he agreed, pleased by the distinction she had made.

"Even as you rescued me from my pointless life," she said, catching his hand.

"If you see it so," he agreed tolerantly. He was well aware she was flirting with him, and pleased that she was doing it well.

"And will you also marry me?"

Hoo! Jolie thought. That was too direct. But of course the girl lacked experience.

"The subject seems to have shifted."

"That is not an answer."

"That is an avoidance," he agreed, pleased again.

She rolled over, lifted her head over his, and kissed him. "I would like an answer."

Still too direct. The girl was in danger of losing it.

"You are being presumptuous."

"That is not an answer."

"We are not two years along, or even one year."

"Is that relevant?"

"You are not yet a woman."

"Yes I am. I have come upon the Curse. That marks the shift."

"You are not breasted."

"Yes I am. They are small as yet, but growing." She caught his hand and guided it.

Jolie marveled again. Boldness had its merits, but this was too much of a gamble. The love amulet was driving her.

Morely tried to withdraw his captive hand. "This is not appropriate."

"You questioned my development. Now you must allow me to make my case."

Her logic was impeccable. He allowed her to set his hand on one small breast, then the other. "You are a woman," he agreed.

"So it can be at any time."

"At any time. Not necessarily now."

"Such a thing must be mutually voluntary," she said. "I am advising you that I have volunteered. Would it help if I said I love you?"

Clever, girl! But a more subtle approach would have been more likely to catch him.

He laughed. "You are learning too well!" But he remained reluctant. She had made a point, not won a battle. He was not a man to be persuaded by mere availability and willingness. She appreciated that, because many of the villages had girls who expressed both, some of them quite fetching, yet he had courteously demurred. He was saving himself for her.

Back off, girl. You can't push him farther.

"I must learn the other legends of the stars," Kerena said. "But I question them."

"There are variants. Mine can not be regarded as definitive."

"I question *all* legends, as you have taught me. It does not seem reasonable that a man, or his wife, or their lovely daughter could sail up into the sky and become stars. Assuming there exists a mechanism, what is the point?"

"So that others will remember them."

"Are they alive or dead?"

"As far as this mortal realm is concerned, I should think they are dead."

"Then do they care about memories?"

"Perhaps not."

"So it may be that the stars have some other origin."

"It may be," he agreed. He was waiting to see where she was going on this.

"As I walk past a tree, my perspective shifts. Near things change more than distant things. But the stars do not shift when I walk; they follow their own limited courses, completely indifferent to my motions."

"True."

"I must conclude that they are very far away. Since distance makes things look smaller, the stars must be larger than they appear. Could they be the size of the sun or moon, only more distant?"

Even Jolie was impressed. The girl was on the right track.

"If they are, how can they keep pace with the sun?" he asked. "Their perspective should shift with respect to it."

"Perhaps it does, if we could but see them at the same time as the sun. But the sun itself is too far away to show any shift of perspective as I walk. I am wondering—this may be heretical—whether the sun does travel around us. Could we instead be traveling around it?"

"You have come across another notion of the ancients: that our Earth is not the center of the universe." She could feel the radiation of his pleasure with her. She had demonstrated a new type of intelligent questioning.

"Does it need to be the center?"

"Not to my mind."

Now was the time. Kerena reached down and removed the figurine from her body. "I love you."

He saw it. "You vixen! You are courting me."

You rogue! How can you pretend surprise? But of course he couldn't hear her any more than Kerena could.

"Take me now, while you are in the mood. You know I am."

As if he hasn't been in the mood throughout.

He laughed. "How prettily she springs the trap. First the body, then the mind." He gazed into her eyes, his amusement phasing into desire. "You didn't even try to conceal your use of the amulet, so I would know your state. I am unable to resist your blandishments."

"If you take me now, you will love me too."

"I already do, from the moment you first met my gaze and I felt your power. I remained clear of you at night so as not to be overwhelmed, but now you have done it anyway."

"Take me," she repeated hungrily.

"There is one more thing. You do not wish to conceive my baby."

"I don't?"

"Not at this time. A child is a lifelong commitment. You are not ready."

She had to agree. "How do I prevent it?"

"There is a spell you must invoke every month. Now would seem to be an excellent time to learn it."

"Teach me."

He taught her. It was merely an utterance, with the force of will behind it. As she spoke it she felt her body shifting in an obscure manner. She was now immune to getting with child, for this month.

"I am ready," she said.

He did not protest further. "There may be some pain, this first time."

"I know. It is a pain I want of you."

Jolie found herself crying. She couldn't help it. There was just something about conquest that got to her.

Morely kissed Kerena avidly. He had accepted her prior kiss without real response; now he had passion. He stroked her slight breasts, evoking special feeling in them. Then he mounted her and set himself, trying to penetrate her slowly so as to minimize the discomfort.

Vain hope.

"Forgive me," he gasped. "I can't wait!"

"Forgiven," she breathed. Her heart was beating hard.

He drove into her. His member was thicker than the figurine, and not angled the careful way she had done. There was sharp pain, as of flesh tearing. Then she felt the balm of his substance coming into her, and forgot the pain in the joy of her accomplishment. She had won him! She had completed the definitive ordeal of womanhood.

Womanhood is a good deal more than that, girl. But this will do for now.

He subsided, and soon got off her and lay beside her on the velvet cloak. "You made me do it," he said. "I tried so hard to wait."

"I wanted your commitment."

"You always had it."

"Now I am sure of it."

"Next time I will make sure you have pleasure too."

He was as good as his word. Now they were lovers, and she discovered far more physical pleasure in the act than she had ever expected. She had supposed that the woman's part was merely to hold and satisfy the man, her pleasure deriving mainly from accomplishing his pleasure.

Some men would have it so.

And her fear of darkness was forever abated. The starry night was her friend, enabling her to win her desire. Now she slept in Morely's embrace, but she could have slept alone without fear.

She tried to return the love figurine to him, but he declined. "Now you know how it works; at some point you may have to recommend it to another woman."

After that, Kerena got a dress that flared out when she twirled, and revealed curvature when she leaned forward. She danced, at first showing mostly her legs, but as her breasts filled out she showed them too. She had become the temptress, and business increased handsomely. She reveled in her apparent power over men, but she was interested in no man's touch except Morely's.

You'll get over that, Jolie thought sadly.

One morning they approached a fork in the trail. Morely took the left one, and Kerena accompanied him. He was the one who knew the way, as this was his familiar route.

Jolie came alert. Something was wrong!

In a moment she realized what it was. The realities were diverging. Her own track was no longer congruent with this track; there was a small but definite difference.

In Jolie's realm, Morely and Kerena took the right fork. Both trails led to the next village, in a similar difference. Why should this matter? Jolie didn't know, but knew that it had to be corrected. She had to keep the two tracks aligned.

She jumped back to the time just before the fork. She put a thought into Kerena's mind, emulating her Seeing ability so as to conceal it's true source. *Take the right fork.*

Morely started left. "This way," Kerena said.

"But I took that last time. I like to vary the route in inconsequential ways."

"But it's new to me," Kerena said firmly. "Humor me."

He shrugged and did so. After all, they were lovers, inclining him to cater to her whim. They took the right fork. The tracks converged. Jolie breathed a ghostly sign of relief.

In time, well supplied with money, they came to Morely's private residence. Here he had something no one else was equipped to understand: a mounted tube with glass at either end. When Kerena looked in the small end, she saw the night sky in greater detail than was possible with the naked eye. This was Morely's greatest secret: a way to look more thoroughly at the stars. She promised not to tell, for ignorant villagers were superstitious about what they did not understand, and might destroy it if they learned of it.

The man's an early astronomer!

It was a discipline the girl eagerly embraced. Soon she was spending as much time looking at the stars as he was. This, too, pleased him. She was an apt match for him.

Kerena occasionally went to the village to purchase staples; this was part of her duty as apprentice and maidservant. The villagers were readily able to accept her presence, and surely assumed she was being sexually used. Why else would a man keep a pretty girl servant? That didn't matter; she was as much user as used.

One day she was late returning, because it had taken unwonted time for a farmer to fetch the grain she needed. It was dark as she made her way back, but she was confident she could handle it. The night was not her enemy; it was her friend. If anyone should follow her, she could readily elude him in the darkness. Sometimes village louts tried; that was a penalty of beauty. She had a knife, and Morely had made sure she knew how to use it, but had also impressed on her that avoidance was far superior. Knowledge, confidence, and darkness were all she needed. She could slip silently into shadow, like a forest sylph.

She came into sight of the house. There was no light, which was odd; normally he left a lamp in the window, a signal that he was waiting for her return. Morely himself was often out peering through his star-tube, especially on a clear moonless night. The stars were endlessly fascinating; she shared his constant amazement.

She went to the house, found the lamp, and lit it from a fireplace ember. "Morely?" she inquired, concerned that he might have overslept or suffered some accident. But he was not in the house.

I have a bad feeling about this.

She took the lamp and looked outside. She made a search pattern, carefully spiraling outward from the house. Such efficiency was typical; she had learned it from Morely and took pride in it. He had to be somewhere; she would find him.

She did not. Instead she found the velvet cloak, with its starry pattern, lying on the ground. Blood spattered it.

She stifled a scream of horror. Something dreadful had happened to Morely.

CHAPTER 2
LADY OF THE EVENING

Kerena wasted little time weeping. She analyzed the situation and planned her approach, exactly as she had been taught to do in any emergency. Morely was gone, but surely not dead, for his body was not there. His Seeing ability and general knowledge should have protected him from almost any ugly surprise. So what had happened?

Obviously he had been tricked in some fashion. Kerena used her Seeing, which had progressed less rapidly than her body or her practical expertise; it had refused to be hurried. But it did enable her to pick up recent physical and emotional events in the area, in a general way. She moved about the house, extending her awareness. Morely had been there, unconcerned as dusk approached. Then he looked out and saw Kerena coming. He went out gladly to meet her.

Uh-oh, Jolie thought.

But Kerena had not arrived back at dusk. She had been a good hour later. That arrival could not have been her.

She went to the cloak, still on the ground. Why had he put it there? Normally he wore it, or spread it on the ground when they lay outside gazing up at the stars. But the dusk today was overcast; there were no stars to be seen.

Or when they made love. They had a good bed inside, but still liked to do it out on the cloak, reenacting their first tryst. She liked to pretend to be seducing him for the first time, and he liked to play along. She even winced at his penetration, though it never hurt later. Somehow the reenactment never got dull.

Along with the drops of blood on the cloak was a fresh stain of sex.

His presence was there by the cloak, along with someone else. Kerena could not fathom the other; it was strange and magical, resistive to her Seeing. Female, but otherwise obscure.

But Morely would not have done it with a strange woman. He had been resolutely loyal to Kerena, even before she seduced him. Especially not on their cloak. Had his business required him to bed a female client he would have done it; she understood about that. She herself might someday have to bed a male client, as business. But never in this manner.

Yet it seemed he had. How could that be?

Think magic, girl.

The answer came in a blinding nonmagical flash of insight. Morely had gone out to meet Kerena, and had spread the cloak. He had sought to love her. *He had thought it was her.*

Someone had timed it for when Kerena should normally have arrived, and somehow emulated her, and indicated she was ready for love. He would not have questioned that; he did love her, and making love (now sex and love really did merge) was their chief joy together. He had gladly joined the imposter—and she had drugged him or enchanted him and taken him away. The drops of blood on the cloak—perhaps a poisoned needle, stabbing him, drawing blood, then paralyzing him. He would not have been wary while clasping Kerena; he would have embraced her, and maybe hardly felt the prick of the needle as he climaxed within her.

"I betrayed him!" she exclaimed, appalled. "My semblance deceived him, made him unwary. He walked blithely into the only trap that could have snared him. Because of me." Tears of outrage and guilt flowed.

Not your fault, girl.

Kerena picked up the cloak. She shook it and brushed it off, but did not go after the stains. Whatever there was of Morely was there, and she valued it.

There must have been more than one person, because a woman petite enough to emulate Kerena would not have had the strength to carry away an unconscious man. Indeed, someone must have carried him, because now she found indentations in the ground beside the spot the cloak had lain, leading away from the house. She tried to follow them, but the ground turned hard and they disappeared. Her Seeing was blocked; she could not divine the trail. They must have known she would try to follow, and prevented it. They had had time to get well away; there could have been a horse nearby.

Why had they done it? Possible reasons abounded. The husband of a client could finally have discovered the connection, and come to extract revenge by imprisoning and torturing Morely. A rival Seer could have sought to enslave him, making Morely's powers his own. Some town or village might have wanted a Seer, and known he would not remain there voluntarily. Obviously they had known about Kerena, and not wanted her; she was the apprentice, as yet only the shadow of the master.

Where could they have taken him? Not to any nearby village; the locals knew and respected him, and in any event his abduction would be immediately known in the area, so no nearby village would be able to get away with it. Where, then?

That perhaps gave her a clue. Most folk remained close to home; travelers stood out. Any local villager anywhere could spot and remember a stranger. It was like perspective: the closer it was, the more obvious the change. They would have to take Morely far away to make him anonymous, for he was known throughout this region. If she could track the motions of travelers, maybe she could find him.

How could she track travelers? She needed to find a contact, someone who knew how to do it. A trader, perhaps, in a big town or city. Meanwhile, she had to make her living while remaining uncommitted. She knew how to do that, though she did not relish the prospect.

She spent a lonely night. In the morning she closed up the house and set off with her meager belongings and the cloak. She had hidden Morely's gold where only he was likely to find it, should he return. She took only enough to get her where she had to go. She would never steal from him.

In due course she arrived in the shining capital city. Naturally it had a rotten underbelly. This was where she could be anonymous yet in touch.

At dusk the streetwalkers came out. Kerena approached one. Her Seeing demurred; this was not a good contact. She veered away and went on along the street. Her Seeing did not inform her whether another person was of good or ill character, only whether association would benefit her.

The third streetwalker was good. Kerena addressed her. "I am new here. Where is the best house?"

The woman eyed her appraisingly. "You look young and clean. Do you have experience?"

"Only with one man."

"Ideal. Come with me."

Kerena started to. Jolie came alert. The tracks were diverging.

Jolie skipped back to the time before the approach. *Not this one*, she thought firmly.

Kerena hesitated. Her seeing was divided; it indicated that this woman was good, yet that she was not.

She's a good woman, but there's a better one ahead, Jolie thought strongly.

Reluctantly, Kerena passed the woman by.

Several women farther along she found another good one. She spoke to her. The dialogue was similar to the first, and they walked together.

The two tracks remained converged. Jolie relaxed. She had gotten them through another crisis point. This time had been more of a challenge, because now it was apparent that Kerena's Seeing was not identical to the alignment.

The woman led her to the back entrance to an ordinary-seeming house jammed in amidst many. A forbidding woman appeared. "Here is a prospect," the streetwalker said, holding out her hand.

The madam sized Kerena up with a single glance. She put a piece of silver into the streetwalker's hand, and the woman vanished. "You'll start with Blake. He'll decide your value. Understand?"

"Yes."

"Wait here." The madam deposited Kerena in a small waiting room and departed.

"Oh, you're new." The speaker was a sweet-faced girl barely older than Kerena.

"New," Kerena agreed. "I am Rena."

"I'm Molly. Let's be friends."

There was a certain charm about the girl's straightforwardness. Her Seeing suggested it was honest. "All right. Is this a good place to be?"

"Oh, sure. They don't cheat you here, and if a client roughs you up, they'll do something about it. But you do have to perform."

"I expect to." She had never wanted to practice her studied wiles on any man but Morely, but now she would have to. She knew he would approve, ironically.

"Do your very best with Blake; his report counts."

"I will try." They talked further, and Kerena learned that Molly was a local girl whose family could not support her, so had sold her to the brothel. She was in the process of earning out her stake. In time she would make it, and be free, because this house was honest.

The madam reappeared. "Molly—take the lord to your chamber now."

The girl jumped up. "Fare well, Rena," she said as she went to intercept her client. "I'll see you again soon."

"Come with me," the madam said to Kerena. "Blake is ready."

Blake was a gruff swarthy man who turned out to be surprisingly competent as a sexual partner. He stripped her and tried her in several positions, which she accommodated immediately. He did not climax; this was not pleasure but business. "Fair face. Good young body," he remarked. He had not even removed his clothing, baring only his business member. "Age?"

"I'm fourteen."

He lay back on the bed. "Seduce me."

Kerena smiled at him, then put her face to his and kissed him lingeringly on the mouth. Then she unbuttoned his shirt and kissed his hairy chest. She took his hands and set them on her breasts. She took down his trousers and kissed his member, bringing it erect. "I want you," she whispered. "Take me." It was all an act, as he knew; the question was how appealing it would seem to a client.

He clasped her, put her face down on the bed, and straddled her from behind. He plunged into her, stroking until he climaxed. Then he got off her, turned her over, and smiled. "You're good. Pretty, plush, malleable, skilled. You made me enjoy it."

"Thank you."

"Dress. You're done here."

The madam reappeared. She had probably been watching. Blake gave her an emphatic thumbs-up.

"You'll get our top room," the madam said. "That's an avenue to outside work with wealthy clients. Treat them well and you will do well. We take half your earnings in-house, none out-house. We provide your costumes, food, private bed during your time off. No sadism; if anyone hurts you, yell for Blake and be sure it won't happen again. What's your name?"

"Rena."

They were at the assigned room. It was well appointed, with curtains, cushions, a couch, and pictures on the wall. It was obviously meant to make a wealthy or high class man feel comfortable. There was a covered potty discreetly in an alcove. "Put this on," the madam said, taking a glittering dress off a hook. "We have a high class clientele. Your first client is a lord of the king's court." She winked. "Low-level, but with money. We call them all lords. Lord X, anonymous, though we know who they are. Make them feel big. Never hurry them; if they stay overtime, they pay more. If they want to talk, listen attentively, but keep their secrets. Discretion is invaluable. If they like you, word will spread. Some of our girls have married their clients and become ladies. We keep their secret; they will never be blackmailed. Keep that in mind."

Kerena barely had time to clean up after Blake and don the glittery dress, which had no underclothing, before Lord X appeared. He looked like a fop, but he was extremely potent, having at her three times in half an hour.

Kerena suffered a wave of doubt. What was she doing here? This was not her proper way of life!

The thought caused the tracks to blur. *But you want to question the men about their travels,* Jolie thought. *This is the way to meet many men, and to get them to talk.*

Kerena nodded internally. She was not one to make commitments, then renege. She would stay the course.

The blurring ceased. Alignment had been maintained.

Kerena got a break. Molly found her and guided her to the kitchen for bread and jam. "We have to eat when we can; the clients always come first."

"So I gather."

Another girl was there, older and somewhat worn. "How come you got the best room, new bitch?" she demanded of Kerena.

"Shut up, Nix," Molly snapped. "You know Blake decided, and new is what the old clients like, for the novelty."

Nix shut up, effectively refuted. Molly's friendship was already paying off.

That day she accommodated three lords, then got to eat with several other girls, and sleep. Molly helped her throughout, introducing her, defending her, showing her around. It would have been far less comfortable without the friendly girl. It wasn't much of a life, but it would do until something better offered.

Word did spread. "We have three waiting in line for you," the madam informed her in the morning. "Don't hurry; I will space them. I suspect you will not be with us long."

Kerena knew that it was her youth and dawning beauty that constituted her appeal. But she intended to augment it with personality, and begin her search for news of travelers. She talked with her clients between bouts of sex, and they responded, flattered by her interest. She handled eight clients that day.

Muted jealousy of her early success showed in the other girls, but Molly fended them off. "They hate anyone new and young," she confided. "Because you make them look old and the men notice."

Obviously Molly knew exactly how it was, being the youngest and prettiest of the other girls. "But aren't *you* jealous?" Kerena asked.

"No. I decided not to let them do to you what they did to me."

Kerena resolved then to see that Molly never regretted befriending her.

The third day there were so many clients the madam had to turn some away if they couldn't be diverted to other girls. Kerena's share of the money was posted as an account from which she could draw when she chose. She could spend it on her day off. One of the benefits of a high class house was that it did not need to cheat its girls.

Jolie was halfway bemused. When Kerena had sex, so did she, for she had the girl's awareness. This life really was as new to her as to the girl. But not actually a bad life, all things considered.

Kerena went out shopping with Molly when they had time, and the girl was as adept at showing her around the town as around the brothel. They had a fine time.

The procession of men was in one sense numbing, as there were too many to remember as individuals, even if they had had real names. But Kerena used the experience to practice her wiles. There were differences, and what subtly turned on one man had little effect on another. She made it a point to attune to each as an individual, the brief time she was with him, making each feel special. On occasion she wore a long-hair wig to change her aspect, looking like a different woman. She was mastering the nuances of appeal and seduction. Soon she was getting repeat business, as prior clients asked for her again.

Sometimes the liaisons verged into something approaching affection. One repeat client was late for their agreed appointment, but she delayed, knowing he would be there. "Thank you," he said when he hurried in. "I would never want to miss my date with you. This damned incontinence held me up."

She hadn't known of that. She drew on her knowledge of folklore. "It is just a story, a superstation, but some believe there is a cure."

"I believe in anything," he said. "What is it?"

"Those who suffer from a weak bladder must stand astride at the head of an open grave, after the coffin is lowered but before the dirt is filled in. Then walk backwards to the foot of that grave, bestriding it. But I am not sure of the logic, unless it is that the malady is thus passed along to the dead person, who won't notice."

"I'll try it," he said eagerly. "Even if it doesn't work, I'll be thinking of you."

"Don't do that," she cautioned him with mock seriousness. "You'll get stiff and annoy the corpse."

He laughed heartily. "How true!" Then he completed the act, in a good mood.

Thereafter she developed a reputation for clever advice and humor, and was more in demand than ever. It seemed the men really liked having some small relationship along with the sex.

"You're really good," Molly said. "You're bringing extra business to the house. That means more for the rest of us, too."

That explained the grudging acceptance by the other girls. They realized that they were better off with Kerena participating than they would be without her.

She made sure to invoke her non-baby spell each month. This had a convenient side effect: it suppressed her periods, so she was able to service men continuously. If the madam noticed, she did not object.

"I'm in a hurry, but I had to see you," one client told her. "How fast can you do me?"

"Give me the lead and we'll see."

"Done."

"Stand where you are." She opened his shirt and his trousers without removing either. She embraced him, pressing her bare breasts against his chest as she kissed him. His member came erect, and she guided it in and closed her thighs below it. She squeezed internally, applying a technique Morely had taught her. He erupted. When he was spent, she dismounted, used her hand to milk his member of remaining fluid, wiped him off, and put his clothing back together. It had taken perhaps two minutes.

"You are amazing!" He departed, in good time for his business.

Even the madam was surprised. "He paid for an hour, and demanded no refund," she said.

"I gave him what he asked for."

"I am going to give you to our most important client. He has special tastes, but if you can accommodate him, you will not regret it."

"I can accommodate him."

"We shall see."

"You're getting Lord H!" Molly said. "He can make your fortune, but he's a challenge."

"How so?"

"He's fine for the first fuck. It's the second one that freaks the girls out. It's always different, but weird. He's never taken the same girl twice, and they don't mind."

They talked, and Kerena began to get a glimmer of the problem, though Molly herself did not quite fathom it. She prepared herself emotionally.

The man turned out to be portly, of middle age, and quite well dressed. The moment she approached him, Kerena's Seeing flashed. This was a significant contact.

He took her in the normal fashion, almost causing her to wonder why the madam had cautioned her. But Molly's discussion kept her alert. They talked, remaining naked, and he was well read and intelligent, with opinions on many subjects. Kerena did not try to conceal her fascination.

"You seem smart," he remarked. "Are you literate?"

"Oh, I wish I could read!" she exclaimed. "I know there is so much to learn from books."

"Perhaps it will come to pass." He glanced at her with a certain hesitation. "There is an aspect of me that some women have difficulty adjusting to."

"You have aroused my curiosity." Whatever it was, she would accommodate it, because she needed to be with him. Jolie agreed; the tracks remained aligned.

"I like reversals."

"My apology, Lord X. I don't think I understand." But she was closer to understanding than she let on.

"Call me Hirsh. I need no personal anonymity, as I do not work for the king."

"Thank you for giving me your name, Hirsh. I am Rena."

"I wish to exchange roles, for a time."

She acted perplexed. "Please explain this further."

"I would like to put on your clothing, and vice versa."

She was careful not to smile. "I think the fit would not be perfect."

"True. It is a temporary expedient."

"Then let's do it." She was curious where this would lead; Molly's information had not gone beyond this point. Merely exchanging clothing should not freak out experienced whores.

Hirsh donned her dress, which fit better than might have been expected, and she put on his fine clothing. When she set his hat on her head, he asked her to tuck her hair out of sight under it, to make her look more masculine. She obliged, then risked an initiative: "If I may, Hirsh." She took the wig and put it carefully on his head, then held up the polished metal mirror for him to see his reflection.

"Perfect!" he exclaimed. He lay on the bed. "Take me."

Role reversal: now she understood. The girls were schooled to be the objects of men's passions, not to take the initiative. But Kerena could play this game. "Woman, you are mine," she said as gruffly as she could manage. "Spread your legs."

He spread his legs, feigning reluctance. She was reminded of her games with Morely, as she pretended pain on penetration.

She got down on hands and knees, straddling him. "Let me see your stuff, you bad girl." She drew up the skirt to show his reviving member. "Just as I thought: you haven't been fucked enough. I'm going to plumb you to the core, wench."

"I beg you, master, no," he whimpered, his member stiffening.

She opened her trousers, then threaded the needle, as it were, making the awkward connection. She jammed down on him, bouncing. It could not be entirely comfortable for him, but it was as close as she could come to emulating the masculine brutality. Then she brought her body down, putting her weight on him, and forced a hard kiss. "Put out, girl!"

He did. She felt his reaction as she pushed against him, still kissing his mouth bruisingly. His passion was greater this time than it had been in the normal mode.

He lay unmoving for a while after it was done. When she judged it time, she disengaged, got off him, and removed his clothing. She was uncertain whether she had pleased him or pushed it too far; it was a new experience and she was not attuned. But her Seeing suggested that it was good.

Jolie agreed. She had not before reversed roles either, but it seemed harmless.

Finally he stirred. "I like sex twice a day, the second time as a variant. Would you like to come home with me? I will provide a stipend."

Home duty, instead of servicing ten or more men a day. "What would be my duties?"

"This, in several forms. No household drudgery; I have servants. They are circumspect."

She appreciated how that would be important. "Would I be free to go about, when not with you?"

"Of course. Anything you wish."

"I have an interest. I am trying to discover where my former lover went—he was abducted—by tracking traveling."

"I will help you track. I have resources."

"Then yes, I would like to go home with you."

He smiled as he removed her dress. "Very good. I will notify my wife."

Kerena froze. "Your wife!" It had not occurred to her that he could be married, though she could have divined it by Seeing. She had been careless in that respect.

"Do not be alarmed. She understands. She merely does not care to accommodate my tastes."

Maybe that made sense. "I will not want to stay, if she objects."

"She won't. Inform the madam; I will send a cart for you this afternoon."

"He's taking you home!" Molly exclaimed. "Congratulations."

"I will visit you when I can," Kerena promised. She liked Molly, and did not want to lose her friendship.

Thus it was arranged. Kerena explained to the madam, who took it in stride. "He is a man we want very much to please. He provides goods we can't get elsewhere. If he tires of you, you will be welcome to return here. You have been excellent for business. Here is your gold." She presented a bag.

Kerena could tell by its size and heft that everything was there: her half share of all the payments for her liaisons. Morely had taught her to weigh copper, silver, and gold by hand. Only gold weighed this much in such small size. She had half expected to be cheated despite assurances, but did not care to say so. "Thank you."

The cart arrived, drawn by a single horse guided by a horseman. Kerena got on, and rode through the streets of the city in bumpy style.

Hirsh's house was at the edge of the city, with a yard filled with attractive trees. A woman came out to meet her. "I am Ona. You will have a chamber adjacent to Hirsh's room, so as to be readily available at night. His needs can be erratic."

So she gathered. "I will accommodate."

"You will need a better wardrobe. Come with me."

"First, I really ought to meet his wife. I am concerned lest she not approve."

The woman smiled. "I am his wife."

Kerena smiled ruefully, blushing. "I took you for a servant." Again, she should have Seen. This remarkable shift of situation was making her unpardonably thoughtless.

"You are charming. This way."

Kerena went with Ona to the kitchen, evidently the center of household activity. "This is Rena, who will be with Hirsh," Ona said to the fat cook. "She is not a servant."

The cook nodded.

Ona took her to a room with many hanging dresses. "Some of these should fit you. Try them on. The seamstress will make adjustments."

Kerena was increasingly nervous. "Please, I think I don't understand. Why are you helping me?"

"My husband is a good man and an excellent provider, and we love each other in our fashion. But sex is uncomfortable for me. I tried to ameliorate it with balms, but they are not sufficient. Hirsh has the desire twice or thrice a day. It is entirely beyond me. I told him to get it elsewhere until we could find one to accommodate him here. Other girls have not been able to keep the pace. He believes you can. I hope that is the case."

"And what is to be the relationship between the two of us?" Kerena asked. "Should I try to stay out of your sight?"

"By no means. You will do what I would do for my husband, were I able. We will introduce you to outsiders as a young relative temporarily in our care. The rest is no one else's business."

"But do you resent the—the need? I do not wish to be the source of dissension."

The woman smiled. "This, too, becomes you. I shall be glad to have the company. Hirsh says you are a bright girl in search of a lost lover."

"Yes.

Hirsh appeared. "Go with him now," Ona said, with no sign of rancor.

Kerena went with him. "Can your wife really not resent me?"

"She dreads my need. As long as you abate that, she will be your friend."

"This is not a thing I am well equipped to understand." Yet her Seeing suggested it was so.

"It is an unusual situation."

They entered his room. It was richly appointed, with an enormous plush bed.

No need to confuse the purpose. "How do you want me?"

"As you are, this time."

They stripped and lay on the bed. To her surprise, Hirsh was not in a hurry. He kissed her, stroked her breasts, squeezed her bottom, and talked. "I have collected recent reports on groups and people that travel. Is there any particular area you wish to verify?"

"You have me naked, and you wish to talk of travel?" she asked, bemused.

"I have you naked, and I want to please you."

It fell into place. He required more than the body; he wanted her pleasure. That was one of his turn-ons.

"Locating the one I lost would please me," she agreed. "I did not think that you would want to address this subject at this time." Men could be possessive about their women, even when they had more than one.

"I love my wife, and would have her here with me if it were possible without her pain. I am not here to love you, and you are not here to love me. I need sex, you need to complete your search. There is no conflict."

She nodded, seeing it. "It means everything to me to recover the one I love."

He asked about the details, and she told him what she knew. "I believe I can help you," he said. "It may take time, but if there have been any unusual travels, we shall become aware of them."

"Thank you!" she said gratefully.

Then he took her for sex, seemingly relishing her appreciation for his help as much as the physical act.

Later in the day they had sex again, this time one of the weird variants. She found it challenging and instructive, but was able to handle it. It was not painful, just different.

Kerena settled into a comfortable situation. She was treated well by Hirsh, Ona, and the household staff. The sex was tolerable and often interesting and challenging. She was free to go into town when there was time, and she did visit Molly, who was amazed and gratified by her success. And Hirsh started teaching her to read.

The reading sessions were typically after sex; it seemed he did not like to spurt and run, but to have more of a relationship. He gave her a handmade alphabet book that illustrated each letter with a picture. A was for Apple, with the A in color, matching the apple. B was for Bum, with a maid's plush bare bottom showing. It was fun. He showed her how the letters combined to form words, which could be sounded out, though many seemed to follow no reasonable rules and simply had to be memorized. It was a challenge, but she loved it, and he in turn liked her ready aptitude.

"You are destined for higher things than being a man's mistress," he remarked.

"What could be higher than being your mistress?" she asked playfully.

And the scene wavered, assuming that fuzziness of outline that indicated a divergence of the timelines. Jolie, on the verge of napping, came alert.

Yet no choice was being made here. Kerena was merely expressing her satisfaction with her present existence.

Which suggested that this was the wrong path. But what else offered?

Jolie scrambled for alternatives, testing each by sending the thought to Kerena. Return to the brothel? The lines fuzzed worse. Seek other employment? Still the fuzz. Disagree with Hirsh? Worse. Agree with him? The lines clarified. Why should that be? She would have to play it through to see where it led.

She returned to Hirsh's statement. "Well, I hope so," Kerena said smoothly. "Though being your mistress is hardly a chore."

"You are kind. Ona really appreciates your effort."

"I am glad of that."

The lines wavered.

Again, Jolie was in a quandary. What was wrong with this amicable discussion? Kerena *was* glad; she knew how difficult Hirsh's wife could have made her existence, had she chosen. Instead she was supportive, and a nice companion. Should she be otherwise?

The lines clarified somewhat. This was the right track.

Jolie returned to the point of divergence. "I am glad of that," Kerena said. "But surely she would be happier if there were no need for my services."

"Surely," he agreed. "But I am as I am, and she is as she is, so we must make the best of it. We are excellently matched in other respects."

The alternates aligned, but now there was a thought in Kerena's mind. They were making the best of a difficult situation, but wouldn't they be better off if the situation improved? So that there was no need for a mistress?

After the session, Kerena went to Ona. "Please, I do not wish to cause you distress, but there is something on my mind."

Ona looked at her with alarm. "The work is too much for you?"

"No, not at all. I have learned Hirsh's ways and they are challenging but not onerous. Betweentimes he is teaching me to read and write. I like it here. But—" She broke off.

"There is ever a 'but,' " Ona said sadly.

"But I fear I am causing you distress merely by the need for my presence. *You* should be with Hirsh, no one else."

"Agreed. But I am long since resigned. It is hardly your fault."

"He—I—I do not know how to say this without risking offense."

"No offense, dear," Ona said patiently. "Say what you must."

"Hirsh is teaching me to read. It is difficult, but I am very glad to learn, knowing it will surely help me later in life. You—if I could teach you how to—"

"Now I appreciate your gist. I know how, but there is pain. As I told you, balms do not suffice. Despite your youth, you have had experience I have not, but this is a physical rather than a knowledge limitation. I could never perform as you do."

"Yet if you could—"

Ona smiled with her habitual sadness. "If I could, I would. But I can't."

"I—when I was new, I feared something similar. That I would hurt, or be wrongly responsive, so as to alienate my lover. But he gave me a remedy, and perhaps it would work for you also."

"Fear is one thing. Confirmation is another. You had the former, I the latter."

Kerena brought out the love figurine. "If you will, sleep with this in your channel, then see what happens. It worked for me."

"I am long past superstition, dear."

"So am I. But this is genuine magic, used by women for countless generations. Please."

Ona sighed. "I will try it one night, then return it to you. Does that seem fair?"

"Yes. One night should be enough to verify or refute its power."

Ona took the figurine, and Kerena returned to her study of the letters and words. She was laboring to make her writing quite clear, so no literate person could misunderstand it. She was adding words to her vocabulary every day. And the realities remained aligned.

In the morning, early, she went to Hirsh's bedroom, as often he liked sex first thing. He nighted alone, as Ona was too much of a temptation when present in dishabille. She did not like to refuse him, and he did not like to hurt her, so they slept apart, with mutual regret. Once Kerena finished with him, it was safe for husband and wife to be together as they dressed. They liked being together, when it was feasible. They were after all in love.

Kerena entered quietly, intending to join him in the bed as usual, to be there as he awakened. She paused, looking at the bed. There was already activity there. Hirsh was having at a woman with gusto, and she was clasping him and moaning with delight. What was going on? Had he brought in another mistress, without telling her?

They rolled over, and the woman came on top, still connected. It was Ona! She was kissing him as her body struggled to squeeze the last of his passion from him. How had this come to pass?

Then Kerena remembered the love figurine. It had worked! Ona must have felt such strong desire that she had come to Hirsh's bed and seduced him, following through with the kind of passion Kerena remembered experiencing with Morely.

Ona lifted her head and spied Kerena. "There you are, on schedule," she said. "I apologize for preempting you. I simply couldn't wait."

"That's all right," Kerena said, half bemused.

"What did you say to her?" Hirsh asked.

"She gave me her magic," Ona said. "It abolished my pain. Now my vulva matches my passion." Then, to Kerena: "You must sell it to me, dear. I have to have it."

"Oh, I wouldn't sell it," Kerena said.

The lines blurred. Jolie focused.

"I will give it to you," Kerena continued, and the lines clarified.

"But there will be no further need for your services here. You must have substance to make your way elsewhere."

"I will find her another position," Hirsh said. "A better one."

"See that you do," Ona said. "She has given me what I most desired. Now let's have at it again."

"But I am spent!"

"Don't make excuses, wretch! I demand performance, or I will bite off your tool and soak it in vinegar and pepper sauce to strengthen it." She lifted the errant member, threatening it with her teeth.

"Please, not that," he begged.

Ona huffed up in simulated anger. "Do you prefer the whip, you laggard? No more excuses!"

They were going into the alternate mode. Ona clearly was competent, now that her pain was gone.

In due course they joined Kerena for breakfast, glowing. The servants were agog, well aware of the change. Jolie was satisfied, as the timelines remained aligned; this change was necessary.

"It is an irony that your kindness costs you your position," Hirsh said. "You will of course remain here until I find the right position. I also have not forgotten the quest for your lost man. Unfortunately no word has reached me on that score."

"Which suggests that a physical search is not enough," Ona said. "Magic may be required, as was the case for me."

"Magic," he echoed. "Are you hinting what I fear?"

"I believe she could handle it. She's smart enough."

"Am I missing something?" Kerena asked.

"There is a woman who has use for talented women," Hirsh said.

"A woman? Not a man?"

"A woman," Ona said. "In the sense that the brothel madam is a woman. This one is far more talented and powerful, and dangerous when thwarted. Perhaps this is not a good idea."

"But she could help me find Morely?"

"If anyone can, she can," Hirsh said. "She could do more good for you than anyone else in the kingdom. But she could also do you more harm. Her temper is unpredictable. This may after all be too dangerous to risk."

Kerena was intrigued. "Who is she?"

"Morgan le Fey. The king's sister."

Kerena felt a chill of premonition. Danger, indeed. "I have heard of her.

Is it true she can cut the heart out of a man without remorse?"

"She can do it without even touching him," Ona said. "No, this is a bad idea. We will find you some other position."

"Agreed," Hirsh said.

Kerena was relieved. She had no idea what use the Fey would want to make of her, but it surely would not be comfortable.

"So that's decided," Ona said. "We will not send you into that lion's den."

A servant appeared. "A coach is here, asking for the Lady Rena."

"What?" Hirsh asked. "Who has the temerity to claim a member of my household?"

"The Lady Fey," the servant replied.

The three of them exchanged glances, similarly appalled. How could the Fey have known of Kerena's presence here, let alone that she was about to be let go? The situation had changed only this morning.

It had to be magic. Kerena knew with a sinking feeling that it would not be denied.

Chapter 3
Cloak and Dagger

The coach conveyed her to a hidden castle in the center of town. It looked like a seedy neighborhood, but as the coach entered its decrepit gate it shifted to become a glorious edifice overlooking a lovely estate. This was of course the magic of illusion. But which was more truly the illusion: the run-down collections of hovels seen from afar, or the massive ramparts seen from close in?

Did it matter? Probably it was some of each. The point was that few would think to look for such a stronghold here. The faerie sister of the king could not be found unless she wanted to be.

The coach halted. Kerena stepped out onto a stone platform and stood there. The coach moved on. Now she saw with surprise that the horse that had drawn it was actually a harnessed griffin: part lion, part eagle. That had to be more illusion, as griffins were too wild to be tamed or harnessed. It was probably the original horse clothed with illusion. Still, the magic was apt. The coach itself was probably mostly illusion too, and was really a wagon with a token covering. What did it matter, as long as the appearance was proper?

No one else was there. Maybe the coach was early and she wasn't expected yet. Uncertain where to go, she decided to find someone and inquire.

She mounted the steps of a winding stone stairway that led up to a high door nestled between rounded turrets. But when she got there, the door was closed and bolted, and no one answered her knock and call. The stair continued up, so she ascended further, around a turret and beside a deep inner court. She peered down to see shrubs growing therein, and perhaps some small trees. But still no sign of human presence.

Jolie was impressed. This was quality magic, of a level she hadn't thought existed this far back. Fortunately the timelines aligned; she wasn't sure how she would have changed them otherwise.

At last the stair brought her to the top of a turret. She stood in this and gazed around the countryside, spread out like a map below. Now there was no town; fields and forests surrounded the castle. The illusion had changed again.

"Welcome, Kerena."

She jumped; the voice was right behind her. She turned to discover a breathtakingly lovely woman wearing a crown-shaped tiara and a gown that hardly concealed her voluptuous form. "Queen Morgan le Fey," she said, curtsying.

Jolie ducked down as low as she could go. She was afraid of the sorceress and did not want to be discovered.

"I will allow one question a day. The rest is business."

"How much is illusion?"

"All of it." Abruptly they were standing in an ordinary room with no view. The Fey, too, was changed, and was now a moderately dull woman of perhaps forty.

"Thank you. I have expended my question, so will not ask what you want of me."

"Smart girl. I have need of information. You will obtain it. In return I will teach you how to locate your lost man, which will require magical arts. Perform well and you will be rewarded."

She did not need to add that failure to perform well would bring punishment. "I am ready."

"Men have secrets, but they will often betray everything to women they desire enough. I can no longer fascinate men to that degree, because illusion alone won't do it. But you are young enough to have the body, nervy enough to use it effectively, and that is most of what matters."

"I understand."

"Sometimes silence is necessary, and the only way to be sure of it is with the dagger's point. You will learn to handle that aspect too."

Kerena stared at the woman, horrified. "I don't think I can do that."

"Not now. But in time you will."

Her first assignment was to seduce a young knight of the king's court, and to learn where a particular cache of silver was hidden. Kerena suspected that the Fey already knew the answer, but was using this as a test case to see how apt Kerena was in this kind of interrogation. Well, she would try her best; she wanted to learn what the Fey could teach her.

The Fey took her to the edge of town just before the knight was due to pass, and faded out. That was a nice trick of illusion; Kerena made a mental note to learn it when she could. Meanwhile she disposed herself in peasant clothing and waited.

The knight was in plain clothes, anonymous, as he was coming into town for a session at the brothel. He was barely 21 and seemed more like fifteen. Kerena had to remind herself that she was only fourteen, though she felt far older in experience. Morely, the brothel, and Hirsh had done that for her.

She stepped out to block his horse. "Kind sir," she called. "Are you going my way?"

He reined in the animal, contemplating her. Kerena's hair was silken long, her face was innocent, and her shift was snug at the waist, accenting her bosom and hips. "That depends."

"I live on market street, near the center of town." That was near the brothel district; he surely was well familiar with the area. "I am a poor maiden afoot, and it is a long walk. I would be most grateful for a ride."

He decided it was a chance worth taking. After all, if she didn't work out, he still would be close to where he was going anyway. "Come on up." He reached a hand down.

She took his hand, and lifted a leg to join her foot to his in the stirrup. In the process, of course, she flashed her bare leg well toward the juncture. The knight's pupils dilated.

It was a bit of a scramble getting up before him, during which her shift got pulled around to show rather too much flesh, and her breasts scraped across his arm. Finally she was there, her bottom pressed against his crotch, and one of his arms around her body just below her breasts. It was not an elegant mounting, but it had familiarized him with all the aspects of her body that might have interested him. Exposive dishabille was a special art.

She engaged him in dialogue, properly impressed by his every remark. By the time they reached the brothel district, he had lost interest in them. They went on to her house, which was at the edge of the Fey's premises, and turned out to be rather nicer inside than it appeared from the outside.

There was no need for him to make known the nature of his interest. They fell on the bed together, their clothing wedged out of the way in the key regions. He was on her and in her before (it seemed) either of them realized.

Then she let him lie there, while she got up and poured him a cup of strong mead. He glugged it appreciatively, not thinking to inquire how it was that a peasant girl possessed such potent brew. Soon he was pleasantly tipsy.

"You must be a really important person," she said enthusiastically. "You have such an authoritative way about you, as well as being handsome and awesomely virile." The approach was transparently obvious, but probably all that was required in this case.

Perhaps in a more sober state he would have realized the shallowness of the flattery. As it was, he became expansive. He confided that he did have key duties in the king's court.

"Oh, you must know all the wonderful secrets," she said, removing her shift as she paced before him. He watched, his interest stirring again. She made sure that her moderate breasts bounced with each step.

By the time she joined him, nude, for the second round of sex, he had told her about the cache of silver, and where it was hidden. She plied him with more mead, and gave him such an experience that it was unlikely that he would remember anything of his evening except that wild business on the bed. That was important: that he not realize what he had blabbed. The Fey did not like to leave her handprints on her mischief.

The Fey was pleased. "You have the touch," she said. "However, some men are resistive to straight seduction, and must be captured subtly."

"Subtly? In my experience, they are all eager for young bodies."

"Not all. Some prefer other men; they are difficult to seduce by flaunting female attributes. Some are interested, but wish to be the initiators; for them, maidenly diffidence is best. Some are old and slow, but do not wish to be reminded. Some are dangerously smart. It is important to ascertain their types before committing. And, on occasion, it is necessary to seduce a woman."

"A woman!" Kerena was amazed. The Fey had been making excellent sense up to that point.

"Women have secrets too. Some are amenable to the gentle suasion of a lovely woman, rather than the crude directness of a rough man. You must be ready to relate to anyone."

"I don't think I could—relate—to a woman."

"Then learn. Try to seduce me."

"I couldn't!" She was appalled.

"Then learn," the Fey repeated evenly. "I will seduce you. Thereafter you will know."

And as Kerena stood bemused, the Fey became fascinating. She engaged her in pleasant dialogue, flattering her, then slowly embraced her and kissed her. Her manner was so exquisitely smooth and enticing that it seemed in order. Before she knew it, they were naked on the bed, stroking each other's breasts and buttocks. The kisses became passionate, first on the mouth, then the breasts, and finally the cleft.

Only when Kerena found herself gloriously climaxing did she appreciate what had happened. She had been completely seduced—and the Fey had used no magic, not even illusion. Everything was technique. There were indeed ways in which sex was better with another woman than with a man.

"Now what did I do?" the Fey asked.

The question reminded Kerena of Morely's efforts to acquaint her with reality rather than impression. That caused her to focus. "You seduced me. We did not make love; you made me be fulfilled. You were not."

The Fey nodded. "I practice sex for business reasons, rather than for pleasure. But if I wanted pleasure, I would take a virile man. The rest is art."

"And I did not realize it until it was done," Kerena said, awed in retrospect. "Now I understand."

The Fey smiled, pleased in much the way Morely would have been by an apt pupil. "But if my taste happened to be in women, you would be the type I preferred. You have a marvelously fresh young body and face. Hone your skills; you should be good with women when that time comes."

"I will try to be," Kerena agreed.

There were other men, and she crafted her skills, managing the marks precisely. She almost invariably gleaned the information desired, and seldom did the men realize what they had revealed. Sometimes the object was not to gain information, but to gain influence. She cast her spell on key men, so that they would act as the Fey desired, resulting in modifications of court procedure that benefited her. It seemed that the Fey never approached her brother directly; in fact he was unaware of her presence at the capital town. She preferred subtlety, and was remarkably successful in accomplishing her designs. Kerena wasn't certain what those designs were; they seemed obscure. But the Fey definitely had an agenda of some sort.

Kerena mused on what that agenda might be. Power? Perhaps, in part. More likely power was but a means to some other inscrutable end. The Fey was said to be half faerie, and once to have seduced her brother the king and conceived a quarter faerie son by him. There were other stories. Kerena knew she could ask, but she doubted that was wise, and in any event she had more than enough other questions to tackle day by day. Such as her quest to find Morely.

"First you must master your cloak," the Fey said. "That will require time. It is a marvelous device, exceptional magic."

"It is Morely's cloak, not mine. I merely hold it until I can return it to him."

The Fey turned a disturbingly intense gaze on her. "Perhaps. Nevertheless, it is the key to your quest. Only when you master it will you be able to locate him."

"You will teach me?"

"It will require several questions and much practice to unriddle it. Meanwhile, of course, you will continue to serve me."

"If the cloak is so valuable, and you understand it so well, I am surprised you do not simply take it from me for yourself."

The Fey made the Morely type of smile. "You are learning to phrase questions correctly. I would of course take it from you if I could. But it is crafted to resist the faerie element that is the source of my power. It is bound to you; the man surely loves you. Were I to seize it, it would crumble into dirt and be useless. If I am to have use of it, I must do so through you. You will be more useful using its powers, until you learn the last of them; then you will go your own way and I will not be able to stop you. So my hold on you is limited. But we can do each other some good in the interim."

Kerena knew the woman spoke literally: she had no love for Kerena or anyone else, but did have use for her. If the cloak helped her be more useful, the Fey would encourage its use. But the cloak would eventually free her from the Fey. So the Fey would be careful about the lessons, and not give the last one until she had to. Meanwhile, they were indeed doing each other some good: the Fey was gaining much information and influence, and Kerena was learning what she needed. It was a worthwhile association. They understood each other.

Kerena normally slept alone when not using her sexuality for business purposes. One night she discovered a dark figure in her room. Had someone sneaked in? "Who are you?"

The figure did not speak. He extended his shadowy hand and touched hers. She was both amazed and thrilled: that touch had more sheer masculine presence than she had felt from anyone in the past.

She didn't speak again. She joined the figure in her bed and they made phenomenal love. Whoever he was, he was the best sexual partner ever. He made her float like a flower on a pool, sail like a leaf in the wind, and quake with the intensity of her pleasure. It was as though they had known and loved each other forever.

Flushed, panting, feeling like an innocent girl, she lay in his embrace after the first session, marveling at the event. "Have we met before?" she asked.

He merely stroked her hand. Even now, that touch sent a thrill through her body. She was a thoroughly experienced woman, yet compared to him she felt amateur.

They made love again, and again, and each episode radiated pleasure though her being. Then he departed, leaving her to sleep and dream of endless rapture.

In the morning she pondered her experience of the night. She had no idea who her visitor had been, but she longed for his return. She did not speak of this to anyone else, somehow knowing that this was a secret she had to keep, lest she lose any continuation.

Alas, her nocturnal lover did not return. Apparently she had been a mere stop on the way to wherever he was going. Her loin ached for lack of his presence. Almost, she was tempted to ask the Fey about him. Almost. It might be some mischief the Fey had wrought, in which case a question would play into her design. But if the Fey did not know of the man, that was surely significant in another manner. How could anyone enter her premises, and she not know?

Jolie had misgivings about this. The identity of the man was a mystery to her too, and she did not like a mystery of this nature. Yet the lines had not blurred, so it had to be a legitimate part of the girl's existence.

Between assignments Kerena visited Molly. The brothel was close to the Fey's castle, so this was convenient. The girl was a pleasant contrast to the mature cynicism of the Fey. Kerena said nothing of her missions, of course, only that she was now being kept by another client.

The cloak's first revealed property was invisibility. This had to be invoked by a special spoken spell, after she related to the cloak itself. "These things are fairly standard," the Fey explained. "You must get close to the cloak, wrapping it about you naked. You must court it."

"Must what?"

"Court it. Profess your love for it. It will respond if it knows you care."

"But it's just a piece of material."

"Hardly that. It is enchanted material, imbued by a sorcerer I would like to meet; he clearly knows his magic. Disrespect it at your peril."

Kerena saw her point. "I do respect it; I first made love upon it."

"That's a good start. Remind it of that. Then when you have its attention, solicit its power by drawing an analogy and forming a triple rhyme with it. Once you invoke it that way, you must always use that specific form; it will not respond to any other, or to any other person."

"An analogy," Kerena repeated, not getting it.

The Fey frowned. "I thought you were a bright girl."

And the lines of reality started to fuzz.

Jolie moved back a minute. *Invisible like the air. Make me glare like the air, with my fair hair. Something like that, only less clumsy.*

"An analogy," Kerena said. "Now I understand." The lines clarified.

Kerena went to her room and tried it. She stripped naked, wrapped the cloak around her, and whispered "Cloak of night, I love you. Make me part of you." She kissed it.

The cloak writhed, clasping her. It was responding! It had never done that before. But of course she had never tried to invoke its magic, not realizing its nature.

"Cloak, hear my prayer," she whispered. "Make us fair, like the air."

Something changed. For a moment she wasn't sure what, then realized that she couldn't see her legs. She couldn't see any part of her body, or the cloak. That was weird.

She walked to the mirror and looked. There was nothing. She was invisible.

She opened the door and walked out around the house. It was actually fairly small; the appearance of the great castle was merely to impress visitors, such as herself, the first time. The Fey didn't bother to generate the illusion at other times, as it required magical energy she didn't care to waste. She went to see the cook, who wasn't aware of her, and the coachman. He was working on a wagon wheel, and suddenly stepped across the room for a nail. And collided with Kerena.

"What?" he asked, amazed as his arms swung around her. "Am I going blind? I see nothing." One hand closed on her left buttock, through the cloth; the other found her right breast, similarly.

"You rogue!" Kerena exclaimed. "You heard me coming!"

"Aye, miss," he agreed, letting her go. "And got a good feel, too."

She had to laugh. "You're used to magic, around here. But suppose you'd done that to the Fey?"

"She'd have sprouted spines and stabbed me. But I know you apart by your tread and smell."

Here was a learning opportunity. "Teach me to mask those, and I'll give you more than a feel."

The man was happy to cooperate. Soon she was managing to step without sound, as she could do in the dark forest, and knew that a thorough body wash would diminish her smell for several hours if she didn't sweat much. She rewarded him with an invisible sexual clasping that left him more than satisfied. It was after all her stock in trade. The coachman had left her alone, surely on the Fey's order, but would not have been a man had he not had a serious hankering for her body.

She returned to her room, and tried to remove the cloak. And failed; it would not come off. She realized that she did not know how to turn off the spell. She remained cloaked and invisible.

She went to the Fey. "Please, I need to know how to end the invisibility."

"You have had your question for today," the woman snapped. "Save it for tomorrow."

"But I'm stuck this way!"

"You should have considered that before invoking it, you silly girl. Never get into something you don't know how to get out of."

It was excellent advice, albeit a bit late. Also a stiff lesson. She would not make that mistake again. Kerena returned to her room. She used her chamber pot, and saw that when she left it, her refuse was visible, no longer masked by the cloak. But she herself could not leave it similarly.

She slept imperfectly, angry with herself for making such a stupid error. But the cloak was comfortable enough, keeping her warm. In the morning she tried to put something on beneath it, but was unable; it clung too tightly to her body. She would have to remain nude until she nullified the spell.

She went back to the Fey. "Repeat the invocation, exactly as you made it," the woman said, not waiting for the question. "It is an on-off latch."

"Thank you, mistress." Kerena retreated to her room, repeated the invocation, and became visible. Now she was able to remove the cloak.

"Next, master protection," the Fey told her later that day. "It should shield you against arrow, blade, or club. That can be useful on occasion."

Kerena went to her room, romanced the cloak, then whispered her impromptu ditty: "Wield a shield, yield the field." It didn't make a lot of sense, but she trusted the cloak to respond to her meaning.

It did. She did not disappear, and the cloak felt no different, but when she went to the coachman she verified it. "Strike me and you can have me," she told him.

"Magic?"

"I hope so."

He curled his fist and tried a cautious punch, not wanting to hurt her. It sheered off harmlessly. He tried again, with greater force; his fist bounced back at him. He tried a third time, with a carriage stay; it jarred from his hand as if caught on an invisible rail. "Can't touch you," he said. "Too bad for me."

"Let's find out." She opened the cloak, exposing her nude body, and stepped into him. Now there was contact. It was the cloak that fended him off, not her body. "Take me anyway; I appreciate your assistance."

He did not argue. In a moment his member was out and in, as it were, as she stood against the wheel of the coach. She had not had to null the invocation; the cloak repelled intrusion only where its fabric was. "You're a nice girl," he gasped. "Not a tease like those others."

"I can tease when I choose. But I might need a ride sometime." She had long since established that the coach was authentic; it seemed the Fey had found it simpler to get a real one, rare and expensive as it was, than to maintain sufficient illusion to fake it.

"Anytime!"

Unfortunately the impromptu tryst mainly served to remind her of the extent to which this man, and any other man, fell short of her lover of the night. She had been spoiled for ordinary men, just as she spoiled ordinary men for other women. Perhaps it served her right, but her loin still ached.

The third power of the cloak was to make solid substance permeable to her progress, even stone. The ditty she worked out seemed stupid, but it was the best she could do at the moment. "Let me jog through fog, unclog the bog."

Nothing seemed to happen, but she tried walking through the bed. There was no resistance; her cloaked lower portion passed through the bed as if it were, yes, a bank of fog.

She tried the wall, and it seemed like illusion. But why wasn't she sinking through the floor? She kneeled—and suddenly was dropping down through the floor and ground. Oops!

She straightened her legs and came to a halt, well below ground level.

She was entirely surrounded by rock. She felt claustrophobic. She didn't dare null the spell, lest she be crushed by the rock. How could she get back to the surface? Her walking produced only forward motion, which didn't solve the problem.

She felt as if she were suffocating. She had to get out of here! But *how?*

The timelines began to blur. Jolie was already alert; now she knew her concern was justified. Kerena had gotten herself in over her head, literally, and needed help if she was not to perish here. She was running out of air; it seemed that all she had was what had accompanied her inside the enclosure of the cloak. There was not much time left.

Jolie remembered that it had been possible to embrace the coachman while the protection spell was on, because it repulsed only where the material was. If that was the case here, how did it relate? Could the girl open the cloak and—what, be buried in solid rock? Still no good.

She had kneeled, and plunged, as the material made the ground below her pervious. Her feet weren't similarly covered, so found the rock solid as usual. That meant, in turn—

Jolie had it. *Stair steps! Lift your feet and ascend.*

Kerena responded. She lifted one foot, poked her toe forward, and found purchase at the higher level. She lifted the other and leaned forward for balance, achieving the higher level. Where the feet projected beyond the enclosure of the cloak, they found solidity. It was like climbing a hill.

Encouraged, the girl adjusted her stepping to become more efficient. She was gasping from lack of air, but was determined to fight her way up and out. If she collapsed, Jolie would have to step back, perhaps preventing her from dropping below the ground level, but that might cause the timelines to separate. So it was better to let her get through herself, if she could.

At last her head poked out of the ground. She panted, sucking in air, recovering. She was in a cellar, having traveled some distance from her point of entry. Fortunately no person was there to see her.

After a time she climbed the rest of the way out, and stood on the cellar floor. Then she walked through the wall toward the Fey's house. This had been another stiff lesson, and another mistake she would not make again. The magic of the cloak had almost killed her, because she had used it improperly.

Meanwhile the Fey had another assignment for her. "I have my own designs," she said seriously. "But there are villagers who once did me a favor, and I do not wish them ill. They are about to be tricked, trapped, killed, raped, and enslaved, depending on their ages, genders and physical appeal. You must prevent that."

"Of course!"

"They mean to travel to Ireland, where greener fields beckon. This is in order. But a pirate slaver ship means to represent itself as their legitimate transport. Once they are aboard it will be too late; any who try to resist will be summarily beaten or killed. The pirates will publicly gang rape the women. Any children who cry will be hurled overboard. It is necessary to prevent this from happening."

"Yes!"

The Fey's smile suggested that she did not share Kerena's feeling. To her, this was merely another business item. "The legitimate ship is sailing from the south, tacking slowly against the winds. The pirate ship is sailing from the north, with the wind. It will arrive a day ahead, and its representative will approach the people to persuade them it is their intended ship. He is silver-tongued and they are trusting; he will succeed. You must intercept him and divert him that day. If you fail, you must kill him. It is the only way."

"But I'm not a killer!"

"What is your preference: to spare the lives of a hundred innocent villagers, or the life of one criminal?"

"There must be another way."

The Fey shrugged. "Perhaps you will find it."

Kerena arrived at the village inn by coach. This was near the Port of Patrick in southern Scotland, where ships sailed for Ireland. "I have come to catch the ship to Ireland," she told the innkeeper. "Am I in time?"

"You are," he agreed.

"How much for a room and a meal?"

He gave an inflated price.

"Oh, I can't afford that," she said. "My family perished of plague in England, and I have barely enough for food and passage to get me to relatives in Ireland. I will have to sleep on the floor." Her nervous voice could be heard throughout the room.

A dapper man rose from a table. "As it happens, I have a room with a bed big enough for two, if you would care to share it."

She gazed at him with large innocent eyes. "My mother told me not to share a bed with any strange man."

"Then come to my table for some food, and we shall talk. Soon you will be satisfied that I am not strange."

She considered, evidently not picking up on the suppressed smirks of a number of other men. This was almost too easy! "Why thank you, kind sir. That seems fair."

They sat at the table, and the innkeeper brought lamb and ale. Kerena, clearly unused to such brew, was soon pleasantly tipsy. Meanwhile she learned that her companion was called Joiner. He made arrangements for things. He was on his way to make a deal for a village traveling to Ireland to obtain passage on the same ship she sought. "Oh, that seems so important!" she exclaimed, much impressed.

In due course, she accompanied him to his room, trustingly and not completely steady. He was soon kissing her and running his hands over her body. She removed her cloak, then her traveling dress. They had urgent sex. Then, as they relaxed, she engaged him in further dialogue. He had taken a fair amount of ale himself, and that and her wonder-filled interest loosened his tongue. He confessed his real mission: to trick the villagers into boarding the pirate ship that had arrived before the legitimate one.

"But that is not nice," she protested. She was playing her role, but she agreed with it. She did not like malicious mischief. "What have those people done to you, that you should treat them thus?"

"Nothing. They are merely marks. They deserve what their idiocy brings them."

Kerena decided to distract him until it was too late to meet the villagers. She was pretty sure she could do it, because she had hardly begun to show him what she could do with her bare body.

The lines blurred.

Jolie moved back a few seconds, revising the thought.

"I must warn them," Kerena said, rising from the bed. The lines clarified.

Joiner realized that he had said too much. "I can't let you do that."

She ran to the door, swooping up her cloak and drawing it about her, lacing it at the neck. "You can't stop me."

He laughed. "I don't need to. You will not make it out of the inn. The others here are pirates on leave from the ship. They will make gang sport of you, and take you with them to the ship so their fellows can finish the job."

"Oh!" she cried in maidenly dismay. "I thought you were nice."

"I was, until you made me talk too much. Now I must kill you. But first I mean to have my way with you again, because you are a really nice morsel with a tight little bum."

"You can't kill me," she said desperately. "That would be murder."

He caught her arm and hauled her back to the bed. "You have no family, and are in a foreign country. So one will miss you until long after my mission with the villagers is done. You should have heeded your mother's advice."

"Oh, I am undone!" she wailed helplessly.

"Therefore I will do you," he said, pressing her down on the bed. Her cloak fell open below the neck, providing access to her breasts and belly.

She tried to resist, but her flailing arms had no power against his restored urgency. She wept as he brutally penetrated her. It was evidently way too late to distract him the necessary time.

"Delightful," he said as he concluded. "I am truly sorry to waste such a beautiful body. But business is business. Now fare well in the other realm." He caught the ends of his kerchief, which he had laid conveniently under her neck, and twisted them together in front, slowly throttling her. Her face reddened as her breathing was cut off. The pirate had no mercy.

Then her hidden dagger plunged into his side, severing blood vessels near his heart. "Aaahh!" he groaned, falling over. The wound was not immediately lethal, but there were no good treatment facilities here, and he would die in a few days. His condition would serve as a distraction so that the other pirates would not think to find another man to tackle the villagers.

Kerena got out from under him. "You should have allowed me to distract you longer," she said. She had not actually been choked; the laced cloak had protected her neck, and she had faked it by holding her breath. She had hoped he would reconsider, then acted when it was clear the hope was vain.

Jolie was also sorry the man had not allowed himself to be distracted longer. Yes she had been the one to prevent that. Why had she had to put Kerena into such a brutal alternative?

The man's warning about the other pirates was surely well taken. Kerena did not risk it. She invoked the cloak's permeability power and walked through the wall. Outside, she canceled it and invoked invisibility. When she was well clear of the inn she returned to normalcy.

The coach was waiting in a secluded glade. The coachman was snoozing as the horse grazed.

"I am done," she said, not loudly.

He came awake. "Miss Rena! How was it?"

Suddenly it struck her. "I killed him! I stabbed him to death."

"Remove your cloak, Miss, and I will comfort you."

She took off the cloak and put it in the coach. Then she accepted his embrace. Of course it would lead to sex, but he had become something of a friend, and did care for her to a reasonable extent. She did need the comfort.

"It was awful," she sobbed. "I wanted to distract him, to talk him out of it, but I messed it up and he raped me and I had to kill him."

"You didn't use the cloak?" the coachman asked alarmed.

"Only to protect my neck when he throttled me. I wanted to occupy him for a night and day, so he would forget, but somehow I didn't. So I had no choice. I am devastated."

"Miss, can you keep a secret?"

What was on his mind? "Yes."

"It's like that, working for the Fey. I have had to do things I didn't like. I know how it is. She forces you not only to do her bidding, but to do it in the way she wants. She makes people fit her moral compass. You couldn't help it."

"I could have distracted him longer. I know it. Somehow I didn't."
Jolie felt guilty.

"I don't think so. Pirates like to rape, loot, and kill; they get almost as much satisfaction from the one as the other. He wouldn't have let you play him along any further than he wanted. The Fey knew that."

"She said I might find another way."

"She knew there wasn't. She let you try your way and fail, so you had no choice but her way. She wanted you to be blooded. To learn to kill. Don't blame yourself; blame her. But don't tell her I told you."

Kerena considered that, and realized it was true. She had been put into a situation with but one likely outcome. Indeed, it had not really been her fault. Still, it hurt.

Yet Jolie knew there had been an alternative. That knowledge hurt her too.

"Cry," the coachman said. "It helps. I know."

She cried into his stout shoulder. It did help.

Then she lifted her face. "You haven't tried to seduce me."

"It doesn't seem right. You are in pain."

"You are a decent man. You deserve your reward. Take me."

He took her, gently, on the coach seat. She kissed him repeatedly, appreciating his concern for her. She had long since learned that though sex was the first thing most men thought of when they saw a figure like hers, they did have other dimensions.

Except, perhaps, for her anonymous lover of the night. He had shown no other interest than sex, yet that had proved to be more than sufficient.

The journey back took time, and she obliged the coachman frequently. It was her main coin, and she realized that his friendship could be useful. Once they got back, the Fey would have other things for both of them to do, so there was a convenient limit to the affair. Meanwhile, it did help distract her from the awfulness of her blooding.

Yet there was worse. Back in town, Kerena went to visit Molly, and learned that the girl was dead. She had been brutally murdered by a client. Blake had gone after the man with a knife, but too late to catch him. Her friend was gone.

"The girl was cursed," the Fey said matter of factly.

"Cursed?"

"Destined to die young and violently. Didn't you know?"

"She never spoke of such a thing."

"Why would she? Her destiny was fixed."

Kerena was hurting from the loss of her friend so soon after the loss of her own innocence about killing. It was as though she had stabbed her friend. "Couldn't the curse have been stopped?

"The time to abate a curse is before it strikes. Or better, before it is made."

Of course it was too late. But Kerena still hurt. Why couldn't she have seen it coming with her Seeing? Maybe she could have, and prevented it, had she just thought to. Had she been there when her friend most needed her. "What can I do now?"

"After she is dead? Reanimation of the dead is beyond my powers and yours, I think."

Surely true. But she still couldn't let it rest. "Where is she now?"

"The victims of such curses normally can't rest, even after death. Not until they manage to abate their curses. She will be a ghost until the final kingdom comes."

Kerena thought about that. If Molly remained here, albeit as a ghost, maybe there was still a chance for her. If there were a way to reanimate her. If Kerena could find it. She had learned much magic; could she somehow learn this?

She didn't know. But she intended to keep it in mind.

CHAPTER 4
SIR GAWAIN

"This case is special," the Fey informed her. "You must corrupt a good man."

"Corruption is easy, if I don't have to kill him." Kerena made no secret of her distaste for killing, but also didn't try to hide the fact that she *had* killed. Her training was proceeding according to form.

"Not in this case. He must not be killed, and he must not know my hand in this. He is intelligent and honorable, dreadfully difficult to sway. Succeed in this, and I will teach you the last great power of your cloak: the ability to orient on its master."

"Morely!"

"You can find him, and with what you have learned, it may now be safe for you to do so. After this mission."

"I will accomplish it," Kerena said, thrilled by the prospect of finally locating her beloved. She was now fifteen, and thoroughly practiced both in the seduction of men and the use of the magic cloak.

"My benighted brother the king seeks the grail." The Fey spoke of Arthur as if he were a dullard, her jealously of his status showing. She surely would have preferred to rule herself, but women weren't allowed at this stage of history.

"The what?"

"It is an ornate cup, said to be the chalice used by Jesus Christ to drink his wine at the Last Supper, and in which some of his blood was caught when he died on the cross. Surely superstition, but my brother believes in it, and has set his knights of the round table to seek it and fetch it to him. The real origin of this talisman is as a female sex symbol whose blood relates to that of the curse of women. Thus men are drawn to it as they are to women, but regard it as pure in a way no women can be. So if there is such a cup, it is unattainable by any man who is not quite pure. In short, a male virgin."

"Those exist?" Kerena asked, surprised.

The Fey smiled. "There are a number of boys below the age of ten who are pure in that foolish manner, and a few retain it to adulthood, if they are not comely. This does not relate to their inevitable experimental spilling of their seed on the ground, only to their genital contact with women. But a handsome, manly virgin is a rarity indeed. Sir Lancelot was one, before the queen corrupted him; that was perhaps her noblest deed, though she got little thanks from the king. Now the leading candidate to find this article is the king's younger cousin Sir Gawain." She accented the name on the first syllable: GA-win.

"Sir Gawain! I have heard of him."

"Everyone has," the Fey agreed wryly. "But no one has seduced him. That will be your chore."

"But he is a famous knight! I couldn't even aspire to touch him."

"He is a man. You are a beautiful young creature. You need not touch him; get him to touch you. Get close to him, and let the chemistry percolate." The term she used was not exactly "chemistry," as that word had not yet come into play, but it was the way Jolie heard it.

"Oh, I couldn't," Kerena said, awed.

"You little fool, what do you think I have been training you for? Those other missions I could have done more expediently with other personnel. I was preparing you for this. Remember the reward I offer."

Kerena remembered. "I will try," she agreed.

The Fey nodded, satisfied to have corralled her balky mare. "It will take time, because he is proof against all ordinary suasions. Do not push it; he must approach you in his own fashion. But when at last his burgeoning desire can no longer be contained, accept it. At that point your work for me will be done."

"That would really deny him the Grail?" Kerena asked dubiously. "Why should an inanimate cup know or care about the sexual status of the man who takes it?"

"As I said, this is mostly superstition. But there is always the chance there is genuine magic there. I will accept it either way: that it can't be touched by other than a virgin, or that the men *believe* it can't be. Then even if Gawain were able to take it after all, my brother would not believe in its authenticity, and would not use it to enhance his power."

Kerena nodded. Like Morely, the Fey knew the distinction between appearance and reality, and was not fooled by the mere semblance of magic. She was out to nullify that cup regardless, thus curbing the power of her brother. The king would never have the use of it, even if it came to sit upon his table.

Sir Gawain liked to gaze at the stars. Other knights thought he was a bit tetched, but Kerena understood; the wonder of so many brilliances still transfixed her when she allowed it. She couldn't help liking a man who liked the night sky, regardless of his status. So she went in the evening to the spot the knight preferred, some distance from the royal town, and joined him in staring raptly at the dark sky.

"Maiden," he said. "Shouldn't you be home?"

"Home is drudgery," she replied. "I prefer to travel. Since I can not safely do it alone, I do it in my imagination, moving among the myriad stars."

"This is an unusual attitude for a young girl. Surely your prospects for achievement and marriage are of greater concern."

"Perhaps, in time. But first I wish I could fathom the world, or as much of it as may be within my reach. There are so many things to know, and a lifetime seems too little to learn them all."

"I agree." He looked at her in the wan starlight, surely able to see no more than her dark silhouette. "However, you can admire the stars from almost any location where there is no nearby lamplight to interfere. Why did you come here?"

Thus did he let her know she wasn't fooling him. "I would like to travel with you, bold knight." She was being easy on the flattery, as he was not the type to be deceived by false words.

He sighed. "For a moment I almost hoped you were not that sort. I have nothing for you."

"I am not approaching you as that sort. I really do want to travel, and believe it would be most safe and rewarding in your company."

"Perhaps I was not clear. I am a chaste knight. I do not wish to dally with the distaff gender, however much I may respect it as a class."

"I am not chaste. I am but fifteen years of age, but have seen solid service in the town brothel district. I would like to be known for something other than my body."

"You are Rena!"

"So you recognize me," she said ruefully. "Though I am sure you never frequented that district."

"I have friends who do. They have reports of a girl who not only indulges their carnal appetites excellently, but also engages their minds. I had not heard tell of her in the past year, however, and assumed she had gone elsewhere."

"Gone to wealthy households."

"Ah. But even if I had that kind of interest, I lack wealth. The acquisition of material value is not for me."

"Consequently on occasion you go hungry."

"That is the way it must be."

She phrased her offer carefully. "I do not wish to affront you with any unkind implication, knowing it would be unfair. But wouldn't it be more convenient for you to travel if there were someone along who was less scrupulous than you are in the practical matters of obtaining food and lodging for you?"

"I am satisfied to endure what fate intends for me."

"And your horses?"

Sir Gawain made a little sigh. "I hate to have them suffer on my behalf." Jolie knew that this was before the time of real squires; knights had to see to the needs of their steeds themselves. In fact they were hardly knights in the manner of legend; they were more like loyal supporters of the king, there to do his will in major or minor ways. They had no metal armor or brightly polished shields blazoned with their shields-of-arms; tough weathered leather sufficed.

"There might be no need, if someone were there to make arrangements for their comfort."

"It is true what they have said: you have an uncanny knack for discovering a man's weaknesses."

"Let me accompany you, and I will devote myself to the sustenance of your horses."

He was silent for a time. "As it happens, I am about to embark on what may be an extended quest. Provender for my horses is uncertain. I would be gratified to be assured of their welfare. Yet I must repeat that I have no intention of treating any young women as anything other than parallel spirits."

"This was my understanding of you. Were I to travel with any other man, I would have to be his mistress."

"Surely true," he agreed. "Even Lancelot—" He broke off, unwilling to speak unkindly of another knight.

Jolie knew what he was thinking of. Sir Lancelot had become notorious for his passion for the king's wife, and it seemed she returned the interest. It was a scandal that somehow had simmered below the awareness of the king. Yet how could the king not have known? The answer, it seemed, was that Lancelot was a very skilled knight the king needed by his side, and the king was willing to overlook certain irregularities to ensure that Lancelot stayed. The queen was the best guarantee of that. It was not as if the king himself had never strayed. So as long as the two were circumspect, the matter was ignored. For now.

"I have a few coins," Kerena said. "I can obtain some feed for your horses. But that will soon be gone. Then I will need to garner more coins, but I don't think it would be appropriate to do that in the manner I have practiced in the past."

"I agree emphatically. Fortunately there is a protocol. I will do some knightly service for a farmer, who will in turn provide some sustenance. The details do not concern me, other than the need to be assured that no one is treated unfairly."

"Of course. I will be glad to dicker with farmers. You will see that the terms are mutually fair."

"Then I believe we have an agreement. Tomorrow I start my quest. If you will join me then—do you know where I reside?"

"Yes. I will be with your horses. I trust your spare will allow me to ride him?"

There was a smile in his voice. "If you feed him, he will allow you anything."

"Thank you. I will be there." She got up and departed without ado. It was a private pleasure to interact with such a clearly honorable man, so different from the great majority. She was sorry she would have to corrupt him.

❦

Kerena went to a grain merchant who was working late and bought two bags of oats. "You can have extra portions, if," he said as he got a fair look at her.

"These are for Sir Gawain's horses."

He said no more, recognizing the name. Everyone in town knew that the knight did not make untoward deals. The same surely went for his maidservant. But she realized it would be better if she concealed her gender hereafter.

She made her way to the stable, found a dry corner, and used the bags as pillow and footrest, the cloak covering all. It was a reasonably comfortable night.

In the morning she found a refuse trench for natural functions, ate the stale bread she had saved, wrapped the cloak closely about her body and head, and brought the bags to the horses. "Who are you?" the stable boy demanded, appearing from a shed.

"I am Sir Gawain's servant, bringing feed for his horses."

"Give it to me. I'll take care of it."

And sell some of it to another knight, she knew. "Thank you, I will handle it myself."

"No you won't," he said, putting a rough hand on her shoulder.

So much for concealment. She turned, let her hood fall back to reveal her face and bosom, and smiled at him. He fell back as if struck. "I thought you were a—a boy."

"I have not recently been mistaken as such." It was such an obvious understatement that he had no response. He went about his business, leaving her to hers.

She opened one bag and held it up to the nose of the lead stallion, a magnificent creature. He munched contentedly; they were good oats. When he was done, she proffered the other bag to the auxiliary horse, a lesser stallion but still a fine animal. If there was one thing a knight was known for, it was the quality of his horses.

Sir Gawain arrived as the second horse was finishing. "Very good," he said. "I trust you know how to ride?"

"I have never been on a horse alone, only when guided by another rider. I hope it is not difficult."

He paused. "Perhaps, then, we should best begin slowly. If you fall, try to get your feet under you. I will put you on Service."

So that was the name of the horse. Sir Gawain led the horses out, and Service stood still while Gawain put his hands on her elbows and lifted her to the blanket saddle. She was surprised by how readily he did it; he had enormous strength of arm.

Then he mounted his lead horse, and they set off. A cord reached back from the lead saddle to Service's halter, and the horse followed without question. So she had no need to guide him. That was a relief.

They walked slowly away from town. Kerena adjusted to the rolling gait, gradually getting comfortable with it. The horse felt the difference, and moved up to walk parallel to the other.

"Service says you are learning," Sir Gawain remarked.

"Service is a good teacher."

They moved more rapidly, and she adjusted to the faster gait. She discovered that there was a certain pleasure in riding. It was somewhat like floating in air, except that she wasn't floating.

They came to a public water trough, and both horses drank deeply. Sir Gawain dismounted, fetched the ladle, and drank. Then he refilled it and brought it to Kerena where she sat, uncertain how to dismount alone.

"But you must not serve me," she protested. "I must serve you."

"Only if you view yourself as servant rather than companion."

"I do."

"As you wish." He took the empty ladle back.

"If I may inquire," she said as they resumed travel, "where are we going?"

"I would answer if I could, but I don't know. I seek the Holy Grail. No one knows where it resides."

"Then how will you find it?"

"I will simply look until it reveals itself to me. That is why this quest may take some time. If you wish to change your mind, I will take you back to town."

"No," she said quickly. "I was not expressing impatience, merely doubt. I am not familiar with this sort of search." But as she spoke, she realized that she was: it mirrored her own search for Morely.

In late afternoon they came to an extensive farmstead. The farmer came out to meet them. "Welcome, Sir Gawain! Have you come for a visit?"

"I have, for one night. What service may I do you, in exchange for food and lodging for myself, my servant, and my horses?"

"There is no need of service. Your fame is known here."

"There is need. I prefer to pay my way."

"Well, if you insist. There are some ruffians camping in my kindling lot that need to be rousted out. I am not a fighting man, so have been unable to do it myself."

"It shall be done," Sir Gawain said.

The farmer showed them where the lot was, and they rode to it. Several surly vagabonds were camping there. "The farmer requests your absence from these premises," Sir Gawain informed them politely. "Please depart."

"Yeah?" one demanded, lifting a wicked looking club. "How would your nag like a clout on the snout?"

Kerena kept her face straight. The lout had threatened the wrong member of the party.

"I see I have not spoken clearly," Sir Gawain said, dismounting. "I apologize, and shall try to rectify the lapse." He drew his sword from a sheath on the horse that Kerena had not noticed before. The bared metal looked long and sharp. "Depart, or I shall be forced to chastise you."

The men stared at the sword. Then the leader suddenly charged, swinging his club.

Sir Gawain's sword flashed. The club flew from the man's hand. Then Kerena saw that this wasn't exactly the case: most of the club had flown. The stub of the handle remained in the man's hand. He was staring at it.

"I hope it is not necessary to draw blood," Sir Gawain said. "I dislike having to clean my blade. Depart forthwith, and do not return, lest my ire be roused."

The squatters had finally gotten the message. They fled.

"You could have cut off his hand—or his head," Kerena said, amazed.

"Fortunately that was not necessary. The warning sufficed."

It had, indeed. Kerena's knees felt weak; it was just as well that she was mounted. She had just seen another side of this supremely polite knight. There was iron under that courteous demeanor.

They returned to the farmer, who had seen the action from a distance. "You didn't kill them."

"I dislike pointless bloodshed. Send a messenger after me, should they return, and I will destroy them. But I doubt it will be necessary."

The farmer nodded, agreeing.

They had an excellent night, beginning with a feast of a meal. Kerena was given a bed in the servant's quarters, while the knight had a room to himself. The horses were well fed and stabled. Her only problem was that her inner thighs were sore from the unaccustomed riding.

"I do see the way of it," Kerena said as they resumed travel next day. "It was a fair trade."

"That is as I prefer." He glanced across at her. "How are your legs?"

"Stiff," she said. "But I will handle it."

"Is there abrasion?"

"Some."

"I regret not realizing. I have some balm that should help." He dismounted, reached into a saddlebag, and produced a glob of something. "Raise your leg."

She lifted her right leg. He mashed the gob between his hands, then smeared it on her inner thigh, reaching up almost to the juncture of her legs. Then he walked around to the other side and repeated the process for her left leg.

Kerena sat and let him do it. Any other man would be slavering at such intimate touching, but he was methodical. Almost immediately the discomfort diminished; the balm was helping. "Thank you."

"Now you must learn to guide the horse." He set a cloth bit in the horse's mouth with reins coming back to her hand. "Be gentle, always; Service knows the signals. Draw right to turn him right, left to turn him left. Draw both to make him halt. Shake them to make him start."

She tried the signals, and they worked; the horse was well trained and responsive. She was in charge now, at least to the extent the horse allowed.

As afternoon came, they sought another farmstead. An old woman came out to meet them. "Let me handle this," Kerena said. She slid off the horse, utilizing a maneuver she had recently learned by observation, and approached the woman. "My master the knight would like food for us and the horses. What is there we can do for you to earn it?"

"I am a poor widow. I have no wood for my hearth. My food is unworthy. All I have is beans."

"Maybe we can bring in some wood from the forest. Beans will do. May the horses graze the night in your fields?"

"Welcome. The fields are part of the commons." The commons was land held in common, available to anyone for use. But locals could get annoyed if folk not of their village made too free with it.

They went into the forest and tied small dry fallen branches together so the horses could drag them. By dusk they had a considerable pile beside the house. The widow was thrilled.

They turned the horses loose to graze on the rich weeds, and settled down to a big pot of beans. They were good enough, but had a gastric effect. They endured it. They spent the night comfortably in the widow's haybarn. Kerena's legs were tired, but the balm had alleviated the soreness. She remembered Sir Gawain's strong, competent, gentle hands stroking them. He had not even looked at their juncture. That impressed her as much as anything else.

Next day they moved on through the forest. Things were fine until a sudden thunderstorm came up. They barely had time to get off the horses and huddle under a tarpaulin Sir Gawain produced. It wasn't quite watertight, but was a lot better than the drenching rain outside it. It also wasn't really large enough for two; she curled up and he put his arms around her, holding the tarp in place. Again, there was no untoward contact; the man was either saintly or sexless.

It became routine as the days passed. They traveled around the countryside, doing chores for sustenance. When they camped out, she would fetch wood, make a fire and heat or cook something for them to eat. Kerena began to doubt that there was any Grail to find, but didn't say anything. After all, if it didn't exist, then her mission had already been accomplished.

Then at dusk, as they were making camp near a forest, close to a town, something happened. Kerena saw a glow hovering at about head height. "What is that?"

Sir Gawain looked. His jaw dropped. "That is the Grail!"

Now she made out some detail. It seemed to be a shining cup, floating not far ahead of them. Sir Gawain walked toward it, and so did Kerena. They did not dare remove their eyes, lest the amazing vision be lost. The cup drifted back, but they were gaining on it, mesmerized.

Then they slipped as they stopped into some sort of pit. They slid down into a large trough filled with—

"Shit!" Kerena exclaimed. She was speaking literally.

It was the town refuse pit. The people dumped their buckets of human manure here, to decay into new soil.

They scrambled out, but the damage was done. Both were soaked in kitchen garbage and fecal matter. They stank.

The image of the Grail, of course, was gone. It occurred to Kerena that it could have been a will-o-wisp, sponsored by the miasma rising from the rotting substance.

"We have to wash," Kerena said urgently. "Everything."

He did not argue.

They spied a river close enough to reach. They hurried to it and plunged in. They removed their sodden clothing and rinsed it repeatedly in the flowing water. They ducked their heads and washed their hair.

Eventually they emerged from the water, naked, chilled, and embarrassed. Night was closing, and their soaking clothing was no good to wear until it dried on the morrow.

"Maybe the horses will share their warmth," Kerena said.

"They need to be free to graze."

"I don't think I can make it through the night like this," she said, shivering violently. "I'll make a fire."

She did so, but there wasn't enough fallen wood in the vicinity to make a big blaze, and they were still shivering.

"We must share body warmth," Gawain said. He fetched the tarpaulin and blankets from the horses and made a bed on the ground next to the small fire.

"I'm not sure this is wise," Kerena said. "You are chaste; can you clasp a naked woman, however innocently?"

"You are suffering; I do not wish that. I will endure."

They lay close together within it, clasping each other for scant warmth. She curled up facing the fire, and he cupped her from behind. It did help; gradually her shivering became less violent. But she knew she was tempting him. One of his arms passed over her and held her close, and one of her breasts touched it. Her bottom was against his groin, and his groin got hot. He desired her, which was hardly surprising; she had grown into a completely seductive young woman. She could probably seduce him now, but she didn't try; it would be a betrayal of his trust in her.

She pondered that in her waking moments. Here she was within reach of her mission, to make this man unchaste, yet she was not grasping it. Why did she care about his trust? Because, she realized with surprise, she was becoming smitten with him. He was a truly noble man, and she respected that and liked him. She did not want to be responsible for his loss of chastity. Which was a crazy attitude, considering her mission.

In the morning they separated. She had hung their clothing on nearby bushes to dry by the fire, and that had been effective. They dressed, and she fixed a breakfast, and checked the horses.

"I have a confession to make," Gawain said as they rode on, circling the dump.

"There is no need." She had a notion of its nature, and preferred to avoid the subject.

"I believe there is, for I value my integrity. Last night as we shared warmth, I had untoward awareness of you."

"You did nothing. I would have known."

"That is not enough. I prefer to be chaste in mind as well as body. I apologize for being mentally unchaste with you."

"Sir Gawain, I am long since unchaste; you cannot wrong me in such fashion, mentally or physically. Had anything happened, it would have been my fault for tempting you unduly. Please have no concern."

"I suppose that is the case. Yet you have been perfect as I have known you, temperate and useful. I would not know your history had you not told me your identity."

"I wish I had no history, so as to be as you would like to see me."

"As far as I am concerned, you are as I see you."

She felt an unaccustomed tear. "I hope never to disappoint you." And what of her mission? Now she hated it.

They traveled, exchanging good deeds for sustenance, and when that was not feasible, camping out. Kerena made sure always to see to the horses, conjuring water when the landscape was too dry. Unfortunately, one day Gawain caught her at it.

"How came you by that water?"

"I have a talent for finding springs."

He merely gazed at her with disappointment.

"A magic talent," she said, amending it. She was unable to lie directly to him. "I have a—a way with the dark arts. I did not want to embarrass you with that information."

"I have known it," he said. "You can strike fire from nothing."

"Yes. But my ability need not sully you; I had it before I knew you, and you have never asked me to practice it."

"You have used it only at need, to serve me or the horses."

"I promised to be useful."

He considered. "I do not consider magic to be unclean, any more than sex is. I am aware that they are common for most people, and often useful. I merely prefer to retain the benefits of abstinence from things that can interfere with my mission."

"That is worthy."

"You are beautiful."

She wasn't sure how to react, and not just because she was in ill-fitting brush-dried apparel, with her hair clumsily knotted and dirt on her feet. "You are kind."

"I am not referring to your appearance, though that is outstanding. In the things that matter, you have been the ideal maiden."

Again she felt the tear. "I am not."

"You believe that your past sullies you. I do not see it that way."

Now tears flowed in earnest. "I am what my history makes me. I can never be ideal."

He put his arms about her, comfortingly. "I apologize for bringing you grief."

"Don't apologize to me!" she flared, pulling away. "I am not worthy of it."

"But you are."

"I am not!" She was in full dismay. That made her reckless. "I will prove it. I am not here on my own. I was sent by Morgan le Fey to seduce you so you could not find the Grail."

That set him back. "I did not know this."

"Now you do. I must leave you, lest I corrupt you." Now she had betrayed her mission. What possessed her?

"You could have done this before now. Why didn't you?"

"Because I love you." Oh, damn! She had let her emotion govern her sense. But that did answer her own question: love possessed her. She couldn't stand to hurt this man, and further silence was bound to do that.

"But don't you have a man you seek?"

"I love him too," she said, bemused by her own state. "I would not hurt either of you. So I must go."

"I know something of the Fey. She is not a nice person. She will punish you if you fail your mission."

"I know. But so it must be."

"I can not allow this. You must stay."

"I want to, but not for proper reason."

"Damn proper reason!" he swore, surprising her. "It is in any event too late."

"I don't understand. If I leave now—"

"I am already corrupted, in my heart. I can not continue my mission without you."

"Oh, Sir Gawain! I am sorry."

"So am I. We have no future together. I could never marry you; my family would not allow it. They would not see the qualities in you that I see. So I have nothing to offer you. But neither can I let you go."

"I must go, for that reason." Kerena came to her difficult decision.

But now the time lines began to blur. Jolie had to intercede. She moved back to just before that decision, suppressing it.

"Then what are we to do?" Kerena asked.

"We must continue. Perhaps I can achieve the Grail before I do with you what I so desperately desire."

That was playing it very fine. But what else was there? "I will try to support you in this."

"Thank you. Do not let me touch you, lest I be overwhelmed."

"I could not resist your touch."

"We must stay apart," he agreed.

They continued to travel, without touching so much as a finger to each other. But Kerena knew this could not continue indefinitely. Not since Morely had she truly wanted to clasp a man in love; all between had been business and convenience. Yet that clasp would ruin his mission. They both knew it.

They came to a broad plain overgrown with tall dried grass. It was fine for the horses to graze on, but there was no water. So Kerena tapped a stone to make it issue water, and caught enough for both animals to drink. Then they moved off, contentedly grazing.

"I don't think I should make a fire," Kerena said. "It is so dry here, the grass might catch, and we might not be able to get it out."

"I agree. We can do without a fire."

They ate what they had, and made ready for the evening. The horses would graze through the night and return in the morning; they required no supervision.

Then Kerena sniffed the air and felt something. "There is fire," she said nervously. "Not of my doing."

"There is," he agreed. "And wind. I fear this is bad news." He tended to understate things.

The fire flared up, racing toward them, consuming the dry grass. They could not outrun it; it was crossing the field in a broad swath, incited by the wind. Flames flew ahead, to ignite grass ahead. It was a thorough conflagration, with smoke roiling above.

"Forgive me," Kerena said. "I must use stronger magic."

"Forgiven!" He was after all a practical man.

She returned to the rock she had evoked to water the horses. This time she intensified the spell. A fountain appeared, jetting up beyond head-height and spreading out. The water splashed back to the ground, forming an expanding puddle. As the fire closed in on them, surrounding them, the water spread out to intercept it. There was a great hissing and an awful smell, but the fire could not reach them.

Yet all through the field it was burning. They could not leave their puddle.

"Pray that the horses found a river," Sir Gawain said.

"Surely they did. They are fast enough to outrun it, and smart enough to avoid it."

There was nothing to do but settle for the night. But their bedding was sodden, and though she had let the fountain subside as the fire burned itself out, all they had to lie down on was mud.

"I would not have you sleep on that," Sir Gawain said gallantly. "I will lie on it, and you may use me as a bed."

"That must not be. We would be touching."

"But fully clothed. That needs must suffice."

"Better we sleep apart. I can survive mud."

"I mislike it. Allow me to do this much for you, Rena. You are precious to me."

"And you to me. That's why we must sleep apart."

"Your mission is to seduce me, yet you oppose it."

"Yes. I want you to have the Grail."

"Though that will cost you the Fey's enmity."

She smiled. "I appreciate the irony."

"Yet if I touch you, you will not oppose me."

"I can't. I desire you intensely, though I curse the cost of you."

"Your diffidence appeals to me as much as your body."

"Oh, this is awful! I am tempting you even as I try to spare you."

"The game is lost. I must have you, though hell betide. Only your nega-tion can stop me, for I would not cross a maiden's will."

"I can't deny you. Stay clear." The words seemed contradictory, but they both knew what she meant.

"I am a man of realism as well as aspiration. You have become more vital to me than the Grail."

"Don't say that!"

"You exist. That may be more than can be said for the famed goblet." He removed his clothing.

Kerena knew she shouldn't, but she couldn't help herself. She removed her own clothing.

They stood facing each other, a small distance apart, mutually naked. Her body was quivering with yearning; his was rampant. Desire suffused them like invisible fire. Then they came together, embracing, kissing, strok-ing, struggling for closer contact. And slipped and fell to the mud.

It didn't matter. He was on her and in her, and she was on him and around him, and they were ardently kissing through the mud that quickly coated them. Taken as a whole, it was glorious.

They spent the rest of the night clasped. There was no counting the times he penetrated her, or the times she took him in. It was seemingly end-less passion.

In the morning the fire had burned out, the horses had returned, and they were so mud-caked as to be virtually unrecognizable. "We shouldn't have done that," Kerena said ruefully.

He laughed. "If I had to become unchaste, this was the appropriate way to do it. Filthy sex."

She joined in, almost hysterically. They certainly looked the part. Yet she was deeply saddened by it too; he had lost his prime mission in life.

She evoked the fountain again, and they took turns stepping into it and rinsing themselves off. It required several rinsings to thin the mud and wash it out of their hair and body crevices.

And of course the sight of their clean wet nudity aroused renewed interest, and they stepped into the fountain together and made love standing amidst the flowing water.

"My emotion is mixed," Sir Gawain said. "Yet I think my joy of possessing you is greater than my grief of losing the Grail."

She did not remind him that he might have had both, had they been able to wait.

In due course they started back the way they had come, as there seemed to be no further point in pursuing the Grail. The journey would take many days, and they did not hurry. Instead they camped out often, and made love more often, catching up on previously suppressed passion. It was the gloriously open expression of their love, which would have to end once they got home. That was why they were satisfied to go slowly.

About two days distant from the capital town, they had another vision. This time there was no garbage pit; the divine Chalice was floating above the middle of the road. There was no doubt of its nature; it was an ornate golden goblet that glowed of its own volition. It was so lovely that both of them stared raptly.

"Do you see it?" Sir Gawain whispered.

"I do see it," she whispered back. "It's the Grail, come to you after all. Take it, beloved!"

Sir Gawain strode forward, reaching for the scintillating cup. It floated away, avoiding him. He could not catch it. "I knew it," he said, crestfallen. "I am not worthy."

It floated toward Kerena. In sudden ire, she picked up a stick and smashed at the goblet. To her amazement, her blow connected. The cup shattered into myriad shards.

Appalled, she stared. Then she stooped to pick up a shard, but it was gone; there were no fragments on the ground. "It was illusion," she said.

"To show me what I lost," he said. "My shame."

"My fault. If I had not—"

"Never your fault," he said quickly. "You were candid about your mission, and tried to depart. It was solely my weakness."

"Still, I'm so sorry."

He held her and kissed her. "I am not. My weakness of character was always within me, and had to be exposed some time. I was never destined to take the Grail. I deceived myself about that. I am glad to have known and loved you, however briefly. You are a treasure."

"I'm the one who corrupted you!"

"You're the one who made me recognize my true nature." He kissed her again.

They found a place and made love beside the road, in full daylight. It was wonderful, as always.

The two days distance somehow took three days, and they made love so many times it felt like five days. Then at last the turrets of the capital town came into view. They used the horses as a shield against discovery and made love once more.

"I will always love you, Rena," he said.

"And I you."

"I think we must see each other never again."

"Never again," she agreed.

They kissed one final time, then reluctantly separated. They rode the horses on toward the town.

Chapter 5
Vampire

"So you were successful, and he did not take the Grail," the Fey said with satisfaction as Kerena concluded her report. The woman had demanded every detail.

"Not because I wanted to be," Kerena said sadly.

"You fell for him, of course. I thought that would make you more eager to clasp him."

Evidently the Fey did not appreciate the self sacrificing quality of true love. Kerena did not argue the case. "Teach me the final secret of the cloak."

The woman nodded. "Your usefulness to me now is ended. It is this: you must wear it and focus exclusively on the thing you most desire. Then speak a standard invocation, and it will orient on that thing. You will feel it turning you to face that direction. When you are distant, it will be a faint impulse; as you get near it will become stronger. It will inevitably lead you there."

So simple, now that she knew. Why hadn't she figured it out for herself? Perhaps because she had not felt quite ready. But now she was more than ready. She had been denied Sir Gawain, but Morely remained. "Thank you."

"I doubt we shall ever meet again," the Fey said. "But if we do, it is likely to be as enemies."

"Enemies? I have never opposed you." Not successfully, at any rate.

"Because you will have too much power. You may not as yet realize your full strength, but I see it, and will not tolerate it in my vicinity. Go from here and do not return."

"But I hardly did any magic, and was clumsy at that."

"You made a dry rock geyser a fountain that flooded the area enough to put out a prairie fire. Most practitioners can manage only a thin squirt."

"Well, the need was great."

"And you rose to it without thinking. What other unrealized potentials do you possess, awaiting your unthinking need? But that was the least of it."

"The least?"

"The Grail. You saw the Grail."

"Well, I was with Sir Gawain. It was his quest."

"He was chaste. You were not. How could *you* see it?"

Kerena's jaw dropped. "I don't know." Actually Sir Gawain had no longer been chaste by then, but certainly he was far closer to purity than Kerena.

"Not only that, you touched it."

"Only with a stick. Anyway, it was illusion."

"Maybe. You shattered it with a blow. No one ever did that, in or out of illusion. You banished it. It should have been impossible for you to affect the image at all."

"I didn't know."

"Here is some advice, in appreciation for the service you have done me: never tell of that episode in this town. They would stone you to death after eviscerating you."

She realized it was true. She had defiled a holy image.

"You may be sure *I* will not tell," the Fey continued. "They would do the same to me, for sending you. So it is to our mutual advantage to have you far from here. You may become a marvelous sorceress, once you realize your full abilities, but you have no future here."

Kerena nodded. The Fey was surely correct.

She bid parting to the cook and coachman, who expressed genuine regret at her departure. Then she set off afoot. Now that her usefulness to the Fey was done, she rated no privileges such as transportation. She could have prevailed on the coachman, but that would have gotten him into trouble.

She had a secret cache she had put away during the Sir Gawain mission, knowing that money was not the key to its success. Now she fetched it.

She rented a room at the edge of town while she considered her prospects. She did not want to return to the brothel, but was not yet ready to commence her major search. She needed time to herself to weather the loss of Sir Gawain. She was being a foolish girl, she knew, but she couldn't seek and face Morely while in the throes of love for another man. She had to let the edge wear off so she could assert emotional control. Then she could do what was necessary.

Two months later she was ready. The memory of Sir Gawain still pained her, but she could handle it. Now she was ready to seek Morely.

She had become familiar with the seedy side of town while working at the brothel. Little there had changed significantly. She walked to a house where several out of work soldiers shared costs. She knocked on the door.

It opened, and a brutish man gazed out at her. "Hey—aren't you Rena? We don't have the coin."

A year after she had retired from the business, they still recognized her. Another girl would have been thrilled. "I am Rena. I come to buy, not to sell.

I want Gordon."

"You don't want Gordon."

"I do." Her Seeing had informed her of the man's nature. It hadn't mattered to her until now.

He rolled his eyes. "Have it your way." He turned his head. "Gordon! Rena wants you."

"The hell she does," Gordon called back.

"Tell her yourself."

Gordon appeared. He was a huge ugly man, massively muscular. "You don't know me," he said gruffly.

"I want to hire you to guard me as I travel. You will pose as my man. I'll pay you and cover costs."

"I'm trying to tell you—"

"I don't want sex. I want to keep the other men off me. You're honest and not for a woman."

His mouth fell open. "You sure?"

She brought out her purse. "You will handle the money. Pay yourself what you're worth." She put it in his hand.

He hefted it, then opened it to peer inside. "Lady, you need to hide this. You're carrying gold."

"Who's going to take it from you?"

"You trust me that far?"

"Yes."

He shrugged, amazed. "When?"

"Now."

"I'll get my weapons."

Jolie was privately impressed. The girl was efficient, once she decided on her mission. She had whipped her own formidable feeling into submission.

They hired a coach and rode out of town. "There is more," Kerena said. They were in the privacy of the passenger chamber. She had not wanted to be seen departing with him.

"I figured as much. I know about you; everybody does. But I didn't think you knew about me."

"Men talk. I listen. I got a notion who was who in this town. I'm not sure whether you're a greater oddity because you don't rape, or because you don't steal. They marvel at your restraint."

"It's just the way I am. I don't need a woman, and I can earn my keep."

"You will have to sleep naked beside me, to make it persuasive. On occasion I will kiss you in public. I will never demand more of you than that, sexually. But others must know that any sexual approach to me will enrage you."

"Got it. That's it?"

"No. I have magic."

"No offense, ma'am, but I don't much believe in magic."

"Call me Rena. I will show you." She drew the cloak closely about her, romanced it, and invoked invisibility. "Find me."

Gordon looked. He smiled, thinking she had slipped aside and hidden. He reached to touch the seat where she had been. His hand was balked by her body, which had not moved. His eyes widened. He felt around her, forming her outline with his roving hands. "That is you, Rena?"

"Yes."

"Now I believe in magic."

She nulled the spell and was visible again. "I have other powers. They are associated with this cloak. If it should ever be stolen, I would be largely bereft of magic. See that it is never stolen."

"Got it." Another man might have tried to steal it for himself. This one would not.

"And try to see that no one else knows about this."

"Now I know why you hired me."

"Why?"

"If you used that magic on your own, you'd be known for a witch. And you'd have to, to protect yourself from rapists and thieves. I can cover for you."

"In several respects," she agreed. "With luck, there will never be any suspicion."

"I don't want to pry, but it would help if I knew where we're going and what you're looking for."

"I am looking for my long lost lover, a Seer named Morely. I do not know where he is, but soon I will invoke my cloak's search utility and orient on him. It may be a long or difficult quest."

"Got it."

The coach stopped. They were out of town. They got out, and it returned they way it had come. More than a short ride in an expensive coach would have invited suspicion.

"I will now invoke the cloak." She kissed the velvet. "I must wreak the unique," she whispered. "Let me speak what I seek." She concentrated on Morely the way she remembered him.

The cloak writhed uncomfortably, as if unable to settle. Something was wrong. Could the Fey have misinformed her?

"Problem?" Gordon asked.

"The cloak seems to be trying, but not orienting."

"How long since you saw him?" Gordon asked.

"Two years."

"You must have changed some in that time."

"From girl to woman," she agreed. Her body had been dawning, with him; it had achieved full daylight thereafter.

"Maybe he did too."

"He was already a grown man."

"People can change other ways."

She considered that. "How?"

"Maybe if he got in a fight, and lost a hand, or something."

"Or something?"

"Sometimes they castrate enemies."

She was appalled. If Morely had been tricked, and ambushed, and cut like that—it would account for why he had never returned to her. He would be ashamed. "I couldn't face that," she said.

"Maybe some other way. It can't find him as he was, but maybe can find him as he is now."

She re-invoked the spell, this time focusing on Morely in a broader manner, allowing for significant change. The cloak rippled, then oriented.

"It got the fix," she said, gratified. "Faintly."

"Which direction?"

"That way," she said, pointing.

"Far away?"

"I think so."

"Then we'd better veer a little to pick up inns to stay in for several days, travel."

"Got it," she said with a smile.

They walked. She had gotten used to riding, but didn't mind walking again. It reminded her of all the walking she had done with Morely. She might have to build up her stamina again, but that was no problem.

In the evening they detoured to find a village and inn. Gordon turned out to be a shrewd negotiator, getting them a good room and good food, with several pieces of silver in exchange for the small gold piece he proffered.

One of the patrons stared at Rena. "Say—I've seen her before."

Gordon faced the man, frowning, his hand touching the hilt of his sword. "Saw who?" he asked menacingly.

"Nobody," the man said quickly.

"Thank you," Kerena said when they were alone in the room.

"If a man wants to night with a pretty woman, it's nobody else's business what's she done in the past."

"Exactly." She stripped and washed at the basin. Then he did. He was not aroused, confirming his lack of interest in women.

By the time he was done, the water was almost black. "We'll need fresh water," Kerena said. "Stay naked as they fetch it."

"Got it." Gordon opened the door. "Hey innkeep! More water."

In a moment the man's plump wife came with a large pitcher and bucket. Gordon opened the door, naked, while Kerena lay on the bed, similarly exposed. The woman said nothing as she dumped the dirty water into the bucket, and refilled the basin with fresh. She departed without looking, closing the door silently.

"Now the whole inn knows we are lovers," Kerena said, satisfied.

"You could have any man you wanted for that."

"Wanted: that's the key. Morely is the only one I want."

"So all that business in the brothel was—"

"Just business."

"Sometimes I wonder what it's like, to want a woman."

"I could evoke your passion, if you wish."

He shuddered. "Please, no. I'd be disgusted."

"You look sexually normal. What do you like?"

"Boys."

"But isn't an undeveloped young woman much like a boy, except for the one organ she lacks?"

"Much like," he agreed. "But neither girl nor grown man appeals to me. Only a boy."

"It's not a thing I understand, but it's your business."

They slept beside each other, naked. If anyone peeked in—and it was likely someone did, for there were crevices in the walls—their status as lovers remained.

Their travel became routine. They left England and moved north into Scotland. Gradually the focus of the cloak grew stronger; Kerena hoped that meant they were getting closer to Morely. She also hoped that Morely was somewhere on the isle, and not beyond it. She didn't want to wrestle with boat passage. It was bad enough roughing it outdoors where there was no human habitation near. They had to use the cloak as cover and share human warmth, as she had with Sir Gawain, but now there was no question of seduction.

Sometimes bands of robbers came at them. Now Gordon showed his mettle. He laid about him with his sword and killed those who refused to flee. Once when there were too many, backed up by archers, Kerena invoked the invulnerability aspect of the cloak and draped it on him so that he could not be struck. It hampered his arms somewhat, but when he saw the arrows bouncing off it he was reconciled. "That's some shield."

"Magic has its uses," she agreed.

Then came a complication. It started with some inexplicable sickness. Kerena would vomit in the morning, then feel better in the afternoon. Once or twice could be a consequence of bad food, but when it continued for ten days, they had to take stock. "It is not good for you to travel this way," Gordon said. "You need to get better."

She paced around their camp as the sun set. "I can't explain it. It is not my way to be like this. I haven't eaten anything poisonous; I know what plants do that." Indeed, she had made a considerable study of medicinal herbs of all types. What was poisonous in large dose could be medicinal in small dose.

Gordon squinted at her. "Oops," he murmured.

"What's the matter?"

"I saw your silhouette in the low sunlight."

"Oh, now you care about female silhouettes?"

"No. That's why I haven't been looking. Your waist has thickened, and I think not from overeating."

"My waist?" Then it came to her. "Oh, no!"

"You are with child."

"I can't be! I haven't—and when I did, I used a spell."

"What about five months ago?"

"I was with Sir Gawain." And it came to her. "I forgot the spell! I was in love and never thought of it."

That slowed them further. Kerena had not sought Sir Gawain's baby, but now that it was inside her, she wanted very much not to hurt it in any way she could avoid. She dared not overstrain herself, or risk going without food in uninhabited territory. Sometimes Gordon carried her across rough terrain. They had to pause to gather food reserves, sometimes for several days at a time, before advancing, and the amount of travel they accomplished in a day was severely diminished. It was further complicated by her urgent desire not to have her pregnancy known by the people they encountered. Thus a distance they might have covered in a week before, now took a month. It was frustratingly inefficient.

"I wouldn't blame you for going home in disgust," she said.

"I am being paid for my time," he reminded her. "And I find I like taking care of you. It is as close as I will ever get to having a family."

"You have had none of the fun part, only the chore part."

"This is the fun part, for me. I like you; I'm sure if I were normal, I would be in love with you. You are pleasant to be with."

"You're such a decent man. It was a great loss to womankind when you were made differently."

He laughed. It was evidently true: he liked the camaraderie, and he even liked her increasing dependence on him. He simply had no interest in ever having sex with her, and love was out of the question. He was a good man, in most of the ways that counted.

At last, as they neared the cold northern coast, the signal grew strong.

"We are almost there," she announced.

Gordon looked around at the empty countryside. "Few people here. Just sheep."

"I'll be satisfied to find just one person."

They came to a rocky slope. A cave penetrated it. The cloak led them to the cave. They would not have found it without guidance; the entry was hidden behind a jagged outcropping of rock, masked by bushes. The opening was small, barely sufficient for a human body to wriggle through.

"Bad things can be in caves," Gordon said.

"I don't want to put you at unnecessary risk. If I don't emerge within a day, go home; all that remains in the money pouch is yours."

"Rena, I can't do that! That would be deserting you."

"You have delivered me where I was going. That is enough."

"Not until you find your man. This is only a cave."

"The cloak will protect me. You will be vulnerable in the confined darkness. That isn't fair to you."

"Even so, I'd rather see you to your man. You don't know what you will find in this cave. He could be a prisoner, or badly injured, near death. Or he may object to your baby, which isn't his. You need to know, before I leave you."

He was making sense. "Very well. Stay with me. I hope things are readily resolved, so you can go home."

They made torches and entered the cave. It slanted deep into the mountain before leveling. There were no stalactites, and the floor was level, once they got past the twisting tunnel of the opening. Now there was room for them to walk upright, abreast.

"This is one weird cave," Gordon said.

"It must be artificial," Kerena said. "It was drilled, or maybe a natural cave was cleared of all irregularities. It's certainly not natural now."

They came to an intersection. Passages went left and right as well as forward. "Where now?" Gordon asked nervously.

Kerena pondered briefly. "This has to be the work of man, and Morely is here. He's down the main hall. But maybe it will be faster to call him."

"And attract attention we may not want."

She nodded. "And our torches will soon gutter out. We'd better go back out. Then I will return here and call."

He shook his head. "If you're going to do it, do it now, while I'm here."

"Morely!" she called. "Kerena is here."

There was a stir. A slender nude woman appeared, shielding her eyes. "Who is Kerena?"

"Morely's beloved, come to reclaim him."

"Impossible. *I* am his beloved."

Kerena took stock. She realized that it was warm down here, so that a person could go without clothing; in fact she herself was becoming uncomfortably hot. She remembered that Morely had said he would tell a girl he loved her, if that was the expedient thing to do. It was a standard way for a man to obtain sex or whatever else he wanted from a woman. Mainly it confirmed that he was here, and evidently not a prisoner.

It was time to set things aright. "Bring him here to choose."

The girl retreated down the passage. Her posterior view was as shapely as her forward view; she certainly had the figure that Kerena now lacked.

"Were I normal," Gordon murmured appreciatively.

"She would certainly do for incidental passion," Kerena agreed sourly.

Morely appeared, naked, shading his eyes as the girl had done. He looked healthy. "Kerena! I feared Vanja was mistaken."

Her pain poured out. "Why did you leave me?"

"That is a difficult story. Please, put out the torches; they pain me."

"We need them to see our way out."

"Then go out now; I will follow, and talk to you at length outside."

That seemed best. She followed Gordon back up the passage, and, in due course, to the surface. It was just as well, for the torches were guttering dangerously. They put them out.

It was dusk. Morely emerged, now clothed in a cloak. He swept Kerena into his embrace, kissing her avidly. "Oh my love, how I have longed for you! But I couldn't come to you."

She was thrilled to be in his embrace again, but now her anguish at being deserted asserted itself. "You seem healthy and well served."

Gordon chuckled. That reminded her. "This is Gordon, who guarded me on my long trek here."

Morely eyed the soldier. "The usual coin?"

"No. Gold. He has no use for women."

"So?" he asked, glancing again at Gordon.

Gordon nodded. "I'm for boys. It seems you aren't."

"Oh, you mean Vanja. That's part of my story."

"So it would seem," Kerena said coldly.

Morely smiled somewhat sadly. "Know this: I do love you and use her. But that is only a scratch on my situation. I doubt that you will like what I have to say."

"Acute observation."

"It was to spare you pain I left you. It grieves me to hurt you now with the news. Kerena, I believe you would be happier departing now, with no further information, and never seeing me again. I urge you to do that."

"And you know I will not."

"I do know, you wonderful creature. I will always love you for your resolve as well as your ability. I wish I could make love to you right now."

"That would be awkward."

"With Vanja watching, yes."

That made Kerena realize two things: the sultry girl had joined them, and Morely did not yet realize Kerena was five months pregnant. "So tell me why you left me."

"I will tell you and show you. Focus so you can see my illusion." A patch of light appeared before them, against the background of the closing darkness. It showed a cloaked figure. "That is me, on that fateful afternoon when you were in town shopping. But then you returned, and I went out gladly to meet you." A second figure appeared: a lovely young woman.

She had not returned at that time, but she already knew it had seemed she had. Her Seeing had shown her that much.

Then his words seemed to merge with the illusion, and the scene replayed itself.

Morely hurried to the Kerena figure, who met him with open arms. They embraced and kissed. "I want you, I need you," she said. "Now!"

He obliged by spreading out his cloak on the ground and doffing his clothing. She got naked with him, and they lay on the cloak, embracing closely. Then he lifted above her, and she brought him into her with arms and legs. In a moment it was done, and he rolled to the side, breathing heavily.

"I love you so much," she said. "I wish I could enter you as you enter me."

"That is not the way of it," he said tolerantly.

"Let me try. Open your mouth."

He did so. She brought her mouth close, then stuck out her tongue. It reached far out, beyond the ability of a human tongue, a long extension. She thrust it into his mouth. He was evidently surprised by the extent of this penetration, but held still for it. She drew it back slightly, then thrust it in again, deeper.

Kerena, watching the illusion, was both amazed and impressed. That was indeed much like a man plunging into a woman, working up to his climax.

After several oscillations, the woman thrust so deeply that their mouths were jammed together. Then she lifted her upper hand, and jammed the heel of it hard against his jaw. That forced him to bite down on her tongue.

He struggled, then, but she clung, keeping her mouth plastered to his. It was only with difficulty that he finally got his face away from hers. Then blood flowed; her tongue had been badly bitten. It had to be extremely painful.

"I'm so sorry!" he said, swallowing and wiping his blood-soaked lips. "Somehow my jaw got knocked, and I bit you. I never meant to do that."

"It will heal," she said complacently. "I do not feel much pain."

"Come into the house," he urged her. "I have balm. I am mortified to have done such a thing."

"No need. Plumb me again; I like it better after a bleeding." She tried to draw him back onto her body.

Now at last he caught on. "I have been blind! You're not Kerena! You're a succubus, a seductive nocturnal spirit."

"Not exactly. I am Vanja, a vampire." Her appearance changed, becoming her own: an extremely shapely strange woman.

"A vampire! But you did not try to suck my blood."

"True. I do not wish to deplete my future husband."

"Husband! I'll not marry you, vamp!" He was scrambling back into his clothes.

"Let me explain," Vanja said patiently. "Meanwhile you might as well plumb me, for we can provide each other much incidental pleasure. Unlike mortal women, we enjoy it as much as the men do, though we cannot make babies."

"Never!"

"It is too late to protest. You have been blooded. You will crave my body increasingly as you become like me. Fighting it will only make you suffer."

He brandished a knife. "If you try to bite me, I will cut your head off!"

"You really should have researched vampires better. Popular superstition is wrong; it is not our bite that converts mortals to our kind. If that were the case, the whole world would soon be vampire. It is the other way around: it is when mortals taste *our* blood that they are transformed. That keeps it under control. We convert only those we choose. You have tasted my blood; now you are mine."

"I am doomed," he said, reluctantly accepting it. "I feel the changes occurring in my body. I do desire you, though I just had you, and now know you are poison."

"Actually there are considerable benefits," she said. "We live virtually eternally, as long as we have regular sips of mortal blood. We suffer little pain, and heal rapidly. We can see well in darkness."

"And can't face the light!" he retorted. "Direct sunlight will kill you."

"Not immediately, but it would blind us and cause our skin to blister. So we prefer to go about by night, which is more convenient for feeding anyway. Now come into me again, before we go home." She reached for him once more.

His reluctance was manifest, but he seemed unable to resist her hold. She drew him down again on the cloak, and in a moment they were having ardent sex, his clothing no hindrance. It was true: her passion equaled his.

"But what of Kerena?" he asked as their mutual joy faded. "The *real*

Kerena? She does not deserve this betrayal."

"Then we must go before she arrives. She would not care to know about the manner you have changed."

"Damn you vixen, it's true. She must not know."

"Come with me. We have a long way to travel." She drew him along, and he remained unable to resist her. They walked away, leaving the cloak on the ground, forgotten.

Now Kerena knew exactly how it had happened. "So you are now a vampire."

"I am."

"Yet if conversion is only by the choice of the vampire, you could have remained with me without converting me."

"I was sorely tempted. But it would have been horribly unfair to you. You would not have liked living with a vampire, and if anyone had learned of it, both of us would have been burned at the stake. I could not stand to put you to that risk."

"And there was Vanja," she said shrewdly.

"Yes. What she said is true. The taste of her blood not only made me a vampire, it attracted me to her personally. I must have sex with her often, or suffer. I love you, but I think you would not long have tolerated my having such a mistress in addition. So it was kinder to end it at the outset."

It was some trap the vampiress had sprung on him. By the time he knew he was not making love to Kerena, he was locked into the new order. He had indeed tried to be kind.

"Why did she want you? She could have done the same to any other man with less difficulty, if not satisfied fornicating with her own kind."

Now Vanja answered. "We are few in number, deliberately, and our society is hierarchical. I was a lowly member, converted at a young age by a man I thought would marry me. He did not; all he wanted was an esthetic mistress. He is Vichard, the current chief of our clan, already married. I seethed when I learned, but I could neither stop being a vampire nor resist his sexual interest, for my desire for him was as strong as his for me. The blooding does it to both. His wife despises me, of course, but she too is locked in."

"So you decided to wrong another innocent person the same way you had been wronged?" Kerena asked acidly.

"Yes. It is the only way out. But I also craved vengeance. So I searched long and hard for a natural leader—one who could displace Vichard as chief. I found Morely, a skilled Seer and magician with excellent qualities of character. I took him. Now he is Vorely."

"The initial letter of a person's name is changed to a V, for vampire," Morely explained. "It is a convenient convention."

Kerena appreciated the situation. In fact, she was compelled to admire Vanja's nerve and strategy. The girl had spunk.

Still, that did not mean Kerena had to accept the situation completely. She still loved Morely, and meant to win him back.

"I have had my own history in the interim," she said carefully. "Bereft of you, but determined to find you, I became a lady of the night, then the mistress of wealthy traders and notable knights. This had a consequence. Put your hand on my belly."

Morely did so. "You are gravid!"

"A love child, yes, but I can not marry the father." she glanced at Vanja, unable to see her now in the darkness, but knowing the woman could see her, Kerena. "Similar in respects to your situation, vampiress. I need to marry, and Morely is the man I want. I did not make the arduous journey only to be lightly balked. I will take Morely back."

"I will kill you!" Vanja said. There was the sound of her motion.

But Gordon, forgotten for the moment, intercepted her. "Let her be, or we shall discover whether vampires can die of conventional causes," he said.

That did make the girl pause. "We can," she said. "We are not immortal if damaged sufficiently. Then let us compromise: he can have you as mistress after your babe is birthed."

"Or you as mistress after he marries me," Kerena said evenly. "I am the one he loves."

"He must choose," Vanja agreed.

"I choose Kerena," Morely said immediately. "I will always love her. It was for love of her I left her."

"Then it is decided," Kerena said, relieved.

The time frames wavered. Jolie reacted almost automatically. She moved back a few seconds, sending a suppressing of Kerena's comment. This time she said nothing, and the frames aligned.

Vanja considered, realizing that she held the losing hand. "Though she birth a baby not yours?"

"Yes. I can't sire a baby now, nor can a vampire woman conceive one. That's a vampire liability you forgot to enumerate when you converted me."

So he felt bitterness too. That gratified Kerena. "I know you love me."

"But the connection with Vanja remains," he said. "I can not eliminate my desire for her. You have to understand and accept this."

"Not necessarily. Didn't Vanja lose Vichard's hold on her when she converted you?"

"Yes, that is the only way," Vanja agreed. "To blood another mortal."

"So if Morely converts me, you will lose your hold on him."

She knew the vampire woman was staring at her. She had analyzed the system rationally and found its weakness. Morely was surely proud of her.

Jolie wondered whether that was the reason the timelines had started to separate: to stop Kerena from converting in order to win Morely back?

"You don't want to be a vampire, Kerena," Morely said. "I would love to have you with me again, but you should remain mortal. That way you have a future in the realm of mortals."

"Yet you would convert me if I asked."

"Yes. I love you. That's why I ask you not to ask me."

Much as Kerena had asked Gawain not to clasp her, though she longed for it. Love was like that. "I will think about it. Where can Gordon and I stay?"

"Not in the warren," Vanja said. "Your stupid torches are a menace."

"In a human village," Kerena said.

"They can't stay there either," Vanja said. "They would reveal our location, and the mortals would invade and destroy us."

"Then we'll camp out," Kerena said.

"But your baby!" Morely protested.

"Isn't due yet. I'll make up my mind before then."

The two vampires left them, and Kerena went with Gordon to find a comfortable camp for the night. It wasn't easy in the darkness, but they managed.

"Do you have an opinion, Gordon?" she asked as they lay under the cloak.

"Vanja is your enemy, but she doesn't know about the cloak. I intercepted her so she wouldn't discover that you are invulnerable."

She smiled. "Thank you. But I mean about my becoming a vampire."

"I don't think you want to become any more like him than like me. Why sacrifice either your mortality or your sexuality?"

"I love him."

"What of your baby?"

"I don't want that to be a vampire. I'll have to take it back to Sir Gawain."

"He may not like that."

"I don't know what else to do."

"Then I will wait until you birth it, then accompany you back to Sir Gawain."

"That is more than you should do. If I turn vampire, you should consider your service over. Is there enough gold left to sustain you?"

"Three times as much as that."

"It is all yours."

"I will keep it—after I finish with you."

"Were you normal, I would be suspicious of your motive."

"I think I do love you, Kerena, in my fashion."

"You wish to kiss me?"

"No. Just to take care of you."

Love was like that too. "So many women would settle for that."

"You will have to settle for my loyalty."

They slept.

Kerena pondered for a week while they camped out. Morely brought them supplies. "Vampires do eat other than blood," he said. "In fact, very little is blood. We need it only every month or so to maintain our vigor. We take it mostly from sheep, and not those grazing close to here."

"You don't seem to have fangs."

"We don't. We make a small cut near a vein, and lick the blood up as it flows. An ounce or so is enough. The sheep hardly misses it."

In the second week Vanja came, bringing the supplies. Kerena was surprised. "Morely let you come?"

"He asked me to come."

"Asked you!"

"He does love you. I come to make a deal."

Kerena distrusted this. "What do you have to offer?"

"I can help you to help him, if you decide to convert."

This was interesting. "Speak your mind."

"I am bound to him regardless what he does. I could break that by converting another mortal man, but we prefer to keep our number low, and I don't think I could find a better man than Vorely. If you convert you will take him. Let me be his mistress. I am ready to settle for that. In return I will show you how he can become chief of the clan, an advantageous position that would benefit us both."

"Better to be the mistress of a chief, than the wife of an ordinary vampire?"

"Equivalent. And if you approved it, he would agree."

Kerena considered. "So it's power you want."

"No. First I want Vorely. I chose him in part because I knew I could love him, and I do. Second I want vengeance on the man who brought me into this. I could have done very well for myself among the mortals."

Kerena knew that with her figure and determination, Vanja could indeed have done very well. Her motives rang true. She had realized that if she hurt Kerena, Morely would turn on her. So she had to make the best of it by making an alliance with her rival. Could she be trusted?

Kerena focused her Seeing, and discovered to her surprise that the vampiress *could* be trusted, for her motives were straightforward. She knew what she wanted and how to get it. She was actually a person Kerena could have liked, had circumstances been different.

"I will consider it," she said at last. "Tell me how you would help him become chief."

"Each year the vampires vote on which among them will be chief for the next year. Vichard has been elected the past twenty years, but dissatisfaction is growing, and now there are only two more votes in his camp than against him."

"Twenty years?" Kerena asked. "How long have you known him?"

"Eighteen years."

"But you look eighteen total!"

"I look as I did when he converted me. I was that age as a mortal."

"So it is true that you retain youth indefinitely."

"It is true. But I would have preferred to remain mortal, had a man and family, and grown children by now. That has been denied me. I do not pretend it is fun to be a vampire. It is merely a different state, with compensations. Vorely gives my limited life meaning. I will do for him what I can."

"So you are of Morely's generation, rather than mine."

"Generations don't much matter, with our kind."

"I am nearing sixteen," Kerena said. "If I converted, I could remain that age, physically."

Vanja smiled. "Yes. You look eighteen, and stunning, but for your pregnancy."

"And if I converted, I would represent one more vote for Morely to be chief. But that would still be one short, not victory."

"I have hitherto voted for Vichard."

Now it came clear. Vanja had been loyal despite her ire, as there was no point in aggravating her lover when there were not enough votes to oust him. But now she had a better prospect, so her change in vote could make the difference. If Kerena joined.

"Let me talk with Morely about this," Kerena said. "If I convert, you can be mistress of the chief. If I do not, I will depart, and you will be wife of the man you love."

"Talk with Vorely," Vanja agreed. She departed.

Alone again, Kerena discussed it with Gordon. "Should I ally with her?"

"I think you should birth your baby, take it to its father, and ask him to marry you."

"He might do that, but I would be a millstone on his neck. I will not do that to him."

"And giving him his bastard child would be no millstone?"

That stung. "Less of one, I think. Siring bastards is a knightly thing to do; many women are enthralled by knights. But marrying a harlot is beyond the pale. I would not ask him to do that."

"Why not raise your baby here among the vampires, then?"

"It is not a choice I care to make for it. I can make it for myself, but my baby must have its chance at mortality."

"Then ally with Vanja and win back your man."

That was the way she was leaning. The idea of remaining her present age forever had a certain appeal, too.

Another night she talked with Morely. "Vanja proffered me a deal: convert, help you become chief, marry you, and let her be your mistress."

"If I converted you, I would have no further compulsion to sexually indulge her. I would want only you."

Kerena was surprised. "Can she be ignorant of that?"

"Maybe she forgot."

Kerena was not sure of that. She would have to discuss it with Vanja. "I never thought it would be so complicated, once I found you. It was difficult enough finding you. I never would have made it without your velvet cloak. It is past time to return it to you."

"Keep it; I am glad it warmed you in my absence."

"And protected me, and guided me," she said. "Why did you not tell me of its marvelous properties?"

"What properties?"

"Invulnerability, for one."

"It is merely a cloak. It provides no invulnerability. If you believed that, you were putting your life in danger."

This was odd. Her Seeing indicated he was not joking. "I will demonstrate."

She invoked invulnerability and wrapped the cloak closely about her. "Now strike me."

"I would not do that."

"Gordon, strike me."

Gordon drew his sword.

"Don't do that!" Morely protested. "This foolishness has gone far enough."

"It's no foolishness, sir," Gordon said. "That cloak has protected me too." But he sheathed the sword. "Try it yourself, with a stick. You will see."

Morely picked up a stick and poked it at Kerena. It shied away. He tried again, with no better success. Surprised, he tried a light blow. It didn't land.

"It's true!" he said, astonished. "There is magic."

"You didn't know?" Kerena asked. "How could you not know?"

"That cloak never protected me like that. I have been buffeted by ruffians many times."

"Well, you have to invoke it, of course."

"It had no such power before. I would have known."

"You are a Seer," she agreed. "You should have known."

"An amazing notion occurs to me," he said. "*You* are doing it, not the cloak."

"But how could I have any such power?"

"As an extension of your power with the elements. You showed much aptitude there, mastering them much faster than I did. I may have seriously misjudged your potential."

"All that I am, apart from my Seeing, I owe to your instruction or your cloak," she said.

"I think not. I think the Fey took you farther than I ever could."

"She merely taught me how to invoke the properties of the cloak. I think she envied you the power you had to invest it with such powers."

"I think she told you that, to limit your awareness of you own potential."

"I can't believe that."

"More experimentation is in order. What other properties did you discover in the cloak?"

"Invisibility, permeability, and orientation on you, its master."

"Doff the cloak. Make yourself permeable."

She humored him. She set aside the cloak, then invoked the permeability spell on herself. "See—I am unchanged."

"Now walk through me."

She shrugged and walked into him, expecting a collision. And through him without resistance. It was as if she had become a ghost.

"Oh, my," she breathed, feeling faint.

"Reverse the spell, so I can comfort you."

She did, and he did. "I never dreamed of this," she said, awed.

"Nor did I. I recognized great potential in you, but never that. I curse myself for my neglect."

"Sir," Gordon said. "You did not recognize it when she was younger because it had not yet developed. It surely came with her maturation."

"Perhaps that explains it," Morely said. "This does somewhat change the picture. Kerena, you must not waste yourself by turning vampire. You have so much more to accomplish in the mortal realm."

"But I want to be with you."

"And I with you. But I tried to train you to be rational. Is it rational for you to handicap yourself this way, when you have so much future elsewhere?"

"No," she whispered.

"It grieves me to come to this conclusion, but it does seem best."

"I have not yet decided."

He paused. "In that case, be sure to let me know when you do. I would at least like to bid you fond parting."

Another night Vanja came again. This time the moon was bright; that light did not bother the vampires. Kerena braced her forthrightly: "If Morely converts me, he will lose his passion for you. That could cost you your association, even if he becomes chief. Had you not thought of that?"

"I had thought of it. But I love him and want what is best for him. If that is to be chief with you, then so it must be. I will still have my vengeance of Vichard, and maybe Vorely will still find me appealing on occasion even if not compelled. You have but to allow it."

Kerena's respect was growing. "I hated you for what you did to Morely. Then I came to understand, without approval. Now I am coming to respect you. You are true to your lights."

"I do what I must."

"Let me study you."

The woman was perplexed. "I will tell you what you want to know."

"This is more than that. I am a Seeress. I can fathom things beyond what others know."

"Yes, that is why Vorely loves you. I can not compete with that."

"I want to look at you with my magic. That may reveal more than you care for."

Vanja shrugged. "I am concealing nothing."

Kerena stood before her, placed her hands on the girl's shoulders, and gazed into her eyes. She extended her awareness.

And was amazed. "Oh," she gasped, falling back.

Gordon leaped to support her. "What did she do?" he demanded angrily.

"Nothing," Kerena said. "I merely saw a path I never expected. I don't understand it, but can't doubt it."

"What path?" Vanja asked. "I felt a jolt, but it wasn't an attack. You have strange power."

Kerena laughed weakly. "So I am coming to appreciate. Here is the way of part of it: you will marry Morely, and I will be his mistress."

"This is humor?"

"This is my Seeing. The proper course to follow. I said I didn't understand it."

"But you have the superior hand. Why should you sacrifice that to give me better status?"

"Because you will convert me."

"Convert you! That's for Vorely to do."

Kerena shook her head, bemused. "It seems not. That is the other part of my Seeing. You must do it."

"But then you and I would be bound to each other. It wouldn't affect Vorely, just us. It wouldn't even change our feelings for him. It would just make us like sisters."

"And lovers, perhaps."

"And lovers," Vanja agreed. "But not strongly, because it does not change sexual orientation, just commitment."

"He would still love me and crave you," Kerena said, working it out. "But we would not betray each other's interests. We could trust each other, and share him."

"We could. This is a much better situation for me. But it makes no sense for you."

"It surely makes sense. I have but to understand it."

"Vorely would say not only not to handicap yourself by converting, but not to give me such an advantage. You are the one he wants to marry."

"It seems that is not to be. I am not gratified."

"You have shaken me with your Seeing. You need to think about it further."

"I shall."

Morely, too, was amazed. "How can you consider such a thing?"

"My Seeing shows it best. What of yours?"

He focused. His jaw went slack. "It agrees. I could not have fathomed this on my own, but guided by your suggestion, I confirm it. It is a proper course. Yet I would prefer to marry you."

Jolie was similarly amazed. She had thought the alignment required Kerena to avoid becoming a vampire. Now it seemed otherwise. What a devious course this was turning out to be!

"One question remains for me," Kerena said. "What of my baby? I do not want it raised among the vampires, but if I convert now, will it also convert?"

"I do not know. I doubt the question has ever arisen before. It may be best to wait until after the birthing."

"Yes. That is sensible."

The frames blurred.

Jolie stepped back, blocking that response.

"Does that make sense?"

"Try your Seeing," he suggested.

Kerena tried it. "I should not wait."

The timelines aligned. Jolie wondered about that, knowing that there was a complication. But it was her job to keep the timelines aligned, regardless of complications. The lines were no longer blurred.

"Still, this is such a significant decision, you must not hurry."

"It is time. I will do it tonight, with Vanja."

"It is of course your decision," he said with deep regret. "I shall be glad to have you with me in whatever capacity you choose. But I think I will never understand why we can't marry."

"I hate that aspect," she agreed. "But I trust my Seeing."

He kissed her and departed.

"What should I do when you convert?" Gordon asked. "You will join them in the warren."

"Let me see." She put her hands on his shoulders and focused. "You must wait in the nearby village until I come for you. So I can take my baby to its father."

"Of course," he agreed.

That evening Vanja came. "Do I have to bite your tongue?" Kerena asked distastefully.

"No. Merely sip a drop of my blood. I will scratch my arm." She paused. "Are you sure? Once done, this can not be undone."

"My vision says I must. Otherwise I would never do it."

"As I never would have done it," Vanja said. "Had I known." She scratched her forearm with a sharp fingernail. Blood welled out. "Quickly, before it heals."

Kerena put her mouth to the scratch and licked up the blood. It had a pungent quality. She swallowed the drop.

Immediately it reacted in her stomach. A curious warmth spread out, suffusing her belly, then her entire being. In fact, she felt good.

"This is not what I anticipated," she said. "I thought it would be like dying. It feels more like truly living."

"It does," Vanja agreed. "But do not be deceived: it does not render you invulnerable to injuries."

"Invulnerable." The word reminded her of her other powers. Did she still have them? "I must try something."

"It will not be complete for an hour or more. It takes time for the body to adjust."

"I will know if it is changing my powers." Kerena invoked the spell of permeability. "Touch my hand."

Vanja did. Their two hands passed through each other. "Oh!" she said, amazed.

"I will test again in an hour. But I think I am retaining my magic."

"I think so."

When the hour was done, Kerena verified all her special abilities. Conversion had cost her nothing in that respect. She was ready to join the vampire community.

Gordon departed for the village, making his way by moonlight. He had plenty of gold to pay his way. He agreed to go out from the village for a walk through the fringe of the forest every day at dusk, so that she could contact him without being known to the villagers. She expected to make that contact in about five months, after the baby was birthed and she had had time to recover.

Kerena's existence as a vampire turned out to be rather dull. She was now Verena, accepted because she was indubitably a vampire and Vorely's beloved. The sipping of the blood of live creatures turned out to range from ten days to a month, and little was needed. The rest of the time she consumed normal food, for which they foraged in the countryside. She ate less than she had before, as the vampire form seemed to be more efficient in processing it, and in conserving energy. This was partly because they rested and slept most of the day, preferring to go out in the cool night. The need for clothing was similarly reduced; they used it only when going out into the cooler nocturnal world. Within the warren all were normally nude.

There was a good deal of sexual activity, as married and "dating" couples entertained themselves. This was fairly open, as there were only ninety residents in this clan and most of them had known each other for decades or longer. They tended to be tolerant about spot liaisons outside established couples, and many liked to travel to neighboring villages to patronize brothels and lonely men. The mortals, of course, did not know the nature of their partners; there was no physical evidence to mark the vampires. They tended to seem young and healthy and highly sexed; few ever thought to question that. They made excellent sexual companions. Kerena, not participating, studied the matter with an experienced eye. It was actually a good deal for the mortals, who were seldom charged much if anything.

Vorely's accession to be chief turned out also to be routine. The votes were tallied, and Kerena's new one, together with Vanja's change of sides, gave it to him by one. That was it; no one argued. If Vichard was disappointed, he was gracious. There was always next year, or next decade. Vampires, it seemed, took the long view.

Soon after becoming chief, Vorely married Vanja. It was a small ceremony in the warren, mainly a mutual statement that they both wished this association. They kissed, and had ritual public sex. Now Vanja's inducement for changing sides was clear, it seemed. Why Verena had agreed to it was less clear, but it was her business. Her obvious pregnancy explained her lack of participation in sexual activity with Vorely. Vanja was clearly willing and able to take up the slack.

Then Verena birthed her child. Here, too, her new state seemed to help; she had little difficulty or pain, and produced a healthy baby boy. He was mortal, not vampire. She nursed him, and this did not convert him. She had been concerned, but her Seeing had suggested it was all right. She named him Gawain.

A month after the birthing she was fully recovered and ready to make the long trek to deliver the boy to his father.

Unfortunately there was something her Seeing had not Seen, because it had never occurred to her to look. She had extended regret ahead.

CHAPTER 6
TAINT

Gordon was in the village, taking evening walks as he had promised. "Rena!" he cried gladly when she appeared before him. "Is all well?"

"All is well," she agreed. "Here is my baby, Gawain the Second."

"He's darling. May I hold him?"

She hesitated, remembering the man's predilection for boys. But her Seeing showed no trouble. She passed the baby over.

"I saw you pause," Gordon said. "The boys I go for are six to eight years old, not babies. Have no fear."

She forced a laugh. "I trust the trip will not take that long."

He handed Gawain back. "Let me pay off my landlord and clear out my things, and I will be with you."

"I will accompany you to the village."

"Is that wise? A woman and baby suddenly appearing?"

"We could be invisible. But do they know your nature?"

"No. As with your kind, I practice my nature elsewhere. Here I am a wealthy widower recovering from bereavement, so not interested in remarriage." He smiled. "However, it has been five months, and the local women believe that six months suffices for mourning. It is about time for me to move on, lest I be openly courted."

"Then I will be your daughter and her child, come to take you to my home, now that I have found you."

"I didn't want to burden you with my morose presence," he agreed. "But it seems Family will not be denied."

"The local women will surely understand."

"They may be annoyed, but know the way of it."

She nodded. "It would be a shame to let your wealth go to waste, when you have a grandchild to spoil."

They both laughed, liking the fiction that served their purposes so well.

She walked with him to the village. They paused to purchase traveling goods, incidentally spreading the story. Then they repaired to his small rented abode.

"How was it with the vampires?" he asked. "You do not seem changed in that manner."

"I am changed, though. I eat less, tolerate light and heat less, and will live indefinitely, as long as I take a sip of fresh mortal blood within every month. I also have a greater desire for the pleasures of sexual congress."

"But you had many such pleasures before."

"No. I gave endless pleasures to men, for pay. That was business, amassing the gold that now is yours. My desire was only for the two men I loved. Now my desire is as strong as theirs. That is quite a different thing."

Gordon looked alarmed. "I hope you do not look to me for such pleasure."

"No more than you look to my baby for yours. We understand each other. But if we should need to persuade a man along the way to do something, I will enjoy that persuasion as much as he does."

"So among the vampires—"

"Vanja and I took turns at Vorely, this past month. He became surfeit, even for a vampire."

"And when you have left the baby—"

"I will return to have at Vorely again, and perhaps other men of the warren."

"That does not seem like much of a life."

"Maybe that's why my Seeing steered me away from marrying him. This leaves me free to wander, at such time as I choose. An eternal life with the same small group surely palls in time."

"Even mortal life can pall. This past year has been more interesting for me than the prior time."

"But now you have gold. That should make a difference."

"It should," he agreed, sounding not quite certain.

They traveled south. When an innkeeper had no room remaining, Kerena put Gawain in Gordon's care and took the man aside for remonstrance. She was so persuasive that he made room for them in his own apartment. When his wife objected, she lent her the baby to coddle while she saw to the man again. Gawain was a little charmer, handsome and friendly, making the woman satisfied with the deal.

"You can twist women as well as men around your finger," Gordon remarked as they trekked next day.

"Persuasion is a useful art. I am always learning."

Another time they were waylaid by three outlaws who blocked the path ahead and behind. "Invoke your cloak," Gordon said grimly. "I will try to tackle them singly."

"That is risky. Let me try persuasion, again." Of course she knew now that it wasn't the cloak it was her, but she could imbue the cloak with the same magic properties.

"They mean to rape you anyway."

"They can't. Take Gawain and the cloak and stand back."

Then, alone, she walked boldly toward the two men ahead. "I will make a deal with you," she said. "I will take you on, all three. When you can no longer fight, you will let us move on without further challenge."

"Fight?" he asked, surprised by her audacity.

"Not with your club," she said, opening her clothing to expose her torso from breasts to crotch.

"Oho!" He embraced her, took her to the ground, and quickly completed the act. Then his companion was on her. Then the third man.

Kerena got up and went for the first man again. "Raise your weapon," she said, stopping into him.

Thus challenged, he did his best, and in due course completed the second act. Then the second man did the same, and the third one.

Kerena went after the first one again. "Where is your weapon?" But this time he was unable to raise it. "Then I am done with you, and shall be moving on."

At this point, bemused, they did not challenge her. Gordon joined her and they left the outlaws behind.

"I never saw the like," Gordon said.

"Wasn't it better than your way?"

"But suppose they had reneged, and tried to hurt you?"

"I would have castrated them."

He was taken aback. "You could do that?"

"Yes. I have magic powers I did not know of before, and know the use of the knife. As it was, I got a nice dose of sex, and you did not have to fight."

"Your way was better."

"Yes, as long as I did not have to use the magic. Had that been necessary, it could have been ugly, as I prefer that my nature not be known."

"So do I!"

The trek to central England took them a month and a half. When they reached the capital city, Kerena went to the spot she had first met Sir Gawain as he gazed up at the stars. He was there, as before, in the early evening.

"Sir Gawain," she said.

He knew her voice instantly. "Rena!"

"You may not like my present mission."

"I still love you, though it damns me."

"But you still can't marry me."

"That is the curse of my existence. Oh, to hold you again."

"That you can do. But first you must know this: I have a son by you."

He was stunned. "You never said!"

"I didn't know. Not until after I left you. I can't keep him; he must be with you. You can give him the life he deserves."

He hesitated hardly a moment. "Of course. If I can't have you, I can at least have him."

"I named him Gawain, after you. Gaw for short. Here he is." She set the baby into his hands.

"There is something about him."

"He relates well to people. He charms the ladies. Can you get a wet nurse?"

That sat him back. "It is not the kind of thing I know about." Then he got an idea. "Would you serve? Until he is weaned? I would pay you."

Somehow Kerena hadn't thought of that. The idea of being with her son longer appealed, as well as that of being with Sir Gawain again. "I would be anonymous," she said.

"Yes, to all others. But to me—Rena, if you would also consent to—"

"I would," she said. "I love you too."

So it was that she dallied longer with Sir Gawain than she had anticipated. She became his hired wet nurse for the son he had discovered, and his secret mistress. If others suspected her dual role, it hardly mattered; pretty wet nurses were fair game for knights, and often they were amenable apart from the pay. This was certainly the case here.

Her status as a vampire didn't matter. She used her magic to direct light around her body so that only part of it actually struck her, making her feel as she were walking in dusk. The diversion made a subtle sparkle around her that others remarked on, on occasion: it was as if she were a bright jewel, scintillating. Meanwhile she was able to tolerate broad daylight, while still able to see well at night.

Gordon departed with the gold. "But if you ever need me again—"

She kissed him on the cheek. "I will find you. You have been wonderful."

He kissed her back. "Now at least I know some of what I am missing."

She stayed with the elder and younger Gawains a year, until the time for weaning approached. Every so often she went out in the evening, found a sheep, cut its skin, and sipped the bit of blood that flowed. The sheep hardly noticed, and healed soon enough. She appreciated the way her Seeing had guided her, so that she was free to do this. It allowed her more time with Sir Gawain and son, and she knew that Morely was well attended.

"Soon your job will no longer be necessary," Sir Gawain said as they lay together after a typically torrid love session. "Then I will lack a pretext to keep you here."

"And I will go," she said. "That was always our understanding."

"Maybe I should renounce my position and marry you. That at least would make me happy. You have such remarkable passion I can barely keep up with you, yet it is a joy trying."

"You owe it to the kingdom to keep your place," she reminded him. "Not to throw it away for a harlot."

"I will slay the man who calls you that."

"Then I had better get me gone before anyone speaks the truth."

"You are entirely too rational."

It was time to change the subject. "I must nurse Gaw."

"That reminds me. There is something about him."

This was new. "I thought you liked him."

"I do. He is bold and beautiful, like you. But there is something eerie, too, like a sour note in a symphony."

"Maybe I should do a Seeing on him."

"Maybe you should. Maybe it can be fixed."

She went to Gaw, nursed him, then set him down and focused her Seeing.

Sir Gawain was right: there was something subtly out of line. It wasn't physical; the boy was supremely robust. It was spiritual. A psychic taint that could cause him mischief.

"What is it?" Sir Gawain asked, seeing her expression.

"There seems to be a kind of curse on him," she said. "Something that will make him unlucky, so that he will die before his time."

"Luck is as a man makes it."

"Perhaps I have the wrong word. There is a spiritual guidance to all our lives. Some of us are destined for great things, some for failure, regardless of our physical or mental potential. Gaw has great potential, but his destiny is compromised. I wish it were not so."

"How can that be? Tell me what ill is fated to befall him, and I will set him on another course."

"This seems to be beyond what human beings can influence. He will ultimately fail in life, and we can not prevent it."

"I can't abide this! My son must succeed."

"Nor can I," she said, her anguish growing. "Yet I don't know what to do about it."

"Your Seeing—can it be focused on a particular aspect? Such as the origin of the curse?"

"I can try." She hadn't thought of that, but it was a good suggestion.

She focused, orienting on the origin. Half to her surprise, she discovered a time when Gaw's fate had changed. Four months before his birth. He had been cursed before ever leaving her body.

Four months. That would have been when—

"Oh, no!" she cried.

"You have found it," Sir Gawain said.

"I have found it. It is my fault." For it was when she became a vampire. She had not told Sir Gawain about that, and did not plan to; the news would not please him, and she thought did not relate to his interests.

"How can that be? You are devoted to him, and have never played him false."

"Not knowingly. But this—it was something I did that affected him while he was still in my belly. I had no idea."

"You ate something poisonous?"

"In a manner of speaking. I ate—something tainted. It affected him. Now the taint is on him. It is too late to take it off."

"Then he is doomed?"

"He can't be doomed!" she cried in tears. "Not because of me!"

"Yet if we can't change it—"

Her desperation summoned a bold idea. "There are spirits we little know. They have powers that can affect us. I will go to them and plead for Gaw. I will save our son."

"I know you will do your best," Sir Gawain said comfortingly.

In due course she weaned Gaw and with deep regret left him and his father. It was time for her to go, lest others wonder why the wet nurse stayed beyond her time. But now she had a mission: to find and address the spirits that could help her.

She went north to the vampire enclave. Vorely remained chief despite the loss of a vote; it would take a majority to displace him, and he was doing a good job, so had actually gained support. He was glad to see her, and not merely for her ardent presence in his bed. "I feared something had happened to you."

"I stayed to nurse Gaw to the weaning. Then I learned he was tainted by my conversion. He will fail in life and die early. I must abate that curse, as it is my fault."

"You didn't know," he reminded her.

"Yet I did it. I should have birthed him before converting. I must change that."

"You can't change the past."

"Can't I? You know so many things; you must know of a way."

He considered. "There is a story, but I have never fully credited it. Rational analysis suggests it is fantasy."

"Tell me that story."

"In the beginning the earth was void and chaos ruled. Then it separated into day and night. Day fragmented into seven major Incarnations of Immortality and many more minor ones, while Night remained inchoate. The Incarnations of Day assumed several major tasks, such as collecting conflicted souls after Death, organizing Time, and manipulating the threads of Fate. They have powers that mortals hardly dream of, but they remain mostly clear of mortal affairs and are difficult to approach. Yet sometimes they do intervene in mortal affairs."

Kerena found this fascinating yet barely credible. "Fragments of Day supervise mortal affairs? That suggests they have minds and awareness. Whence come such consciousness?"

"A rational question," he said, kissing her and proceeding to another round of love. "I bless the day I met you, though your potential extends well beyond mine."

"You are avoiding the question," she said, participating with full vigor.

"Merely remarking on my delight of you. We are near the limit of my knowledge of the Incarnations. I think at some point human beings merged with some or all of them, lending human intellect to their nebulous powers and giving them direction. Thus Death was personified as Thanatos, Time as Chronos, and so on. I know no more."

"So there are people there to deal with. How do I find them?"

"I do not know. It is certainly beyond my power, assuming the story is true and that such folk exist. Perhaps it is not beyond your power."

"There is my challenge. I shall go to meet it."

"Now you are losing rationality."

"How so?"

"How can you go anywhere, when you have no idea where or if they exist? Remain here while you contemplate this challenge; you can do as much in the security of the warren as elsewhere."

"And you will have me in your bed longer."

"Exactly."

"It's so nice to be desired."

"Thank you."

Yet his suggestion made sense. Her desire matched his, and she had nowhere else to go. She remained while she struggled with the question, and bit by bit between horrendous bouts of sex she worked out an approach.

She would use the velvet cloak. By itself it had no power, but it had good associations for her, and she was comfortable with it. It helped her to focus on it, imbuing it with the powers she chose, as she had done while traveling.

But what kind of focus should she apply? That was easy: whatever worked. She tried focusing on life, and found it all through the forest; no differentiation there. She tried focusing on spirits, and after a month or so was able to detect them, but they too were omnipresent: every person and every plant had a spirit of some sort. She adjusted the intensity, and that filtered out most, but still didn't locate anything special.

She was frustrated. Time was frittering away, and while it was fun making out with Vorely, sometimes in tandem with Vanja, her mission to help her baby was getting nowhere. Yet what else could she do?

She discussed it with Morely, but he had exhausted his inspiration on that. It was Vanja who came up with the most promising lead: "They are aspects of Day, you say? So they must draw their power from what we can't face, the light of day. The burning energy of the sun. Can you fix on that?"

"Surely I can," Kerena agreed. "But since that unfiltered energy would destroy me, what is the point?"

"You must denature it, as you do when going abroad by day. Then maybe you can address it."

Kerena tried it. She deflected the light so sharply as to become almost invisible, and went out at noon. She oriented the cloak on the sun itself, aligning with its savage energy, sorting out its special qualities. Most was sheerly physical, the kind that heated ground. Some was nutritious energy that encouraged plants to grow. Some was deadly, destroying qualities of flesh. Step by step she filtered out the irrelevant or dangerous elements and concentrated on the rest. And discovered the underlying component of magic.

That was surely what she wanted. She set the cloak to nullify the rest, allowing only the magic to penetrate. It was everywhere, because sunlight was everywhere by day, but there were areas of special concentration. A high intensity of daylight magic. She tuned it and retuned it, getting the filter just right so that she would be able to orient on such a phenomenon and go to it. If she were correct, the several Incarnations of Day would be found amidst exactly such energy swirls. If.

Finally she was able to narrow it down to seven manifestations, the strongest. Those were the ones she wanted. She hoped.

She realized that she would have to travel far distances, and not want to do them afoot. What alternative was there? She had heard of magical devices like floating carpets or transformation into swift birds, but didn't trust them; she preferred to keep her own form and footing. How could she walk, yet not take a month to pass from Scotland to England? The world was much larger than that, and she had to be prepared to chase the Incarnations throughout the world.

She struggled with this, and finally devised a compromise: she would remain afoot, but phase out most of her mass to enable her to move rapidly through mountains and towns with very little energy expended. Taken to its extreme, she might even magnetize the cloak so that it was attracted by the energy swirls and would carry her there with minimal effort on her part. This might be dangerous, but it would be under her control so she could slow or stop it at any time.

Another year had passed. "I am going after them," she said. "They may be dangerous, so I can't promise to return. But I hope the vampires will welcome me if I do."

"As long as I remain, we will," Vorely said. "You are a remarkable woman, and I will always love you."

"I, too," Vanja agreed.

Kerena kissed them both and departed. She went abroad by night, not because she had any further difficulty with day, but because the swirls of energy were clearer by night because of the contrast.

She stood in the forest, orienting. She was eighteen years old, looking slightly younger physically, but rather older in experience. Much older in information and power. Was it enough? It had to be.

She tuned in on the swirls of energy. They were widely scattered, but one was relatively close. She oriented on that, adjusting the cloak to ignore the others. She phased out most of her mass, and started walking toward it.

She passed through trees with only fog-like resistance. She turned on the cloak's attraction, and it started urging her forward. She phased out further, and allowed herself to be carried forward, her feet no longer walking. She was on her way.

The cloak carried her roughly southwestward, through Scotland. But it didn't stop there. It took her on to the shore and across the heaving sea. This startled her, but she realized that she no longer needed solid ground to walk on; she could walk on water if she needed to. She lightened further, and her body moved faster. She wanted to get where she was going.

She came to another shore. That would be Ireland. She forged giddily though its trees, houses, and mountains. She hoped she didn't have to go beyond Ireland, because she knew there was nothing but broad ocean beyond the isles in this direction. She would go the distance she needed to, but she preferred this first excursion to be short.

The direction changed. This alarmed her; had the cloak lost track? No, she realized; it was that the energy swirl was also moving, so was no longer where it had been when she started. Soon it changed again, but only slightly.

Her awareness of the energy swirl intensified. She was getting close. She increased her mass and decreased the attraction, slowing. When she was very close, she returned to full mass and walked, regaining her equilibrium. She had of course practiced this mode of travel before, but only for very short local hops; this time she had gone vastly faster and farther than ever.

Ahead of her was a vaguely human figure in an encompassing black cloak. Beside it stood a magnificent pale horse with a huge scythe strapped to its side. The figure was leaning over a man lying on the ground. It looked as if the fallen man had had some kind of internal failure, and lost consciousness.

Consciousness? *He had died!* That was why the Incarnation of Death was here. This was the sudden grim confirmation of Vorely's story: the Incarnations of Immortality existed. They were real, and operating in exactly the way conjectured. Or so it seemed.

Death reached down with one hand. The hand swept through the body, pulling something out. Kerena realized that this would be the man's soul being drawn from his body. She shuddered.

Now she was close. "Hello, Thanatos!" she called, feeling vaguely foolish. What did one say to an Incarnation?

Death turned to face her. Within the cloak's dark hood was the fleshless visage of a human skull.

Appalled, Kerena simply stood there staring. *This was Death*, the taker of souls, of life. How could she face him, let alone make any demand of him?

"You see me," Death said, his voice sounding surprisingly human.

"I see you," she echoed numbly.

He glanced at his wrist, where there was what Jolie recognized as an anachronistic timepiece. "You are not on my schedule. Who are you?"

There was nothing to do but answer. "I—I am Kerena. A mother. I come to ask—a favor."

"No." Death turned, mounted the stallion, and murmured a word to it. The horse leaped—and disappeared.

Kerena was left standing alone, amazed. Thanatos hadn't even considered. He had simply denied her.

Her feeling shifted slowly to anger. The Incarnation didn't have to grant her favor, but he should have listened. Her enormous effort to locate him warranted at least that much.

All she had wanted to ask Death was to postpone Gaw's death until a more timely age, so that he would have a chance to live out his life and accomplish whatever great deeds were otherwise destined. Death had rejected her plea without even the courtesy to hear it.

Then her rationality took hold. There were other Incarnations. She could achieve her desire with one of them.

She adjusted the cloak, eliminating the signal that was the Incarnation of Death. Now there were six. She oriented on the closest of those. She resumed traveling.

Now the cloak did take her out across the larger sea. She accelerated, wanting to get clear of the endless water. She zoomed heedlessly across the Atlantic.

Then, suddenly, the energy swirl was close. There was a large island, with the ocean extending on beyond it. What was this?

What, indeed, Jolie wondered. This was the center of the Atlantic, in the vicinity of the Mid-Atlantic mountain range, deep below the surface. She knew her geography. There was not supposed to be any such island here. Yet the timelines were straight.

Kerena slowed, coming to land on the beach. This appeared to be a garden paradise, warm and fair, with plants of every imaginable type. There were animals too, of every species, predators and prey, mingling without fear of each other. Strange indeed.

Jolie's mental jaw dropped. *The Garden of Eden!* It existed here near the Equator, between the continents. Or was it Atlantis? Here until it suddenly sank into the sea, as the great rift shifted. She had not realized that calamity was so recent, barely before European ships started crossing to the New World. No wonder there were persistent legends.

Kerena walked toward the energy whorl. She approached an elegant twentieth century mansion.

But this is the fifth century! Jolie protested. *This can't be here!* Yet obviously it was.

Kerena found the architecture odd, but wasn't concerned, as this was far from England. She knocked on the door.

A man of middle age opened it. Behind him hovered a glowing hourglass: The Hourglass that controlled time. "Will I summon you?" he asked.

"I summoned myself," Kerena said boldly. "You are Chronos?"

"You are esthetic, for an undead," he said, eying her.

So even the Incarnations noticed her body. "I come to ask a favor. You must enable me to return to the point when I inadvertently tainted my son, so I can avoid it. He—"

"No, of course not," he said. "I never interfere with a timestream on the whim of a denizen of the mortal realm; it disturbs the flow."

Kerena was taken aback. "The flow?"

"The flow of time. It is my position to ensure that it is even. A change affects everything following it. I would be aware of such an effect if I am to make it. There is no change; the flow is undisturbed."

Jolie remembered: Chronos lived backward. From the future to the past. Thus he knew the consequences of any act; they were in his memory. So he spoke of what he would do, though it was what had already been done, in the awareness of all the folk of the world. Kerena didn't understand that, but didn't need to.

"But my son," Kerena said. "I must save him!"

Chronos focused on her. "You are a half mortal. How did you come here to Purgatory?"

Purgatory! But that was not on Earth. It was—Jolie didn't know where it was, though she had been there. An alternate dimension, maybe. What was it doing as an island in the Atlantic?

"Purgatory is becoming more primitive as the religion that spawned it approaches its infancy," Chronos said, answering her. "Now it is on this isle, which is near its termination, and in a few mere centuries purgatory will not exist as a separate entity."

"I didn't ask about that," Kerena said. "I am here on behalf of my son."

Chronos focused on her. "What is a ghost from my past doing in you?" he demanded. "This disturbs the flow. I must deal with it." He reached up to grasp the Hourglass.

The timelines blurred badly.

Distract him! Jolie thought violently. The Incarnation of Time had detected her temporal nature, and surely had the power to drive her away from this timeline. He was receiving her thoughts.

Kerena did not understand the sudden urge, but obeyed it. "I am no ghost," she said, opening her clothing. "Let me prove it to you."

"But there is a ghost within you. It—"

Kerena cut him off with a kiss, and bore him back into his mansion. She was extremely good at what she knew how to do. Her body was exquisite, buttressed by her magic Seeing and her considerable experience. In a moment he was indeed distracted. He was after all a man. From the future, living backward when away from Purgatory, but still a man. Now there was nothing in his mind but the divine unmortal body so avidly seducing him.

By the time she was done with him, Chronos had completely forgotten about the ghost. *Now get out of here.*

Kerena got out of there, leaving Chronos blissfully sated. She reduced her mass and oriented the cloak on the next closest energy swirl. She was on her way to the next Incarnation, whatever that might be.

"What is this ghost in me?" she asked. "That forces me to protect its secret?"

Jolie tried to prevent it, but now that she had the hint, Kerena was determined, and she had considerable psychic power. She oriented on the mystery within her, and in a moment had it. "A foreign spirit!"

Jolie considered moving back to just before the girl's discovery, but knew that was no good. Chronos had given it away, and there was no way to avoid that interview, because that would change the timelines. She had done what she had to, and that had worked: the lines were clear again. She would have to face the revelation of her presence, and hope she could manage it in such a way as to maintain the alignment.

A friend, she thought.

"Those other times I changed my mind—that was your doing?"

Yes. But never to harm you. To guide you.

"For what purpose?"

This is complicated to explain.

"Make it simple."

Jolie tried. *This world is headed to a bad end, unless guided to a good end. I am Jolie, from a world just like this one, except it achieved a good end. You are the key to the difference between them. My job is to guide you along the correct course so that your world, too, achieves salvation.*

"What bad end?"

Satan wins control and leads it into destruction. Jolie did not try to explain that the Incarnation of Satan at that time in her world was not an evil man, and wanted to save the world as much as the other Incarnations did. But in the alternate world the Incarnations were different, with God incompetent and Satan truly evil. Kerena could change that.

"How can I believe that?"

Use your Seeing.

Kerena did. "It is true. You are beneficial, and I need your guidance. But there is something else odd about you. What is it?"

I do not yet exist. I will not be born until the year of our lord 1191, in France. But I am independent of time in your world, which I am visiting.

"You feel young, like me. What is your personal history?"

At age fourteen I was sent to serve a powerful man, a sorcerer named Parry. I became his apprentice, then his wife when I was fifteen.

"So you *are* like me! You loved and married young. I feel grief in you; did he die?"

No. I did, when I was seventeen. I was murdered by Crusaders sent by Evil's minion Lucifer. I came to inhabit a drop of blood on Parry's wrist, so I could appear to him as a ghost. He became an influential cleric. Satan sent a demoness to corrupt him, and she did, but she also fell in love with him. When he died she helped him defeat Satan and assume his office as the Incarnation of Evil.

"You *are* like me!" Kerena repeated. "Forever younger than eighteen. And I made an ally of Vanja so Morely could become chief of the vampires."

Good men have that effect on women. There may be a further parallel: the other Incarnations treated him with contempt, as they seem to be treating you, and he swore vengeance on them. He tried to wrest ultimate power from the Incarnation of Good, and in the end succeeded, in his fashion.

"This is your good end? Satan wins?"

I said in his fashion. He fought to prevent the Incarnations from declaring the office of the Incarnation of Good to be vacant. When he lost that, he made his own nomination, and his candidate became the new God.

"Isn't that the same thing? That man is one of Satan's creatures."

No, it was a good ghost woman named Orlene, related to all the Incarnations in some manner so they could not oppose her. She is doing her best to make the world better.

"A ghost woman! *You're* a ghost woman!"

A different one, Jolie agreed. *Orlene's friend. It is really at her behest that I came here. So that she will be the Incarnation of Good in this world too. This is vastly better than the alternative.*

"She's trying to take power here too."

No. She is not power hungry. She merely wants to save this world from the doom that otherwise awaits it.

Kerena considered. "I know you through my Seeing. I like you. But my mission is not yours. I must save my son from the taint on him, so that he can thrive normally.

This is more difficult than you imagine. But there is no necessary conflict with my mission. If your world aligns with mine, you will rescue your son, in a manner.

"In a *manner?* What manner?"

It will happen many generations hence, when—

The timelines blurred.

Jolie tried to move back a step, but could not. Kerena had taken control. That was amazing and alarming.

"What is that?" Kerena demanded. She was now aware of the alternate frames.

What I am telling you is changing the course of your reality. I must not do it, lest the alignment be lost. You must let me revert, to eliminate that telling.

Kerena considered again. "I believe you. My Seeing confirms it. But I mislike this. Am I to be a puppet on a string?"

That is an unkind way to look at it. It is more like a course that will in time achieve what you desire, that you must confirm, lest you lose the way.

Kerena decided. "Go back only the minimum required." She loosed her grip on her timeline.

Jolie moved back to the key question.

"In a *manner?*" Kerena demanded. "What manner?"

I must not tell you, lest the rescue be compromised. I ask you to trust me.

Kerena considered, in this alternate dialogue. "I do trust you, because of my Seeing. But I do not like not knowing."

I understand. It seems your knowing would cause you to change course, and the timelines would no longer align. It is possible that the alternate one would enable you to accomplish your purpose also, but I would not be able to help. I can guide you only toward conformity with my own reality.

Kerena sighed. "So it must be." Then she thought of something else. "Won't Chronos mess with my timeline anyway, now that I have broached him?"

I doubt it, because he said the flow is smooth, and he doesn't want it changed. Also, our contact with him is in his future, as he lives backward. He won't remember it because he hasn't experienced it yet.

"I find that utterly confusing!"

So did Jolie. *Maybe that is imprecise. We are going one direction, he the opposite direction. If we were to meet him again tomorrow, our first meeting would be in his future. He is now going toward our past, and must remember our first meeting as in his past. But surely he will not interfere with your past, because that would stop you from having that encounter with him, denying him what was surely his best amorous outing in centuries. Men are funny about sex.*

Kerena laughed. "Well, I hope it was his best, as a matter of professional pride. But I won't seek him again."

That is safer, Jolie agreed.

Then Kerena thought of something else. "If Chronos lives backward in time, does he exist before his mortal self was born?"

Sharp question! *No, unlike the other Incarnations, his term is limited to his natural lifespan. He must pass the Hourglass on to another before he reaches the date of his birth.*

"Then how could I have given him his best outing in centuries? He would not live that long."

Because he is a vampire, like you. You didn't notice?

"I didn't!" Kerena said, surprised, realizing it was true. No wonder Chronos had recognized her nature.

You were distracted. He's an excellent lover, of course.

They were coming to another shore. "You know geography?" Kerena asked. "Where is this?"

I am not sure I should give you information unknown to your generation.

"Try it. If it fuzzes the lines, untry it."

That made sense. *This is the continent of America, which has had no known contact with Europe in twelve thousand years.*

"No wonder I never heard of it."

Now that Jolie was known to Kerena, and the timelines remained aligned, it was less lonely for each of them. They had much to talk about. Kerena was interested in just about everything, especially secrets of any nature. Jolie told her about America, including the way it had been settled by several waves of colonization from northeast Asia, with the later waves finally obliterating the earlier ones. *The first were sea folk, using their boats as homes, never penetrating far inland. Most of their artifacts were covered by the rising sea. Their boats limited their numbers. The later ones were land dwellers, unlimited, so they prevailed.*

"It would have been better had they just shared the land."

Humans were never much for sharing with other cultures.

They came to the next energy vortex. A mature woman was sitting on a high rocky slope, gazing down at a small village. Kerena came to a stop beside her. "Are you Nature or Fate?"

The woman glanced at her, shifting to old, then young. "Who are you, nymph?"

That's Fate, with three aspects: Clotho, who spins the Threads of Life, Lachesis, who measures them, and Atropos, who cuts them.

"Kerena of England. I have come to beg a favor."

The woman shifted to her middle-aged version, Lachesis. A large colorful tapestry appeared before her. "Kerena," she murmured, her finger hovering over a single thread, which brightened. "My, my: a pretty vampire. But this thread is not due for cutting at this time."

"My son, Gawain, is tainted. Please change my thread so that I do not taint him. That is all I ask."

"You seek to change your fate, you foolish freak?" Lachesis demanded irritably. "Begone!"

"But you see—"

But the woman had changed into a large spider. The spider climbed an invisible line and vanished. Fate was gone.

"Damn it!" Kerena swore. "Why won't they listen?"

It's the arrogance of power. They don't like being pestered by folk of the mortal realm.

"I will not give up," Kerena said with tearful determination. She oriented the cloak on the next vortex.

This took them, in due course, to a battlefield in east Asia. An armored man with a giant red sword stood contemplating the action. This of course was the Incarnation of War, known by many names.

"I don't think this one can help me," Kerena said, disappointed.

I'm not sure. The relations between vampires and mortals could be considered a war between types. If so, Mars might affect it.

"Maybe so," Kerena agreed, recovering hope.

She approached the warrior. "Excuse me, War. I have a favor to—"

"Begone, rabble!" the Incarnation snapped without looking at her. "I am busy."

"But if you could just—"

The Incarnation drew the red sword, turning toward her.

Kerena made herself begone.

"This isn't going well," she said as she oriented on the next vortex.

These are not the Incarnations I know. They seem to have no sense of responsibility to others.

Kerena was grim. "I noticed."

The next vortex was in what Jolie recognized as Africa. It was a huge thick-trunked tree with such thick foliage it seemed like a forest in itself. Within that foliage was a surprisingly capacious residence. A solid woman was there, watching a collection of termites building a small mound.

Nature, Jolie said. *She could surely fix the taint.*

"Madam Nature," Kerena said. "I need a favor—"

"And I need food for my flesh-eating termites," the woman said. "How nice of you to volunteer."

Get out of here!

Kerena was already on her way.

"I didn't think they would do it for nothing," Kerena said. "I'm ready to serve some onerous duty. But they have no interest at all."

Two remain, Jolie reminded her. But whatever faith the might have had in the Incarnations of this time was fading.

"I will query them."

The cloak went south. Jolie was amazed when it left Africa and went out across the cold southern ocean. There was nothing down there but frozen Antarctica.

But it turned out that under the mountain of ice was a hot subterranean realm: Hell. As with Purgatory, this was at this time a physical location, not yet refined into an alternate realm. That meant that they should be able to leave it as readily as they entered it.

Kerena came to Satan's office. This was a crude chamber somewhat isolated from the flames of the main portion. Satan was relaxing in an easy chair, watching the activity through a window.

"Satan," Kerena said. "I—"

He faced her, smiling. "Of course, you lovely creature. What can I do for you?"

For a moment she was silent, caught off-guard by this response. He was ready to help?

Ask him to erase the evil of the taint, Jolie prompted.

"Please erase the evil of the taint," Kerena said. "My son Gawain—"

"Certainly," Satan said. "Come sit on my lap, beautiful vampire." His clothing disappeared.

I distrust this. He may seek to use you, then renege. Remember, he is the Incarnation of Evil. Deception and cheating are natural to him.

"Naturally, ghost," Satan said. "But it seems you will just have to gamble on my fidelity, since the other Incarnations won't help you."

Kerena made a quick compromise. "You can have me once now, and again after you eliminate the evil from my son."

"So you really are a whore."

Kerena refused to be shamed. "Whatever it takes."

"Very well. Step into my bedroom." He indicated a doorway to an adjacent chamber that was filled by a huge bed.

Kerena took a step toward it.

Don't go there! That's a trap. You'll never get free.

"But I can phase through solid rock," Kerena said.

That's not rock. It's the boundary of Hell proper, constructed to prevent tortured souls from escaping. I recognize it.

"Ghost, you are becoming obnoxious," Satan said.

The warning was sufficient. "Here, in this office," Kerena said.

"As you wish." Satan approached her. His masculine member swelled hugely, becoming a thick knobby club.

That's illusion. He's trying to freak you out, so you'll renege. Then he'll have pretext to incarcerate you in Hell.

Satan sent a ball of fire at Jolie. But she was familiar with this trick too, and didn't budge. She had, after all, associated with a later Incarnation of Evil, and learned as he learned. *Why don't you just oblige her request, and trust to her gratitude to oblige you in turn?* she asked him.

"That would be no fun. I want her unwilling."

"She's right," Kerena said. "Give me what I want, and I will give you what you want, within reason."

"Within reason. There's the rub. I am not reasonable. I want to rape you, and have my top demons rape you, until you scream for release."

"Abolish the taint from my son, and I will enter that room," Kerena said evenly. "Then you can torture me all you want."

"But that makes it voluntary, ruining it. No deal."

"Then I will gamble by trusting you," Kerena said. Before Jolie could stop her, she marched into the bedroom and threw herself down on the bed.

On, no! You fool!

Satan shook his head. "It is the foolishness of nobility. I can't touch her."

"Touch me!" Kerena cried. "I am in your power."

He can't, Jolie thought. *Your motive is pure, unselfish, without deceptive intent. There is no evil for him to exploit.*

"Therefore no deal we can make," Satan agreed. "Begone, vampire. Return when you have some evil for me to indulge."

Kerena got up. "Then will you cure my son?"

"Of course not. I'll merely use you mercilessly. You can never glean good from evil."

"Damn!"

Satan laughed. "Even your swearing doesn't taint you, luscious creature. Your frustration is justified."

Kerena walked out of the chamber, and out of Hell, disappointed. "I would have done it, for Gaw," she said tearfully.

Exactly.

One swirl remained. "Surely the Incarnation of Good will heed my plea."

Jolie was deeply uncertain of that. In her time, God had tuned out, paying no attention to the affairs of the world. That was why he had been removed. This was fifteen hundred years before then. Was God more responsive now?

They slid north. Of course any direction was north from the south pole, but they were roughly retracing their course to Africa, then on to Asia Minor. Jolie was curious to know where the Incarnation of Good might be at this time, since the other Incarnations were not where she had known them. Was there a true Heaven?

They stopped at eastern Turkey, as Jolie remembered it from the time she had left. Now it was—she concentrated, remembering history—part of the Eastern Roman Empire, or the western edge of the Persian Empire. And this was—Mount Ararat, where Noah's Ark landed after the Flood.

"Where is this?" Kerena asked, confused.

Jolie explained. *It seems that this early in Christianity, the several locations are not as far removed from the Earthly sphere as they are in my time. The Incarnation of Good is still in this vicinity, liking mountain tops.*

Kerena stood atop the mountain. "Incarnation of Good," she called. "Where are you?"

There was no answer.

She extended her Seeing, searching for the swirl. It was there, in space; this was merely a local connection, as it were. But it seemed to be a vacant number.

God has tuned out, Jolie explained. *That was true in my time too. It seems He hasn't been paying attention for a long while. We finally replaced Him.*

The lines wavered. It seemed she was telling too much about the future, and that would influence Kerena wrongly.

Jolie hastily backtracked. *It seems he's not interested,* she thought instead, and the lines firmed.

Kerena was disappointed and disgusted. "None of the Incarnations of Immortality will help me. I'm going home."

Maybe there is some other way to remove the taint. But Jolie was almost certain there wasn't. This was pain this woman was destined to suffer.

"Whatever it is, I'll find it." They were on their way back to Scotland, moving rapidly. Kerena had gained skill with practice.

Soon they were there. Kerena phased back in beside the outcropping at the entrance to the vampire warren. And paused. "There's something odd."

The trees are larger.

"That's it. How can that be?"

Jolie suddenly remembered something. *Purgatory—the Incarnations—the passage of time can become different. We may have been absent longer than we thought.*

Kerena entered the warren. "Vorely! Vanja!" she called. "It is Verena, returned."

Almost immediately both appeared, looking the same. "We feared you dead," Vorely said, embracing her.

"How long has it been?"

"Thirty years."

"Thirty years! I thought it was a day or two."

"Where were you?" Vanja asked.

"I visited the Incarnations of Immortality, seeking help for my loss, as I planned."

"We knew you were going to try," Vorely said. "But when you did not return, we feared that Death found you before you found Death, as it were."

Kerena settled in for the day, talking with them both while she had avid sex with Vorely. She acquainted them with her excursion and failure. "So now I need to find another way," she concluded.

"But thirty years," Vanja said. "Your son is a grown man."

Somehow Kerena hadn't realized that. "Yet still my son."

Next day she traveled to England, doing it in minutes. She checked, and confirmed that Gordon had died several years before. "But you would not have had much luck with him," the man said, smirking. He took her for her apparent age of eighteen.

"Of course not. I'm his daughter." That left the man silent.

The kingdom had suffered a calamitous defeat, and the knights were scattered or dead. Sir Gawain was dead. So, it turned out, was his son. That stunned her. Even had she gained the intercession of an Incarnation, she was too late to save him.

Kerena's Seeing located his widow, a comely woman of twenty five. Kerena introduced herself as a woman who had once known him passingly: her mother had wet-nursed him. "How did he die?"

"Oh, he was a bold and wonderful man," the widow said. "All the ladies loved him, and I most of all. But he was cursed by bad luck. He was killed last year by a rogue horse. Fortunately I have somewhat to remember him by."

"He left you a token?"

"Not exactly." The woman went to a covered crib and lifted out a healthy baby boy. "Meet Gaw Three."

Kerena was amazed. Her Seeing should have picked up on this, but she hadn't thought to check. Gaw had sired a son! "Oh, he looks just like his father!"

"Yes he does," the woman agreed fondly. "But there's something awry."

Kerena used her Seeing now. The taint was there! It had been passed along from father to son.

She said nothing of this to the widow, and soon departed. Her emotions were whirling. She had lost Gaw Two, but now there was Gaw Three, just like him even in the curse. What was she to make of this?

She couldn't decide, but the pain continued. She had lost many of the things that had been dear to her, and had nothing to show for it. What remained for her in life?

Her pain slowly converted to seething anger. The Incarnations of Immortality could have helped her save Gaw, but had dismissed her plea contemptuously. None of them had considered it fairly; all had rejected it out of hand. They had simply let it happen.

They had been derelict, and it had cost her. Even her effort to plead with them had sacrificed any further contact she might have had with her son. The Incarnations had by that avenue deprived her of her motherhood.

They deserved to pay for their arrogant neglect. "I swear to have vengeance on each of the Incarnations of Immortality," she said with true feeling.

It might have been laughable, for what could a lone vampire do to make any impression on the mighty Incarnations, let alone punish them? But what shook Jolie was that the timelines never wavered. This was no empty threat.

CHAPTER 7
GHOSTS

Kerena returned to the warren. She had made her oath; now she needed to figure out how to implement it. She needed advice, and Morely was the one she most trusted.

"You need a base," he told her. "Something equivalent to an Incarnation, but apart from the existing ones."

"What could that be? The greater and lesser Incarnations make up the full complement, as I understand it."

"Maybe there is an alternative," Vanja said.

Kerena was ready to grasp at any straw. "What one?"

"Vorely said the first separation was into Day and Night. All known Incarnations are aspects of Day. What of Night?"

Kerena considered that. "There may be one more Incarnation I can appeal to!"

"There may be," Morely agreed. "But I have never heard of that one. I assumed that Night remains inchoate."

Kerena focused her Seeing. The Incarnations of Day were there, scattered about the world, but there was no similar swirl of power for the night. "It seems so," she agreed, disappointed.

"You have great power," Vanja said. "Maybe you could draw on Night to smite the fragments of Day."

Kerena liked the way Vanja's mind worked. "Let me study Night for a while."

She did. She remained at the warren, sharing Vorely with Vanja, and on occasion making love with Vanja directly, while she tried to discover a key to the power that might reside in night. But it was elusive, if it existed at all. She walked out in the night, extending her awareness, but it was unable to fix on anything specific.

Vanja helped again. "Where does your power come from, when you bend light around you or wade through rock?"

"I don't know. It just seems to be there."

"It must have a source."

"What are you thinking of?"

"Could your power come from Night? As the Incarnations draw from Day, could you be drawing from Night?"

"It seems possible. If Night is inchoate, that power may be there to be drawn on."

"So if you could discover the specific source of your power, you might then know how to address Night."

"And there may be as much power in Night as in Day," Kerena said. "If I could only harness it. Then I would be in a position to counter the Incarnations."

"Then you might," Vanja agreed.

"You are being very helpful."

"Vengeance is a thing I understand. You helped me obtain mine against Vichard."

"What happened to him? He is no longer here."

"He left the warren, and was killed elsewhere. I am not sorry."

"So your vengeance is complete."

"I suppose. I would be an old woman in my sixties now, had he let me be."

"Instead of a lovely creature."

"I would have children and grandchildren."

Kerena sighed. "There can be imperfect satisfaction in that." Yet she understood Vanja's disquiet. She had been denied the conventional life, and what she lacked had the appeal of lost fancy. People generally did favor what they lacked more than what they had.

She focused on the source of her powers. When she guided light around herself so as to tolerate full day, or to become invisible, what did she draw on?

She found it impossible to focus on that; she was too busy achieving the effects themselves. If she focused on the process, she lost it. She needed a less direct way.

"The library," Vanja said.

"The what?"

"The vampire library of the occult. It has existed as long as vampires have, all the ancient information preserved. There should be answers there."

Kerena found herself getting to like the vampire girl for more than her body, just as she had once gotten to like Molly in the brothel. "The library," she agreed.

The library consisted of many ancient scrolls, maintained by a dedicated vampire named Keeper. He was enormously gratified to have the facilities used. "So few care, any more," he said. "All this arcane knowledge going to waste. We have scrolls rescued from Alexandria before the Arab conquest, cuneiform tablets from Sumerian times—"

"Alexandria hasn't been sacked yet," Vanja reminded him gently. "Not for another century, at least."

"Pardon, I do lose track. But they are worthy documents."

"You have scrolls from the future?" Kerena asked, surprised.

"No, they exist today, or they wouldn't be physical. But they are destined to be lost, so we rescued them. Such things have to be done before the fact."

"Just as curses have to be nulled before they take effect," Kerena said, seeing a parallel.

"Exactly. Now how can I help you?"

"I'm sure you will be able to guide me in apt directions," Kerena said, stepping close and kissing him. Vanja had warned her that his assistance was much more useful when he was well motivated, and that he had expressed admiration for Verena's form and manner. So she was prepared to keep him motivated by being his appreciative mistress while in the library. It was not only easy for her, she enjoyed it, so no fakery was necessary.

Jolie found this interesting too. She had known Kerena possessed special skills and had a special destiny; that was of course why she was here to keep it on track. But she hadn't known the intricate details of it. A library that wasn't necessarily restricted to the present, kept by vampires: who would have thought it?

There turned out to be an enormous amount of relevant material. The vampires had been much concerned, historically, about the forces of night, because vampires were creatures of the night. Their powers stemmed from darkness, just as their liabilities stemmed from light. But Kerena needed more. She had powers of her own, such as Seeing and making useful transformations of the velvet cloak. From where did these stem?

But now she encountered an obscure balking. Somehow the scrolls did not ever quite address these powers, other than to acknowledge their existence. Some references referred to others for further information, but those others were not in the library. "This is more spotty than I realized," Keeper said apologetically. "Prior interest has been in vampire powers, and we have excellent definition on those. But phasing through stone—somehow it seems those scrolls did not come into our possession."

Vanja was annoyed. "There seems to be a barrier between you and the knowledge you seek," she said. "Can this be coincidence?"

Kerena started to laugh, but quickly stifled it, because her Seeing suggested that this was indeed the case. Something was preventing her from gleaning her answers here. Yet how could the long-term library have been limited to balk her—before her arrival on the scene? That was what had seemed funny, for a moment.

"There is a force opposing the fathoming of this mystery, by anyone," she said. "We are not meant to know."

"A hostile force?" Keeper asked. "Who governs such force?"

"I don't think anyone does," Kerena said. "It's just there, an intangible wall. But I mean to surmount it, one way or another."

"Was there similar opposition to the formation of the Incarnations of Day?" Vanja asked.

"I wonder." They dived into it. The library was not strong on the powers of Day, but did suggest that for every power of Day, there was an equivalent power of Night. So by studying Day, they might glean useful information on Night. That was an indirect approach, but very well might get around the wall.

But of course they couldn't go and ask the Incarnations of Day exactly how their powers had come to be harnessed, assuming they knew. It had to be done separately.

Still, there were indications. Each Incarnation was different, but there were some similarities. It seemed that each had become Incarnated when a human being demonstrated that he or she was more capable of performing the task than the original mindless force was. That human had stepped into the swirl of energy and thereafter personified it. This was true for the major and the minor Incarnations.

But no one had stepped into the force of Night. It remained mindless. Except that it resisted exploration.

"Did the first human Incarnations have to overcome opposition to take their positions?" Kerena asked, returning to Vanja's question.

"It seems likely," Keeper replied.

"Is it really?" Vanja asked, now taking another tack. "There's one big distinction between Day and Night: Day is visible, Night is invisible."

Kerena pondered that. Things could be seen by day, but not by night, unless some light was brought in, an aspect of day. "You think it is Night's nature to keep secrets?"

"What else? And the secret you want to fathom is how to save your son's son from the taint."

So it seemed. "But I think the answer is not in this library. I need another source of information."

Vanja shrugged. "Maybe you could ask a ghost. They have access anywhere."

"A ghost," Kerena said thoughtfully.

"I was joking."

"Nevertheless, it may be a good idea. Do you know of any local ghosts?"

"Well, there's Lilah. She hangs around. I think she finds the undead more compatible than the fully living. But she's not a nice person."

"I don't want a friend, I want information. I will see if I can contact her."

"This may not be wise," Keeper said. "Ghosts can be dangerous."

"How so, since they can't do anything physical?"

"Most of them crave life, and would take over the bodies of the living if they could. That's why the living don't trust them."

"Fortunately I am no longer truly living," Kerena said. "I am undead."

"Still, it's a risk. There's no certainty a ghost couldn't govern an undead person, given the chance."

"I need information. I am willing to take a risk to obtain it. If the ghost wants to borrow my body for a while, I will do it—if she gives me what I want."

Jolie shared Keeper's misgiving. She was a ghost herself, and did not want to share Kerena's body with another, though it was possible. Suppose the ghost started influencing the woman the way Jolie did? It might become impossible to keep the timelines aligned. Yet if interaction with a ghost was part of the proper history, it would have to be done. So she would stay out of it, unless a divergence occurred.

What do you think? Kerena asked internally.

So much for staying out of it! *If I participate in any way other than aligning the timelines, I will be causing a divergence myself. I am a ghost, and have an opinion, but I think must not answer you or assist you in this respect.*

To her half surprise, Kerena accepted that. "How do I summon Lilah?" she asked Vanja.

"You can't. She's independent. But I will tell her of your interest the next time I encounter her."

The next day when Kerena was out foraging for food, and for a taste of the blood of a distant sheep, she became aware of a presence. It was shadowy, though of course there were no firm shadows in the night, and significantly masculine. "Hello, lover," she said, recognizing the aura despite the passage of two or thirty two years, depending on whether it was her time or the world's time.

He came to her, and a softly lighted bower formed around them as he embraced her. "So you have external magic too," she murmured as she kissed him.

He did not reply. He simply bore her down on the thick cushions that floored the bower. Her loin yearned to him; she was eager for his divine penetration. But she had another mission, and decided to gamble in the hope of making progress.

She locked her legs together. She knew this would not stop him long; the mere touch of his conducive member would cause her to open them wide in welcome. But she hoped to bluff him. "First talk to me. Who are you?"

He paused, seeming amused. Then, to her half surprise, he spoke. "You seek to bargain, half-mortal girl?"

Victory! "You can have me unwilling, if you prefer. But if you want me joyful, you must meet me part way."

"You have unusual spirit."

"Who are you?" she repeated firmly.

"Merely an anonymous afreet."

"A what?"

"An air demon from Arabia. There is no precise equivalent in occidental mythology."

She extended her Seeing, but the man remained opaque. She had no power over him. He was obviously supernatural. She relaxed, having gotten as much as it seemed she could. She was desperate for the completion of his embrace.

He took her swiftly, thrilling her has he had before, and she participated fully. "You are the most luscious creature I have encountered in years."

"Then come to me more often," she said.

"Perhaps I shall." He paused, perhaps in thought, then changed the subject. "Is your existence ordinary, pretty vampire?"

"No. I have a case against the Incarnations of Day."

"Ah. What is that?"

There seemed to be no harm in telling him that much. "My baby has a taint, a curse. They refused even to listen to my plea for help."

"They are arrogant," he agreed. "But neither mortal nor half mortal can make much of an impression on them. It is the other way around: they control your lives and deaths."

"What could make an impression?"

He smiled. "Another Incarnation."

Did he know what she was seeking? She could not be sure. "I sought all those I could find."

"So you did. A remarkable achievement. You are correct: your existence is not ordinary. Perhaps that is why you intrigue me. Yet it seems you have been balked."

"So it seems," she agreed.

"Has anything supernatural actively interfered with your life course?"

That was an interesting way to phrase it. "I am aware only of tacit balkiness. But I am determined to overcome it."

"Perhaps you will." Then he proceeded to another bout of love, which she was more than glad to oblige. It was evident that he possessed supernatural potency, that incited her complementary passion.

She slept in his strong embrace. When she woke, he and the bower were gone. She was lying on the leafy forest floor. But it had not been imagination; the evidence of his passion was in her body. The lingering fluid was like a warming balm, generating both satisfaction and new hunger. It spread from her channel into her body, pleasantly diffusing.

Jolie remained wary of the afreet, if that was really what he was. He had enormous magical power, and seemed to know a lot. Yet he had been questioning Kerena, and she suspected she knew what he was seeking: information about Jolie herself. *She* had been interfering with the girl's life. What was his interest? She was not at all easy about this.

Yet the timelines had not blurred. Whatever effect the afreet had, was in accordance with the proper course of history. All she could do was let it be. But this was another disquietingly odd turn. Jolie had had no idea that there would be such mysteries connected with her mission.

A few days later, as Kerena was pondering approaches, she became aware of a presence via her Seeing. "Lilah," she said immediately.

The presence floated close. Kerena put out one hand, touching the region. *Lilah,* the ghost agreed.

"Can you help me fathom the powers of Night?"

The ghost took faint form as a strikingly lovely woman. "Why should I?" Her thought was not audible, but as Kerena attuned she was able to receive it as such.

"I can lend you my body for a time."

Lilah considered. "It is undead."

"But indistinguishable from living, when among the living, and as responsive as ever."

"Give me half your time."

Kerena laughed. "What, my waking time? You'll get no more than the time you give me, providing information. An hour."

"An hour among the living, an hour at a time, at my choice, until the time matches."

"Far from here, where I am not known. I must maintain anonymity."

"Agreed."

This was too easy. "And I must agree to the hour you want, so that it is convenient to my schedule."

"Agreed."

Kerena didn't quite trust this, but if the ghost reneged on anything, the deal would end. "Agreed. Now tell me who you are. Your personal history."

"That counts as time."

"Agreed, within reason."

"I am Lilah, a version of Lilith, a once mortal woman. I was Adam's first wife, until he rejected me and took that feckless slut Eve instead. I swore vengeance."

"But Adam was the first man, and Eve the first woman."

"Revisionist history. *I* was the first woman. I gave him the hottest sex he could imagine. But the fool wanted a virgin, and I was cast aside and banned from Eden. But I got him back: I sent the serpent to tempt the innocent girl with the knowledge of good and evil. After that she was no more virginal than I. God was angry; he blasted me to bits. But he still had to expel them, because Eden is not for the knowledgeable."

Kerena was amazed. If this was to be believed, this was no ordinary ghost. This was a historic nemesis.

"You doubt?" Lilah inquired. "I see you are a sexual innocent."

Kerena realized she was being baited, and refused to rise to it. "Go on with your history; it interests me."

"Now that Eve was no longer innocent, she had at it with Adam, and they begat dozens of brats. Cain was an early one; I whispered in his ear, infuriating him over a childish argument, and he slew his annoying brother Able. Further vengeance. When he was banished for that, I came to him as a child of Nod and taught him what sexual passion was all about, and bore him more dozens of brats, as I had done with Nod before him."

"But you were the age of his mother," Kerena protested.

"Older; remember, I was the first woman. But we lived a long time in those years. I was as sexy as I am now." The ghost did a little dance with breasts and bottom, showing both bouncing as she spun around. Her figure was fuller than Kerena's, and the rippling flesh was impressive. "Except that I didn't; he got a notion for a young virgin, as his lout of a father had—what *is* it about virgins?—so I slew her, and the ungrateful lout slew me. I was furious."

Kerena was coming to appreciate that this was one mean spirited entity. But one with no hesitation expressing herself. If she knew any secrets, she would surely tell them. "Furious," she echoed.

"So I hung around as a ghost, observing secrets, studying techniques, and every so often I was able to animate the body of an unwary girl and make her perform as never before. Some of them got themselves stoned as witches, but what a time I had before it came to that. I remember infiltrating Lilah, a formerly cow-like creature with nothing to recommend her other than her voluptuous body. I gave her initiative and guile, causing the Philistines to recruit her for a key mission. She then seduced that muscular ignorant Israelite Samson and betrayed him to the Philistines. They blinded him, chained him to a wall, and used him for stud duty to generate sturdy dull boys like himself. But me they ignored, after I accomplished my mission. So I tempted an official, and whispered in his ear, and got him to anchor Samson between two columns of their temple during a festival. Naturally the brute heaved hard enough to bring the temple down on his head and on all the celebrants, including those who had ignored me. I never tire of vengeance against idiots."

And she didn't like to be ignored, Jolie saw. Lilah's history was an exercise in braggadocio, for all that that term would not be coined for another thousand years. She knew Lila, as the variant spelling went, from her own timeline, a notorious creature, but hadn't realized that Kerena had associated with her.

"I think I have the essence," Kerena said. "What do you know of the powers of Night?"

"Everything, of course. But first give me my hour."

Kerena considered, and concluded it was best to do that now, to keep the cynical ghost cooperative. "Do you have a distant setting in mind?"

"Eastern Roman Empire, where decadence exists in style. Constantinople."

Kerena had never heard of it, but was amenable. "What direction?"

"Southeast."

Kerena dressed, oriented and phased down for rapid travel. The ghost followed. Kerena wasn't sure exactly how ghosts moved, but wasn't surprised.

Soon they came to the great decadent city. It was far larger than any Kerena knew. It was surrounded by a great wall, but it was hard to imagine an army large enough to represent a threat to such a vast metropolis.

Beyond the city was a large estate with a villa. Murals on the walls depicted fabulous erotic scenes. People were arriving; it seemed it was time for a party. The ghost evidently knew how to sniff out such events.

"Now," the ghost said as Kerena stood in an empty chamber admiring a scene wherein three nymphly maidens were seducing a willing man.

"Take it—for an hour," Kerena said, and let Lilah in.

"Well now," Lilah said, assuming control of the body. "I forgot the costume; your primitive rags won't do. Fortunately slaves are nude for this type of service." She removed the dress and stood bare.

A robed man entered the chamber, wearing bright jewelry: apparently a member of the governing class. "Ho—I don't recognize you," he said. He spoke in Greek, but Kerena discovered she could understand it. The ghost's control had evidently lent her knowledge of the language, or she had somehow assimilated it from the context. There were things about magic she had yet to fathom.

"I am a slave from afar," Lilah said, winsomely. "Just in today, for this event."

"Ah. Let me look at you." He took hold of her and eyed her torso, which she eagerly displayed to advantage. "You'll do." He bore her back and pro-

ceeded to sex without further preliminary. There was no pretense of mutu-
ality; it was all for himself, but Lilah cooperated enthusiastically.

"It's good to have a body again," she said as the man got off her and
went off in search of wine.

So it seemed. Kerena had shared in the sensations of the act, but as sex
went, this was not much. The man's dry member had been abrasive until
liquifying, and technique had been absent.

But as it turned out, there was a good deal more to be had at this party.
In the next hour Lilah managed to set up a two man, three woman conjunc-
tion that did indeed have aspects Kerena hadn't seen before. It seemed the
Romans and the ghost took their sex seriously. It was a considerable orgy.

"Your hour is done," Kerena said.

"I don't think so."

"Oh, it is. Time to go home and study the forces of Night."

"No it isn't."

"What are you talk about? We made a deal."

"I lied. I know nothing about the forces of Night, and I am keeping this
body. It's a good one, despite being not fully alive."

"That does it. I'm taking it back now." Kerena moved to do so.

And was balked. The ghost refused to relinquish control, and she had
experience with this kind of conflict. Possession provided power. "You fool
innocent girl, you threw it away. It's mine now."

Kerena realized that she had walked into a trap. She had blithely assumed that a given deal would be honored by both parties. She had indeed
been a fool.

Yet Jolie noted that the timelines were not fudging. This sequence was
true to both realities. This was one Kerena had to fight through on her own.

She did. The ghost had taken control of the actions of the body, but not
its substance. Kerena thinned it down to ghostly texture, then steered it
through a wall and away. She was gone, leaving the ghost behind, as there
was no longer any substance to hold on to. She was free.

How did you know to do that? Jolie asked, surprised.

"Morely taught me, when I told him of my plan to negotiate with a
ghost. He warned me of their tricks."

That was a revelation to Jolie, who had not picked up on Morely's more
recent instruction. *You could have done it with me, too.*

"I trust you."

There it was: she remained with this woman by tolerance, not right or
ability. Kerena was far from the innocent girl she once had been. *Thank you.
But I can't help you study Night.*

They were headed back toward England. "I need a local ghost I can
trust. A friend." She brightened. "Molly!"

Jolie did not speak. As it happened, she knew Molly very well; they were associate ghosts in her own reality. She was an excellent choice. But she did not dare provide information that might change the timelines.

In due course Kerena sought Molly. She went to the old town where Molly had died. The experience with Lilah had at least taught her how to interact with ghosts.

Kerena wasn't sure exactly where to find the ghost, so started at the obvious place: the brothel where they both had worked. It was under subsequent management, the daughter of the madam Kerena had known, who of course did not recognize this pretty stranger as a former house girl. "Why yes, we do have a ghost. That's Molly, who worked here but was killed by a client. We gave her a room out of sentiment. Some of our older clients remember her, and she's shapely and friendly."

"I'm not a client, but I would like to talk with her. I'll pay a client's fee." She proffered silver.

"You have the room for an hour," the woman said, gratified.

The room was small but nice; they were taking proper care of their ghost. Molly's presence probably enhanced their reputation.

Kerena stood beside the bed. "Molly, do you know me?"

There was a swirl of mist. Kerena extended one hand to touch it. There was a faint shock of recognition.

"Rena! It's you! But what happened to you?"

"I became a vampire. That has its liabilities, but on the whole is a benefit, because I retain my youth." Actually she had in effect jumped thirty years, but that was more complicated than she cared to get into at present.

"You are lovely! You have filled out since we were companions. But why are you here?"

"I believe I have a deal to make. I will help you if you will help me."

"We don't need to make a deal, Rena; we're friends. But there's not a lot I can do as a ghost."

"I think there is. I want to learn how to use the powers of Night. I need a test subject I can trust."

"A test subject? I don't understand."

"I am studying magic, but lack access to the secrets of Night. I think a ghost could find them more readily. More than that, I want to learn to transform a ghost to something more solid, and not have her turn on me."

Molly was interested. "Can you give me back my body?"

"I don't think so. Not your living body. But maybe I could give you some solidity, so you might emulate the living state. I don't know whether there would be danger for you."

"What danger could there be for one already dead?"

"Dabbling in such arts is thought to be evil. You might get sent to Hell."

"I am in Hell already, foully murdered and unable to seek vengeance. No risk there."

"I might be able to help you achieve vengeance. I don't know."

"No, it's too late for that."

"I can lend you my body for some renewed experience of living."

"That would be wonderful! But I will help you regardless. You're my friend."

"Then come with me, and we shall see what we can accomplish."

"Gladly! But I must bid farewell to those I know here."

"You can do it in physical form, though me. But when I need my body back, I expect you to yield it."

"Of course." The ghost nodded. "Suddenly I appreciate why you want a friend. You can't trust just any ghost."

"So I found. Do you know Lilah?"

"Don't mess with her! She's dangerous."

"So I found," Kerena repeated. "I think we understand each other. But there is one other thing: I already have a ghost. Ignore her."

"But maybe I know her."

"No. She needs to be ignored. Trust me."

The timelines didn't waver. Kerena knew what was what. Molly and Jolie were friends in T1, but Jolie did not yet exist in T2.

Molly joined them. Kerena gave her the body, and she walked to the mirror, adjusting herself. Molly did not look at all like Kerena, apart from being of a similar age, but as she fixed the hair and assumed an expression, the image in the mirror came to resemble the ghost to a remarkable extent. "I am ready," she said.

Molly went to the madam. "I appreciate what you and your mother have done for me," she said. "Now I am departing with a friend, for a special mission, so my room can be used by another girl."

The woman stared. "Molly! Can it be?"

"I am still a ghost, merely with a temporary host. I don't know how long I'll be gone. Thank you for accepting me, after my death."

The women looked bemused. "Congratulations. You well be welcome back when your mission is done."

"That is kind of you. Tell the girls I wish them well." She departed.

Outside, Molly relinquished the body. "That felt wonderful! It's so nice to be alive again, even if only in surrogate. Thank you so much."

"Welcome," Kerena said, resuming control. "Now I must travel north, but we can talk meanwhile. Please tell me your history. You never mentioned your curse when I knew you alive."

"I preferred that it be unknown, as nothing could be done about it. It started with my mother. She was a beautiful woman. She was courted by a sorceress, but she was not of that persuasion, so declined and married a man. The man was one the sorceress desired also, which made it worse. The sorceress was angry, so retaliated by cursing the child of that union: me. This was calculated to hurt my mother worse than anything else, and indeed she wept, but could not change it. So I was destined to die young and violently."

"Young and violently," Kerena repeated, remembering something. "Who was the sorceress?"

"The king's sister, the Fey."

That was what Morgan le Fey hadn't told her: that she was responsible for the curse that killed Molly. Kerena's anger surged; indeed, they would be enemies. "I worked with the Fey," Kerena said. "I was with her when you died. She never said."

"The curse was from fifteen years before. Maybe she forgot about it."

"No, she mentioned it to me. The bitch."

"I wanted vengeance, but now she is dead or gone, so it's too late. That really irks me. Not that I ever had any way to accomplish it."

"I had to turn vampire to accomplish my desire, yet today I am satisfied to be so. Maybe you can find some satisfaction in your ghostly status, in time. We never know where fate will lead us."

How very true, Jolie thought. Kerena had as yet no idea of the phenomenal course she was destined to follow, just as Molly had no notion of her own.

"What's that?" Molly asked. "What phenomenal course?" And the lines blurred.

Jolie jumped back to stifle her own thought, and the lines clarified. She would have to be more careful; the other ghost could tune in on her otherwise, especially when her thoughts were on that ghost.

"I hope my fate has something more interesting in mind than stasis."

"Oh? What is it that ghosts do, when not interacting with the living?"

"Nothing. We simply settle in place and tune out of minutes, years, or decades. I would love to have things interesting enough so that I don't have to tune out much."

"I hope to have far more interesting things," Kerena said.

They arrived at the warren. Kerena solidified and went to Morely's chamber. He was there, asleep, embracing Vanja, who lay naked on top of him.

"This is already interesting," Molly said, observing detail knowledgeably. "He is in her, but asleep. She must be pretty dull."

"Not at all. But they practice sex an enormous amount here. They must have felt more comfortable sleeping together, as it were."

"This is your man? He evidently doesn't miss you much."

"He's with his wife. I'm his mistress. I've been busy elsewhere." Kerena nudged Vanja's pert rear with a foot. "Wake up, sleepy bottom," she said aloud.

Vanja did. She lifted her head. "Oh, hello Rena. Did you find her?"

"Yes. Molly is with me now. She says you must be pretty dull if Morely fell asleep at the helm."

Vanja laughed. That woke Morely. He made as it to disengage, but Vanja refused to let him. "Finish your business first, lover. *Then* you can see to her."

Morely did not require further urging. He completed the act with style, while Kerena and the ghosts observed. It was surprising how many nuance variants there could be for a straightforward act.

"I think I like these people," Molly said internally. "They truly appreciate sex."

In due course Kerena formally introduced Molly, and lent her the body briefly. Then it was time to explore the ghostly aspects. "Lilah said she knew everything, but I'm not sure she did," Kerena said. "How much do ghosts know of Night?"

"Depends on the ghost," Molly said. "I tried to learn things in order to pursue vengeance, but found mostly interesting by-paths like the Carnival of Ghosts. I could introduce you to more knowledgeable ghosts, I suppose."

"That may help. But I'd rather start without them, because of the trust issue."

"Lilah was one of the worst choices, but any ghost will try to take your body," Molly agreed. "I would be tempted, if I weren't your friend."

"Which is why I sought you. But I'll try to make it worth your while. What do you want, apart from vengeance?"

"To have a living body, of course. But—"

"What about someone else's body? If we could find a girl who doesn't want to live, so you could take over?"

"Depends on the body, but yes, I'd like that."

"Now what's this carnival you mentioned?"

"The Carnival of Ghosts. That's a regular event, where we all get together for fun. We dance, have contests, make love, see sideshows, tour time—"

"Tour time?"

"Ghosts aren't limited the way mortals are. We can go where we want."

"To the future?"

"Yes, but I don't do that; it makes me dizzy. There are so many alternates, I'm afraid I'll get lost. The future really isn't fixed, so what you see there may not actually happen if you don't stay on the right timeline. I prefer to visit the past, which is fixed."

Jolie found this interesting. She knew it, of course, but had thought such awareness was a more recent thing. Evidently not. And of course even the past was malleable, if touched by a visitor from a divergent timeline. She had not said anything about this to Kerena, lest that make the lines diverge, but now that a person of this timeline had done so, it was all right.

"I want two things," Kerena said. "To save my son, now my grandson, from the taint I inadvertently put on him, and to have vengeance against all the Incarnations of Day for not helping me accomplish that. Maybe a visit to the future could show me weaknesses they will have, that I could exploit. But if I can't be sure that what I see will really happen, that won't help. Still, if the past can't be changed, that doesn't help either."

"Vengeance against the Incarnations! I think that's impossible. I didn't even know of them until after I died, but now I know they are untouchable. They wield powers beyond those of any mortal magician, and can destroy mortals at whim. If Fate cuts your thread, or Death takes your soul—"

"I'll risk it," Kerena said grimly. "They are arrogant and uncaring, and deserve to be dispatched."

"Maybe so. Still, how can you hope to accomplish any such thing?"

"I was able to locate them using powers I have developed as a mortal and as a vampire. If I can tame the powers of Night, I should be able to do much more. Those powers should match all those of Day. But there seems to be resistance; something prevents me from approaching those powers. I need to find a way to get around that resistance."

"Well, its inherent," Molly said. "Things don't like to be handled. A boulder doesn't like to be moved; the wind doesn't like to be balked. Night doesn't like to be exposed."

Kerena paused, surprised. Could it be that simple? The inertia of forces long left alone? That had never occurred to her. "Could a ghost locate and define those powers, even if they are resistive to exposure?"

"I don't know. It's not something I ever thought of doing."

"This carnival—there are many ghosts there? Could I talk with them? To learn if any know what I need?"

"Oh, sure, I could take you there. But they won't necessarily tell you the truth. Not unless you pay more than you want."

"Would they tell *you* the truth?"

"Maybe. I have nothing to be cheated out of."

"I want to go to the carnival. Can I go?"

"Yes, as my guest. But you would be the only part-mortal there; it could be uncomfortable. They would notice, and maybe tease you cruelly."

"I'll risk it," Kerena said again.

CHAPTER 8
NIGHT

The Carnival of Ghosts was a wondrous thing. It was set up like a pitched camp, with assorted tents of various sizes, barkers at each entrance, and throngs of ordinary looking folk. Kerena saw the top of some kind of wooden mountain with tracks on it, an oddity.

A roller coaster, Jolie thought. *They will be invented a thousand years or so hence. Evidently the ghosts are truly timeless, and take their pleasures wherever they find them.*

"They are all ghosts," Molly assured Kerena, "All but you. Don't let them get to you."

They approached the main entrance. "What's this dung?" the ticket man demanded. "We don't let her kind in here."

"Well, make an exception, pinhead," Molly snapped, floating out from Kerena to assume her full ghost form. "She's with me."

"And how is she going to pay for the ticket, cutie?"

"I'll buy the ticket."

"No you won't. She has to buy her own."

"That's not in the rules, you lecherous leech."

Kerena caught on to what the ghost wanted: sex with a live woman. This was hardly a burden, considering her history, and she had been without sex for several hours, so was getting hungry for it. "I'll do it. Tell me how."

"Just stand there," the male ghost said. He stepped up to her and embraced her, his outline barely touching. He kissed her, and she felt the tenuous impact of his lips on hers. Then she felt a similarly tenuous penetration below. Her clothing made no difference; he ignored it. He worked his way into the spot, evidently feeling as much contact as he needed. She would not have felt anything, had she not been alert for it. Had she moved, what faint interaction there was would have been lost, as there was no physical component. That was why he needed her acquiescence.

He thrust and panted, and she felt the motion, like a feather made of bubbles, faintly tickling her interior. He climaxed, and it was like a driblet of thin mist. Maybe it was her own moisture, stirred by her awareness of sex. It was enough to get her interested, but not enough to allow her a climax.

He finished and withdrew, leaving her unsatisfied. "Here's your ticket," he said, presenting a ghostly piece of paper.

So she had just had sex with a ghost. It wasn't much, but at least she had seen his figure and felt a little. Maybe if she practiced she would be able to get more from it. "Thank you."

"It's not as much for him as with another ghost," Molly confided as they entered the Carnival. "A lady ghost is on the same plane, so the sensation is real. But they're all thrilled by the notion of doing it with a real live body. Lady ghosts like doing it with living men, too, though they have to move carefully to keep the anatomy in place."

So it turned out to be. Every side show had its ticket taker, and the price was the same for her: stand and be addressed. So she stood and felt their faint ardors. As sex went, it was puny. But neither did it bother her, because as sex went, it was also about as convenient as it could be. She didn't have to do anything but stand for a moment for the barely-felt plumbing. Then she encountered a female ghost barker, and had to stand still for kissing, breast stroking, and genital rubbing. Well, she had had experience with that, too, before and after turning vampire.

The shows and activities were fun. Kerena saw all manner of exotic animals and insects, and participated in wonderfully structured costume dances, and tasted ghostly pastries and wines. Gradually she perfected the ghostly semblance, so that the sensations became first real, then potent. At last, drunk on spirits in more than one sense, she had a sexual fling with a truly manly spook on a public stage that was fully satisfactory. Only the fancy rides were beyond her: the roller ghoster, the cart through the horror house, and the water mountain.

"It can be arranged, for a price," a pair of young looking men informed her. Apparent age was determined by the time in life they died, so was deceptive, as was her own appearance. "What ride do you want?"

"All three," she said, interested.

"Done." A third young man came over, and she realized that it was one man per ride. So be it.

"This will be some experience," Molly warned. "I'll watch." She separated into her own form.

Kerena sat on an isolated chair. Then illusion surrounded her: the cart and tracks of the first ride. She was not moving, but the image was, so that she seemed to be rolling forward. She let her mind accept it, beginning to feel the motion.

Men appeared on either side of her, and the third bestriding her. So it was to be all three at once. So be it, again. She was able to see through the one on top, so he didn't interfere with the experience of the ride.

The scene tilted, as the cart was hauled steeply upward by a stout rope. The side men fondled her breasts and the top man kissed her lingeringly, his translucent skull framing her view.

The cart reached the top of the wood mountain, then angled to roll down the other side. It was awesome, like a long fall. The tracks descended to a seeming lake, and the cart plunged into it with a great loud splash. She seemed to feel the coursing water, though probably it was merely the questing mouths of the men as they kissed her breasts.

There were monsters under the surface: giant toothy fish, spectacular jellyfish with trailing sting lines, and huge squid with sucker-lined tentacles. One squid grabbed her with several arms and brought its deadly beak down to bite her face. All three men kissed her mouth and ears at that moment, making it seem more than real; a small cry escaped her, pleasing them. Girls were supposed to scream in horror scenes.

By the time the ride was done, so were the three men. She had had considerable multiple seeming plumbing. But also a phenomenal ride experience. "I must do that again, sometime," she said dazedly as the track returned to the open court and the illusion faded, leaving her sitting alone.

It was Molly who called her to account. "You have acclimatized. You came here for a purpose."

"So I did," Kerena agreed, remembering. She threw off the daze of wine and illusion and concentrated. "Who here knows things I need to learn?"

"Many. But remember, you can't trust them. It will be better to see for yourself."

"I don't even know where to look."

"Why not start with the origin of the Incarnations?"

"And how they became offices. Yes! How do I see that?"

"You travel back in time. But you will need a better guide than I can be. Someone who derives from those times."

"Who would that be?"

A lovely ghost forged out of the throng. "That would be me."

Oh, no! "Lilah!"

"Lilith, originally. The first woman."

"You tried to keep my body."

"Of course. A fool and her body are soon parted."

"You aren't even embarrassed about it."

Lilah frowned. "Listen, you naïve creature. I was the first feminist."

"First what?"

"An anachronism in terminology, not in practice. I refused to consider myself Adam's inferior, so I left him, and was expelled from Eden. I stand by my stance: women are at least the equal of men, and far less crude."

"You said Adam wanted a virgin."

"Well, I was one, until that first fuck, for which he was as responsible as I. But it was the virginity of the mind and spirit that counted. He wanted his woman to be inferior to him. That was laughable, and I would have none of it. Neither should you."

Despite her ire at the betrayal, Kerena found herself warming to this woman. She was open and direct, and proud of her gender. "How can I trust you?"

"You can't, until you are as cynical as I. That will require centuries. But you can be sure I will honor a deal that provides something I want. Make me that deal."

"What do you want, aside from my body?"

"Next best is demon substance. That comes from the raw material of chaos. I can't go that far myself, but maybe you can. Get me some of that so I can be a demoness and assume partial solidity when I want to."

"Partial solidity? Why do you want that?"

"So I can have at men physically again, obviously. I won't be able to stay solid full time, but an hour at a time will be fine. It will expand my potential enormously."

"For this you will guide me to the origin of the Incarnations?"

"Exactly. That is near chaos."

"How can you trust me to deliver, after you guide me?"

"You can be trusted, you naïve tart. I am the one who can't be."

This was making uncomfortable sense. "What do you think, Molly?"

"She's right. Set it up so she has to trust you, and you don't have to trust her. She can be useful, for a price."

So it seemed. "But I want you along, Molly."

"Of course. I wouldn't let you go with her alone. She'd find a way to cheat you, because you really are too trusting." Molly merged again, disappearing into her body. Her presence was distinctly feminine and yielding, in contrast to the eager hard lust of the male ghosts.

"I am more like Eve than Lilith," Kerena agreed with resignation. She found that an oddity, considering how many men she had serviced sexually, and her status as a vampire. "Very well: I will make that deal."

"This way," Lilah said. She began to move backward. Not exactly physically.

Kerena's Seeing picked up on how she did it, and emulated it. She followed Lilah, and Molly followed her. They slid slowly back in time. It was like thinning and traveling across the globe, only in another direction. They were not moving spacially, but their surroundings were changing, as they had for the ghost ride. This, however, was not illusion. Darkness came, and light, and darkness, the nights and days of the recent past. Then the seasons changed, faster as they accelerated, until they flicked by in much the way the days and nights had before.

The Carnival of Ghosts was in a glade in a forest. The surrounding trees diminished, growing younger. New old trees appeared, filling in the glade. The forest became thick, overlapping Kerena's space, but she was insubstantial and did not feel any impact of the trunks. The forest was a living thing, its parts shrinking while its whole remained. Everywhere trees appeared, shrank into shrubs, and disappeared into the ground.

Then the forest changed its nature, the leafed trees giving way reluctantly to firs. The pace increased, so that a tree that started as several centuries in girth descended into nothing in the space of a few seeming seconds. Hundreds of years were being traversed, then thousands.

Jolie was amazed and fascinated. This was an excursion beyond her expectation. Far farther back in time than ever. What would be seen at the end of this journey? Or the beginning, as it were.

Suddenly it stopped. They stood in a lush garden where all manner of fruiting trees grew. Tame-seeming animals grazed, unafraid of molestation. Indeed, there was a lion and lamb resting under a spreading tree. "Garden of Eden," Lilah said. "We drifted a little in space to find it, as well as time. It's in Africa."

"But weren't you banned from it?" Kerena asked.

"This is the Garden after Adam and Eve were booted. It's empty of human beings. Nobody's paying attention to ghosts anyway. This is as far as I can go. Only my pre-ban self appears here before this. You'll have to continue back on your own."

Kerena hesitated. "Why can't you go farther back, skipping over Eden?"

"I can't go to the time before I existed."

"How is it that I can, then?"

"You're not a ghost, for one thing. You have special powers, for another. You lack normal limits. That's why I had my eye on you. No one knows your potential."

Jolie was a ghost, but not in her own timeline, so was able to break the normal rules also. But Kerena was rapidly outstripping Jolie's abilities. Jolie was no longer riding a kitten, but a tigress.

"No normal limits," Kerena murmured thoughtfully. That was interesting, but this wasn't the time to dwell on it. "How do I find the way?"

"Just keep moving back. You can't miss chaos when you find it. I'll be here when you return; there's more to see."

Kerena nodded and concentrated. She resumed traveling back, slowly. Lilah disappeared.

"Let's move near the Tree of Knowledge," Molly said. She was a ghost without special powers, but evidently could be carried along with Kerena's sufference. "That's where the action mostly happens."

Kerena hadn't thought they could talk while time traveling, but realized that they were in the same framework. She adjusted her focus, and they angled toward the center of the Garden. There stood a giant tree with many different fruits: apples, pears, peaches, plums, oranges, bananas, cherries, pineapples, blackberries—everything Kerena had ever seen was there, and many more varieties. They all looked delicious.

"But don't eat any," Molly warned, mentally smiling.

Then they saw a man and a woman approaching the tree, backward. He discarded a fig leaf, putting it back on its tree. Now the man was naked and handsome, the woman clothed in a skirt of leaves but without upper clothing. They were trying ineffectively to cover their bareness with their hands. The man held a banana, which he was uneating; the fruit grew with each mouthful. Finally he reached up and put it in the tree, where it anchored. That was Adam, of course. He and Eve then faced the tree and backed away from it, he no longer ashamed of his lack of clothing.

Later (earlier) it was Eve alone who backed to the tree, discarding her improvised skirt, where she handed the apple she was uneating to the serpent that slithered backwards to receive it. She backed away from it, now nude and lovely. Her temptation and loss of innocence had just unhappened.

Evidently the visitors, as time traveling ghosts, were not apparent to the denizens of this wondrous garden. So Kerena followed the man and woman. They were completely unaffected, eating, sleeping, defecating, and having sex without inhibition. Their age of innocence.

Yet Kerena noticed that Eve never initiated a sexual encounter. She waited until Adam thought of it, then gracefully acquiesced. She seemed to enjoy it, but only by providing him his joy.

Eve disappeared and Adam was alone for a while. Then the original Lilah/Lilith appeared, backing haughtily up to Adam to have some kind of argument with him. She raised her arm and he unstruck it. So he had tried to resort to violence, but she had balked him there too. Kerena found herself privately applauding the woman. Why should she have to accept abuse from her man? It was Adam who should have been banished, not Lilith. The seed of his violence had passed along to his son Cain, who slew his brother. Instead, in the patriarchal scheme, she had been punished for defending herself.

But later (earlier) they were considerably more friendly. When it came to sex, Lilith was evidently the expert, throwing herself into it with seeming abandon. She would come to him, evidently demanding it, choosing the manner of it. He seemed to be not entirely satisfied with this, though he did participate. In time (earlier) Adam came to really like it, right up to the first encounter, where they mutually discovered the kind of interaction their bodies were capable of.

"Oooo, I wish I was doing that," Molly moaned.

"Me too," Kerena agreed.

Jolie agreed too. There was something about that first, innocent, tentative joy of union that was extremely seductive, surely by no coincidence. Yet it seemed Adam had in time blamed her for it, perhaps resenting her evident delight in it. It was, it seemed, only his joy that counted, not hers. In that respect, Eve had been better for him.

Then they were gone, and before long, so was the garden. There seemed to be nothing.

Kerena accelerated, trying to get beyond the blank spot. Suddenly she passed a flurry of odd action, and realized that she had overshot. She slowed, then reversed, so as to pick up the events in time-forward manner.

"This must be Chaos," Molly said.

So it seemed. Around them the universe was without form and void, a chaotic (naturally) mixture of light and darkness. Kerena tried to make sense of it, and slowly there came to be two overlapping scenes. One was of patches of light and darkness flying through space, coming from some monstrous distant explosion, coalescing into points of light which were actually giant hot balls of fire, admixed with great dark clouds of dusty vapors. As she strained to see more of this confusion, a bit of substance formed from a collapsing cloud and became a ball of hot rock. This bubbled and cooled, forming vapor around it, and later was coated with slime that became plants and creatures. Finally fish crawled out of the seas and became animals, and one of the animals was mankind.

"I can't make any sense of this," Kerena complained.

"You're looking at one scene; I'm looking at the other," Molly said. "Mine makes some sense."

Kerena adjusted her vision to tune in on the other scene. In this one, Chaos became a huge animate living thing that heaved and hurled out two lesser things. One of the two was vaguely male, the other vaguely female, both clothed in darkness. They writhed, forming semblances that enhanced their genders: a monstrous phallus, a similarly monstrous vulva. They came together, their parts merging repeatedly. Then the female squeezed out a blob of energy that drifted away. She issued another, that also departed. Another, and another, until there were ten or more.

"She's birthing babies!" Molly exclaimed.

Then Kerena saw it, like a huge mother, copulating with her brother and generating children. They weren't children, of course, but swirls of energy that sought their own regions.

Two of the swirls came together and mated, and from the female issued plants and animals that came to inhabit a garden that came into being, and two human beings.

"The Garden of Eden!" Molly said.

"And Adam and Lilith," Kerena agreed.

"They were birthed by Nature. By Gaea."

"By Mother Nature. Father Good made the Garden and established the rules," Kerena said, working it out. "And dictated the forms of the human beings: they were modeled after his own chosen semblance, and Gaea's. He must have set up the Garden as a kind of playground, entertaining himself by acts of creation. Things were fine until Lilith got assertive."

"What about Nod?" Molly asked.

"He must have been an earlier experiment, not quite right to govern the world, so he was set aside, and God and Gaea tried again. They were satisfied with Adam, but Lilith still missed the mark and had to be replaced." Kerena smiled somewhat ruefully. "So Lilith went east of Eden and married Nod, surely satisfying him sexually and fooling him about her fidelity. Even so, there were subtle problems in Adam and Eve's line, that took time to show, such as Cain's violence. But by then God must have been tired of tinkering, and humanity has just had to live with his imperfect state ever since."

"Agitated by the admixture of the blood of Nod and Lilith," Molly agreed. "That explains a lot."

"An awful lot," Kerena agreed. "You are surely a daughter of Eve, as it were. Morgan le Fey would be a daughter of Lilith."

So now they had seen the origin of living things, in one scene. Kerena shifted focus to the other scene. Similar living creatures were there, as apes lifted their bodies to walk on two feet, lost their body fur, and evolved into human beings. There seemed to be no Garden of Eden, unless that was the continent of Africa.

"So all the creatures were created in a short time," Kerena said. "Or they evolved over a long time. Depending in which scene you view. The end result is much the same."

"But the Incarnations of Immortality don't yet exist."

"Not as we know them now. They could hardly have human proprietors before humans existed," Kerena pointed out. "That's the next thing we want to see: how they were taken over. That must be what Lilah is waiting to show us." That reminded her. "I need to get some substance from Chaos."

She reversed course, moved back to the void, and scooped up an armful of chaos. She wasn't sure how to handle it, but the blob seemed to stay with her readily enough. It lacked much will of its own, so responded to hers. She moved on forward, to the Garden, past Adam and Eve, and to the time just after the expulsion.

There was Lilah. "You got it!" she exclaimed, grabbing for the blob of chaos.

"Not so fast, ghost," Molly said, intercepting her. "You still have to show her the investing of the Incarnations."

"I was going to," Lilah snarled.

Kerena nodded. It was obvious that the ghost would have taken off with the chaos substance and reneged on the rest, had Molly not been alert. That was much of the point of having a friend along.

"This way," Lilah said grudgingly. She led them downtime and slant-wise across the terrain. "Here is the first one: the Incarnation of Good."

The swirl of inchoate energy was resting at the top of a mountain, evidently tuning out. A holy man climbed the mountain, discovered the swirl, and stepped into it. He became transfigured, with glorious light surrounding him. He had assumed the mantle, but did not seem to know exactly what to make of it.

"It takes him about a thousand years to get it straight," Lilah said. "I could have done it faster, had I been interested in doing good."

She took them to the next, some time later. This time an evil man fleeing pursuit decided to hide in a dry well. In that well was a swirl. The man merged with it, became charged, and floated up and away, amazed at his newfound ability. "The Incarnation of Evil," Lilah said. "If only I had known that swirl was there, it could have been mine."

"The people didn't know about the swirls before they encountered them?" Kerena asked.

"Right. The things were just drifting around, doing whatever they do naturally and not very efficiently. Even Good and Nature reverted to somewhat chaotic status after their mixed results with early people. They must have pretty well used up their initiative. But once humans got into them, they had human will and intelligence. That made a difference. Good started forming Heaven and Evil started forming Hell, and recruiting souls to inhabit them. In time it developed into something of a system, supported by the mortals who got a glimmer."

The third one to be invested was Nature, taken over by a mature woman who had a fair idea what was what. "But Gaea birthed all the animals, and Adam and Eve," Molly said. "Now she's taken over by one of her great granddaughters?"

"And she birthed Nod and me. Why not?" Lilah asked wryly. "The whole system is incestuously nepotistic. Erebus and Nox were brother and sister; they got together and generated all the other Incarnations. Father God and Mother Gaea are siblings, and so were Nod, Adam, Eve and me. Both my brothers fucked me."

"Erebus?" Molly asked.

"Chaos' son. I don't know what happened to him or Nox; maybe they're still drifting around somewhere, having fucked themselves out."

But Kerena was paying attention to another aspect. "So all the humans did was step into the swirls, and became the Incarnations of Immortality?"

"That's all, at the beginning," Lilah agreed. "It wasn't very cosmopolitan, early on. Anyone could have done it. Later they developed more sophisticated rules of transfer."

"I have seen enough. Here is your chaos." Kerena pushed the blob toward the ghost.

"Got it." Lilah stepped into the blob, became a solid naked woman, and stretched luxuriantly. Then she vanished.

"See, she skipped out," Molly said.

"That's all right. I'm through with her. She's not the easiest person to take, in more than small doses." Kerena reversed course and headed back uptime.

"What are you up to?"

"I am going to invest the powers of Night. No one else has."

"Which one is that?"

"Nox. The one who mated with her brother and birthed the other powers."

"You're going to become an Incarnation?"

"I'm going to try. Before someone else does. I need those powers."

"That's why you are so hot on ancient history!"

"I knew the powers were there. The kind I need to do what I mean to do."

"I never knew!"

"I didn't know it was possible, until now."

"But can you do it before humans existed?"

"I doubt it. I mean to trace Nox to human times, then brace her."

"But she's the mother of the others! I think you're younger than any of the humans who took over. Not counting your vampire time."

"That doesn't matter. Age doesn't matter. Just possession. If I understand this correctly." Kerena hoped she did.

They returned to the giant birthing. Then Kerena moved forward, following the mother swirl. It drifted aimlessly. She followed it as the Garden of Eden was formed, and the plants and animals. It floated across the continent of Australia. Now was the time.

She moved in. The swirl of energy was invisible, neither dark nor light, but Kerena oriented on it with her Seeing. She had not been able to do it before, not realizing that the absence of human presence fundamentally changed the swirl. Now she knew exactly what it was, and had no further difficulty. She solidified. And hesitated. "Molly, if something goes wrong—"

"I will tell Morely and Vanja."

"Thank you." Kerena nerved herself and stepped into the swirl.

She suffered immediate disorientation. She clung to her human awareness, struggling to avoid being overwhelmed. Belatedly she realized that others might have stepped into swirls and lost their identities instead of taking
over. Was she strong enough?

She recovered equilibrium and looked around. There was Molly. "You
changed your mind?" the ghost asked.

Kerena looked behind her. There was the swirl. She had passed though
it without investing it.

She turned about and tried again. And failed again. "I can't do it," she
said. "It's as if we are on different planes."

"Maybe you are," Molly agreed. "What year is it?"

"About 3,000 BC." As she spoke, she realized: "Way before my time! I
can't do anything before I exist."

"All we can do is look," Molly agreed. "I forgot."

"So did I. Fortunately that is readily remedied. I will return to my present
time."

She did so, tracking the swirl so as not to lose it. It drifted all across the
world, which Kerena realized was a round ball rather than a flat plate, preferring night without being limited to it. It had no governing direction. Apparently once it had mated and birthed the Incarnations of Day—if that was
really the right name for them—it had little remaining purpose. In that respect it resembled Good and Nature, lacking continuing initiative on its own.

They returned to the Carnival of Ghosts, completing their excursion
into the past. But now Kerena knew where the swirl was. They left the Carnival and she phased down and zoomed back to Australia, where the swirl
had coincidentally drifted again. It was resting in the shadowed lee of an
isolated mountain. She solidified and walked toward it.

Another figure appeared, solidifying similarly beside the swirl. It waved.
"Oh, Rena—fancy meeting you here."

"Lilah!" Kerena was not pleased. What was the demoness up to?

"I thought if there's an Incarnation to be taken, I might as well take it,"
Lilah explained. "So nice of you to locate it for me."

"You bitch!" Molly exclaimed. "That's Rena's chance."

"Oh, really? I must not have gotten the word." Lilah stepped into the
swirl.

There was a scintillation as body and energy overlapped. Then the body
was hurled out, landing limply on the sand.

Kerena hurried over. "Are you well?" she asked, kneeling beside the
form.

"Don't waste time on her," Molly urged. "Take the Incarnation. It's your
chance."

"But she may be injured. I have to help if I can."

"You're being a fool! *She tried to take your chance.*"

The demoness opened an eye. "Who are you?"

"A fool," Kerena said.

"Who am I?"

"The demoness Lilah. You were just hurled a distance. Maybe if you desolidify you'll feel better."

Lilah sat up, her substance dissipating. "Do I have a history?"

"You were Adam's first wife, and Samson's temptress. You're the original feminist. You were a ghost; now you're a demoness."

Lilah nodded. "I begin to remember. What happened to me?"

"You tried to become an Incarnation, and got ejected."

"Now I remember more. I tried to steal your chance. Why are you tending to me?"

"You seemed to need help."

"You *are* a fool."

"Whatever," Kerena agreed.

"A daughter of Eve," Molly said.

"You must suppose I owe you one, now."

Kerena laughed. "I know better. That's not the way you think."

"Here is the way I think: you will not do me harm, but may do me good. I am likely to be better off on the right side of you, as there may be some important favor you can do me in the future."

"I have no awareness of that."

"So I will return the favor, at such time as is convenient, as a matter of cynical calculation. I will not be your enemy, though I can't be your friend. I prefer to have you neutral or owing me; it could pay off, as you have unusual powers and may acquire more."

Was that the truth, or did the demoness have a faint modicum of gratitude or decency in her? Kerena didn't argue the case; Lilah was surely ashamed of any good qualities she possessed. "I don't even know what happened to you."

"I couldn't Incarnate because I was not a proper match for the role. I have too much selfishness and meanness. I surely could have taken the swirl of Evil, had I had the chance, but this is not that. But you are generous and good; you may be be able to do it. So I—"

Kerena was amazed by a wild thought. "Are you saying you want to be my friend after all?"

"I don't want to be anyone's friend!" Lilah flared. "Friendships are wearisome."

"To be sure," Kerena agreed carefully. "Whatever way you prefer."

"I prefer to depart." She faded out.

"That was weird," Molly said. "She masks appreciation with cynical reasoning. I think she likes you."

Kerena smiled. "Promise never to tell."

"You want it that way?"

"She might one day do me some good."

They both laughed, understanding. Then Kerena approached the swirl, cautioned by Lilah's rejection. Would it hurl her out similarly?

She stepped in. The energy swirled about her and through her, infusing her, lifting her, tugging her in several directions, none of them physical. She took another step.

And found herself out the other side. The swirl hadn't thrown her out, but neither had it accepted her. What did it mean?

"It didn't work?" Molly asked.

"It didn't work," Kerena agreed. "Yet it didn't manhandle me either."

"So maybe you're halfway there."

Kerena had another idea. "The resistance I have encountered to obtaining or even learning about the powers of Night—could it be that it is simply that I am not yet where I need to be? That there is something else I need to get or do before I can assume the office?"

"It is putting you through a test?"

"I don't think so. But obviously it doesn't just accept whoever approaches it. There must be qualities that align with its nature, and I have some but not all of them."

"What would those qualities be?"

Kerena sighed. "I think that's what I have to find out."

"But you are what you are. How can you be something else?"

"Maybe I have to practice," Kerena said with resignation.

"Did it offer any hint? You were in it for a moment; maybe there's something."

"No just a sort of nonphysical urgency. A lot of feeling, but I can't say what kind. Raw emotion."

"Like chaos, before the fragmentation into assorted aspects. The ten children."

"Perhaps. Whatever is left to Nox."

"Secrets!" Molly exclaimed. "That's what Night has."

"Secrets," Kerena repeated thoughtfully. "Maybe that's it. But what secrets?"

"Your Seeing. Can you use that?"

"Not on something that intangible."

"On the Night Swirl. It's still there."

Kerena looked. "Try Seeing the swirl," she said, intrigued. "What have I to lose?"

"You may lose it if you don't."

Kerena approached the swirl. She extended her Seeing, and stepped into it again.

Again the energy of it suffused her being. Again she found herself beyond it. But this time she had a notion.

"Secrets," she agreed. "You were right. To merge with it I must learn to control secrets. To expose those it wants to hide, and hide those it wants to reveal."

"What are those?" Molly asked, excited.

Kerena smiled ruefully. "I don't know. They are secret."

Molly laughed. "Is this thing teasing you?"

"Not intentionally. I simply don't yet understand its nature well enough to merge with it."

"I think we need to go home and think for a while."

"That does seem best."

They returned to the warren. This time decades had not passed there; Kerena had gone to the past and returned to the present, and the present remained the present. She was relieved.

She had some sessions with Morely, and talked with Vanja. "Secrets?" the vampire asked. "That makes sense. Our existence is mostly secret, necessarily."

"But I haven't fathomed what secrets to expose or hide."

"Well, let's reason it out. What's the most sensitive secret a girl can have?"

"News of a crime?"

"People steal bread all the time without shame. But they hide their sexual activity. We vampires don't, but we're different. Real people hate to have it exposed."

"People hate to have their toilet activities exposed too," Kerena said. "But everyone knows they perform them."

"Embarrassment, literally. You sit on the pot, you don't want tourists peeking at your effort. But that's not optional; you have to do it sometime. Sex is optional, so can be canceled if the occasion is not private enough. That makes it more sensitive; they don't provide public facilities for sex, apart from the brothels."

"Still, just about everyone does it, and since normally two do it together, it can't be entirely secret."

"I suppose not," Vanja agreed. "That leaves you without a secret. Maybe the library could help."

Kerena brightened. "I'll try it."

She went to the library, and this time used her Seeing to orient on the appropriate scroll. She found it—and was baffled again. Had Night balked her once more?

The scroll she found had no text, just three pictures. A coin. A stage. A group of people.

"What does it mean?" Vanja asked.

"I wish I knew! None of these seem exactly secret. Coins are used for money, a stage is used for a public address, and people are everywhere. Yet my Seeing suggests this is the hint I need."

They discussed it with Morely. "An audience," he said. "That's what the people are. An audience for whoever is on the stage. And the coin is what the people pay to hear the speaker. He must be an entertainer."

"But what is secret about that?" Kerena asked.

"Nothing. It's a public event."

Still, it seemed to be progress, of a sort.

"Maybe we should put on a show," Vanja said. "I always like those. I'd love to be a star."

"What can you do?" Morely asked. "Can you sing or dance? Tell jokes?"

"Not well. I suppose I'd have to demonstrate how seductive I can be. And I'd be ashamed to do that in public. So it's a bad idea."

"I love to see you seductive," Morely said. "Why shouldn't the world appreciate it as well?"

"The world might call me a whore."

"What's wrong with being a whore?" Molly demanded. She remained with Kerena, but hadn't participated in the dialogue until now. "I was a good whore. Rena was a better one."

Morely laughed. "Good question. Men value whores for sex, but feel constrained to disparage them at other times. It's sheer hypocrisy, but widespread."

Kerena was intrigued. "Why do men condemn what they like best?"

"It's religious. Sex is one of our strongest drives, but often socially condemned. So we have to have it, but also have to deny it. To pretend that we don't really desire what we desire. We must love and hate women for it."

"I want to be loved, not hated," Vanja said.

"You are," Morely said.

"Can that be the key?" Kerena asked. "Sex is most desired, but also most feared if it is exposed? Surely there are more secrets concerning sex than anything else."

"That can explain the stage and audience," Vanja said. "But not the coin. It can pay for sex, or for a show, but there's not much shame in that; anything can be bought."

"A coin is also an agent of chance," Morely said. "When it is flipped. It spins in air and where it stops is theoretically unknown." He produced a Roman coin, one of those left over from the days of Roman occupation of

Britain, and flipped it. It landed on the floor, bounced, and came to rest before Kerena.

"Chance," Kerena said, staring at the coin. "What's the connection between Night and Chance?"

"A strong one, I suspect. If Night shrouds the unknown, nothing is more unknown than the outcome of pure chance."

"So the coin could be the symbol of chance. But how does that relate to a performance on a stage for an audience?"

"Oh, it can relate," he said. "When there is a performance, no one can be sure ahead what the reaction will be. They may love it or hate it, for indecipherable reason."

"I wouldn't dare risk the stage," Vanja said, "if my success or failure depended on the flip of a coin. I'd be mortified by a loss."

Hell had no fury like that of a woman scorned, Jolie remembered. That thought might be anachronistic here, but related. No woman wanted to be rejected or deemed to be worthless.

"Yet the coin is mindless," Morely said. "It has no values. You shouldn't care."

"I *do* care. Horribly."

"You're cute when you're nervous." He caught hold of her and began stroking her. She resisted a moment, then participated, as there was no doubt of his interest and she was a lusty vampire.

Kerena had been flirting with a realization. Now that she was alone, in a manner, she concentrated. Sex—a stage—audience reaction—chance—Night—secrecy. How did it all fit together?

She picked up the coin. One side had the head of a bygone Roman emperor, the other the designation of its amount. Heads and tails. A win or a loss.

"Let's find a stage and an audience," Molly said.

"Somewhere," Kerena agreed.

She went to the central hall of the warren, where there was a stage. Several vampires were there, conversing between sexual efforts. They glanced up as she entered.

She mounted the stage. Then, acting on a prompting by her Seeing, she flipped the coin high in the air. It spun, trying to scintillate though there was no significant light here; the vampire vision could see it well in the dark. It seemed to slow, hanging in the air, turning in a leisurely manner. Time was pausing.

Kerena started an impromptu performance: a sexual dance. She moved her body sensuously, spreading her arms in seeming invitation, quivering enough to make her breasts ripple. She turned, making her hair fling out, showing her bottom. She was trying to make herself desirable to this spot audience. If the coin landed heads, perhaps she would succeed and be thrilled. If it landed tails, she might fail, and be chagrined. Suddenly it was important that she win, proving herself to be lovely and worthy. It would be awful if she lost; she would want to die. Yet her chances were even. It depended on the unpredictable coin. Her life depended on its uncaring chance.

The coin descended, turning. Perhaps it already knew which way it was going to land, carelessly sealing her fate one way or the other. Everything depended on it. If it landed right, she would be a brilliant success, warmly applauded. If it landed wrong, she would have to flee the stage, humiliated. Chance.

To merge with Night she needed to fathom a secret Night was trying to hide, and hide one Night wanted to expose. To be a public success, or a private failure. The coin was random, but Night was not; it controlled its secrets.

Yet they were two sides of the same coin. Heads and tails, publicity and privacy, success and failure, joy and chagrin, all and nothing. They existed together, opposite aspects of the same concepts.

It wasn't sex that powered human emotion, or accomplishment. It was feeling. Success was to be loved by others; failure was to be scorned. Yet to achieve applause, a person had to risk condemnation. The verdict of chance.

The coin stopped in the air. Kerena stepped forward and caught it in her hand, not looking at it. She had conquered chance, by realizing that secrecy was the necessary underside of the human drive for recognition. She had fathomed what Night had tried to hide, and now she would hide whatever she chose.

She stood still, spreading her arms. "Come to me," she murmured, expanding not merely her Seeing but her discovered power.

The swirl of amorphous energy came, attracted from far away as to a magnet. It overlapped her body, merging with her. This time there was no disorientation. She felt its power, and controlled it. She was Home.

She had become Nox, the Incarnation of Night, mistress of secrecy.

CHAPTER 9
DATABASE

But it was soon apparent that though she had become the Incarnation of Night, she was not nearly close to being mistress of the Office. The secrets were now open to her, but there were so many that she simply could not keep track, or grasp the larger picture. It wasn't just those of people, but those of the other Incarnations she was now able to fathom: Exactly what made souls be judged good or evil, the province of Thanatos. The nuances and paradoxes of time that Chronos had to manage, as he made his way backwards. He started with legions of selves, one for each timeline, which merged as he progressed; when he finally reached the beginning, all would be one. The devious interactions of the myriad threads of Fate. The ultimate causes and futility of War. The living processes of Nature. All those folk remedies she had studied with Morely were but the shadow of natural processes no person comprehended. Indeed, most of them should never be opened to mankind, lest he use them to exploit nature into destruction.

"I am Nox," she told Morely and Vanja. "But the scope is huge. I feel like a bird riding the back of a heedless ox. How do I make it mind?"

"You can't simply fathom and use any secret you need?" Vanja asked.

"I can do that. But now I am aware of the larger picture. Every action I take as Nox has consequences, like a ripple spreading out from a pebble flipped into a lake. Those consequences have consequences, and may lead to things I do not wish to be responsible for. So I dare not do anything."

Morely nodded. "You have too much power, too quickly. You need time to grow into it. Fortunately you will have the time; you can take centuries to study the situation."

"I don't even know what to study. I need a guideline before I can start."

"Maybe you should catalogue your information, as I catalogued magic folk remedies."

"You have a better memory than I, and my challenge is far greater. There are more secrets than folk remedies." How vastly she was understating the case!

"The other Incarnations must have similar problems," Morely said. "We should consider how they handle them."

"They have powerful tools," Kerena said. "Death has the Scythe and Mortis the Death-Horse. Time has the Hourglass. War has the Red Sword."

"And it seems Fate has the Tapestry of the Threads of Life," he agreed. "Which she may weave in the form of a spider. The others surely have equivalent tools. How did they come by those dread symbols of their Offices?"

Kerena was taken aback. "Why, I'm not sure. They just seem to be there."

"I saw," Molly said. "The humans made them when they became Incarnations, or soon thereafter. I think Death converted an ordinary horse. I think they had some leftover chaos substance."

"That is surely potent stuff," Morely said.

"It is," Kerena agreed. "It adapted Lilah from a ghost to a demoness. It would account for the powers of those symbols, as you call them."

"Yes. They would be defined by the first Office holders, then passed along to their successors," he agreed. "Or their predecessors, in the case of Chronos. So perhaps you should develop a similar symbol."

"I should," Kerena agreed, liking the notion. "But what?"

"The cloak, of course," Vanja said. "You have been using its powers all along."

"Those weren't really its powers," Kerena reminded her. "I only thought they were, deceived by the Fey."

"Yes, they are your powers. You imbued the cloak with them. Now you can do it more. Make it the Nox Symbol."

That was appealing. "Should I?"

"Yes," Molly said. "Symbols are classy."

"I agree," Morely said. "I would be proud to see my old cloak become eternal."

"I'll do it." She brought out the cloak, and put it on. She found surrounding left-over chaos stuff, and imbued the cloak with it. The old cloth developed a sparkle, then a deep shadow.

"The stars!" Vanja exclaimed. "It shows the stars!"

Indeed it did. The chaos element made the cloak's surface fade out, and it showed the scintillating sky of night, with the stars as they were, slowly moving in their courses. Then the moon appeared, a crescent, followed by the first brightening of dawn.

"Enough," Morely said. "Don't burn us."

Kerena took off the Cloak and folded it, stifling its growing radiance. She could control its cycles, but was satisfied to have her Symbol: the velvet Cloak of Night. "But this won't enable me to remember myriad secrets," she said.

"I wonder," Vanja said. "We seem to know more now than our ancestors did. Will our descendants know more than we do?"

"Surely so," Morely agreed. "But Verena's problem is now."

"But if she can travel in time, maybe she can go see how they track things in the future. It might help."

Kerena was intrigued but dubious. "Could our descendants tell me how to remember better?"

"Why don't you go look and see?" Vanja asked.

"Can I do that?" Kerena asked Molly.

"Well, you can't be sure that what you see will really happen," the ghost replied. "Because even your knowing about it can change it."

"She doesn't need to know the specific future," Morely said. "She merely needs to observe and learn a superior technique."

"She should be able to do that," Molly said.

Kerena remained unconvinced, but was willing to give it a try. "Then let's go look."

Jolie was interested. She could travel in time, because this was not truly *her* time; there was no necessary paradox. But if Kerena went to the future and brought something back, wouldn't that invite paradox? Still, the lines were not fudging, so she could relax and see.

"Do they wear clothing in the future?" Kerena asked.

"Surely they do," Morely said. "For warmth, protection, display, and privacy. But it probably won't resemble what you wear today. There's probably no point in taking any current clothing, as it would only mark you as a foreigner."

"I will take the Velvet Cloak. That's is my symbol, and I have imbued it with significant magic."

"Of course, he agreed. "But you won't want to cut that up for future fashion."

"Never!" she agreed, horrified by the notion.

"I can help," Molly said. "I learned sewing before I died, a maidenly skill I thought might one day be useful as a mother." Then she was quiet, remembering that her death had forfeited all of that.

"Take cloth, shears, needles, thread," Morely said. "Then let Molly make what you need when you know the style."

Vanja set her up with a knapsack filled with the essentials, including some food and a vial of blood. She put it on and looked in the mirror. "A nude girl with a backpack," she said, bemused. The Cloak was neatly folded inside the pack.

"A lovely nude girl," Morely said. "The contrast is suggestive. I wonder—?"

"Do it swiftly," she said, laughing. "I'm ready to travel."

He embraced her, bearing her back against the wall, standing. She braced against the knapsack and thrust her groin against his, meeting him thrust for thrust. It was indeed swift, almost instant, but intense and gratifying. She was pleased to note that her new status as the Incarnation of Night had not depleted her ardor; she could still respond as rapidly and intensely as a man, and retained her interest in doing it frequently. Then she kissed him, disengaged, and mopped up.

"I'm jealous," Vanja said. "You never did me that way. You were so turned on I feared she would sail into the air when you climaxed."

"Then fetch a knapsack, girl," Kerena said as she phased down and oriented on the future. She was pleased to see the accelerating forms of the man and woman indulging as she moved forward in time, both wearing knapsacks.

"You have invented a new mode of sex," Molly said. "Now all the vamps will be doing it in knapsacks."

"I'll lend you the body and knapsack so you can do it too, when there's a suitable man."

"Thank you," Molly agreed, laughing.

She had started traveling in the warren. Now she slid upward to reach the ground, preferring to see what was passing outside. It was the forest, the trees this time growing larger, aging, disappearing, being replaced by sprouts and saplings filling in the places.

Then the trees were gone. Only bare ground remained. "What happened?" Molly asked, surprised.

Kerena slowed, stopped, and solidified. She stood on he wreckage of the forest. Only brush remained. There were a number of decaying flat-topped stumps. "They cut them down," she said, appalled. "All of them."

"Why would they do that?"

"They must have wanted the wood."

"But now there won't be any more wood. They left none to grow."

"It does seem nonsensical," Kerena agreed. "Maybe when I learn to fully handle my powers I'll be able to stop the cutting, and save the forest."

They resumed travel into the future, drifting across the terrain to get away from the lost forest. Buildings appeared, aged, and vanished, to be replaced by larger ones. "There must be a lot of people living here," Molly said.

"There must be," Kerena agreed, not entirely pleased. She would rather have kept the forest.

She accelerated, so as to spare them further sights along the way. She used her Seeing to orient on what she wanted: a way to keep track of all the information she would now be able to gather. She didn't know how far into the future she was going, but her impression was a thousand years or more. Maybe fifteen hundred.

Her Seeing found its object. She slowed, and stopped.

She stood on a city street, naked except for her knapsack. She hastily made herself invisible and inaudible, as she suspected her appearance in this manner of garb would attract more attention than she liked.

Now they studied the sights of the street. There were floating carriages that moved without being drawn by horses. There were stores with fancy windows showing their wares. People appeared before the stores to look, then went inside if they felt inclined. Some appeared in the street, then floated to one of the upper stories, where there were doors. Obviously magic, and everybody had it.

"No horses, no workmen," Molly noted. "I think we're not in Scotland any more."

"We're in Scotland, but not the one we know. They evidently have magic for everything. They must conjure their food and supplies, or just float to wherever the things they need are."

Jolie was interested. This was what in her day was called Hi-Tech magic. But there had to be something to power it. Magic wasn't free; there was always a cost, just as there was with science. Also, was her awareness of the alignment of timelines operative here in the future? She doubted it, as this was a tenuous future, rather than a fixed one. Yet it could affect the alignment by changing Kerena's outlook in her own time. Well, maybe Jolie would be able to verify the alignment when they returned.

A handsome man wearing a turban appeared before them. "May I be of service, pretty maiden? I see you are without a companion."

Kerena extended her Seeing—and recoiled. This was a demon! What was he doing out of Hell? Her invisibility was useless against that kind. But she masked her reaction. "What did you have in mind?"

"Oh, the usual fair exchange of desire. I fulfill your worldly needs, you fulfill my sexual needs."

Kerena was surprised despite her caution. So was Jolie, for different reason. It was known that demons desired mortal humans for sex, but normally this was confined to the punishments of Hell. Massively endowed male demons perpetually ravished the souls and tight vaginas of prudish women, while winsome bare female demons tempted eager men without ever granting them release. Sometimes, it was hinted, mortal male and female souls were then put together naked while demons watched and made bets on the outcome. Hell was not a nice place. "You openly proffer a deal like that?"

He squinted at her. "You're a vampire! What are you doing here?"

"Just looking around," Kerena replied evenly. "Demons are prejudiced against vampires?"

"No. Mortals are. Here come the police." Uniformed men appeared, surrounding them. "There she stands," the demon told them indignantly. "A shameless loose bare vampire."

"Fetch a stake," the head policeman said as he advanced on Kerena. "No, first we'll have to torture her for information. There's obviously been a leak in the tank." He brandished a bright silver cross as his other hand went to the front fastening of his trousers.

Kerena didn't know exactly what he was talking about, but she shot backward in time, escaping the threat.

"What do you think?" she asked Molly as she came to a stop a few years earlier.

"They tame demons," Molly said. "Demons must do all the magic for them, in return for sex. Why demons want sex so much with mortals I don't understand, but that seems to be the deal. You could make it readily enough."

"Every male wants sex with personable young live women," Kerena said. "You saw how eager the ghosts are."

"True. And demons are twice as sex obsessed as ghosts. So you have a ready means of exchange."

"But they kill vampires. I can't risk that."

"You can't," Molly agreed. "And we didn't even learn if they can remember things."

"Maybe they don't need to, in an all magic realm." But she reconsidered immediately. "My Seeing brought me there, so they must have a way. Maybe the demons do it all. But I wouldn't trust a demon for that; I want to have complete control myself, always."

"I wouldn't trust a demon for anything. They're all like Lilah, if not worse. But what is there, if not a magic way?"

"Morely taught me that there are usually alternatives to magic, like science. He never used magic if there was another way. He studied the stars without magic."

"Did he count the stars? There are so many."

"Even more than we can see. Myriads, he said."

"Could there be a—a science way to keep track of them, or other things?"

"I wonder. I can try to visit a science future, though I don't know whether that would interfere with my magic."

"Is Night limited to magic?"

Kerena considered. Then she used her Seeing. "No," she said, surprised. "Nox can fathom any secret, regardless of the universe it is in. I was limiting my thinking, not being rational. Morely will chide me."

"Horrors," Molly said pleasantly. "Something else: shouldn't the language change in fifteen hundred years? That demon spoke just like us."

"The gift of tongues," Kerena said, abruptly discovering another Nox ability. "Night knows all languages. It was actually rather different from ours." But she remembered something vaguely unsettling: she had understood other languages when visiting Rome with Lilah. Had she been picking up on the powers of Night before becoming Nox? That suggested that her course was guided rather than coincidental.

Jolie, too, wondered. She remembered how the ghost woman Orlene had begun assuming some of the powers of the Incarnation of Good before she had been voted into the Office. Indeed, before she had an inkling of it. Was individual choice more apparent than real? Or did the ambiance of such status extend backwards as well as forwards?

"I'm glad you became Nox before traveling this far," Molly said.

"Blind luck. Let's call it foresight."

"Naturally."

She followed her Seeing. That took her back a thousand years, then forward on another track. This brought them to what appeared to be the same city street. There were floating coaches and stores with window displays.

"Are you sure it worked?" Molly asked as Kerena hastily made herself undetectable.

"It is the same place, but has to be a different future," Kerena said uncertainly. "I will use my Seeing again." She concentrated, willing herself to become aware of the proper course.

A coach paused, and a rather muscular handsome young man stepped out. The coach floated away, leaving him standing on the walk. He wore an iridescently green shirt and metallic shorts, with what looked like wooden boots. "Hello," he said. "Is someone here?"

Kerena stared. Her Seeing indicated that he was what she was looking for. But did she dare make herself apparent, after what had happened before?"

"I received a telepathic signal," the man said. "It indicated that I would find it well worthwhile to befriend a girl I would find here. Was that mistaken?"

"If you don't want him, I do," Molly said. "He is surely a fantastic lover."

Molly decided, she hoped not for that reason. She had not encountered the concept of telepathy before, but gathered that it meant he had somehow received her mental presence. That, she hoped, was a good sign. She made herself appear. "That must have been mine."

He looked. His pupils expanded. "Well, now!"

Kerena remembered belatedly that she was still nude with her knapsack. Well, maybe that was suitable to impress the man. "I could use some help."

"You're beautiful!"

"I could use some clothing," she said. "I may indeed need a friend."

"You wish to make a stipulation of friendship with me?"

Her Seeing remained positive. "Yes."

"To what degree? What term?"

She avoided showing her confusion. "What do you prefer?"

"Need you inquire? Of course I want romance. How about a fortnight renewable term?"

Fourteen days! Kerena was appalled. She intended to be here only hours. Yet her Seeing remained amenable. She had to do it. It wasn't as if it would make a difference when she returned, as she would go to the time she had left. She could manage time far better than she had when visiting the Incarnations. And the man *was* handsome. "Yes."

"Wonderful! I hope you are as fetching as you appear. I am Kermit."

"I am Kerena." Was that sheer coincidence, or confirmation that they were slated to be together?

A screen appeared before him. "Kermit and Kerena committing to a fortnight romance," he said.

A woman's face appeared on the screen. "Kermit is listed. Kerena is not. More detail, please."

That set him back. "How can she be unlisted? She is standing here before me."

Oops. Of course Kerena did not exist in this future; she was from its past. Yet this challenge demonstrated that this culture had a way to check every person in it, immediately. That was exactly the kind of thing she had come for. "Please, can we withdraw, for the moment?"

"Withdrawn," Kermit said to the screen, and it disappeared.

"That looks like a magic mirror to me," Molly said.

Kermit turned back to Kerena. "You have an explanation? I assumed you were registered. Everyone is."

"I'm not. I don't think you would believe what I am."

"For the sake of a term romance with a woman as lovely as you, I am ready to believe almost anything."

She laughed, aware by the intensity of his gaze that the way this shook her flesh excited him. He was a completely normal and manageable male in this respect. "I am a woman, and I do want to be with you. The rest is complicated. Is there somewhere we can go for a private dialogue?"

"A slow coach is private."

"A slow coach," she agreed.

He lifted his hand, which now she saw held a small key. The square screen appeared in the air before him. "Slow coach, here, now, destination home."

A coach appeared behind him, floating. "Just like that," Kerena murmured appreciatively. "That's hardly slow."

"I gather you are unfamiliar with our society," he said as he guided her onto the step and into the coach. It was plush and dark inside, very comfort-

UNDER A VELVET CLOAK • 155

able.

They sat on facing couches as the door shut and the coach floated onward. She noted with satisfaction that his gaze was unable to remain clear of her bare legs. It was another confirmation that he was a typical young man, regardless of the future culture. That was important. "I am. For example, I don't know exactly what a term romance entails, but am ready to accommodate it. Sex?"

He licked his lips. "If we choose."

"Let's do that first. Then I must see about obtaining suitable clothing."

"If you really don't know our culture, you may not be aware of the range and degree of sexual expression we indulge in. If you prefer to discuss it first—"

She lifted her bare rear, swung it about, and set it on his lap. "I believe I can handle it," she murmured, nibbling on his ear.

Things proceeded rapidly thereafter. Soon Kermit was naked and panting beside her on the bed that the merging seats had formed, her breasts still pressing against his chest. His delightfully urgent young ardor was spent for the moment. He was in every respect sexually ordinary, and she was perfectly equipped to accommodate his fondest ambitions. Now she had the social advantage, having verified that she could manage him satisfactorily.

"That signal I received was right," he said. "You have given me more joy in less time than any girl I have been with."

She slid up so as to put her breasts at his face. She drew him in, his flushed cheek nestled between them. "I am a woman," she repeated firmly, conscious of the parallel between her tone and her flesh. His sexual urgency had been abated, but breasts had effects on men that went beyond that. She wanted him pacified as she told him what she needed to, to ensure his informed cooperation. "I am older than I look."

"I guess you must be, because you certainly know what you're doing. Will you tell me where you are from?"

She kept her Seeing attuned. So far it indicated that she could trust him. "The key is not where, but when."

"I don't understand."

She used her hand to press her upper breast more closely against his face, so that it brushed his mouth in a reverse kiss. She felt his groin stir. Good; his critical mind would be filtered through his recovering desire. He had spoken truly when he said he was ready to believe anything for a relationship with her; men's minds were opportunistic when sex was in the picture. "I am from your distant past."

"I think I would have remembered you, even if I knew you when I was three years old."

She tweaked her breast again. "I mean your culture's past. About fifteen hundred years."

He reacted, first trying to laugh, then shocked. She stifled both reactions with her breast, until he relaxed. "You're not joking, are you?"

"No. I have traveled far into my own future to learn something I need to. I wore no clothing because mine would have given me away as fabulously out of fashion."

Now he did laugh, and she let him. "I don't think I should believe you, but there's something persuasive about you." He kissed her conducive breast as his groin heated. "What do you need to know?"

"How to keep track of a huge number of secrets."

"That's easy. You need a database. A relational database."

"I have no idea what that is. I don't think such things exist in my time."

"Nor computers," he agreed. "I can tell you the basics, but I'm not expert. You'd need to take a class to get competent."

"If you could arrange that, despite my lack of registration, I would be most appreciative." She nudged him with her breast again. It had exactly the volume and quality required to be properly persuasive.

"I—Oh, Kerena, can we—?"

She was well ahead of him. "Lie on your back."

He did. She straddled him and took him in for another effort, letting him hold her breasts as it progressed. "I believe everything!" he cried as he climaxed.

"I think I would prefer to be anonymous as far as others are concerned," she said as he lay again in spent bliss. "So that you alone understand my nature. I shall be happy to fulfill all the conditions of a term romance, despite it being unregistered."

"I'll say you are an anonymous acquaintance. That is an accepted status for those who prefer not to be known, such as ones having conflicts of interest."

"Such as being married?"

He looked at her with alarm. "You're married?"

"No. Not at all. But I wouldn't mind if others assumed that. It would prevent them asking awkward questions."

He smiled. "Yes. I'll register you as an anonymous illicit romance, and no one will inquire further. How jealous the boys will be! You don't mind my pride in that?"

"Not at all. But I assume that this romance limits us to each other."

"A closed romance does. Good enough. I'll do it now." He fetched his key from his clothing and made the screen appear. "Kermit and Kerena committing to a fortnight romance, she illicitly anonymous."

"Screen name Kerena, illicitly anonymous," the woman agreed. She glanced at Kerena. "Mutually agreed?"

Kerena realized that this was to be sure there was no coercion. "Yes."

"Registered," the woman said to Kermit. She smiled. "Congratulations. She's spectacular."

"Thanks." The screen vanished. "See—even the clerk sees I have a good thing. She can't figure why a creature like you would waste her time on a nothing like me."

"But you're a handsome man!"

"I have not yet graduated from trade college, and my grades are mediocre. My family has no political power. My face is my fortune, and that's not enough for ambitious girls. I am not even a great lover."

That was an advantage, for Kerena, because she could readily lead him. "You are fine for me."

He glanced at her cannily. "Like an older man tackling an innocent girl, delighting in her virginal naïveté?"

"I'll never tell." She drew him in for a languorous kiss. Actually, there was much truth in the analogy. She did like seducing a relative innocent. That type was far more malleable than cynically experienced older men.

By the time the slow coach conveyed them to his home, they had achieved sex a third time, and he was thoroughly committed to her privacy and welfare. As with any young man, he was smitten with her. This was an advantage of the term romance: he knew there was a limit, so breaking up with him would not be ugly. This was a social concept she would take back with her.

Kermit's family was nice about his sudden term romance, in part because they too were struck by Kerena's young beauty. They let her share his room, and they provided her with suitable clothing: iridescent blouses, metallic skirts, and wooden boots. She was uncertain about those last.

"They are floaters," Kermit explained. "So you can step across flowerbeds, ponds, whatever. You had better practice to get control of them. Folk would wonder if you floated out of control." He demonstrated, rising from the floor. "You apply them slowly, and use your calves to keep yourself steady."

Kerena tried it—and promptly landed on the bed, her feet flying up. Those boots really did float!

"I love the view," Kermit said as he helped her get her legs down. "But just barely press your toes on the contacts, slowly, slowly. You'll get the hang of it."

She did, and did use the sturdy upper sections of the boots to brace her body upright. That was why they were so solid: to take the strain off the ankles. These were very nice seemingly magic boots, and quite comfortable inside.

But there was something that interested her more. "That key that makes the picture—what is that?"

"Oh, that's my spot projector. It's a virtual communicator."

"A what?"

He nodded. "I guess those didn't exist in 500 AD. Here, I'll show you." He held up the key. It had little buttons along its sides. "Press here to log on to the Net." He pressed, and the square screen appeared, this time with no woman's face. "Here to project my computer." A panel marked with assorted symbols in jumbled order appeared. Kerena, used to script, could barely decipher them, until she realized that they were stylized versions of the alphabet. He touched his fingertips rapidly to the panel, and letters appeared on the screen above it.

"Could those be shown in script?" Kerena asked.

"Sure." He touched a combination, and suddenly the text was in legible script. **I love you Kerena**.

"Oh!" He had caught her by surprise.

"Yes, I know: you have to go in two weeks. But in that time, what an emotional fling I'll have! In fact—"

She moved into him, kissed him, and took him down on the bed, obliging his so readily roused ardor. But she was careful never to indicate that her sex drive was as strong as his; she wanted always to seem to be doing him a favor.

"As if that mature man with the teen girl is obliging her passion, rather than his," Molly remarked enviously. "Very nice trick if you can maintain the pretense."

"Who spoke?" Kermit asked.

Oops. Kerena would have jumped back a few seconds, but wasn't quite sure that would be enough, considering his occasional ability to receive thoughts. "I have a confession. There is someone else with me."

"In your mind?"

"Yes. The ghost of another woman, my friend Molly. She likes you too."

"There are no ghosts."

"You might call her a telepathic projection. An alternate personality."

"Do you have multiple personality disorder?"

"I prefer to consider her the ghost of a friend."

He smiled. "Very well. What is this about obliging passion?"

Kerena wasn't sure what was safe. Some men did not like the notion of women having sex drives. "I am not pretending when I enjoy sex with you. It's fun for me too."

"And for Molly?"

"Yes!" Molly said.

He gazed at her. "I received that. If Molly is one of your personalities, then it would not be a violation of our term romance if she participated."

"I'm a personality," Molly agreed quickly.

Kerena decided not to argue. "You were showing me your—computer."

"So I was. You type on the virtual keyboard, and the virtual screen shows it. It's good for writing notes to friends. Of course it's easier to speak it instead."

"To speak it?"

"Now I have two girlfriends: Kerena and Molly," he said. As he spoke, the words appeared on the screen, in script.

"Oh!" Kerena exclaimed, delighted. "Can I do that?"

"Speak."

"I love this magic." Her words appeared on the script screen. The word "magic" was marked in color.

"That means the syntax program is querying whether that is the correct word, there being no such thing as magic."

That was another case Kerena decided not to argue. "Science," she said, and suddenly that word replaced the other. "Whatever it is, I still love it. But can it be rendered into a scroll?"

"And you lacked printed books in your day, of course," Kermit said. "Let me print it out as a scroll. For this, a virtual device won't do, because I presume you want it physical."

"Yes, because that way I can keep it."

Something made a whirring noise in the corner of the room. Paper emerged from a slit. It was a small scroll. On it was written **I love this science**.

Amazed, Kerena hugged the paper.

"But you know, that's an archaic way of saving information," Kermit said. "A database is better, as I said before. Not only is it more convenient, it can store more information that a whole library building of physical books."

"I want to learn about that."

"Then probably you should take a course in it. Then you'll know more than you'll ever need."

"A course. Is that like apprenticing?"

He smiled. "You really *are* out of touch. Why don't I just sign you up for the course?"

"Yes, please, do. That's what I came here for, I'm sure. I'm so pleased."

"And here we've just made love, so I can't take advantage of the moment."

Sex, of course, was never far from a young man's mind. But the excitement had turned her on too. "A change of partners can work wonders. Try it with Molly."

"Oooo!" Molly said enthusiastically.

Kerena gave Molly the body, and they went at it. Meanwhile Kerena considered what she had learned. The tiny key was an avenue to all manner of communications, including what she needed: a way to save a great deal of information. Yet how could all that fit inside the key? She didn't quite trust this; there must be something she hadn't yet discovered.

"Glorious!" Molly said as they climaxed together. "Where were you when I existed alive?"

"One and a half millennia downtime," Kermit said, kissing her. "But we're together now."

Molly kissed him back, avidly. "Oh, yes!"

Next day Kerena registered for the database class. Because she was anonymous here she couldn't receive college credit for it, but otherwise she was a full participant. There were nineteen other students in the class, boys and girls in their late teens, few of whom seemed really interested. It turned out they were taking it for required credit and hardly cared about the subject. Kermit joined her, his interest having been stimulated by hers. Also, she half suspected, he wanted to be sure she developed no other male interest there. Considering her appearance, readily the prettiest girl in the class, this precaution seemed sensible. She preferred having him there, because she was not at all comfortable on her own in this odd advanced culture.

"I realize that not all of you are truly devoted to anything as dull as database management," the professor said. He reminded Kerena vaguely of Morely, which helped. "So we are offering an inducement: the outstanding student will receive the demonstration unit we use here in class, hardware and software. It is superior in all respects, state of the art."

As an inducement it seemed to fall flat. It seemed that most students were satisfied with their own units, and never intended to look at a database again after this. But Kerena was intensely interested: she wanted that unit, as she lacked her own. What she had was one Kermit had rented for her. It was, he assured her, serviceable. But it wasn't *hers*; she couldn't take it back with her.

That was a private qualm: she had traveled back in time, but could she take a future artifact into the past? She hoped she could, because she would keep it secret, allowing no one else even to know of it, let alone use it, so it would have no effect on the ordinary world. But she wouldn't know for sure until she actually tried it.

"Now for basic definitions," the professor said. "We are here to learn to understand and use the standard relational database. A database is essentially a collection of information organized into a table: times, costs, stock numbers, orientations, sources, addresses, cautions, whatever. A relational database is two or more tables operating in tandem, when the total information is too complicated for a single table. We'll review examples of every type."

The class evinced polite boredom, but Kerena was fascinated. She quickly discovered that a table in this context was not a support for a meal, but a criss-cross pattern of lines forming cells in which the bits of information were stored. It could be just about anything; it would certainly do for storing secrets, once she figured out how to properly record them.

Day by day the professor took them through it. Each student used an individual computer unit to project the selected type of database on a virtual screen, and manipulated the words and figures there. Kerena's were in script; it didn't matter. From the first day the professor picked up on her attitude, appreciating her extreme interest, and gave her leeway. Often she had questions that seemed stupid to some of the others, and might have been so, but he answered them carefully. She had started from abysmal ignorance, but rapidly forged toward the head of the class.

Between the daily sessions, she did homework with Kermit, visited the many wonders of this realm, and made love with him. Often, for he was quite conscious of the brevity of their romantic association: pleasure postponed was pleasure lost. Taken as a whole, it was a glorious week.

She won the database unit, of course, as the outstanding student. The professor made to shake her hand as he gave it to her, but she leaned forward and naughtily kissed him on the mouth. The class applauded; they knew that not only was it a cute gesture, it would give him several nights of restless dreams. Her standard issue blouse had somehow managed to flash interesting frontal curvature, just as her short skirt flashed fascinating nether curvature as she sat. Other girls in class, observing her, had made open notes on more than database techniques.

"It's a nice unit," Kermit remarked when they were alone. "Enough storage to hold a small universe, yet small as a coin." For the unit was a disk that could be set on the tip of a finger without overlapping much. "Powered by a mini-nuke."

"A what?"

"A tiny nuclear power plant that will last indefinitely. This will never need an external power source."

"That's nice," Kerena agreed, understanding only that it was a desirable feature.

"Fissionable, too."

"Fishing?"

He smiled. "I love it when you tease me. Fission. That means it splits." He demonstrated by squeezing it correctly, so that it fell into two thinner disks. "Entangled, of course. That means that whatever happens to one, happens also to the other. So you have instant automatic backup. That's useful, if you happen to mislay one." He squeezed them back together.

Kerena had learned a prodigious amount about databasing, but had somehow not picked up on this feature. She liked it.

But now their time together was coming to an end; the term was almost done. "You know I—is there any chance—" he started, abruptly awkward. He was more than smitten with her.

"I really do have to return to my own time," she said.

"But can you visit? I'll never forget you."

Kerena considered. Why not? She liked him and this future; it would be a nice safe place to relax on occasion. "When I can," she promised.

They made love. Then Kerena addressed another matter. "I want to keep this database with me always, but I don't want folk of my time to know. How can I do that?"

"Easy. Hide it in plain sight where no one will see it."

"Isn't that an oxymoron?"

"Not at all. For example, if you wear it as a bauble at your bosom it will be taken as jewelry to attract the eye, and the eye will immediately forget it in favor of your divine breasts."

That seemed to have merit. "But it's recognizable as what it is, a database."

"A token computer," he said. "That would hardly be noticed here, but if there are no computers where you live, that could be a problem. Maybe you could hide it inside an ornament."

Kerena had an idea. She produced Morely's Roman coin, which she had kept for sentimental reason. "What about this?"

"Ideal! A replica of an ancient artifact. People wear those too."

They worked on it, and managed to fasten the disk onto the back of the coin so it didn't show. The coin was attached to a thin chain around her neck. Kerena opened her shirt and let it dangle down between her breasts. "Thus?"

"Ideal!" he repeated, leaning down to kiss a breast. "I've forgotten it already."

Kerena had one more thing to do before she left this future. She wanted to make her first relational database entry, to be sure the device was in order. When she was by herself, she selected the introductory secret: her own. She had never told anyone, and never wanted any to know, but she had been horribly jealous of her lovely older sister Katherine, the magnet for men when Kerena was nothing.

She touched the disk. The virtual screen and keyboard appeared before her. She typed the verbal indexing component: Kerena—jealousy—Katherine. Subject person, emotion, object person. The script appeared on the screen. She checked it and saved it, closing it.

She summoned the image of her sister Katherine as she had been then, lovely at age fifteen. Since then of course the girl had aged, borne children, become a stout grandmother, and of course lost her youthful beauty. There was no jealousy any more. But the fact that it had once existed remained secret, and Kerena never wanted it known. With an act of will she transferred the image to the screen, where it appeared holographically, three dimensional. She saved the picture and closed it.

Then she focused on that emotion, putting herself back into it, feeling the ugly feeling. The intangible essence of it appeared on the screen, a dusky pattern of textures with muted fire hidden underground. She concentrated, and it digested down into computer coding and saved it to the database.

Three aspects: description, image, feeling. Three databases that related to define the whole. She had done it. She shut down the virtual computer.

Now to verify that she could summon it back at will. She reactivated the virtual computer. "Kerena, jealousy, Katherine," she murmured, touching the disk.

The picture of her sister appeared, smiling as though alive. The feeling returned, suffusing her. It had definitely been recorded. Her first entry was complete.

Jolie, observing, was highly impressed. Nox was developing a formidable tool for her office.

And you must never tell, Kerena thought to her. *It is a trade secret that must never be known by any other, lest the paradox of anachronism be invoked.* Jolie had to agree.

She had gotten what she had come for. With this device she could record every secret she encountered, and recover it when she chose. Because the secrets would be indexed by any system she chose, she would be able to locate them at need.

She made love to Kermit one more time, and so did Molly. Then she got by herself and faded out of this scene, returning to her own time.

Chapter 10
Niobe

Kerena did not return straight to the warren and her friends there. She paused on the way to take stock. Because of the danger of anachronism, she had to keep the database secret from all but Molly, who would never betray her because of personal loyalty, and Jolie, who would not do it because it was her mission to protect the timelines. Yet she had to be free to use it, or it would be no good to her.

She also suffered from a peculiar unrest. Maybe it was merely the dislocation of returning to her own time, but it seemed like more. There was something she had to do, but she didn't know what it was. She couldn't rest until she found out.

She slowed her backward travel and spied a lovely land around her. This was Ireland, centuries after her own time.

She hovered, invisible, looking for a nice and private place to rest. She was aware of forest, field, village, and lake. One region attracted her; it was somehow compatible. She floated there and discovered a dense swamp with a faint path leading to a huge water oak tree inhabited by a hamadryad, a tree nymph. That seemed ideal.

But there was something else. There was a huge nexus of significance associated with that spot. Kerena was drawn to it like a moth to a lamp. What was so important about this isolated site and time?

She phased in to the small dry region by the trunk of the water oak, becoming tangible.

"Oh!" It was a startled girl. Kerena, distracted by her awareness of the larger import, had not noticed the pedestrian aspect: the person sitting by the tree.

She would have to bluff through and depart. "I apologize for disturbing you. I wasn't looking where I was going."

"You popped out of nowhere! And you have strange clothing."

How could she explain either the popping or the futuristic dress? She should have taken out the Cloak and used it to mask her presence. "I was traveling in a different mode. I didn't mean to intrude."

"That's all right," the girl said, recovering. She was about Kerena's physical age—fifteen—and startlingly beautiful. In fact she reminded Kerena of her lovely sister at that age. She had honey colored hair and sky blue eyes, fine features, and a body the shape of man's desire.

And, Kerena realized with a shock, she was the focus of the significance. This lovely creature was destined to change the world in some remarkable fashion.

"Is something wrong?" the girl asked. "You are staring."

Kerena hastily averted her gaze. "I apologize again, for being rude. There is something about you that fascinates me."

The girl laughed, like the music of a trickling brook. "I am nothing. But you—you're the prettiest girl I've ever seen. And you're magic. Like the hamadryad."

Kerena glanced up into the tree, spying the tree nymph, who nodded. One magical creature knew another.

This threatened to get complicated. "I believe I should leave now," Kerena said.

The timelines fudged. Jolie stepped in, moving them back a few seconds.

"I hate it when she does that," Molly said.

"I have no choice," Jolie said to Kerena. "You were diverging."

That brief dialogue was internal. Kerena spoke again, externally. "I am magic," she agreed. "But not like the dryad." This time, to her surprise, there was no timeline trouble. Was she supposed to tell this girl the truth?

"I'm surprised too," Jolie said. "I'm sure you mustn't tell her about me, but maybe the rest aligns."

"There's something about you," the girl said. "As if we are destined to be good friends."

"That is not possible," Kerena said. And the boundaries fudged.

Jolie moved them back to try again. "Perhaps so," Kerena said. "Yet I am not free to tell you very much about myself."

The lines fudged. What was this? Nox was supposed to be secret.

"I know," Molly said. "You have to tell her—then make her forget. There must be some reason."

"Tell her only to make her forget? This is ridiculous!" But the the lines fudged again.

"I don't understand it either," Jolie said. "But it may be so."

"Well, I'll try it," Kerena said dubiously. And the timelines straightened out.

Jolie took them back for another try.

"...destined to be good friends," the girl was saying.

"Maybe we are," Kerena agreed. "There is enormous significance associated with you."

The girl laughed again. "If you were a boy, I'd be suspicious of your motive."

Kerena joined the laugh. "I have had my own experiences with boys. They have only three things in mind, and two of them are on my chest."

"And the third under your skirt." The girl smiled, and it was like sunshine in the glade. "I'm Niobe."

"I'm Kerena." They shook hands, then hugged; it seemed natural.

"Do you know, seeing you, I can begin to appreciate what the boys are after," Niobe said. "I don't think I ever saw a prettier girl."

"That's because you must lack a good mirror. You're the prettiest I've seen."

"Are you teasing me?"

"No." Kerena glanced up into the tree. "I see you have befriended the dryad. Ask her."

Niobe turned to face the tree. "Come down, dryad, if you think it's safe."

The nymph of the tree came down. That impressed Kerena; dryads were extremely shy of mortal folk; the girl *had* succeeded in befriending her. She was their height, without clothes, and lovely in the manner only her kind could be.

"Which of us is prettier?" Niobe asked. This wasn't any competitiveness on her part, but genuine curiosity.

The nymph studied them. She shook her head and made gestures with her hands.

"She says we aren't comparable," Niobe said. "Because I'm innocent, and you're—" She didn't finish, flushing.

"I'm not innocent," Kerena said. "True. I am very far from that, however I may look. Still, judging physically alone, she might reach a verdict."

Niobe looked at the dryad. "Can you do that?" Kerena realized that the girl's naiveté enabled her to relate much better to the tree nymph than Kerena herself could. The nymph did not hesitate to approach Niobe, but was politely wary of Kerena. Ah, the precious innocence of youth.

The hamadryad considered. Then she gestured as if removing clothing.

Clear enough. Both Kerena and Niobe doffed their clothing and set it on the ground. Kerena quietly lifted the chain from her neck and put the coin with her clothing, not wanting it to attract attention. Then they stood beside each other nude, for the nymph's inspection.

The dryad shook her head. She gestured them both to stand on either side of her before a clear pool of water at the base of the tree. They did so and looked down into the water.

There were three virtually identical reflections. They were all visions of man's fondest desire. No wonder the nymph had been unable to choose.

"Call it a draw," Kerena suggested as the nymph returned to her tree. "I became perhaps the prettiest of my generation, and you are surely the prettiest of yours."

"Maybe that's why we were attracted to each other," Niobe said.

"I don't think so. There was something drawing me here before I saw you." Kerena returned to her clothing and picked up her iridescent blouse. She would have to hide that the moment she got home, as there was nothing like it in her time. Interesting that her future clothing traveled with her, not disappearing when she went before its time. Maybe that was another aspect of the power of Night.

The coin slipped off and plunked into the dark water of the swamp, drawing its chain behind it.

"Oh!" Kerena cried, dismayed. How could she have forgotten that! Her invaluable database, the whole point of her travel into the future.

"What is it?" Niobe asked, alarmed by her outcry.

"I dropped a—a coin into the water. It is very precious to me. I must find it." Already she was plunging her hand into the murky water. Of course she couldn't tell the girl the real nature of the coin.

"Let me help." Niobe came and put her hand in.

They searched desperately, but all they came up with were roots and mud. The coin had found a horribly effective hiding place. What was she to do?

"I fear it doesn't want to be found," Kerena said. "It may be avoiding us." Because she had let it go out of the immediate presence of Nox, and it had become anachronistic in this setting. She had been so foolish!

"I know," Niobe said. "The dryad can find it. She knows every part of her tree, roots and all. The roots will tell her where."

"And she's magical," Kerena agreed. She looked at the dryad. "Please— can you do this?"

Now the dryad did hesitate. She gestured to Niobe.

"She says she would like to—to exchange favors."

Kerena suffered a siege of caution. "Does she know my nature?" For it was important that Niobe not know that.

"Yes. She says you are—I don't know the word, but it seems like Knocks. I must have it wrong."

Nox. The hamadryad knew, all right. "What favor?" Kerena asked grimly.

"Her tree—she wants to know its future. She's afraid some logger will cut it down. I don't see how anyone could know such a—"

"Done." Kerena was desperate to keep the girl from catching on. But she had to recover that database. The dryad's wish to know the fate of her tree was quite reasonable; that would be her fate too.

Kerena stood back, and the nymph came back down from the tree. She went to the spot where the coin had fallen and reached into the water. Immediately she brought up the chained coin. She gave it to Niobe and retreated back to the tree.

Niobe brought the coin to Kerena. "Can you do what she wants?"

Kerena accepted the precious disk and put the wet chain over her head so that the coin came to rest again at her breast. She would not remove it again. "Yes."

Kerena stood beside the tree, touched its bark with a finger, and moved into the future. She followed the tree to the present time as she knew it. Then its outlines fuzzed. She knew why: this alternate timeline was not assured of survival beyond that time. Only if it remained aligned with her own could it, and therefore the tree, remain beyond danger.

She returned to the time she had left. "The future becomes uncertain," she announced. "But the tree remains for a century hence, and longer if this world remains. No one cuts it down."

The dryad looked greatly relieved. She knew Nox spoke the truth.

"That's wonderful," Niobe said. "But how could you know such a thing?"

This complication with the coin had lead to a complication with Niobe. How could she safely explain her power? Maybe she could change the subject. "As I said before, there is something that drew me to you. I have special abilities; surely you do too."

"But I'm just an ordinary girl," Niobe protested. "I'm not smart or well educated, while I can see that you have extraordinary powers. My face is all of my fortune."

That seemed to be the case, essentially. Yet the tremendous aura of significance surrounded her. There was certainly something about her. Kerena, as Nox, could probably fathom it—but was that the right thing to do? Surely not; it was not wise to interfere with a situation as potent as this. "I think I need to be on my way."

The lines fudged dramatically. *You mustn't do that,* Jolie thought, alarmed.

Even if I make her forget, this is dangerous, Kerena said.

Not as dangerous as breaking off now.

Well, she would try it, and stop when Jolie saw the lines diverging. Jolie moved them back.

"But I'm just an ordinary girl," Niobe protested.

"You are hardly that, Niobe."

"Do you know something I don't? Please tell me!"

Still no divergence. This was weird. "First I must tell you something of myself," Kerena said. "I am not of this time. I come from a past time—about fourteen hundred years ago."

"I don't understand." The girl was evidently too polite to call her untruthful or deranged.

"It's not a thing I can prove directly. But I can demonstrate other things. I do have some magic powers. I can turn invisible." She did so, briefly. "I can float in air." She did so. "I can travel in time."

"I am beginning to believe, Niobe said, amazed.

Still no divergence. So she went for the rest. "I am Nox, the Incarnation of Night."

"I didn't know there was an Incarnation of Night!" But she saw the hamadryad nodding.

"That's not surprising. I am the keeper of secrets. I am returning to my own time after a visit to the future of a hundred or more years from this time."

"You do know the future?"

"I know *a* future, or two. The future is not fixed."

"Can you see *my* future? Oh, please tell me!"

Could she do that? Kerena realized she probably could.

But there were constraints. "If I tell you your future, that knowledge will cause you to change it. Then what I tell you won't be valid."

"I don't understand. Why should I change it? I just want to know, in case there's something bad."

"She really is of ordinary intelligence," Molly said in her head. "As I was, before I had several decades without a body to think about things."

"Suppose there *is* something bad," Kerena said to Niobe. "What would you do?"

"Why I would avoid it, of course." Then she paused. "Oh, now I see. That would change it, and everything might be different. Still, maybe not as bad as it would have been."

"But possibly worse. We toy with fate at our risk."

"Still, I so much want to know. Even if it changes."

And Kerena was quite curious too. Niobe seemed like a perfectly ordinary girl, apart from her stunning beauty. What was the overwhelming significance associated with her? So she compromised: "I also have power over memories, because secrets are made from them. I can cause you to forget what you learn here. So you may not be able to keep your knowledge."

"Tell me, and if it seems I must not keep it, then take it away," Niobe said. "At least I'll know it briefly."

"Even your knowledge of my visit here may have to go, because that could change your future too. You would know there was something, and you would search for it."

Niobe blanched, but nodded. "Do what you must do, Nox."

Kerena traveled into the future, following Niobe's individual timeline.

What she discovered astonished her. Niobe was destined to have more impact on the future than anyone else except Kerena herself—and their fates were indeed intertwined. No wonder she had felt the attraction.

Jolie, too, was amazed. Now she recognized this innocent girl as the grandmother of Orlene, with whom she had seriously interacted. No wonder there was significance here; this girl was in a manner the start of a phenomenal series of developments. But it was no simple course; the skein of life was almost hopelessly tangled. Which was of course why Jolie was here to guide Kerena through the tangle. She did not hide her thoughts from Kerena. Awed, Kerena returned to the glade.

"I have looked," Kerena said.

"I saw you flicker."

"I was traveling to your future. It is amazing and complicated, and there is early tragedy. It might be kinder not to reveal it to you."

"Oh, please, you must tell me!"

Kerena sighed inwardly. She had to do it. "I must drastically summarize, because there is so much. You will live here uneventfully about five more years, and become recognized as the loveliest woman of your generation. Then you will be married against your will to a boy five years your junior. He—"

"What?"

"That is only the beginning," Kerena said grimly. "He turns out to be an extremely smart, strong young man, and you do come to love him. But Satan means to kill you, and your husband takes your place, dying in your stead, to foil that evil plot. That breaks your heart. You give your baby son to his father's family and go on to become an Aspect of the Incarnation of Fate. Clotho, who spins the Threads of Life." Jolie had of course known Fate, but had not properly tracked her mortal origins, as it were. Clotho had simply been Clotho, learning and performing her office.

"An Incarnation!"

"Later you leave that office to marry a mortal man, your son's cousin, and bear him a daughter, whose daughter will die, then become the Incarnation of Good." How straightforward it seemed, phrasing it that way! Niobe's granddaughter Orlene, a fine sensitive ghost and good friend to the ghost that was Jolie, on her way to the miraculous destiny none of them had foreseen. "So you are to be the grandmother of God."

"The grandmother of—" The girl couldn't finish.

"God, or Good, too, is an office. They are all offices, except those that have not been animated by people. In one way or another, you are to be related to all the major Incarnations of Immortality."

"I can't believe this!"

"Perhaps I can show you some of it. I will take you on a spot tour of some of your relatives, as seen from this one site. I think I can safely take you there if I don't try to move you physically. You won't be able to speak to them or affect them, but you will see them briefly."

Niobe simply stared at her.

"Take my hand," Kerena said firmly. "Traveling will seem strange, but you can not be harmed because you will not really be there. Only your spirit will see."

Awed, Niobe took her hand.

Kerena phased them both out and moved forward, tracing Niobe's life as she had done before, except that she remained by the water oak tree. That was a blur, as Niobe's visits to the tree were brief, until Kerena stopped to show an episode at its normal pace. Then they could both see the Niobe of the future, stunningly beautiful.

Thus they saw this same glade, anchored by the great tree, where a handsome and powerful young man took Niobe's hand and sang to her. "That is Cedric Kaftan, your husband, a very fine young man who loves you absolutely."

"But you say he dies!"

"To save you. What finer love can there be?"

A tear formed in Niobe's eye. "I can't let him sacrifice himself for me."

"That's why you must forget. Your future must be as it is fated to be, or your universe may suffer horrendously."

They moved on, and paused again as Niobe brought a boy baby and left him by the tree. "What is she doing!" Niobe demanded. "She can't leave him alone there!"

But then they saw how the dryad came down from her perch in the tree and took care of the little boy. "The nymph can't have children of her own," Kerena explained. "That is a price of her near immortality and youth. But she loves children, and will approach them and help them while mortal adults remain clear. She is teaching him magic. He is destined to become a great Magician."

Indeed, they saw how the child was gleefully learning magic tricks the dryad showed him. It was a highly compatible association.

They moved farther forward. Kerena stopped when two little girls visited with the dryad, also learning magic. "The one with buckwheat-honey hair is Orb, your daughter by your second husband. The one with clover-honey hair is Luna, your granddaughter by another man, Cedric."

"But they look like twins!"

"They are nevertheless more like cousins, once removed. It is a complicated relationship. Later in life you found love again, but that was about forty years later, with Cedric's younger cousin. The two girls were born only days apart, and you took care of them both."

"I see," Niobe agreed, seeing herself come in due course to take them home. "But forty years? I look twenty!"

"Twenty three. You didn't age while you were an Incarnation. But now, as a renewed mortal, you age normally again." That was another key to Jolie's initial nonrecognition: she remembered Niobe as the middle-aged Aspect of Fate, Lachesis, her once phenomenal figure lost.

They watched other visits to the tree, as the girls grew and leaned, and Niobe aged. She gradually became a middle aged woman, a bit heavyset, no longer lovely. "Oh, I wish I had stayed in shape!"

"That is hard to do, when you are mortal. Once the girls went out on their own, you return to become the second Aspect of Fate, Lachesis, who measures the threads of life. As far as I know, you are the only one ever to have occupied two such offices."

"What did I do after that?"

"Nothing. You remain Lachesis in my time."

Niobe thought about that. "Are we friends, then?"

"We can be," Kerena said. "I haven't gotten there yet."

"Let's be friends then."

"But I must take away your memory now, so that none of this well be changed."

"Will you restore it, then?"

Kerena was taken aback. Would that be possible, most of a century later? Why not, if she saved them? "But by then you will know all this, from living it."

"My memory of this meeting."

Ah. "Yes, if I can. If I can't, I will tell you about it, so you'll know."

"Thank you."

Kerena glanced at the hamadryad. "You will not tell?"

The nymph shook her head, agreeing not to tell.

Kerena touched Niobe and drew out her memory of this occasion. Then, before the girl could see her again, she resumed her travel into the past.

"But if she has no memory of it," Molly asked as they traveled, "Why was it so important for you to talk with her?"

"I wish I knew," Kerena said.

Jolie didn't know either. The contact with young Niobe had been a phenomenal revelation to them all, but in terms of her mission, what was the point? Why had Kerena been drawn to that site at that time? Why had the lines of alignment faltered only when she tried to avoid it? Evidently it was a necessary thing, but it seemed to make no sense.

"And you never did get to settle down to think things through," Molly said.

"I think I no longer need to. Now I know that this whole business is more complicated than I had imagined. That provides perspective."

Could *that* be the reason, Jolie wondered. Somehow she doubted it. Perspective could be gained in simpler, less risky ways.

They returned to the warren. Kerena meant to make it an instant after she left for her future venture, but found herself balked. She was unable to settle into normal mode until two weeks after her departure.

"How was it?" Morely asked as they made love.

"Tell us everything," Vanja said as she watched.

Kerena did. "But I don't understand why I couldn't return to a time of my choosing. I did when I traveled into the past."

"I have no problem with that," Morely said. "You traveled only spiritually into the past, but physically into the future. You actually lived those two weeks. So your sundial was moving, as it were. It's the same as if you had visited London for two weeks."

"But when I sought the Incarnations, I returned thirty years later."

"Then you visited purgatory, and interacted with supernatural beings whose time-scales aren't fully of this world. Now that you are an Incarnation yourself, you control your own time. You probably won't suffer any more such lapses unless you choose to."

It made sense when he analyzed it. "Thank you."

"Always glad to be of service," he said, smiling with the pun as he completed his act with her.

"Will you show us the device from the science future?" Vanja asked.

Kerena lifted the coin and touched the disk embedded in it. The screen appeared in the air between them. She realized that it had another nice feature: it could be read from the other side as well as her side. Her sister's lovely face appeared on it. "My first entry," Kerena explained. "My secret jealousy of my older sister's beauty."

"But you are lovelier than she," Vanja said.

"It seems I became so," Kerena agreed. "All I needed was time to mature, and the love of a good man." She kissed Morely. "But that secret feeling remained. Now all I have to do is fathom and record the secrets of everyone else in the world."

"Why?" Vanja asked.

"Because that is what Nox does: keeps the secrets. That will be the basis of my power."

"Naturally our secrets will be your next entries," Morely said. "Can you fathom them?"

Kerena focused on him, exerting her newfound power. "Hoo!" she exclaimed.

"Why do I suspect you are not bluffing?" Morely asked, evidently intrigued.

"Because your Seeing knows I have it."

Vanja's eyes glittered. "Tell us what he never told me."

"When he was a boy of ten, his family had to travel briefly without him, so they left him in the care of a neighbor. She was a handsome woman, and he had a secret crush on her. He had never spoken of it to anyone, for fear of ridicule, but he longed to possess her to the extent he was able. When it got cold at night she kept him warm in the normal manner by sharing her blanket and body heat with him, holding him close. Her bare breasts against him were marvelously soft and exciting. Then when she slept he got his groin close to hers and managed to wedge his stiffened member into her warm damp cleft. There was no fluid from him, but he had a glorious sensation and possible climax. Thus he had his will of her. She never knew, and of course he never told; she would have been appalled by such abuse of her hospitality. It was his deepest secret."

"And I trust you will keep that secret," Morely said tightly. "It has been a lifetime, and she may no longer live, but I would not have it known what I did."

"It was no secret from her," Vanja said. "She knew."

"How can you be sure of that?"

"The same way I know when you have your will of me as I sleep," she told him. "A woman does. Your crush would have been as subtle as dog poop on your foot. She surely liked you, and was intrigued to see whether you could manage it. But she had to pretend oblivion, lest she be charged with molesting a child."

"She wanted it," Morely breathed, realizing. "That's why she shared her blanket with me; she could have made me sleep alone and shivering. Oh, those breasts! Her man had died; she must have missed his embrace."

"So she clasped you close, pillowed your head with her conducive bosom, and feigned sleep, giving you leave. She kept her legs a little apart so as to promote access. She was gratified by her evident sexual power over you. But she surely never told."

"Surely not," he agreed. "All this time I thought it was my secret alone."

"And now it is mine," Kerena said, classifying it and putting picture and feeling into the database.

"Now fathom Vanja's secret," Morely said, licking his lips.

"There is no need," Vanja said quickly.

"Yes there is. You heard mine; it's your turn."

"Damn." But the woman remained still as Kerena oriented on her.

"Her older brother forced her into sex, but that isn't really her secret," Kerena said. "She didn't like it because it hurt, and hated him, but didn't tell lest he beat her up worse. Then when they were out picking berries, the pickings were small, so they ranged into unfamiliar territory. He slipped and fell into an old well; she heard the splash. The sides were slippery and he couldn't climb out. But instead of going for help, she hauled branches to cover the hole, concealing it, then went home and pretended she had been sleeping. They never found him, having no idea where to look. She got away with murder."

Vanja cringed, awaiting Morely's reaction.

"He molested you?" Morely asked.

"Almost daily," she said. "It was easier to let him do it than try to fight him. I learned to moisten my cleft with balm so it wouldn't hurt so much."

"Then it wasn't murder so much as retribution. He brought it on himself."

"You believe that? You don't hate me for it?"

"Yes. You did what you had to do."

"What a relief!" Vanja moved into him, pushing him down, and they were promptly into sex while Kerena recorded the secret.

"But how are you going to proceed?" Morely inquired when Vanja let him up. "Even if you read a secret every minute, there are too many people to interview. You'll never catch up, and meanwhile more are being born and old ones dying."

"I hadn't thought of that." Kerena considered. "I surely have the power to achieve it, if I can figure out how to use it."

"There need to be many of you," Vanja said, smiling.

"Now that may be feasible," Morely said. "Do the powers of Night include multiplying yourself?"

Kerena investigated. Then she split into three copies of herself. "Yes," the three said together.

Morely was not really surprised. "But can they act independently?"

The three pondered a moment. Then the one on the right went to Morely, the one of the left to Vanja, and the middle one with the coin at her chest spoke. "Yes." The right one kissed Morely, and the left one hugged Vanja. All three were solid and conscious.

Jolie was not reproduced. She remained with the middle figure, the one with the coin. That had to be the original Nox. Just as well; she wasn't sure she wanted to be constantly duplicated. It might have a confusing effect on her identity.

"Me too," Molly agreed. She had remained single as well, as far as they knew.

"And can you then recombine," Morely inquired, "so the landscape isn't littered with sexy girls?"

The three walked together and merged into one. "Yes."

Now Jolie was aware of the perspectives of the other two selves. It was as if the original self had done three slightly different things in turn. It might have been confusing, but wasn't. This also verified that there had been no Jolie or Molly copies made. It was strictly Nox.

"So you can split into as many copies as required to get the job done," Morely said, satisfied. "And one of them can remain with me to make perpetual love."

"Hey!" Vanja said. "What of me?"

"Correction," he said equably. "Two for us, the other to make love with Vanja."

They dissolved into laughter, pretending not to remember that Kerena and Vanja did make love often enough. It was fun discovering her powers. "But one thing nags me," Kerena said. "Why did I have to tell the girl Niobe everything, then erase her memory so that her course was unchanged? What sense does that make?"

Morely nodded. "I agree that the rationale is elusive. The Incarnation of Good is said to be omniscient; maybe you should ask him."

"God? He refused to answer me before. That's why I want to get him replaced. I want them all replaced."

"Vengeance," Vanja said approvingly.

"But then you were mortal," Morely said. "Now you are an Incarnation yourself. You should be able to compel a response."

Kerena nodded. "Maybe so. I'll try for God again." She phased down and moved toward Mount Ararat.

She stopped there and extended her Seeing, tuning into the Incarnation of Good. As before, there was no response. But this time she brought the powers of Night. *Answer me, God, or I will tell your secret to the world: that you are hopelessly tuned out.* She was not bluffing. She had the power to reveal secrets as well as fathom them.

A shining handsome male figure appeared before her. "A greeting, Nox."

She focused her Seeing. "And to you, Angel Gabriel."

Molly was amazed. "What's he doing here?"

Jolie wondered too. She hadn't known that Gabriel existed this far back.

"I was created to handle the routine business of Good, Ladies," Gabriel answered. "So that the Incarnation need not be bothered with trivia. I have existed since God was formed as a separate entity from Chaos."

It seemed that Kerena did have as much of God's attention as was available. "Then perhaps you will do. I wish to talk."

"Of course." Gabriel gazed at her directly, and she felt the impact of his scrutiny. "You are a remarkably esthetic woman."

Kerena smiled. So he was a typical male in at least one respect. She knew exactly how to play on that. "I was preserved at my age of blooming. I presume you were created according to the template for the ideal man."

"True, in every respect."

Well, now. Kerena was experienced in recognizing male interest, and he was confirming it. Sex was not something promoted in Heaven. "I know a private place not associated with your business."

"That would be appreciated."

"This way." She phased down and led the way rapidly back to the warren. When there, she split into two, and her second self went to locate Morely or Vanja and ask them to protect the privacy of their chamber for an hour. Meanwhile Kerena stripped away her futuristic clothing.

Gabriel's robe faded out, leaving him gloriously naked. He was well endowed and perfectly proportioned. They came together, and there followed a considerable sexual session. His member had the property of conveying intense delight by its internal contact, enhancing her pleasure of the occasion. He was very soon aware of her matching desire, and not at all turned off by it.

After several rounds, as it were, they lay beside each other, sated for the moment. "That's the best I've had in a century," he said, speaking literally.

"I confess to taking a certain pride in my sexual expertise," she said. "So many secrets concern sex, that I need to understand its nuances well."

"Heaven is, in this respect, sterile. I dislike slumming, but the women of Heaven are not interested in carnal activity. They prefer to assume the likenesses of their most esthetic youth, but also affect complete innocence about the erotic appeal of such fine bodies. At times it causes me to envy the attention of the smoldering damsels of Hell, who have no such diffidence. Yet I distrust demonesses for obvious reason. So I have to mask myself and take up with unknowing but willing mortal girls. I have to hide the full nature of my ardor, lest they be overwhelmed. It's a nuisance, especially since news of it would not be well received in Heaven."

"Fortunately I will never go to Heaven," Kerena said. "But what of the female Incarnations?"

"Only Clotho, the youngest Aspect of Fate, is appealing in this respect, and her interest in such liaisons is slight."

"My interest is considerable, and I can be discreet." It was an offer.

"I am at your disposal." Accepted. They would meet for future liaisons, unadvertised. Kerena's early experience with brothel clients was serving her well; she had excellent universal currency, as it were.

"I am new to my position, and seem to have much to learn. I would appreciate a source of private advice."

"I am not omniscient, but do know a fair amount."

"I had contact with a woman named Niobe."

"I am not familiar with that name. But there are so many names I lose track."

"She exists about fourteen hundred years hence."

178 • PIERS ANTHONY

"That would explain it. I do not travel in time."

She had not anticipated this complication. How could Gabriel know the answer she craved? But she gave it a try. "I do, on occasion, backward and forward. The past is fixed, but the future has many alternates. I call them timelines. I discovered that I needed to examine her future, and tell her of it, then erase her memory of it, so as not to cause her to change that future. What mystifies me is why I had to do that, instead of simply leaving her alone."

"This woman has significant effect on her timeline?" He was quick to pick up the terminology.

"Extremely."

"Have you considered that the point of the exercise was less for her than for you?"

"For me? How so?"

"To fix her identity and nature in your mind. Her memory was cleared, but yours remains. You need to be sure not to mistake her, at such time as you contact her again."

"*My* memory," Kerena said, seeing it. "It affects me, not her. Yet I am not sure how."

"Or perhaps it is my memory that counts, in this case," Gabriel said. "There may be an occasion when I need to know that her import is critical. I would not know it, except for your travel in time and your report to me."

"How would you affect her?"

"I do not know, but perhaps I will recognize the occasion when it comes. It is clear that she is an essential link in your ghost's alignment to the timelines, so as to save this one from destruction. I will not forget."

Jolie jumped, in her fashion. She knew Gabriel had been aware of her, but not that he had read her full mission. No wonder he caught on so readily. Fortunately he had no objection to her role.

Kerena extended her Seeing, and found confirmation. It was *Gabriel's* memory that counted. "This seems to be true. Thus you have after all explained the mystery."

"I am happy to have done so. It is a pleasure assisting so lovely and circumspect a lady."

It was a hint she responded to immediately, for the pleasure was mutual. They had another bout of quite rewarding sex.

Then they talked again. "It occurs to me that we could do each other some good, apart from private pleasure," Kerena said. "I can use advice, as I mentioned, and perhaps I have something to offer in exchange."

He frowned. "I assumed this liaison was for mutual satisfaction without onus."

"It was. I have something else in mind. Do you know what a database is?"

"No."

"It is a mechanical or electrical file of information. For example, I am collecting secrets of all living people and storing them in my database."

"You are storing all secrets?"

"It is my business," she reminded him gently.

"There are times when it would be helpful to know secrets, especially when processing in new souls for Heaven. They tend to try to hide things that count against them."

"That was my thought. I can provide you with a copy of all secrets."

He laughed. "I would have no way to keep track of them."

"Let me tell you more about the nature and operation of the database." She did, eliciting his considerable interest. Then she split apart the facets of her disk. "These two are entangled; whatever is in one, is also in the other. You will have all my secrets, as they are recorded."

"I would need instruction how to use it."

"I will give you that, until you are competent."

He nodded. "And for this you desire—?"

"Your continuing good will and advice, for the next fifteen centuries." For this was an extremely intelligent and knowledgeable male, in a position of considerable importance. For her purpose, quite possibly better than God Himself.

"We would maintain our liaisons for that time?"

"Of course. They would perhaps be the pretext for our meetings."

"I am completely at your service, in any manner that does not interfere with the performance of my duties."

"You have a staff of angels, I presume."

"Yes, and growing as the population of Heaven grows."

"You therefore have expertise in personnel management."

"To be sure. But I doubt you need a staff, as you are not managing people or souls."

"I will have, not a staff, but copies of myself, perhaps in great number. I am not entirely sure how to organize them."

"Copies of yourself?"

Kerena split into four selves. "In this manner," the one with the coin said, while three went to kiss and stroke Gabriel. They were perfectly coordinated. This led to another sexual episode that clearly amazed and delighted him. Kerena was intrigued herself; this had been a spur of the moment notion, and she liked it.

Once that was done, Gabriel gave her basic rules of organization and dispersal, so that she could make most efficient use of her selves. He did indeed have expertise, and she appreciated it. It would enable her to fetch in secrets efficiently, and record them without confusion.

She gave him the other half of the database. Later this was to become known as the marvelous and amazingly informed Purgatory Computer. The secret of its origin was kept throughout.

And the fate of the sweet pretty girl Niobe was secure. Kerena was especially glad of that, and not merely because it meant the likely salvation of this universe.

Chapter 11
Incarnations

Nox split into several thousand selves and went out to fathom all the key secrets of the population. She organized the selves according to the advice Gabriel gave, and developed a technique of recording data in the database so that one secret was entered every second, day and night. Even so, the job took thirty years full time, before they caught up to every living person. Then they were able to relax, merely keeping up with the new secrets that incoming people had, while focusing on the secrets of Nature and the other Incarnations. That promised to keep them busy for further decades. Everything was open to Night, though Kerena tried to see that other Incarnations did not realize what she was up to. Her power lay in knowing what they did not.

Meanwhile she maintained relations with several males, including Morely in the warren, Kermit in the future, and Gabriel. Morely she loved, Kermit was cute and sweet, and Gabriel was lustily appreciative. She let Molly take over the body sometimes, as the men liked the variety. Molly especially liked Kermit, and did her best to make him happy. Morely was good for intellectual discussion, between bouts, and Gabriel had tremendous practical expertise to share. Overall, her social life was satisfactory. Except that she missed the afreet: the supremely masculine anonymous lover who had come to her only twice, and thrilled her like no other. She loved Morely, and had loved Sir Gawain, and she liked the others, but somehow the demon lover was supreme in her sexual fancy. Molly didn't like him, and Jolie didn't trust him, but since when did liking or trusting matter when it came to pure lust? He was the one she dreamed of. If only he would come to her more often.

Every so often some trivial detail caused the timelines to diverge, and Jolie put her back on track. Once, curious, Kerena checked the alternate future, and verified that it led surprisingly quickly to the destruction of the world by the collision of a meteor. How an unfortunate spoken word caused that to happen was beyond them to comprehend, but it was so.

Morely, who continued his astronomical studies, offered the most likely explanation: "The divergence is not merely of actions or people, or even of worlds, but of universes as we are slowly coming to understand them. Each is its own separate reality. In some universes things are different from ours. In some there are devastating collisions. This is one of those alternates."

Neither Kerena nor Molly could quite grasp that concept, but Jolie, who had seen more of alternate universes, almost did. It wasn't cause and effect so much as shifting to the wrong cosmos. At any rate, it confirmed the need to keep the timelines aligned. Disaster otherwise lurked.

Kerena had two overriding imperatives: to achieve vengeance against the Incarnations who had refused to help her, and to cure her son Gawain, of whatever generation, of the psychic malady she had inadvertently given him. Unfortunately she found she was unable to act on either objective directly; as Nox she fathomed and kept all secrets, but she could not do anything about them herself. The powers of her office came with limitations. She had to act through others, thus protecting knowledge of her hand in events. She wasn't a ghost, yet her impact was ghostlike. That complicated her projects.

She tackled vengeance first. She examined countless futures, employing selves that were no longer needed to fathom secrets, and located one that would accomplish the most with the least continuing effort on her part. Then she summoned the Demoness Lilah.

"No one summons me," Lilah protested as she materialized. "I come simply because I am curious what's on your half-mortal mind."

"I have located a nexus where you can betray another important man and have enormous impact on subsequent worldly affairs."

"I am interested, of course. It has been some time since Samson, and I miss the action. What do you demand for this information?"

"I have no demand. You owe me for your demon substance; this will expiate that debt."

"There's got to be a catch. Why should you show me a delightful situation and call it expiation?"

"Because it serves my purpose."

"Still—"

"I want you to go to work for the Incarnation of Evil."

"To serve Lucifer? I don't want to be locked in Hell."

"As an assistant and mistress. He has just had a housecleaning, as it were, and is in need of new personnel he can trust."

"But he can't trust me."

"Need he know that?"

Lilah considered. "If you don't tell, I won't."

Kerena smiled. "Go fascinate him, bitch."

Lilah vanished. Kerena followed her career over the course of the next six centuries. She served Lucifer loyally as a thoroughly sexual creature, until he sent her to corrupt a mortal cleric named Parry in the year 1242, which she did most effectively.

"Parry!" Jolie exclaimed. "My love!"

"You've been dead 34 years," Kerena reminded her.

"He's still my love, in this world as well as my own. I hate seeing that slutty creature mess him up." Yet of course it was necessary to maintain the alignment. She had to watch while Lilah used her chaos-enhanced body and powers to tempt him to distraction. This was almost as painful as watching her own brief life and love and death, and she tried to tune out of it. This was not her story, but Kerena's.

Parry fought valiantly, trying to deny the impact of her super-seductive body and manner, but Lilah nailed him: "Every lie you tell, brings you closer to Hell." It was inevitable that he succumb; she had too much expertise and sex appeal. A man was helpless before a woman's apt appeal to his gonads.

But that was hardly the whole of the story. After corrupting Parry, Lilah fell in love with him, to her chagrin, and finally betrayed Lucifer and helped Parry take over as the Incarnation of Evil, now called Satan. Thereafter she served Satan loyally, in her fashion.

Kerena smiled grimly. One Incarnation down. Not just any one, but the one who would be treated despicably by the other Incarnations, and swear vengeance against them, exactly as Kerena had. And Parry could act more directly than she could to accomplish his purpose.

Initially he tried to be forthright, as she learned from Gabriel at a subsequent tryst. He went to talk with the Angel about replacing God. They finally made a deal: if Satan could corrupt a particular mortal person, or that person's child or grandchild, Satan would win. Otherwise he would give up his campaign to take power.

"Agreed," Parry said at last. "Tell me the name."

"Niobe Kaftan." Who would not come into existence until five centuries later. Gabriel, prompted by Nox, had delivered, in the process outsmarting the father of lies.

"Thank you, Angel," Kerena told him.

"Well, it does give me five centuries of relative peace."

"As if this realm can ever be truly peaceful."

"I suspect—this is a secret—that God finally got tired of the constant bickering that passes for human social relations, and tuned out in disgust."

"I can't blame Him," she said, surprised to discover that it was true. She was long since disgusted with the cheap selfishness that passed for the average person's secrets.

The five centuries passed quickly enough, punctuated by a few memorable events. Kerena still collected the secrets of mortals and filed them in the database, which both Gabriel and Parry found useful when assessing the merit of souls entering Heaven or Hell. She still formed multiple selves at need, and contracted them when the need passed. Each self was individual, but generally aware of the others; they shared a common consciousness. There was no confusion when they formed, and no regret when they merged; they were all her, and she was all of them.

In the course of that time, the girl grew into the role, and became all that Nox could be. She left Jolie's comprehension far behind; the ghost was now like a gnat riding the shoulder of a giant. But she retained the one thing Kerena lacked: awareness of the alignment of timelines.

The afreet came every year or so, always a delight, but she couldn't wheedle any real information from him. Neither did she tell him of Jolie despite his efforts to get her to reveal her secret. He clearly suspected something but couldn't prove it. Meanwhile the sex was phenomenal.

An oddity about that was that he didn't seem surprised about her change of status, the first time he visited after her ascension. He understood that she had become Nox, the Incarnation of Night, but it made no difference to him. He was not at all awed. In fact he seemed to take it for granted. "I have been enjoying you for millennia," he said.

"But I have lived only a century or so," she protested.

"And that makes you better yet. There is now a firmness about you that I missed before."

"He was having sex with Nox before you came!" Molly said when they were alone, amazed. "He's some afreet. I don't trust him at all."

Neither did Jolie. But the mysterious male was part of Kerena's life.

Every so often the timelines tried to diverge, but Jolie put them back into alignment. It was surprising how readily they could change, in trifling ways that nevertheless led to ultimate disaster. It was almost as if this reality wanted to be doomed, a curious notion.

Then, abruptly, shockingly, Morely was gone. That was only part of it; the entire warren had been wiped out. Kerena returned from a tryst to discover Vanja gazing at the ruin in grief. "I was delayed returning," she said. "And found this."

The warren had been destroyed. The entrance was rubble. The vampires were not trapped inside; their bodies were hung on the branches of trees, horribly mutilated. Superstition had it that a vampire had to be killed by burying it with a stake through its heart; the fact was that simple hacking apart would do it, and it had been done.

Kerena traveled back in time to discover what had happened. A villager out hunting had discovered the entrance, and lurked, watching. He had seen the vampires come and go, and had recognized their nature. The villagers had organized and struck in force at noon, when the vampires were in their chambers. They had charged inside with torches and knives, blinding and slashing the occupants, driving or dragging them out. Then they had used explosives to collapse the warren. It was a disciplined slaughter, well planned and executed.

"Why do they hate us?" Vanja asked. "We never hurt them."

"Superstition," Kerena said. "They hate what they don't understand, and they don't want to understand." She was choking with grief too. She had loved Morely for centuries.

She took Vanja to a private apartment she maintained for convenience, and arranged for a new identity for her. As Nox she had ways to do such minor things. Vanja was her one remaining living or half-living friend from her original time.

Once Kerena had handled the necessary details, she retreated to a private place and suffered. Morely, who had first recognized her Seeing, similar to his own. Morely, the early astronomer and chemist. The one who had taught her to think rationally. Who had taught her sex. Who had always been there for her intellectual considerations. How could she exist without him?

She wept for perhaps a week, and in that time the gathering of secrets did not proceed, for she did not divide into other selves. All of them would have been as grief-stricken as the original. She mourned him with abandon, caring for nothing else. Molly and Jolie stayed out of it; they had had griefs of their own, and knew there was no amelioration but time.

Slowly her grief shifted to something else: anger. Those ignorant villagers had destroyed one who had never done them harm. Why should they be allowed to live when they had killed him? They should be made to pay.

"Kerena," Molly said. "I don't think it's my place to object, but—"

"Then don't!" Kerena snapped.

Jolie stayed out of this too, because the timelines were not fudging. Whatever was to happen, was to happen. She had to let it be. But it promised to be ugly.

For the first time Kerena used her power as Nox for personal vengeance. She went to the village by night, divided into more than a hundred selves, and visited each sleeping person. She put the knowledge of another person's secret into the dream of each, firmly enough to be remembered on waking. Then she settled back to watch. Her indirection was about to become savagely direct, through the actions of the dreamers.

A mother learned that her brother had been sexually abusing her daughter. A man learned that his son had been torturing small animals. A woman learned that her diffident lover was homosexual. A poor man learned that his cousin had cheated him of his inheritance. A rich man learned that his wife was plotting to poison him. A woman learned that her married lover was also having sex with her sister and her best friend. A grandfather learned that neither his grandson nor his son were his own; he had been cuckolded throughout.

There was a kind of pause when day came, as the villagers pondered the dirty secrets that had come to them. They knew they were true, because Nox had instilled absolute belief—and because they *were* true. They questioned, they verified, they reacted. Then the mayhem commenced.

On the first day several villagers committed suicide when they found their guilty secrets exposed. Several more were killed in crimes of passion. Others were so severely shamed they had to leave the village, never to return. On the second day the retaliations began, for the outrages of the first day. Day by day the carnage continued, until the village was but a hollow shadow of its former self.

Yet somehow vengeance didn't feel sweet. Like the urgency of sex, it seemed less reasonable once satisfied.

"I think it is time for me to be moving on," Molly said. Kerena knew that the siege of ugliness had turned her off, though she was too polite to say so directly.

There was nothing for Kerena to do but oblige her friend's wish to be separate from her. It was part of her own punishment for misusing her power. She resolved never to do that again. She still missed Morely, but recognized too late that this was not the way to honor his memory. It had not brought her relief, and had cost her a friend.

Then she found a situation for Molly. A handsome young woman in the Irish city of Dublin had lost her mind and would soon die if not helped. She was a fishmonger, selling cockles and mussels in the street from her wooden wheelbarrow. It was dull, dingy work, but it paid her way.

Molly took over the vacant body, restored to life. "But you know my curse will catch up with me," she reminded Kerena.

"But maybe not for years. Meanwhile you will have life, and so will a body that would otherwise have died much sooner."

By day Molly the fishmonger wheeled her wheelbarrow through the streets of the city, crying out her wares for sale. But by night she reverted to her own early trade, becoming a pricey courtesan and making a lot more money. She reveled in it, knowing she was good at it.

But after a decade the curse did catch up, and she was brutally murdered. Kerena, attuned, came immediately to claim her soul, and she returned as the ghost companion she had been. She was philosophic about it, and appreciated the years of renewed life she had been granted.

But her story wasn't over. The officials of the city, appalled by the double life revealed and embarrassed because a number of them had been Molly's nocturnal patrons, did their best to erase all evidence of her existence. They pretended she had never existed, and that even the legend of her double life was fake. "As if there could ever be a fake legend!" Kerena said, laughing. Indeed, the common folk remembered, and the legend refused to fade. It even became a song.

Then the American-Irish city of Kilvarough, seeking tokens of authenticity, offered Molly a position there, as a ghost. It wasn't a perfect spell, because Molly could truly interact only with those who were approaching death. But it was better than nothing, and had its own recognition. Kerena visited her on occasion, and she was satisfied.

Thereafter the afreet had disturbing news. "I have studied you, Nox, and discovered something. Your reality is not constant. It deviates from its proper course."

"I don't understand," Kerena said. Of course she understood the truth of his observation perfectly; what she didn't understand was how he could know of this. Would he finally tell her?

"I have made something of a study of the timelines," he said. "There are many of them, each traveling its destined course. But yours is unnatural; it shifts into alternates. Do you have any idea why?"

Kerena was sure she did not want him to know the truth. He was a great lover, but she had no notion of his ultimate nature or aims. Her Seeing did not help her in this respect; his background was a frustrating secret from her. So she played the innocent. "What is a timeline? Is it like a row of clocks? I don't believe I have seen anything like that."

His mouth smiled, but his eyes smiled not at all. "You are the mistress of secrets, of course, and you are keeping them well. I am sorry that you do not trust me enough to tell me the truth."

Jolie was outraged. This ultimately secretive entity expected to be trusted? Sheer hubris!

"I don't know who you are!" Kerena flared. "You have never even given me a name, let along revealed your true nature. How can I trust you?"

"Perhaps in time." He faded out. She tried to use her Seeing to track his essence, but he was totally gone.

"The afreet is more than he seems," Jolie said. "He knows I am adjusting the timelines to make this one conform to mine. But I don't fathom his motive. Does he know what happens to the timelines that don't conform?"

"I don't know," Kerena said. "He's such a great lover that I have been hesitant to challenge him, but the fact that he takes Nox in stride makes me nervous. Who or what could do that?"

"An Incarnation," Jolie said. "An angel. A demon. A ghost."

"He is none of these, as far as I can tell. He's not an afreet, either; I'm sure of that now."

"So am I," Jolie said.

Kerena continued to watch, and saw the woman Niobe come on the scene. Now was coming the time of the changing of Incarnations. But she remained clear of Niobe, not interfering with her at all. She had done enough of that five centuries before, via Gabriel.

In 1917 Niobe gave her baby boy into the care of her dead husband's brother's family and became Clotho, an Aspect of Fate. Actually the three Offices of Fate had already changed in the interim, so that aspect of Kerena's vengeance had already been accomplished. In any event, she was no longer so keen on vengeance. For one thing, it distracted her from her main personal mission: somehow removing the taint from the lineage of her son.

Forty years later, Niobe stepped out of the Clotho role and married a mortal, Pacian Kaftan, then of middle age. Niobe was still physically 23, the age she had been when she became Fate. The following year she birthed her daughter Luna, destined to be a prominent politician. In 1980 Zane shot Death and assumed the office, becoming Thanatos, and began his association with Luna, then 22.

In 1981, after Pacian died, Niobe returned to Fate, this time as the Aspect Lachesis. She was now 46 physically, no longer a beauty, but a solidly responsible woman. She had finally had the experience she had missed before: that of raising her child.

Meanwhile Niobe's granddaughter Orb had been active. An accomplished musician, she sought the Llano, the potent set of melodies that could be called the operating system of the cosmos. She loved Mym from the east, but his royal family broke up their affair, not knowing that she was pregnant. In due course she birthed a daughter, Orlene. Mym learned of that only after he became the Incarnation of War. By that time they each had other social interests. Orb became the Incarnation of Nature and took an interest in Parry, who remained physically a young man. When she discovered his identity as Satan, she destroyed humanity in a fit of rage. Kerena understood about that sort of thing. But Chronos, the Incarnation of Time, who lived backward in time, reversed it, saving the world. Parry had courted her for a purpose, but fell in love with her, though it was not acceptable for the Incarnations of Nature and Evil to be a couple. Nevertheless, they married. Love was love, regardless of rules or the approval of others.

Orlene grew up and entered into a key relationship: a ghost marriage to Kerena's descendant Gawain, who had died of the curse before she met him. It would be her duty to conceive a baby of a living man, to inherit Gawain's name and fortune. The ghost of Gawain located a man named Norton and sent him to impregnate his bride. From this affair came Gawain the nth, who became known as Gaw2. His father appealed to Gaea to change his genetic pattern to match Gawain's, and she, not realizing the significance or the consequence, obliged. Thus Gaw2 acquired the Taint, and died as a baby.

Orlene, distraught, committed suicide, determined to follow and somehow rescue her baby. Norton, desolate, would later take the Hourglass and became the Incarnation of Time.

The turnover of the Incarnations was complete or accounted for, except for the Incarnation of Good. God. Jolie felt relief; she had guided Kerena almost to salvation for her timeline.

Then something changed.

It was the afreet who did it. He made glorious sex with her as always, then hit her with it.

"I have investigated. You have been having your timelines changed. There is a malignant ghost doing it, costing you grievously."

"So you say," Kerena said, determined not to let him trick her into revealing the truth.

"Her name is Jolie. She is determined to bring you to ruin."

Jolie jumped, figuratively. How had he learned her identity?

"How do you know such a thing?" Kerena asked.

"I visited her home timeline and saw her cross over. She has been interfering with you for some time."

"And you say this supposed ghost is malignant? Why?"

He smiled grimly. "Because she caused you to lose your lover, Morely. And before that, your baby, to the taint."

Now Kerena jumped. "I don't believe it!"

"I shall be happy to explain. She nudges your reality from one timeline into another. In the originals you suffered neither of these horrors."

"That can't be!"

He shrugged with affected nonchalance. "Travel back in time, Nox, and verify it for yourself." He faded out.

"I am not malign," Jolie said angrily.

"I am sure you are not," Kerena agreed. "But I must check."

She checked. She phased down and moved back in time to check what she had not thought to check before: the connection between one of Jolie's alignment nudges and the slaughter of the vampires. She attuned to the closest such change before the event, then traced the alternate timeline—the one not taken.

It was a routine meeting of Kerena and Vanja. Kerena, as Nox, was away from the warren most of the time, but she tried to check in with both Morely and Vanja frequently. In this instance, Vanja was out seeking a sheep for her necessary token taste of blood. The day was overcast, with rain threatening, so she was comfortable in the light. Kerena appeared before her, solidified, embraced her, asked after Morely, then remarked that she had seen a sheep nearby.

Jolie stepped in and erased that as a deviance. So Kerena did not mention the sheep, and they parted. Vanja quested farther out, found another sheep, and returned to the warren in good order. That was all. All that had changed had been her harvesting a few drops of blood from a different sheep. No one else had been affected.

Meanwhile the hunter had stumbled upon the entrance to the warren, observed it, and in due course roused the villagers to their mayhem.

This time Kerena followed the other timeline: the one she had deviated from. In that one, Vanja went to intercept the closer sheep, tasted its blood, and moved on. The sheep hardly noticed, and went on grazing. Vanja headed for home.

And intercepted the hunter. Realizing that he was ranging awkwardly close to the warren entrance, she did what came naturally. She pretended to be an innocent wood nymph, which wasn't difficult because she was already nude and shapely. She acted timid, retreating from the hunter in maidenly caution. He pursued her, and when they were fairly distant from the warren, she let him catch her for a fast crude plumbing, which she discovered she liked, once she experienced it. He was, she indicated in her silent nymphly way, a truly manly man. Well pleased with his conquest, the hunter soon recovered enough passion to do it again, before going on home to his compact wife. Naturally he did not mention the forest encounter to her, and his associate menfolk did not believe him on the following day. Everyone knew that forest nymphs could not be caught unless they wished to be, and why would such a creature ever want to be caught by *him*?

And he never found the warren entrance. It had been pure chance, which chance Vanja had distracted him from. She had unknowingly saved the warren from destruction.

Kerena did not follow the timeline farther. She knew it would end in destruction somewhere down the line, perhaps in centuries, but inevitably. The cost of saving it had, in some devious manner, been the murder of all the other vampires.

All because Kerena had said or not said a thing that put or did not put Vanja in the way of the hunter at the right moment. It was really Kerena's fault. The afreet was painfully correct.

She suffered another siege of grief for Morely and the others, for the moment not regretting her vengeance against the villagers. Then she resumed time traveling.

This time she moved all the way back to the deviance closest before her conversion to vampire. That was the act that had introduced the taint. Sure enough, it was a dialogue wherein she said something that caused Morely to think of a possible consequence to her baby. Jolie had erased it, and the matter had not come up. Kerena could have waited for her conversion until after birthing her baby, had she considered that aspect. But Jolie had steered her into the other course, and the major horror of her early life had happened.

"I didn't know!" Jolie protested. "I meant you no mischief."

Kerena understood that. She also knew that had she not started her long quest to save her baby, she would not have become the Incarnation of Night, and acted in ways that helped save the timeline. Gaw-Two's Taint was the price of that.

Yet if she had known, and avoided it, she would have been a far happier mother. How would she have chosen, had she seen the alternate consequences at the time of decision? She didn't know. After all, her life would have probably have run its course before the end of the timeline came. She might have had nothing personal to lose.

"I have paid serious consequences for saving the timeline," Kerena said. "I am not sure I want to continue that. Who else in the world even cares about my sacrifices?"

"I'm sorry," Jolie said lamely. "It's the only way we know. I didn't think it would cost what it did."

Kerena didn't answer, but she doubted that was enough.

A few days later there came another divergence. This time Kerena did not simply accept it. "I want to know what the consequences of each choice are."

"Salvation versus doom," Jolie said. "Not immediately, but inevitably in the future."

"The short-term consequences," Kerena said grimly.

The point of divergence was seemingly innocuous, as they all were. Kerena was about to pay a routine visit to Vanja, who had settled in Kilvarough with a male vampire she had encountered, and was working as a night clerk. She had made a decent half-life for herself, and had largely recovered from the horror of the massacre. The two of them remained close friends, and Kerena often spent the night, giving extra pleasure to the husband. He resembled Morely, surely not entirely by coincidence; she closed her eyes and pretended. It was something they understood.

She phased in to Vanja's day room, in the early evening. "Hello," she said. "Is anyone home?"

Vanja appeared, garbed in a fetching nightie. "Kerena!" The two came together for a hug and kiss—and the lines blurred. Jolie immediately jumped it back to just before Kerena spoke.

"Hold," Kerena told her. "I need to know."

She held herself still in time and traced the course of the timeline she had been about to take. It proceeded to a hug by the two women, followed by a friendly dialogue, then a session where the two of them tackled the husband to see how often they could make him climax in exactly one hour.

Kerena slept with them, and departed in the morning, satisfied with the friendly outing. No problems there.

Then she followed the alternate timeline. In this one she paused a moment, then spoke. "Hello. Is anyone home?"

Vanja appeared. "Kerena!" The two ran together, embracing and kissing. "I was just about to get it on with Hubby. Come join us."

Kerena did, and Hubby was highly appreciative. It was almost like old times with Morely. Kerena loved relaxing with folk of her own nature, keeping the necessary secrets. No one else in Kilvarough knew they were vampires, and Hubby did not know that Kerena was Nox. That was for his own safety, so that he could never inadvertently betray his knowledge of her and attract dangerous interest. He thought she was merely a vampire friend with traveling magic.

Nothing untoward here. Kerena tracked it farther—and saw that Vanja and Hubby got arrested two days later, charged as vampires, and slated for execution.

"That can't be!" she told Jolie, who kept quiet. "Vanja is my last ancient friend."

Kerena rechecked the first timeline. There there was no arrest. So the short term consequences were clear: the lives or deaths of her friends.

But why should such a trifling difference, a mere pause, change the realities so painfully? Kerena went back to the divergence point and extended her Seeing. And there it was: there was a neighbor woman who happened to glance in the window at just the moment that Kerena passed it. The neighbor evidently wondered how such a visitor had arrived without being seen at the walk outside. The neighbor was working in the adjacent garden, and would have noticed. Curious, she investigated—and discovered that there was something about her neighbor. That led to the query to the police, their checking of records, and discovery of Vanja's background.

That pause doomed Vanja.

"No," Kerena said. "I refuse to let any action of mine doom my last old friend."

"But the alternate leads to doom for the timeline," Jolie reminded her.

"We can't be sure of that."

"Check it."

Kerena did, and found that the survival of the vampire couple did deviously lead to the destruction of the timeline. But she still refused to accept it. "If a small deviance from my natural timeline leads to the deaths of my friends, a small deviance from the other timeline should lead to its salvation. I just need to find the way. We are now so close to your 'present' that there should be many avenues to salvation."

"I don't advise this," Jolie said. "I understand why you want to save

Vanja; I have known her as long as you have, in my fashion. But to trade her life for the whole timeline is unthinkable."

"I'll risk it," Kerena said. She blocked Jolie's effort, and proceeded to the first timeline, saving her friend. She said nothing of this to the vampire couple; it was just something she had to do.

When she returned to her home, she had a visitor.

"So you finally did it," the afreet said.

Kerena was not totally pleased. "What do you know?"

"That you refused a deviation. Now you have doomed this timeline."

"I have done nothing of the kind! I'll find a way to change it back, with my friends alive."

He smiled, again with no more than his mouth. "When you are satisfied that you can't save it, call me."

"Why?"

"Because there may be a way after all, if you have the gumption."

"I have the gumption." She was annoyed by his presumption, but that did not change the fact that he was her best of lovers. "Now is that the extent of your interest at the moment?"

"Such a lovely invitation." He swept her in, and proceeded to the kind of passion that only he could generate.

Thereafter Kerena searched for ways to save the timeline. She discovered that key divergences were few; most accomplished nothing worthwhile. The course of the timeline was surprisingly stable. It proceeded slowly, subtly, but inevitably to its ultimate destruction.

There had to be a way! The destruction was not immediate; it would take a century for the subtleties to become obviously damning. So she proceeded with her other project, hoping that she could discover a world-saving avenue along the way. If that failed, well, she would ask the too-knowledgeable afreet. She didn't want to do that; he was a great lover, but his attitude irritated her. It was as if he thought that a woman could not accomplish what a man could.

Jolie stayed out of it. She agreed with Kerena, and sympathized with her desire to save her friend. But she feared very much for her timeline. She sincerely hoped there was a way to get back on track. It seemed that while every person on the globe was constantly making decisions, only those of Nox, and of Kerena before she assumed the Office of Night, affected the timeline in this manner. The hidden powers of Night were awesome, and invisible to others, even the Incarnations.

"I mean to emulate your timeline as closely as possible," Kerena told Jolie. "I may no longer be exactly on it, but if I follow it closely I may be able to discover a way to cross back to it. I hope you will let me know where I deviate."

"I will try," Jolie agreed. It did seem sensible, in the circumstance. As it happened, her active part in her own timeline was just about to commence; that should facilitate this. But there was a tricky aspect.

Niobe's granddaughter Orlene had lost her baby, Gaw-Two, and committed suicide. Orlene was Jolie's friend, and she had come immediately to try to help the young woman. That meant that the Jolie of this second timeline was here with Orlene, and Jolie of the first timeline would be interacting with her other self.

"It's not hard," Kerena said with a passing trace of amusement. "Think of it as dividing into two selves. You both have similar minds and experience, so she should understand readily enough." Then she reconsidered. "But will that foul the alignment?"

"If it does, I'll know it." But as she spoke, Jolie realized it wasn't true. The timelines were no longer perfectly aligned. "No, I won't know it. Maybe I should hide myself from her, so as to avoid affecting her."

"No need. Since we are out of alignment, the worst you can do is put it further out—and if it is already doomed, that shouldn't make much difference. Maybe your interaction will bring the timelines closer together. That could spare us both some serious mischief."

So it might. But Jolie decided to remain clear for the time being. They joined the just-formed ghost Orlene, undetectably.

Jolie Two was there. "Orlene, let go! You will float directly to Heaven!"

Orlene's soul writhed. "No, no, I must not go."

"Orlene, it is Jolie, your dream friend. I would not guide you falsely. You are good; you have nothing to fear from the Afterlife."

"I must not," the soul protested, clinging.

The skeletal Death appeared. He spied Jolie and paused, surprised. "You know this client?" Jolie, having served as Gaea's messenger, knew all the Incarnations.

"She is my friend, almost my child. I don't know why she died."

Thanatos clarified that Orlene's baby had been tainted, and died early. Orlene wanted to recover him, even in death.

"Let me try to help her, Thanatos," Jolie Two said. "Does she have to go to Heaven right away?"

"She does not," Death answered. "Her balance is close. She was born illegitimate, had an extramarital affair, and committed suicide. Those three sins would have been enough to send her to Hell, were she not otherwise almost completely good. I leave the matter in your hands."

"Thank you, Thanatos."

The cowled figure nodded, then walked through the wall. Jolie Two had charge of this soul.

Jolie One nodded too. "I remember," she told Kerena. "This is almost identical. The alignment is perhaps close enough to be restored."

Kerena extended her Seeing. "That baby is now in Purgatory. I must fetch it."

"You would deny a grieving mother her baby, even in death?" Then Jolie remembered. "Oh, of course. You're Nox!"

"You forgot?" Kerena inquired wryly as they moved off.

"I did, for the moment. In Timeline One I did not understand your motive."

"And what is my purpose?"

"To recover and heal your baby at last, and to promote the ghost Orlene to the office of the Incarnation of Good. If you can accomplish that here in Timeline Two, we may yet save this world."

"You forget that my search into the future shows that I do accomplish that, but the timeline remains doomed."

"I forgot, again," Jolie agreed ruefully. "I am suffering a confusion of perspectives, now that my T2 self is active on the scene."

They went to Purgatory, where Nox picked up the soul of the baby Gaw-Two. She was not challenged; the Angel Gabriel understood her mission. As a ghost, the boy required no feeding or cleaning up. She folded him into her bosom, where he slept in comfort. "Now at last I will save my baby, using his immediate mother to appeal to the Incarnations, in the process preparing her for her ultimate destiny."

"First she will seek you, as Nox," Jolie said.

"Yes. That is the apparent reason I took the baby."

And *only* the apparent reason, Jolie now knew. Kerena's history with the Taint went back fifteen hundred years.

Nox had a mountain estate associated with Purgatory, an incidental property set up a few centuries before to establish her presence and legitimacy. Apart from that she had remained largely aloof from the other Incarnations. She prided herself on being mysterious even to them. Now she was set to interact rather more forcefully.

The ghosts Orlene and Jolie had the semblance of their original living bodies, here, and seemed solid to the mountain and each other. That was part of their challenge.

The mountain was shaped like a giant diamond, and its Afterlife substance was diamond. There were several impediments along the way, but these were mere diversions, to generate the semblance of resistance to intrusion. The real challenge was to Orlene: as she progressed up the steep slope, she was gradually masculinized in the crudest manner. Unused to the form and drives of a man, she attempted to rape her companion Jolie.

"I remember," Jolie One said, wincing.

Then Nox appeared to them, in the form of a woman made of mist.

"Come to me, man-thing," she said. She spoke to them in the ineffable mode they perceived, <Come to me,> but now Jolie One recognized it as ordinary dialogue. Perspective made a difference.

Orlene-Man did so. She/he embraced the lovely figure and proceeded to try to have sex with it. Then Nox changed her back to female. "Remember," she said. For that was the lesson: that the genders differed, and a woman should not condemn the passions of a man without understanding them. Orlene, appalled, now understood.

"How can I endure this shame?" Orlene demanded, and fainted.

Jolie Two ran to her, but it was Nox she addressed. "Why do you play with us, Incarnation of Night?"

"You have much to learn," Nox replied. A significant understatement.

"All she wants is her baby, Gaw-Two. Please return him, now that you have humiliated us."

Jolie One winced again. She had, understandably, not understood when she played this scene herself. Now she did: the prior Incarnation of Good and many of the other Incarnations had had overweening arrogance. Nox meant to see that the next God understood humiliation, and would never forget. That, and a little empathy, would go far in preventing indifference to human concerns in the future.

"I have her baby," Nox agreed. "His malady continues in his Afterlife." How well she knew!

"Give him back to her! We'll cure him somehow."

And there was the challenge. Orlene could do what Nox could not, for she could act directly in the ordinary universe, whether living or dead. She was the necessary tool. Nox spelled it out: "Fetch a blank soul from Death, a grain of Hourglass sand from Time, a thread of Life from Fate, a seed of violence from War, a tear from Nature, a curse from Evil, and a blessing from Good. Bring these items to me and I will restore him." Before they could respond, Nox departed.

It seemed like an impossible requirement, yet Jolie One knew it was necessary, both for the salvation of the baby and for Orlene's preparation to become the Incarnation of Good. She also knew that Orlene would struggle through, suffering further heartaches, until at last she achieved the fate she had never dreamed of, and had to give up her baby after all. It was a culmination Nox had crafted most carefully.

Now they went to talk with the Incarnation of Evil. Kerena, as Nox, broached him in Hell; she was of course immune to its fire and its reluctance to let any soul go. "Satan."

"Nox," he agreed. "I though your taste ran more to angels." He was of course teasing her about her affair with the Angel Gabriel, and implying that she had come to him for sexual purpose.

That was an incidental challenge. "My taste is eclectic," she said, coalescing into her lovely physical body. "What do you do for relief when Gaea is absent?" She was teasing him in turn about his affair with the Incarnation of Nature.

Lilah appeared behind him, in luscious dishabille. "What do you think, mistress of secrets?"

"What, haven't you betrayed him yet?"

"Not quite yet," the demoness agreed. The two came together and hugged. They were not friends, quite, but knew that their continuing association had benefits. Lilah was also the mistress of the Incarnation of War; she got around.

"Hey!" Satan protested, as if jealous. "Just whom did you come to seduce?"

"You, of course," Kerena said, leaving Lilah and moving into him. "I bring Jolie." Jolie had been his first love, and the two retained feelings for each other.

He was of course more than willing. But he demurred. "You don't do much for nothing, vampire vixen. What will it cost me?"

"Merely a dialogue about a deal."

"A dialogue," he agreed. "Not a deal."

"Not yet," she agreed. She turned the body over to Jolie.

Then they went at it. Satan was good at sex, having had much experience with Lilah, and Jolie had learned much in the course of her associations with Nature and Night. But the dominant passion was love. Satan was professionally the master of hate, but one of his secrets was love: a secret he knew Nox would keep.

In due course the two were satisfied. Jolie returned the body to Kerena, and Satan was ready for the dialogue. "You drive a hard bargain, you nocturnal temptation. What is your concern?"

"I want my baby." She drew Gaw-Two from her bosom, where he had slept without substance.

Satan smiled. "I think I might have guessed."

"You want to achieve power, in accordance with your deal with Gabriel, by corrupting Niobe's granddaughter Orlene. She is your last chance, and little time remains."

"She is not corruptible. Your angel lover outmaneuvered me on that deal."

"That is my hope. But I must be sure. There is one way she might be corrupted: via her ill baby. She died to follow him, and means to save him. In the course of that effort she will come to you, begging a curse. Here is the deal I proffer: you may use Orlene's baby to corrupt her, if you can, and thus achieve dominance in this realm. If you can not corrupt her, then you will support my candidate for the replacement of the Incarnation of Good."

Satan considered. "This is interesting. You will provide me my last chance for victory. If I flub it, I will promote your victory."

"Yes. As you know, I do not act directly, but only through intermediaries. I want you to be mine for this occasion."

"This may be a first: Satan as an agent for good. I am not sure I could stomach that."

"You forget I know all secrets. Yours is that you are at heart a good man."

"Damn your information!" he swore, and a ball of fire flew out of his mouth.

"You're so cute when you're mad."

"Negative passion is much the same as positive. Abate it as yourself while I ponder."

"What, me?" she asked innocently.

"You do wish me to take your deal seriously?"

She moved into him, retaining possession of the body. "Can Nature do this?" she inquired as her hands stroked him with very special expertise.

"Hoo! Not yet, I think." He reacted as he had to, and they were soon in the throes of an explosive mutual climax. It was all gaming; both of them wanted it, and both knew it. He as the male had the option of professing desire, and she as the female the option of professing avoidance. Such pretexts were no more than ornaments on a foregone commitment.

Thereafter they talked again. "Who is your nominee?"

"The same one you Tempt: Orlene."

"Hoo!" he repeated. "Fate's granddaughter, Nature's daughter, War's daughter, Time's lover, Death's lover's great niece—"

"And your lover's daughter," Kerena concluded. "Who among all of you will turn her down—if you nominate her?"

"But she is a good woman! How can I, in evil conscience, support her?"

"She is a bastard, an adulteress, a rapist, and a suicide. What more need she be, to fit your profile?"

Satan nodded. "You make a formidable case, Nox. I would love to see such ludicrous definitions of evil overthrown. I will make that deal."

Kerena was relieved. She had thought he would agree, but not been quite sure. This was not the same timeline as Jolie's, and was no longer in alignment. "Shall we shake hands on it?"

"The hell we will! We'll fuck on it."

"Oh, my," she said, with feigned reluctance. "So soon again. Such language. How can I ever endure the shame?"

Lilah burst out laughing, holding her ribs and floating. And of course they went at it again. She would have to visit Satan more often; he was a good sport.

Jolie Two took Orlene to animate a teenaged prostitute on spelled H, one of the worst of addictive drugs. This was to help Luna, who needed to save this girl for reasons relating to the welfare of the timeline, and to give Orlene a temporary living body to occupy. Thereafter the two ghosts were based in the girl name Vita, helping her escape her addiction and profession while still pursuing Orlene's mission.

Death was no easy mark. He took them to a newborn baby in a Dumpster doomed to die soon of exposure, and gave Orlene in Vita's body the power to take its soul for her purpose. Since the baby was doomed anyway, the soul was available.

And Orlene balked. She couldn't hasten the death of the innocent, help-less baby. "I can't!" she cried in anguish.

Death fixed her with his eyeless gaze. "I ask you to consider just how serious you are about your quest for your own baby," he said. "If you do not care to do what is necessary—"

"Oh, Thanatos, I would give my own soul! But I cannot sacrifice this innocent one to my purpose."

Instead she took the baby to a hospital and left it for care and adoption. She had saved the baby, to Fate's momentary annoyance as she hastily recrafted its Thread of Life. Orlene thought she had thrown away her chance, on her first test of resolve. But Death, satisfied about the quality of her conscience, agreed to obtain another clean soul for her. "I would not yield a soul to a person who did not properly appreciate its value."

So she had passed after all, because of the quality of her character, as Jolie One had known she would.

She tackled Time, Fate, War, and Nature, and these were no easier, for different reasons. Time had been her lover before assuming the Hourglass, and wanted her to return to him, even in this different body. But he lived backward, she forward, so it was not possible. An Aspect of Fate was her grandmother, but Fate was in a process of transition that complicated it. War was her natural father, but arranged to show her rather directly the nature and stress of his business. Gaea was her natural mother, but required an ugly service of her. They were all participating in her savage impromptu education.

And Satan tempted her cruelly, providing her a painful tour of Hell and offering to recover her baby for her if she cooperated with his designs. He wasn't bluffing; one of his secrets was that he always honored his deals to the letter, however deceptive that letter might be. Again she struggled, but again declined. Then she did Satan a service in return for his curse, hoping somehow to win her baby the hard way.

But with God she failed, because He did not meet with her or respond to her prayer. She could not get the Blessing.

The Incarnations voted to declare the Office of the Incarnation of Good vacated. But they could not agree on a person to take over the Office. That was when Satan, honoring his deal with Nox and his private preference, nominated Orlene, to her amazement. And Orlene became God. Unable to take Gaw Two with her, she allowed Nox to keep him, with the hard-won items obtained from the other Incarnations. Including God's Blessing, which she herself was now equipped to give. The dread Taint would be cured at last.

God, soon thereafter, sent Jolie to try to save Timeline Two. They had at last reached the present time.

"But there is a difference," the afreet said, appearing in Nox's abode. "Timeline One will survive. Timeline Two is doomed. The differences appear small at the moment, but they will steadily grow until the inevitable happens."

Kerena and Jolie knew it was true. They had run the full course, but the one change had nullified it.

"And you have come to bargain," Kerena said evenly to him. "What is your case?"

"First I must reveal my identity. I suspect you knew I was no simple demon."

"We did," Kerena agreed. "Who are you?"

"I am the Incarnation of Darkness."

They stared at him, not understanding.

Chapter 12
Erebus

"I see I must clarify," he said. "I am Erebus."

"Erebus!" Kerena exclaimed. "Nox's ancient brother!" Lilah had mentioned him, but the distractions of becoming the Incarnation of Night had put that in the background.

"The same. You are the Incarnation of Night. I am the Incarnation of Darkness. They are not identical. Rather, they are the two salient Aspects of the situation. Just as the Fate has three Aspects, we have two. Male and female."

Kerena was appalled. "I've been having sex with my brother?"

He laughed. "Indeed. And we generated all the following Incarnations, back at the dawn of timelines. We are the first siblings and lovers, parents of the rest. It wasn't as if there was much choice in partners, at the outset."

"But I traced all the existing Incarnations. I never found evidence of that one."

"You aren't the only Incarnation who can hide, sister. I was never on anybody's radar."

"Who animates your office?" Jolie asked shrewdly. "The way Kerena animates Nox."

"One of the first true men: Cain."

"Cain! Who slew his brother?"

"The same. I am good at slaying."

Kerena felt dizzy with these revelations, but she regrouped. "Why Cain?"

"As you know, when I slew my impertinent brother, who really brought it on himself, our parents were annoyed, and banished me from their land. I went and dwelt among the Children of Nod. You understand, aspects of the early history are figurative; Adam and Eve were the first officially recognized man and woman, but of course there were others, such as Lilah and Nod. They lacked recognition, but were human in all other respects. So I got me a nice obliging girl, and did all right for myself."

"That so-called girl was Lilah, your father's mistress," Jolie said.

"Lilith, then. And one sexy wench, at first," Cain agreed. "She did well, hiding her age, bearing me a number of brats, until I found a more suitable virgin. Then she had the temerity to dispatch the true child of Nod before I could enjoy her. I was annoyed."

"So you killed Lilith," Kerena said, remembering the ghost's story.

"She was a bitch. I hadn't known her identity at first. She was Nod's mistress, then pretended to be his daughter. That was a bit too unvirginal for me."

Kerena realized that the man had a case, of sorts. He had learned late that his wife was both his father's and his father-in-law's mistress too. It was also true that Lilah could be rather assertive and annoying, in her murderous manner. "I mean, why did the Office accept you? You were bad seed from the start, surely unfit for the power of an Incarnation."

"Because we share a grudge against mankind. Erebus is the dark side; he means to destroy all that Nox has wrought, and I am happy to facilitate his effort. I am perfectly fit for that."

"But Erebus is the father of the Incarnations," Jolie said. "Just as Nox is the mother. What could he have against his own children?"

"They are Nox's children, and Nox's worlds."

"But they are Erebus' children too, by definition," Kerena said.

"I see I need to be more specific," he said, as if she were being stupid. "They were not merely children, but timelines, alternate realities. Each generated multiple new lines, each of which contained all the other characters, including Nox. But not Erebus. They were her worlds."

Now, indeed, Kerena felt stupid, and so did Jolie. "Not Erebus' worlds too?"

"Not," he agreed. "She exists in all. He exists only in the original."

Kerena used her Seeing to trace this back. "Because as the mother she could make offspring, sharing her substance with them, while you were a separate entity, not a child. But you could join them by separating into many selves, as she could."

"Not the same. Selves are all parts of the one, not entities in themselves. They were intruders in realms in which they did not exist naturally."

Kerena nodded. It was true. "But this is inherent. Why should you resent it?"

"I resent being excluded. Wouldn't you?"

Again, he had a certain case. "I'm sorry."

"No need. I am taking care of it in my own fashion."

"By destroying the other timelines?" Jolie demanded.

"Yes, of course. Then we are both excluded equally."

"This reminds me of the story of the dog in the manger."

"I see it as mere fairness."

Kerena was growing angry. "All those dooms of the timelines that deviate from the original one—that is your doing?"

"Yes. Nox is the generator; I am the destroyer. Our powers are equal and opposite. The positive and negative aspects of Night."

They reflected on that. "Why didn't Erebus simply decline to contribute to those offspring timelines?"

"And miss out on all that great sex? It wasn't as if he had anywhere else to get it, back then. He wanted Nox to stifle her damned fertility, but she wouldn't. So the battle was on. It has been quite a job, canceling all those alternates. Have you any idea how many there were?"

"Theoretically an infinite number," Jolie said.

"And I have had to extend myself almost infinitely to stop them all." He smiled again, with only his mouth. "Fortunately since Nox turned human, you have not realized her full capacity, so there have been no more Incarnations generated. That simplifies things somewhat. It is much easier to clip a timeline that is a minor twig, than to prune back a branch sponsored by an Incarnation."

Kerena's feelings were dangerously mixed. "Just for the sex! That's all you came for."

"Not all," he said, amused. "I also needed to keep track of your activity, so as to catch the simpler variants that constantly spun off. Everything Nox does has the potential to make new timelines, and they must be readily curbed when caught early, as I said."

"To spy on me!"

"Of course. But you like the sex too. Shall we go at it now?"

The awful thing was that Kerena was sorely tempted. This man, this demon, this Incarnation, gave her the best sex ever, always. "But you're my brother!" she protested.

"Your brother and your lover," he agreed, touching her hand. The touch thrilled her despite her ire.

"He's your brother," Jolie told her. "He's your lover. *He's not your friend.*"

"Well spoken, ghost," Erebus said. Then, to Kerena: "And with that understanding, shall we indulge?"

Kerena was minded to refuse angrily, knowing he could not force her. But he had not yet told her what she needed to know. If she obliged him (and herself) she might have a better chance to learn what she sought. She could dazzle any ordinary man with sex; the Incarnation of Darkness was beyond that, but might still be affected. "We shall indulge," she agreed grimly.

And the sex was awfully, wonderfully, impossibly exciting and fulfilling. Erebus was indeed the match of Nox in this respect, as it seemed in others. There was even a certain frisson in the knowledge that he was her brother and perhaps enemy.

In due course they separated, sated for the moment. "You surely have more to tell me," Kerena said. "I don't expect to like it."

"Yes, I enjoy making you accept what you wish to reject. You will really hate my offer."

"She's not a mouse to be toyed with!" Jolie snapped.

Erebus affected surprise. "She isn't?"

"He's getting to you," Kerena murmured.

"And you are important to my designs, Jolie," Erebus said. "You, too, will be properly appalled."

"You are angling for me to give her the body for your next effort?" Kerena asked mischievously.

"Kerena!" Jolie was not as shocked as she pretended; they were putting on a small show to divert the man and perhaps recover control of the dialogue.

Erebus shook his head. "I would love to dally longer for your teasing, ladies, but I have other timelines to terminate and must be on my way soon. So we had better complete our present business, unless you prefer to end our discussion now."

And of course they couldn't do that. They had to know what was on his devious mind. "Speak," Kerena said.

"A bit more clarification, first. The larger universe is a comparatively grand endeavor, with several notable aspects. What concerns us at the moment is the Tree of Life."

"In the Garden of Eden," Kerena said. "We know of it."

"This is somewhat more," he said with that infuriatingly superior attitude. "It is a useful analogy for concepts otherwise too complex for distaff minds to assimilate."

He was trying to get to them again. What was most annoying was that he was succeeding. "Let's try the complex version," Kerena said, sure she would regret it.

"There are a perhaps infinite number of very large approximately parallel membranes stretched across the larger universe. They are close enough together so that sometimes two 'branes brush against each other, generating ripples of matter and energy from the point source of their contact. To the eventual residents of the region this appears to be an explosion of existence emerging from nothing: a concept they find difficult, as they believe in the continuity of matter and energy, which are actually different forms of the same thing. Regardless, the ripples continue to expand outward, generating eddy currents along the way that assume visible or invisible status. The denizens perceive only the visible, yet are dimly aware of the rest, and are frustrated by their ignorance. Therefore they devise assorted theories of relativity, quantum mechanics, string, and other fanciful explanations to mask their ignorance. In that minor segment of the visible cosmos that is suitably solid, life appears and assumes several forms. This has its own mysteries, for which alternate explanations are devised. One is evolution, which states that incredibly complicated creatures can evolve from very small variations and very large periods of time, facilitated by natural selectivity." He paused. "You follow perfectly, of course."

"Of course," Kerena echoed faintly. Both women were utterly baffled by this complicated nonsense, as he knew. "But for expedience, let's try the simple analogy of the Tree."

"For expedience," he agreed smugly. "When Chaos formed the known cosmos, he generated a giant tree. It diverged into three main branches or trunks, to accommodate the contrasting aspects of existence. One we shall call the Science trunk, whereon all things followed strict patterns of non-magical development. That is, chemicals formed and mixed and became the first primitive types of life. Life followed evolutionary principles of divergence and natural selection, with the unfit variants getting eliminated and the fit ones surviving. Continued radiations and selections eventually evolved into the entire modern panoply of funguses, plants, and animals, including human beings, the animal with a naked body and an overdeveloped brain."

Both Jolie and Kerena managed to stifle their threatened outbursts of outrage at this revolting notion. "Fascinating viewpoint," Kerena said tightly.

"Another stem we shall call the Magic trunk," Erebus continued equably. "This was created approximately six thousand years ago, complete with all creatures and plants, and mankind was put in charge. There were even large old bones buried in the ground to make it seem as if giant lizards had once walked the earth long before the present order, fooling those who did not pay sufficient attention to the holy book that spelled out the only truth. All things there are accomplished magically, and the Supreme Deity keeps a beneficent eye on the proceedings so as to better select those good souls destined for Heaven and the bad ones condemned to Hell. Yet such is the perversity of the species that bad folk still appear and prosper, and require punishment in the Afterlife."

"Of course," Kerena agreed. This description was more familiar, but did not wholly align with the real world.

"The third trunk grows between the others, and shares aspects of each," Erebus continued. "Much of it is magic, and of course there are the Incarnations of Immortality to assist it along its destined course. But there are also rogues of the Science persuasion, who build machines and perform feats of chemistry to improve their lives. The aspects of Magic and Science are thus in chronic competition, neither achieving real dominance. A person is free, for example, to travel by airplane or by magic carpet, and Hell itself advertises its advantages, such as sexual and gluttonous gratification that are of course unknown in Heaven. This is the trunk we know."

"We do," Kerena said, relieved to be back on familiar ground, as it were. "But what has this three-trunked Tree of Life analogy to do with us?"

"Everything. This is the trunk I mean to eliminate, leaving only the two extreme Science and Magic trunks."

They stared at him, not trying to conceal their dismay.

"Here is the key," he said. "If I can eliminate all the branches of this middle trunk, it will wither away, and devolve back into chaos. Then we can start over, this time with rules that favor me. Nox will be my plaything, limited to a single timeline, while Erebus will be everywhere. Ultimate power will be mine."

"Will it?" Kerena asked. "How can you be sure it won't develop similar to this one?"

"It may," Erebus agreed. "In which case I will prune it back again, and try again, and again, until I get what I want. The process may require a number of millennia, but eventually there should be something worthwhile."

"And you expect us to go along with this?"

"Not willingly."

"What, then, is your proffered bargain?"

"Ah, yes. I have pruned this trunk down essentially to a single strand. It is a sorry looking thing, compared to the fully spreading trunks on either side. But I am unable to prune the remaining central strand, because the Nox there has caught on and balks me. In fact she was the one who alerted the Incarnation of Good to the threat, causing her not only to defend her own reality, but to send an emissary to the adjacent one, in an effort to save it also."

"That's why Orlene sent me!" Jolie explained.

Kerena extended her Seeing, and verified it. "And we almost saved this one too. But for my determination to spare my friend Vanja, it would have been secure."

"Well, you are womanishly weak, understandably," he agreed contemptuously. "It took me some time to realize that I was being actively balked. There are so many timelines to handle, so similar, I assumed the self assigned to this one had overlooked it. Each self handled several timelines, so that's understandable. So I diverted it again, and later discovered that too had been balked. Finally I investigated more directly, and discovered the interference of the ghost. That was a surprise, as normally individuals can't cross between timelines."

"How is it than you can, then?" Jolie asked.

"Because there are no other Erebuses there. The presence of a home-grown self prevents another from entering. Nox can't cross, for example."

"But I did," Jolie said.

"There was no Jolie there, as you crossed before your self in this second timeline existed."

"But I remained to see myself come into existence, and to become a ghost again. In fact I facilitated it by holding to the alignment."

"Yes. That was what I overlooked. It seems that a ghost doesn't count, at least not as much. You crossed to where you did not exist, then remained, and the presence of the new Jolie was not enough to drive you out. It might have prevented you from crossing to your own time, but your inertia held you here. So I did not suspect until later, and then I thought you were a local ghost. I was a fool."

Was that an invitation for them to gloat? Neither trusted it. "So we have learned of a partial exception," Kerena said. "Evidently Nox in T1 knew, though."

"She put it by me," he agreed. "All our trysts, and she never let on."

"You trysted with her too?" Kerena asked, not wholly pleased.

"Of course. Consider your alignment: how could I have done otherwise, without fudging the lines?"

"And you were trysting with all the other Noxes. That's why you came to me so rarely."

"Correct. That has been the one advantage of being the only male Erebus on this trunk."

"But now that we are down to so few branches, there are only me and the Nox of T1. That's why you have come more often recently."

"Exactly," he said, not at all embarrassed.

Kerena had had enough. "What is your deal?"

"First we must establish the parameters. Nox can not save any timeline but the first; all others are doomed. I can not eliminate that one, because of the active opposition of that one's Nox. So we are at impasse. I need your cooperation to eliminate T1."

Kerena smiled, emulating his mouth-only expression. "I am the Nox of doomed T2. I can't help you there."

"But you are very like the Nox of T1, by no particular coincidence. In fact you are almost identical. What persuades you will persuade her."

"I am in no mood to be persuaded to doom the final timeline."

He looked at her, springing his trap. "But if you had the chance to save T2, and perhaps others? As you may, with my cooperation."

Kerena felt a shiver of excitement. "How?"

"We make a double or nothing deal. Both timelines, or neither."

Kerena worked it out. "You would make this deal in order to get at T1 and make your victory complete, abolishing the last live branch of the central Tree. I would make the deal in order to save T2 and whatever other timelines remain."

"If T2 is saved, it would in turn act to save T3," he said. "By sending its ghost Jolie there to its past to make it align, and so on for T4, T5, and on. The process would be unstoppable, and the entire original foliage would recover."

"All or nothing," Jolie said. "These are fair stakes."

"How would the issue be settled?" Kerena asked suspiciously.

"A contest between the two of us. The winner takes the timeline."

"Between you and Nox1," Kerena said.

"Actually, no. Nox1 will not compete. She needs to remain in place to enforce compliance. You, who are otherwise doomed, will compete."

"Why would she honor that?"

"Because you would. She trusts you."

Kerena's head was spinning. "Why would *you* trust her?"

"We are both masters of deceit, but we can't deceive each other. We are the two Aspects of Night. The winner will in effect incorporate the other, preventing any further resistance. It will be a fair contest, and the decision will be honored."

"But if I contest with you and win, what does it matter whether I merge with you, making you part of me? I am bound to this timeline."

"Not if you win. You will assume my power of crossing, being twice what you were. You will then cross and merge with your other selves. There will be a single Nox governing the whole. Your victory will be complete."

"As will yours, if you win."

"Exactly."

"I am interested," Kerena said. "But I doubt it is a decision I can make alone, or my sister self in T1 can make. When the new Incarnation of Good was chosen, all the other Incarnations and a mortal woman participated. They would have to be consulted again."

"And Ghost Jolie will return to T1 and make the case," he said. "As she did when proposing Orlene to be God."

"I hardly feel qualified," Jolie said.

"You will cross back and consult with Nox1, who will convene the Incarnations. I will be there, but of course they will not trust me. You are the one who has been on this scene, here in T2. You will make the case."

Jolie saw it. "They may not agree."

Erebus shrugged. "Then the impasse remains, and T1 will be the only survivor."

"Shouldn't the Incarnations of T2 have some say?" Kerena asked.

"They're irrelevant," Erebus said. "They have no way to alleviate their doom. Only those of T1 count for this."

That seemed to be true, unkind as it was. But now Jolie remembered something. "There is a thing Nox1 wants from you, Erebus."

"She can tell me that herself, next time I visit her."

"No, because Nox2 must implement it."

"A message from my other self?" Kerena asked, surprised.

"In a manner. She has cured Gaw Two—that is, her baby in that timeline—and wants an Office for him. Only you can enable her to generate that Office."

"She wants her son to be an Incarnation, as of old," Erebus said. "It is true that she can't generate that from copulation with a mere mortal. Why does she think I would cooperate in that, since it would only complicate my elimination of the resulting chain of new timelines?"

"Not just for the sake of the sex," Jolie said. "As a condition of the contest."

Erebus visibly took stock. "She knew it would come to this when she sent you?"

"She saw you coming," Jolie agreed. "In more than one sense."

"And she knew it would at last come to this," Kerena said, seeing it. "As I would have known, had I kept the timeline aligned."

"It won't make any difference, if I win," Erebus said. "That Incarnation will be doomed along with the others."

"It will make a difference to me if I win," Kerena said.

He considered. "What Incarnation?"

"Dreams," Kerena answered.

Jolie saw the nicety of it. Kerena had dreamed for centuries of saving her tainted baby. Now he could become the Incarnation of Dreams.

"The contest can occur only if the Incarnations of T1 agree," Erebus said.

"And if I agree," Kerena said. "This is my separate price." She agreed completely with her other's self's notion.

"Let's have another bout of sex before I decide."

Kerena reined in her burgeoning desire. "Decide before the sex, because it will generate the Office."

"No. You don't get the Office unless you agree to the contest. I finally learned how to stifle the generative aspect of the interaction."

"Free sex now, Office sex for the contest."

"A sexual contest!" he agreed, delighted.

"We shall have to work out the details."

"Between clasps," he agreed.

"Go make the case," Kerena told Jolie. "Return with their answer. Assuming you can return, with a Jolie now here at T2."

"She can," Erebus said. "As a ghost with an established bridge."

The two Incarnations of Night and Darkness came eagerly together as Jolie crossed back to T1. She envied them their phenomenal sexual interest and ability. They were indeed well matched.

There was only a kind of flicker as the timelines changed. Then she was with Nox1, who was having sex with Erebus. Had she made it across?"

"Yes, this is T1," Nox told her. "This is an alternate self of Erebus, aligning the timelines."

"And I know all that my other self knows," Erebus said, without pausing in his effort.

"But I do not," Nox said, not abating her own effort. "So in a moment you will acquaint me with it, as I do not trust my brother."

Which was perhaps an incidental irony: Nox was enthusiastically indulging in sex with a man she couldn't afford to trust. The mistress of secrets could not directly fathom the major one required.

They concluded their bout, with Jolie participating by sharing Kerena's sensations. Then Erebus faded out.

Jolie acquainted Kerena with the situation. "So Erebus proffers a contest between himself and Nox2 to decide the issue. Nox2 has agreed, provided he enable her to generate the Office of the Incarnation of Dreams for Gaw Two to assume. But the final decision must be made by the informed Incarnations of T1."

"Of course," Kerena1 agreed. "We'll convene them now."

"You can convene them on your whim?"

"Nox's whims have force."

The floor became a soft, firm white quilt. No, it was cloud stuff, except that it was solid enough to stand on, slightly spongy. Nox sat on a glittering dark stone throne, shrouded by the starry Cloak of Night. Arranged in a circle before her were several other thrones of different hues, iridescent in the soft sunlight from above. On each throne an Incarnation sat: Death, Time, Fate, War, Nature, Evil, and Good, each appropriately garbed. Jolie knew them all, but had never before seen them all together in their official splendor.

The Angel Gabriel stood beside God's throne, and assorted lesser Incarnations and assistants stood by the thrones of the others. This was truly a complete gathering.

Orlene, the Incarnation of Good, spoke first. "Nox, the mother of all our Offices, mistress of secrets, became aware of a secret that concerns us: there are many alternate timelines, each a reality similar in some degree to our own. But most of the others have been destroyed. I asked the ghost Jolie to undertake a special mission: to align the adjacent timeline with ours. In this manner we hoped to save it from the doom that otherwise threatened, and perhaps initiate a chain reaction that would save many others. Unfortunately the situation is worse that we supposed, and that timeline, too, is doomed. Nox will explain."

Nox nodded. "I defer to Jolie, who was on the scene. Jolie, tell them of Erebus and his offer. Be complete; time is suspended." She nodded toward Chronos, whose shining Hourglass glowed.

Suddenly Jolie was the cynosure. For a moment she quailed, then rallied. She described her excursion to T2, her long association with Kerena, the manner Kerena had influenced the placements of all the other Incarnations, the discovery of Erebus, and his concluding offer. "It seems that this is Timeline One, the original, that Erebus can't destroy directly without our acquiescence," she concluded. "We must decide whether to accept his offer, in the hope of recovering the other timelines, at the risk of our own."

Orlene glanced at Nox's throne. "Erebus. We grant you no vote here, but has the case been fairly presented?"

Erebus appeared beside the throne of Night. "Aye." He faded. Jolie was surprised; he had said he would be present, but she had for the moment forgotten. He really could, as he claimed, hide even from Incarnations.

Orlene glanced around, then spoke. "We will have a chain of votes, until we reach consensus. Do we accept Erebus's offer? Thanatos."

Death spoke. "This risks not the mere death of individuals, whose souls are preserved, but our reality itself. That is too much. Nay."

"Chronos."

"This is not a manipulation of time, but the possible destruction of time itself. Nay."

"Clotho, Lachesis, Atropos."

Niobe, the central aspect of Fate, spoke. "This risks Fate itself, destroying the entire tapestry. We are agreed: nay."

"Mars."

"There can be no War if there is no cosmos. Nay."

"Gaea."

Orb spoke. "Nature prefers to leave nothing to pure chance. Nay."

"Satan."

"Hell is a better risk than nonexistence. Nay."

"God," Orlene said, calling on her own office. "Heaven, too, is better than nonexistence. Nay." She looked at Kerena. "Nox." The Incarnation of Night had not participated directly in the vote for the new God, but was this time.

Kerena spoke. "Aye." She glanced at Jolie. "Speak to my case."

Again, Jolie was caught by surprise. The vote was seven to one against accepting the offer, and she was supposed to argue for the one? How could she even attempt it?

The eight Incarnations gazed silently at her. They seemed neither concerned nor impatient.

Then it came together. Jolie asked a question of her own: "Are we to be safe and selfish?"

Satan shook his head. "Trust my ancient beloved to find the key. What point safety, if we are heedless of the welfare of others? This is not the kind of evil I advocate; there is no justice in it, no redemption. I reverse: Aye."

"I am shamed," Gaea said. "I would not doom my alternate selves for my own benefit. Aye."

"I, too, am shamed," Orlene said. "I gave up my life for my child. Will I not risk it for the universe as we now know it, the Tree? Aye."

The Death figure spoke. "I once asked Orlene to consider how seriously she viewed her mission. She refused to take the selfish route, and thereby gained her objective that she thought lost. How can I do otherwise? Aye."

"One timeline risked," Chronos said. "A myriad to be gained, though I will not see them. Aye."

"We of Fate, too, reconsider," Niobe said. "I owe my position, ultimately, to Nox. We prefer to join her. Aye."

"And there will be war," Mars said. "Between the two Aspects of the Incarnation of Night. Given fair rules of engagement, Aye."

"We accept the offer," Orlene said without other comment. "Now we will negotiate for the rules of engagement."

☙❧

The rules of engagement were weird. Someone, probably Satan with Lilah's advice, had invented a new competition to fit the need, simple but tricky. Erebus and Nox met in a dream, in free-fall, floating in a misty environment, naked. The surrounding fog alternated at irregular intervals averaging three minutes between blue and pink. Blue was Erebus's color, favoring him, the male; pink favored female Nox. The object was to have the sex required to fertilize her with the Incarnation of Dreams in a chosen environment. If it occurred in blue fog, Erebus won; in pink fog, Nox won. They had merely to keep their eyes out for the color, and seek the act in the right one.

Each of them had loops affixed to their hands and feet. Her pink loops would immobilize any part of his body they encircled, from the point of contact to the end. If she looped his neck, all of his body would lose volition, making him helpless. The paralysis would last one minute, then abate, and the loop would need to rest for a minute before its power was restored. So it was not a contest of strength so much as timing and dexterity. She needed to immobilize him in pink fog, make the connection, and hold it for one minute. He needed to do the same to her in blue.

The problem was that they could never be sure how long a color would hold. It might be six minutes or ten seconds, randomly generated. The three minute average was only a crude guideline. A perfect hold would be wasted if the color changed. Chance was a major factor. In this dream state they had no powers of phasing out or checking the future; it was all blindly ongoing. No database or advice from the sideline. They were purely now and physical, Kerena and Cain. For as long as it took.

Because the game was newly devised, they had no experience with it. That made it even, in that sense. Neither of them had been playing entertainment games in the past millennium; their games had been all business, seeking advantage or accomplishment.

The fog was pink. Kerena stalked Cain, finding that she was able to move in the direction she wished despite having no firm ground. She swung her loops to get the proper feel of them; they were flexible and controlled by her will. She looped his left wrist, but at the same time he looped her unguarded left wrist. Her hand went numb. She threw herself back, to withdraw her hand by hauling it clear with the rest of her body, but the loop had closed firmly. Meanwhile he did escape her loop, which she had failed to tighten. A pox on the initial learning curve!

Cain looped her right arm at the elbow, and pulled it tight. Now she could not escape. He held her before him, his member erect; he was quite ready for sex. But it was not his time, while the fog remained pink.

Then the fog changed to blue, fading to neutral in the course of five seconds, and taking the new color in another five. Now Cain had her by hand and arm, and it was his turn. He hauled her in, angling for entry.

But her legs were free. She lifted them and set her feet against his hips, holding him out from her body. He pushed forward but was balked. He could not penetrate her while her feet were free. Then he twisted to the side, and her feet slid off, allowing him to get his body close to hers. He grinned, savoring his victory.

Her left hand recovered its feeling. The minute was up; the loop's effect had worn off. Quickly she slipped it free and looped his right hand, reversing the hold. Her right arm followed, recovering. But he caught on, and whipped his hand and loop away. She had the advantage, but not enough, and the fog remained blue.

By the time the fog was pink again, her loop had lost its effect and Cain was free. But they had both learned things. Looping hands or arms was not enough; the legs had to be immobilized too, and at the right time. Better yet, loop the neck, and have the whole body vulnerable; then there could be no counter-attack. For a minute, at least. Longer, if one neck-loop could be switched for another after a minute. Loop time management could be critical.

She looped one of his feet, but he looped one of her arms again, and the position was indeterminate. He couldn't pin her during his color, and she couldn't pin him during hers. They were evenly matched, in their inexperience, as physical strength counted for little. Both protected their heads, and while one tried to loop one limb, the other went for another limb. At one point she looped his right arm with her left foot-loop, and his left arm with her right hand loop, and the color was hers, but the position was too awkward to manage. She couldn't do anything with one foot held up against his elbow and his lower body free to swing away. Then her loops lost strength, and he reversed it and pressed in close to her as the color changed. But the color changed again in thirty seconds, forcing him to stop, and soon his loops lost effect.

She realized that more was required than mere sparring. She needed a larger strategy. How could she succeed in immobilizing him at just the right time? The chances were close to even that the color would change, giving him the advantage at just the wrong time.

Cain formed a huge foot loop and whipped it at her leg. She countered by snapping her legs together so that one could not be caught. That turned out to be disaster; the loop circled both legs and tightened about her waist. Suddenly all of her body below the waist lost volition. He bent his knee and came close as her powerless legs drifted apart. The fog was blue.

"Now take it, loser," he said. His form became that of a gorilla. He intended to make it clear that she was being ravished.

Kerena was so surprised that she forgot to resist for a moment, and he looped one of her hands. He could change form? No, as he touched her she realized that it was illusion. She countered by assuming the seeming of a crocodile, snapping at his face with her long toothy snout. That made him jerk back, before he realized that this, too, was illusion.

Then the loops lost power, and she was free. The one remained about her waist but had no further effect; he would have to remove it to let it recover. She tried to keep tension on it so he couldn't get it off her, but it foiled her and fell away. Meanwhile she went for his head. He blocked that with his arm, and the loop slid aside. The color changed to pink. They were even again.

But that gave her an idea. Cain didn't merely want to win, he wanted to win with style. To make her suffer worse by being seemingly ravished by a monster. That could be a dangerous distraction on his part.

She sparred, foiling him and being foiled by him. She tried a kick at his groin, but her foot shied away; that kind of combat was not allowed. He was similarly unable to strike at her breasts or pull her hair. The loops were the only physical weapons.

She would have to gamble horrendously, but if she had figured him correctly, it would give her a better than even chance of winning. That was the edge she needed.

She came at him during the blue fog, focusing on both his arms together. She got one, but missed the other, and that gave him an opening. He lifted his free hand and dropped its loop over her head. It became snug, and her entire body became inert.

"Fool!" he said. He assumed the form of a bear, pulled her close, and penetrated her unresisting body.

Only her head was free. She screamed piercingly. "No! No!" She whipped her head about, causing her hair to flair.

"Scream. Struggle," he said approvingly. He brought his seeming snout down for a kiss. But he did not forget what counted: he was holding the nether connection for the minute required.

"No! Please!" she cried, trying to avoid his cruel kiss. Her face was the only part of her capable of resisting his embrace.

"Delightful," he said. "I think I like you better this way, hating your loss." He tried again for a kiss.

This time she met him, kissing him back. That surprised him, but he held it, enjoying it. He didn't know what ploy she could be trying, but refused to be distracted from the vital action below.

At last he lifted his head, savoring his victory. "I think the minute has passed." Then he froze: the fog was pink. "How long—?"

"Thirty seconds," she said. "You did not complete your minute. Now you're on mine."

He tried to jerk away—and discovered that not only had the color changed, his loop had lost its potency. She had quietly looped his arms and wrapped her legs around his hips. He struggled, but could not escape. In this setting her strength matched his. She held him as the next thirty seconds passed, bringing her to the completion of her minute. Connected and in pink.

He had been distracted trying to torture her, and not seen the color change in time. She had continued crying past the resumption of her freedom, as if remaining caught. She had deceived him. And won.

"Damn," he said.

"Come into me, Erebus," she said as her powers recovered beyond the dream. She sucked him into her, like a reverse birth, making him part of her body. She became the whole of Night and Darkness.

Then she birthed the baby he had become, for there were no human delays with the Incarnations. She squeezed him out: the Incarnation of Dreams. She had accomplished the rest of her mission.

The dream framework dissolved. Nox was back in her own chamber, with the baby. Jolie was there, amazed. "Tell them I won," she said. "All of us won."

It was an elaborate hall, decorated for a party. Kerena was in a translucent evening gown, her hair loose and half floating. She looked devastatingly lovely.

Jolie was in a gown too, looking her best. Perhaps slightly better than her best in life. "Where are we?"

"In Erebus," Kerena said.

"But I thought you absorbed him."

"I did, and birthed his substance as the Incarnation of Dreams. Then I locked him into a region between the mortal realm and Hades. He has become Erebus the place."

"But isn't that dangerous? Suppose he locks us in?"

"He can't. I deprived him of that power. But it hardly matters; this is not the literal place, but a communal dream recreation of it. I needed an ambiance that anyone can visit, for this special party."

"Party?"

"To celebrate the salvation of my timeline—and all the others. It has been a long and sometimes difficult chore, as you know."

Jolie studied the hall. "It is a very well appointed dream. But where is it? I mean, in which timeline?"

"In no specific timeline, because some guests will be from the first, some from the second. Most can't cross, but the dream has no such restriction."

"Guests?"

"They will be arriving soon. Most are from T1, as are you. But I am from T2, and a few others. There will be no problem."

"No problem," Jolie agreed uncertainly.

A handsome young man appeared. He reminded Jolie strongly of Sir Gawain of old. "Thank you, Jolie."

"Meet Gaw Two, in his adult form," Kerena said. "He crafted this dream, of course."

Music started. "Will you honor me with the first dance, Grandmother?"

"By all means." The two danced, perfectly, an extraordinarily handsome couple. Mother and son, grandson, great grandson on through the centuries, at last reunited, he cured and eternal as an Incarnation.

A man appeared. "May I cut in?"

"Of course, Morely." And as Kerena entered his embrace, Jolie saw that it was true. Her first lover had returned. That was an advantage of a dream setting: life and death no longer mattered. Morely had spent some time in Purgatory but finally made it to Heaven, and of course his soul had been released for this occasion.

"I always knew you had promise," Morely told her. "Now you have saved the central trunk of the Tree of Life."

Gaw Two turned to Jolie with a flourish. They danced, and he was the perfect partner. Jolie smiled. "I knew you when you were a baby," she said. "More than once."

"I am the culmination of fifteen hundred years of babies," he agreed. "Grandmother, bless her, simply would not give over until she had restored me."

"Well, she loves you."

They finished the dance and went to sit on the sideline. "Mother has an impressive guest list," he remarked. Mother was Orlene, the Incarnation of Good, who had fought as hard to save him in her way as Kerena had in hers. She had coordinated with Nox to set this up.

A pretty young woman appeared. "Molly!" Kerena cried, hurrying to embrace her old young friend.

"Congratulations on saving the timeline. Lovely party."

"Would you object if I invited Morgan le Fey also?"

Molly paused. "I never achieved vengeance against her."

"This would not be for that purpose. I am inviting those who had significance in my life or career."

Molly shrugged. "It's your party."

Morgan le Fey appeared, also eloquently garbed. "Thank you, dear," she said to Molly.

"You put a curse on me! Before I was even born."

"And have you never cursed innocents?" the Fey inquired. "Those you spoke to on the streets of Kilvarough, doomed to die soon?" She turned to Kerena. "I was correct. You had too much potential to remain with me."

"I did learn much from you," Kerena said.

"Of course."

"Not all of it was true."

"Of course. Have you never deceived others in the line of business?" And of course Nox was the mistress of secrets and deception, and was guilty.

Morely approached. "Fey, you are a fascinating sociopath."

"Of course." She moved into his arms for the next dance, her décolletage drifting artfully downward. She had put on her most seductive figure for this occasion.

Molly shook her head. "She has grace and nerve, but I don't want to be like her, even in death."

"You will never be like her," Kerena said.

The original Sir Gawain appeared. "I would have married you if I could have," he said, embracing Kerena.

"I know it." She kissed him. "I finally saved our son."

"So I see." He kissed her again. "Oh, Rena, I wish we could—"

"We can," she said. "Take over as hostess, Jolie." The two faded out.

Jolie nodded to herself. So this was to be that kind of a party. But there could be complications.

Vanja appeared. "Kerena sends you this," Jolie said, hugging her. "And wants you to know that Morely is yours, for the moment."

"Ah, delight!" She turned, caught Morely's eye, and the two faded from their separate locations, leaving the Fey without a dancing partner. It seemed the dream had many chambers.

Lilah appeared. She looked surprised. "I'm on the guest list?"

"It includes all those who had significance in her life or career. You helped her handle Lucifer."

"I did," Lilah agreed. "Because I fell in love with his successor. Now if only—"

Satan appeared. "I see Nox is busy at the moment, so you will have to do, demoness."

"I'm second to her?" she demanded.

"Third. My true love is Gaea, but I don't find her here."

Lilah was outraged. "Parry, I refuse—"

"Refuse what? You're War's concubine now. You can hardly object to being second when you yourself are straying."

"Well, you were going to destroy me for failing to corrupt War."

"I was angry. But later I remembered how sexy you can be when you try, and forgave you in my fashion."

"So I discovered subsequently. Many times. Your fashion is certainly virile. But being third is beneath my station, and I don't belong to you any more."

"But you do still love me."

"That's irrelevant. You never loved me. I was just your sex slave."

"An excellent one," he agreed.

"I'm not sorry I got back at you for heartlessly using me." The demoness evidently enjoyed playing the wronged maiden.

"I am after all the Incarnation of Evil." He glanced sidelong at her. "You got back at me by not corrupting War?"

"That, too. I also told Thanatos that you had never released a soul from Hell."

"I released five souls in the fourteenth century."

"I know. It was a wonderful lie. Thanatos believed it and told Nox, and she put it in the database, thus also the Purgatory Computer, so everyone believed you never released souls."

"You lied about the Father of Lies!"

"My supreme achievement," Lilah agreed. "So as I said, I refuse to oblige your selfish carnal passion again. In fact I refuse—"

He caught her and kissed her.

"To wait any longer," she finished, and the two faded out. The game could play out only so long.

Kermit appeared, from his future science timeline. "Kerena welcomes you," Jolie said. "But she is busy at the moment. However, Molly is here, in her own form."

"You're still such a handsome man," Molly said, stepping into him. They faded.

Fate appeared, in the Aspect of Lachesis. "Welcome, Niobe!" Jolie said. "Nox is—"

"She was always more physical than I was," Niobe said. "And more mysterious. I am here for the party." Soon she was mixing with the guests who remained in the scene.

Gaea appeared. "Welcome, Orb!" Jolie said. "I'm so glad you could join the party. This is Gaw Two grown, and Morgan le Fey, and of course you know your mother Niobe."

But Orb had something else on her mind at the moment. "Where is Parry?"

The Fey smiled cruelly. "With the erotic demoness, of course, who wasn't his second choice. They interact marvelously."

That was the connection Jolie had sought to conceal. Naturally the evil sorceress had clarified it, in a misleading manner.

There was a rumble of not-very-distant thunder. "Oh?"

Orlene appeared. "Please, Mother, don't make a scene. You know how tangled our relationships are."

"Yes, daughter," Niobe said. "It ill behooves Nature to go awry."

Orb sighed. "It seems Nature must give way to the Incarnations of Good and Fate." She hugged both. "It is good to see you both, informally."

Gabriel appeared. "Am I late?"

"Not at all, Angel," the Fey said. "I'm sure Nox will join you when she finishes with the knight."

Orlene turned to Gabriel, frowning. "What is your interest in Nox?"

He was taken aback. "Um—"

Then they couldn't hold it back any longer. They all laughed. Of course all the Incarnations and their associates knew who related to whom in what ways; the mischievous Purgatory Computer was quite current, naturally. Tolerance was endemic.

Gaw Two approached the Fey. "Naturally I have no idea what the humor is, having grown up in the past hour, but I suspect you have interesting explanations. Shall we dance?"

"I shall be happy to enhance your imagination," the Fey said, stepping rather too closely into his embrace as her gown threatened to fall apart at strategic seams. "Have you encountered dirty dancing yet?"

"The distaff hound!" Gabriel swore. "She will never be admitted to Heaven."

"Considering that she is on temporary leave from Hell," Jolie said, "that seems likely."

"I must say, it's an interesting dance," Gabriel said, observing closely.

"I am familiar with it," Jolie said. "Would you like a demonstration?"

He nodded. "Of course you would be conversant, Bride of Satan. Yes, I would." He took her hand as they moved onto the dance floor.

"This is the first time I have embraced you in my own likeness," Jolie said as she moved in close to demonstrate the moves. "Always before I have been with Kerena."

"You are interesting in your own right. We certainly appreciate what you have done for the second timeline." He was rapidly catching on to the moves.

Was he suggesting a tryst? He was, as she knew from prior observation, considerably male beneath the extreme caution his position in Heaven required. Jolie was definitely interested. "The dance merely emulates movements better performed without clothing."

"Why settle for mere emulation?"

Then the other dancing couple faded out. Fate, Nature, and Good stared, aghast.

"Damn," Jolie murmured, seeing opportunity lost.

"I could not have said it," Gabriel said. "Thank you."

"I believe it is time to call the meeting to order," Orlene said grimly. "Gabriel?"

The naughty side of the dream had definitely been aborted. "Of course," Gabriel agreed regretfully. He was ever the loyal and efficient right hand of God. He disengaged from Jolie's torso and clapped his hands.

Suddenly all fifteen at the party were present, seated in the meeting hall that the dance hall had become. Several looked somewhat surprised and disheveled. Gaw Two seemed amazed and the Fey angry; Orlene had evidently acted in time to preserve a bit of her child's innocence. Parry and Orb now sat blithely together and Lilah was in a waitress' uniform, serving refreshments. Things had been firmly set in order.

"May I introduce the Incarnation of Night," Gabriel said smoothly. "Nox, the mistress of this particular dream."

"Thank you, Angel," Kerena said. She had evidently had the time she needed to complete her business with Sir Gawain and put herself back in order. Probably she had peeked ahead along the timeline and made sure of it. "We have secured the first and second timelines. It was easy to do once Erebus was vanquished."

"That's something I don't understand," Vanja said. "Timeline Two was doomed, because you saved me instead of aligning it to Timeline One. How did that change?"

"I can answer that," Morely said. "The default is the original timeline. It is always easier to make it conform than to change it. That is why Jolie was able to keep the lines straight; Erebus could not make his changes hold as long as Nox supported alignment. But once she accepted a deviation, that became the primary course, and she could not subsequently revise it without his acquiescence. Since he was determined to channel it into destruction, only his elimination enabled her to save it. She made the necessary changes, and it is now no longer doomed."

"But it isn't identical," Vanja said. "I died in the original, and lived in the second."

"There are many routes to salvation," Niobe said. "The timelines don't have to be identical any more. Identity was the only way to be sure of saving Timeline Two while Erebus was trying to steer it wrong. Now we have more freedom."

"But there is still a considerable job to do," Kerena said. "We have secured two, but there is an infinite number of others that are doomed unless they too are revised to eliminate the deviations Erebus caused. There will have to be a knowledgeable emissary from T2 to attend to T3, and thereafter from T3 to T4 and so on, as we discussed before."

Jolie had almost forgotten that. "I will do it, of course. Or my T2 self will."

Orlene nodded approvingly. "We certainly appreciate it. Go with our Blessing."

✐▪▰

It was the time of a great king who ruled from a shining city. In a small village in this kingdom was a family with two daughters. Jolie Two searched for the younger daughter. She had a mission to accomplish.

A great central tree had been trimmed of most of its branches. Now they were reappearing, one by one. In time and space, with diligence and conscience, it would be restored.

Author's Note

The Incarnations of Immortality series started with Death. Not merely the novel; my concern with the subject. I am, by my definition, mildly depressive, and I think about death a lot. So finally I made something of it, and wrote *On a Pale Horse*, a novel featuring Death as the central character. It has a story, of course, but the essence of it was the thoughts along the way, touching on various aspects of death. My breakthrough was in devising death as an office rather than merely a role, so that an ordinary person could step into it. Once I had that concept, I realized it was possible to go onto other key aspects of existence: Time, Fate, War, Nature, Evil, and Good.

Originally I planned to stop at five novels, because I thought readers would consider it unacceptable to address Satan and God fictively. But as reader responses came in, I found no such concern, so I decided to complete the roster. Thus I added two more, and that completed the series, I thought. But readers didn't want to let it go. They urged me to write more, tackling the minor Incarnations, perhaps with a collection of stories, or a novel about Nox, the Incarnation of Night. I demurred, because I felt that after God anything else would be anticlimactic. It would require considerable effort to review the complicated novels and get forgotten elements straight, and the effort might not be appreciated anyway. Thus it continued for about 15 years.

Then two things happened. I learned of a chronology a reader, "Phoenix," had made for the series. He had worked out the dates of events from clues in the novels and put it all together as consistently as was feasible. That timeline is available on the Internet: http://www.spundreams.net/~phoenix/IoIChron.html. This did much of my homework for me; instead of having to do copious rereading and note-taking, I could use this as an excellent starting point. The other was a long letter from Stephen Smith, who not only suggested Nox, but had three pages of summary for the novel he proposed, *Under a Velvet Cloak*. I considered that, and concluded that it was feasible: it would indeed make a novel.

So I queried my readers via my bimonthly column at my http://www.hipiers.com website. What about it: did they favor or disfavor such a project? The vote was overwhelmingly positive: they favored it. Accordingly

I decided to write the novel, and worry about marketing it later.

One contributing factor was that at this time there was a motion picture option on the first novel in the series, with Disney working on it. A movie would probably increase the market for a new novel, making it more likely that my effort would not be wasted: I would be able to find a publisher. Many readers think that a successful author can sell anything he writes; that's not the case. The market is highly competitive, and the dubious judgment of editors is notorious. I had a number of unsold novels that I was marketing or self publishing, and they're not stinkers. I wanted them to be available for reading, one way or another. So this movie option made a difference.

An option doesn't necessarily mean there will be a movie; it is in essence a reservation placed on the book for a year or more while the option holder explores the prospects: screenplay, financing, location, studio, suitable actors, prospective audience, and related aspects. If everything falls into place, the option is exercised and the movie made. They don't want to do all that work only to discover that in the interim someone else has grabbed it for a movie. The option guarantees that such a thing can't happen. They pay for the option, and if they don't make the movie, the author keeps the option money. Options are free cash for writers. Exercised options are barrels of money for the authors. Sure, they may change things all around, perhaps ruining it, but the average writer needs the money. That's why the standard advice is to take the money and run.

Thus early in 2004 I started writing, following Stephen Smith's summary. This is the only time I have done this: writing a novel based on a summary by a reader. His thoughts were not always mine, and increasingly as I went I added elements of my own, finally leaving the summary and going entirely on my own. So in general the first part of the novel is as conceived by him, and the last part is mine. But the novel would not have come to be at all without his summary.

Stephen had analyzed the first seven volumes of the series, and used logic, interpolation, extrapolation, intuition, and imagination to fill in the blanks. "I think now is the appropriate time for this story to be revealed," he said. But a story based on a careful study of a series is necessarily derivative, and despite the claims of critics, that's not the kind of thing I write. I needed a story that fit the existing parameters but was not merely a restatement of familiar themes. I needed to widen the compass, including novelty and new perspective, without departing too far from the original framework. It is an ongoing judgment call for series writing. So there are aspects that are neither in the summary nor the prior novels, such as the multiple Timelines of the Tree of Life. This is part of the creative process for such a project.

I did spot research to buttress my references, and this got into aspects of the Arthurian legend to get Morgan le Fey and Sir Gawain straight. In the process I realized what a tangled skein those legends are. For example, King Arthur's wife Guinevere falls in love with his chief knight Sir Lancelot. That forbidden love aspect is found in other knights and in variants of the same ones, depending on who is retelling the tale. In one version, Lancelot is loved by two women, both named Elaine. In another it is Tristan with two Iseults, one the wife of the king he serves. I tried to steer generally clear of the main legend, catching it peripherally, as this novel is about Nox, not Arthur.

Another reader, Tim Bruening, was at this time reading my series and sending me up to three emails a day asking awkward questions. Some were about this series. In *On a Pale Horse*, Chronos mentions Adolf Hitler, but in *For Love of Evil* Chronos eliminates the Nazi Holocaust. "How can he do that without eliminating Hitler as leader of the Axis?" I answered that Hitler may have been diverted, so didn't get around to the Jewish pogrom. He asked how come Luna's hair ranged from bright chestnut to dull brown in different novels. I answered that Luna's natural hair was honey blonde; she dyed it to fool Satan, and must have used different dyes at different times that didn't quite match. In *Bearing an Hourglass*, magic has a range of about one Earth diameter, so how could a magic-powered saucer fly to the moon? I answered that magic, like gravity, surely faded gradually with distance; the original figure would have been an approximation for full-effect magic, not the ultimate limit.

A simpler explanation would be that in the course of seven complicated novels, the author lost track of some details. They were written before the days of the personal computer, so I couldn't do a Find to verify prior references. In fact they were written in pencil, then typed for sending to the agent and publisher. I considered trying to address such questions in this 8th novel, but concluded that one omnibus answer would have to do: there are many timelines, differing from each other in slight or significant manner, so that just about every possible combination of human event, science/magic effect, or hair color is to be found somewhere. The Incarnations have superior powers, and may catch glimpses of alternate timelines, accounting for stray references. Meanwhile I made sure to get Tim's feedback on this present novel, and try to correct errors before they appear in print.

Fantasy is generally low-research writing, but this novel required a lot of background thought and some spot research. A decade back Patricia Telesco sent me her book *Folkways—Reclaiming the Magic & Wisdom*. I saved it for future research, and used it for some of the folk wisdom and belief Kerena learned from Morely. Of course there's a great deal more in the volume than the tidbits I used. It really pays to have the right reference at the right time.

I also had an idea I wanted to use somewhere: the virtual computer, projected from a tiny cube, with the virtual parts such as screen and keyboard working in the normal manner. I was watching a movie in a theater when it abruptly jelled: that would fit in this science/magic framework. That was actually the point when I decided to write the novel; it tipped the balance. So that computer is there, concealed as Nox's coin, and I hope that before too long something like it exists in our own realm. True convenience: carry it in your pocket or on your wrist, expand it by virtual projection when you need to use it while traveling, eating, taking a bath, in bed or wherever. Almost like magic.

In each of the prior novels of this series, the events of my life seemed to echo the subjects of the novels. Was that the case with this one, tackled fifteen years later? I'm not sure, but perhaps I can make a case. By this time I am pushing 70 in age, my children are long gone into their adult lives, and my career as a best-selling author is over a decade past. My wife and I and a big dog, Obsidian, live in a house on our tree farm, coming up on our 48th anniversary in reasonable health considering our retirement age. It's really a pretty dull life, aside from my writing career.

That career, however, may be changing. In that post-best-seller decade I made a sustained effort to get my books consideration by the motion picture industry, and at this time—mid 2004—have three serious movie options on three series, and interest in one or two more. A movie can make a big difference, and a good movie can make a huge difference. So there is a reasonable chance that I will live to see a restoration of my former success. Does that relate to the way Nox manages to rescue the other timelines from destruction? Well, it was a thought.

At any rate, I think this novel does conclude the series, though perhaps only Nox knows for sure, and she's not telling.

—Piers Anthony,

ABOUT THE AUTHOR

Piers Anthony is one of the world's most prolific and popular authors. His fantasy Xanth novels have been read and loved by millions of readers around the world, and have appeared on the *New York Times* Best Seller list 21 times.

Although Piers is mostly known for fantasy and science fiction, he has written novels in other genres as well, including historical fiction, martial arts, and horror.

Piers Anthony's official website is HI PIERS at www.hipiers.com, where he publishes his bi-monthly online newsletter. Piers lives with his wife in a secret forest, hidden deep in Central Florida.

THE BEST IN FANTASY

PIERS ANTHONY

The ChroMagic Series
Key to Chroma
Key to Destiny
Key to Havoc
Key to Liberty
Key to Survival

Of Man and Manta Series
Omnivore
Orn
OX

Macroscope

Tortoise Reform

Under a Velvet Cloak
(Incarnations of Immortality Book 8)

❧

PIERS ANTHONY & ROBERT E. MARGROFF

The Roundear Prophecy Series
Dragon's Gold
Serpent's Silver
Chimaera's Copper
Orc's Opal
Mouvar's Magic

Printed in the United States
214045BV00001B/67/A

9 781594 262944